FLIGHT INTO JEOP[illegible]

ALISON BURKE

LILY DALE PRESS

alison@alisonburkefictionwriter.com

Cover design by Lynnums

To Aunty Betty, who loved a romance.

1

Guadeloupe, mid-December 1802

In the heavy air of the tropical night, an urgent whisper broke her sleep.

'Wake up. Lucienne, you must wake up.' There was moonlight and she saw Bett, fully dressed and with two-year-old Alain slung across her body in a shawl. 'Be quick,' she whispered. 'There are men in the house, downstairs. We have to get away."

At once Lucienne was wide awake and out of bed. 'My father! He'll know what to do. Didn't you wake him?'

Bett thrust a dress into her hand, 'Put this on and keep your voice down. I tried to rouse him but he, your stepmother as well, they must have been given something' She broke off to catch hold of Lucienne as she darted forward.

'Let go of me, Bett, I'm eighteen now, not eight. I'm going to try for myself.' She broke loose, flung open the door and darted out on to the landing.

At once a pall of black smoke, acrid with the smell of burning palm oil, enveloped her. In a blast of heat, flames streaked up the broad wooden staircase and she fell back in terror as a wall of fire sprang up between herself and her parents' bedchamber. Fumes scorched her throat as she ran back into the room.

'Quick, Bett, the backstairs. Hold your breath and run.'

Clutching the little boy, the housekeeper rushed past her, fleeing into the pitch darkness of the passageway towards the back of the house and calling for her to follow. But for a few seconds Lucienne couldn't move. There must be something she could do to save her father and dear Chantelle. But the fire was three-fold now. Long tongues of flame licked the wooden panels of the walls up to the ceiling and devoured the sisal carpet on the floor.

From outside the house! From outside there might still be a way. If they got a ladder up to the bedroom window, broke the netting and climbed inside there might still be a chance to get them out. She turned and ran after Bett.

In total darkness, pursued by foul-smelling smoke, coughing, gasping for air, she groped her way along the wall of the passageway. It seemed endless. Her eyes were streaming, and her heart hammering in her chest by the time she found the narrow opening to the back stairs and stumbled down the first flight. Mercifully the fumes faded as she went lower and reached a small, moonlit landing. She gulped deep breaths of fresh air from the open window while Bett comforted Alain, whose little face she had pressed to her bosom to save him from the smoke.

'Thank God you are safe, Lucienne. Put your dress on over your nightdress. We must get right away from here. If I am not mistaken, fire is not the only danger we face tonight.'

Her hands shaking so she could barely fasten the buttons of the bodice, Lucienne struggled into the dress, dreadful thoughts racing through her head as she followed Bett down the next flight of narrow stairs. They reached the closed door that led through to the kitchen.

'Bett,' she whispered, 'We can't just leave them there asleep. What if they wake up with fire all around them and can't escape? We must get to them somehow, wake them and...'

Bett put her strong, capable hand on the girl's arm and said softly, 'They will not wake. Something was put into their food last night, or perhaps the wine. When I went to them, they had already left this life.'

'Dead! You mean they were both dead?' Grief-stricken, Lucienne started to cry. Not so much for her father, who the last few years had shown to be a hard, thoughtless man, but for Chantelle, the sweet young step-mother she had grown to love. 'To do such a dreadful thing!'

'Lucienne,' Bett broke in urgently, 'There is no time for this now. We must get to the stables, rouse the groom to take us.'

'No Bett.' The horror of her parents' death was suddenly swept aside by frightening thoughts of what they were caught up in. Was the fire started by the slaves from their own plantation, goaded to take revenge for the cruel treatment meted out to them? Or it could be part of what all the plantation owners dreaded? An uprising of the slaves throughout the islands of Guadeloupe. Either way, they were in grave danger, and she was terrified.

'Bett,' she said, feigning a calmness she didn't feel, 'I think all the servants will have run away. Besides, the road might not be safe. Best if we make our way to the river, take the rowing boat, get to the overseer's house to

warn him, and take shelter there.' She heard a sniff of disapproval. They both hated the man for his brutality to the slaves on the sugar plantation her father managed here on the island of Guadeloupe.

'If he is our only hope, then yes, we must go to him,' Bett muttered as she pushed open the door and led the way into the kitchen.

There was no sign of the fire here yet, though the servants must have left in a hurry because an oil lamp still burned on the kitchen table. By its light, Lucienne found a pair of her shoes, brought down to be cleaned. She slipped them on while Bett snatched up shawls for them both from the laundry room.

Cautiously, afraid of what might await them outside, Lucienne opened the back door. On the threshold they waited, peering out into the night, dreading to see the figures of men lurking close by, listening for the sound of voices. At first, they could hear only the faint buzzing of night insects, then a growing crackle, then the roar of fire raging towards them through the ground floor of the house.

'Whatever is outside, we can't stay here,' she whispered, and they slipped out into the garden, knowing their way to the river well enough to find it in the dark. The moon had gone behind a cloud and almost at once Lucienne stumbled over the body of Rufus, her father's big hunting dog.

'Poisoned! No wonder he didn't bark to warn us,' Bett murmured as they made their way swiftly across the open grass towards the trees that lay between them and the river.

They saw no one and, at the forest edge, Lucienne turned back to look at the place that had been her home for the last seven years. The grand house of the Belle

Chance plantation, with sweeping roofs and wide verandas, stone-built in the days when Guadeloupe was vastly rich from the sugar trade. A house meant to last forever, but the elaborate wooden interior was easy prey to the inferno that now consumed it and the windows glowed like fiery beacons in the night. Aghast, she turned to Bett.

'So quick to be destroyed! And poor Chantelle,' she sobbed. 'I can't bear to think of it. Of her being in there. My father too of course.'

'Come on, Lucienne. We've got to get away,' Bett took her arm and hurried her on to the path. 'Follow me, close behind. Remember, there are steps. And let's hope the boat is still there.'

The moon was out again now and faint shafts of silvery light pierced the canopy of leaves, casting weird shadows across a path that seemed longer and steeper than in daylight. Shuddering at what might lurk among the dark trees on either side, she kept her eyes fixed on Bett's shadowy form ahead of her as they hurried through the strange silence of the forest night until they came out on to the bank of the broad, swiftly flowing river.

Thankfully, the rowing boat was still there. Holding it steady for Bett to clamber on board, Lucienne remembered how, seven years ago when they had first come from France to join her father here, he had taught her to handle a small boat like this. Trying not to think how her last words to him had been shouted in anger, she climbed on board, sat down, and pulled away into the midstream.

Once there, she rested the oars in the rowlocks and let the current take them as she swotted away the flying insects that had found them now that they were sitting down.

'We'd better rub some of this on to get rid of them,' Bett was saying as she reached into her bag for the small bottle of cinnamon-oil she always kept handy. Alain was asleep again and she smoothed it lightly onto his face, neck, and limbs, then handed it to Lucienne.

'The overseer's house is close to the riverbank, less than half a kilometre away,' she remarked, 'So let us hope the moon stays bright or we might go past it.'

'I'm sure we won't. But Bett,' Lucienne asked, as she handed back the precious oil 'What happened back there? Were you awake when they got into the house?'

'No. One of them came into my room and woke me, said that I must get away or I would be killed. I couldn't see, but I think it was one of the young boys from the settlement.'

'Well, that follows, after the way they were treated' Lucienne said bitterly. The river ran through the Belle Chance estate. Two weeks ago, freed slaves, who were settled on a strip of poor land nearby, were refused access to water their cattle. When their headman had come, humbly, to ask for this to be reconsidered, the overseer set the dogs to run him off the property.

Her mind went back to the scene last night when they sat down to dine at the long table, she at one end, her father at the other with Chantelle silent and anxious beside him as another quarrel erupted between her step-daughter and her husband. She heard her own voice, angry and protesting.

'You must know it was wicked to deny those poor people water. All they have is a little stream and that dries up when it doesn't rain. You are master here and you should have stopped your overseer from doing such a dreadful thing.'

Richard Deverell downed his glass of wine and said sharply, 'The man's been here all his life, Lucienne. He knows how to deal with these people. It's not for you, with your stupid ideals, to tell me or him what to do. Now keep quiet and eat your food or get out of my sight.'

In answer, she'd pushed her chair away, jumped to her feet, sent her plate of food crashing to the floor, and ran from the room. The last time she heard her father's voice, he was shouting to the servant to stop the dog from injuring his mouth on the pieces of broken plate as it gobbled down the food she hadn't even started to eat.

If she had eaten it, would she too have been dead when Bett came to waken her?

Sick with horror at the thought, she heard Bett saying, 'Yes, I'm sure it was a boy from the settlement who came to save me, and I thank the good lord that your stepmother left all the housekeeping to me. I believe what little kindness I was able to show those Africans over the years, in food and medicines, has paid for our lives tonight.'

About to answer, Lucienne realised that they were drifting towards the bank. She freed the oars and was pulling the boat back into midstream when she picked up the smell of smoke. For a moment she thought it was from the fire at Belle Chance, then realised that it was coming from the other direction. From the stricken look on Bett's face, she must have noticed it too, and sure enough, a little way along the river, the dying embers of the overseer's house glowed red in the night.

Her mind reeling under the realisation that their last hope of finding help close to home was gone, Lucienne pulled on the oars with all her strength to get them past the scene of devastation, knowing there was nowhere else nearby for them to seek help and shelter. Their closest neighbour, another plantation owner, lived over five kilometres of wild country away, a hazardous journey on foot even in daylight.

'We'll have to go on,' she heard herself say with a confidence she didn't feel and saw the look of horror on Bett's face when she added 'We must get to Chantelle's uncle at Sacré Eulalia.'

'But Lucienne, that is so far away, right down on the coast. And in this small boat! Will we be safe?'

Swallowing hard to keep the fear out of her voice, Lucienne demanded, 'What else can we do? We won't be safe if we stay here, and if we stop anywhere on the way we could run into danger. Anyway, I know my father took Chantelle on a river trip to visit her uncle years ago, so there can't be any rapids or waterfalls. And we're going with the current. It's a long way, but we should be safe.'

Safe, she thought desperately, unless it starts to rain, and the boat fills up and sinks because we have nothing to bail out with. Safe, unless the moon disappears, and I can't see what I'm doing. Safe, unless I fall asleep and loose the oars. Safe, unless we run into the bank, get trapped in reeds, or capsize in turbulence if a tributary joins this main river. Safe, unless...

'We may be safe while it's dark,' Bett was saying nervously, 'but it must be after midnight already and day breaks so early these mornings. One of the traders said it was a seven-hour journey to the coast and if there really is an uprising all over the island and we can be seen—'

Lucienne broke in, 'Chantelle's uncle warned my father that, when trouble comes, it always starts in remote places like Belle Chance, then gradually spreads to the towns. If we have as much as three or four hours under cover of darkness to get away from here, that should take us far enough to be out of danger. And, besides, we don't know for certain that there is any wide-spread trouble,' she added hopefully.

She rested on her oars to gaze at her brother's little

face, pale in the moonlight, and wondered how he could have slept through so much of what had happened. One thing was certain. When he did wake, he wouldn't cry for his parents. They loved the little boy, born after many lost pregnancies, but were so wrapped up in each other that leaving his day-to-day care to his half-sister and the housekeeper had seemed natural to them.

A sudden image of them, locked in each other's arms as the flames consumed them, sickened her and she took up the oars and started to row again, squeezing her eyes tight shut to stop the tears escaping down her cheeks. Inwardly she shuddered. Despite her reassurances to Bett, it was hard to ignore the possibility that they may yet meet with violence. Still, she must concentrate on handling the boat, be glad of the strong current carrying them along, and rely on Bett to pray for deliverance. And then what?

'Bett, we can't stay here in Guadeloupe,' she said with sudden determination. 'Not now that such a dreadful thing has happened. We must get back to France somehow. We were happy there when I was little, even though we were so short of money. Now I am grown up, I could give lessons in piano and English to help earn our keep.'

Bett's face creased in a hopeful smile. 'Perhaps Chantelle's uncle will help us. Pay our passage back to Europe. Do you think he would?

'He's very wealthy and he can be generous when it suits him, so he might do that. But first I will have to tell him what happened to poor Chantelle and I'm am dreading it. He loved her so.'

It had been light for several hours when they came to a landing stage and climbed the stone steps up the steep riverbank to the gardens of the Sacré Eulalia estate. Bett had managed to snatch a few hours' sleep, but Lucienne, watchful throughout the night, was so tired that she could barely reach the top. She felt unsteady as they made their way towards glorious beds of flowers, cut into grass as smooth as velvet, where gardeners knelt to pick up every leaf and blossom fallen from the frangipani trees.

Knowing what she had to do, she said softly, 'It's better if I go to speak to Chantelle's uncle alone. Please take Alain to look at the fishpond until I call you.'

Approaching the magnificent old house, she paused when she caught sight of Chantelle's uncle, Maurice de Lesseps, sitting on a wide veranda, reading a newspaper. Steeling herself, she took a deep breath and called his name as she went forward. He looked up, caught sight of her and at once stood up. An elegant and handsome gentleman, despite his eighty years, he hurried down the steps to take her hand.

'My dear child! What has happened to you? Why are you here! You are dishevelled? Your parents—?'

And standing there, on his well-tended lawn in the bright morning sunlight, she held back tears and told him, briefly as she could, what had happened in the dark of that terrible night at Belle Chance. At first, she thought the shock had been too much for him. His body seemed to crumble as he fell back against the wooden rails of the veranda, covering his face with his hands. She went forward to support him but, seeming to pull himself together with tremendous effort, he brushed her gently aside, turned and went slowly up the veranda steps, silent tears streaming down his face. Not looking back, he called out that he would send someone to attend to her, then disappeared into the house.

She called for Bett to join her, and they sank gratefully into the comfort of the rattan chairs on the veranda where, almost at once, one servant appeared with a carafe of iced water and another with a breakfast tray. Eagerly, because they had eaten nothing that day, Bett spread guava jam on to a croissant for Alain, then poured two cups of the fragrant coffee, and handed one to Lucienne. She took it, but her hand shook as she held the cup to her lips.

'What is it? You are shivering. Are you cold?' Bett got up and draped her shawl over Lucienne's shoulders. 'Does it feel like a fever coming on?'

'No. I think it's reaction now that we are safely here and then seeing poor Uncle Maurice so stricken with grief. I feel as though all my strength is gone and I'm so tired, but my head is full of thoughts and fears, I don't think I could sleep—'

'What you need, my poor child, is a good cry.' Bett's own voice was breaking. 'Such terrible things have happened, and you've scarcely shed a tear. You need to weep and get it out of your system.'

'You are probably right,' Lucienne told her, 'But not now, with darling little Alain standing here, looking up at me. Whatever happens, I mustn't let him see me cry.' She swallowed hard and some of her natural spirit came back as he smiled up at her and offered her his half-eaten croissant.

Later that morning, bathed and rested, they were out on the veranda again when Maurice de Lesseps joined them. Apart from appearing a little more subdued than usual he seemed, outwardly, to have adjusted to the tragic news better than Lucienne would have thought possible.

'In a long life where so many loved ones have been lost, I have gained resilience,' he said, as if reading her thoughts, 'And now we must deal with your immediate situation. Tell me what you want to do, and I will help you in any way I can.'

He listened while she told him of their plans to return to France, then said, 'I could ask you to think again, to stay here under my protection, but I am an old man. The lord might call me at any time, making your future here less secure.' He paused, then added, 'That is unless you allow me to find you a strong young husband to look after you.'

Knowing that, to him, an advantageous marriage was the one achievement for which all young women should aim, she managed not to speak her mind. No use to point out that to her, whose mother had died in childbirth, marriage seemed no safe haven. Instead, she looked down and shook her head.

He nodded, 'No, I thought not, so it may be best for you to get away. A messenger from the town today brought news of more violent incidents in the interior, too many and too serious for coincidence. Such risings of the slaves have always been subdued by the garrison of French troops we have on the island, but there will still be great danger before these wicked rebels are crushed.'

Despite a warning glance from Bett, Lucienne couldn't stop herself from asking, 'But can't you see how it has come to this? For slavery to have been abolished after the Republic was formed in France and then, less than ten years later, for it to be brought back again. How could that be right?'

'Right has nothing to do with it,' he said with the fierce energy of total conviction. 'The abolition of slavery ruined our trade in sugar and threw these islands into chaos. The idealists of the revolution didn't concern themselves with the loss of revenue to the French exchequer. It was Bonaparte, the new First Consul, needing money from our taxes to fund his reform of France and to subdue her enemies Europe, it was he who saw the need to bring back slavery so that our plantations again begin to prosper. And that, my dear young lady, is the way of the world.'

Before Lucienne could utter the reply burning on her lips, he went on, more calmly, 'Now let us go back to your own situation. You want to leave this island and, for that reason, I will not immediately report the terrible events at Belle Chance. If I did, the authorities would expect you both to stay here to give evidence that the fire was started deliberately when the perpetrators are caught and brought to justice. That may never happen, so best you slip away while you can.'

'Thank you, Uncle Maurice, but do you know how soon a ship will arrive from France to take us back there?'

'No, because cholera has broken out in the town and a red flag warns all ships not to dock here. Passengers and cargo can be ferried ashore, but no passengers are taken on board for fear the disease goes with them. Even local trade between the islands is forbidden.'

'Then what are we to do?'

'Trading vessels still slip out in secret from along the coast. One of those I know to be sailing in a few days for Kingstown, Jamaica.'

'Surely that is a long way and in the wrong direction,' Lucienne began to protest.

'My dear child, if you want to leave this island, you must get away by whatever means possible. Kingstown is a major port for ships coming in from Europe. As it is in the hands of the British, I cannot vouch for frequency of

French ships, but you will certainly be able to take passage on an English ship to the English port of Plymouth. From there you could make a much shorter journey by sea to France.'

'And you would help us to do that?'

'I know for a fact that your father always exceeded his income, so somebody must help you. I will pay the passage to France for the three of you, though what you intend to do when you get there I cannot imagine.'

'I have brothers in Le Havre,' Bett broke in eagerly. 'They are in business making leather goods, at their own factory. I am sure they will help us.'

As if she hadn't spoken, he demanded, 'Lucienne, have you thought of contacting your father's family in England?'

'No, Uncle Maurice, I have not. My father never spoke of them. I don't think he'd had contact with them for many years.'

'I can assure you he had. Twice each year he received a remittance of money from your grandfather's estate in the English county of Devon. I know this because, when he came here to marry my niece, I enquired into his ability to support her. He told me recently that it was not enough, but he still receives it.'

She stared at him. 'I had no idea of this. But if I wanted to contact my grandfather, how could I do that without an address?'

'I kept a letter I received from the agent dealing with the transfer of your father's money when I first enabled him to have it sent to Guadeloupe. The address was that of a Mr Albert Bazley, a lawyer in a place called Castlebridge, also in the county of Devon. I suggest that, on arriving in France, you write to this lawyer, identify yourself and ask for your grandfather's address.'

'But there must have been some sort of quarrel because my father never mentioned his family. Perhaps my grandfather will not want to know us.'

He shrugged impatiently, 'I don't know how you envisage your own future in France, Lucienne, but consider Alain. His father was from the English gentry, my niece descended from a long line of French aristocrats. Is their son to be apprenticed to a shoemaker in a few years' time? Or will you at least attempt to have him recognised and educated as a gentleman by his father's family?' When she didn't answer, he went on, 'Consider that Lucienne, while I send a message to find out precisely when the trader leaves for Jamaica, and to make some other arrangements to help you on your way.'

When he rose and left them, Lucienne got up and went to put her arm about Bett's shoulders. 'I am sorry he was so snobbish about your brothers.'

'No surprise though. If I'd thought before I spoke, I would have held my tongue,' Bett said dismissively. 'But Lucienne, thinking back, I do remember hearing your father tell Chantelle he expected to come into money when his father passed away. So, if your grandfather is wealthy, he might well be prepared to help you.'

'I shall certainly write to him from France, but however kind my father's family might turn out to be, you are my true family, Bett and always will be. And, for Chantelle's sake, I will never be parted from Alain. I will keep him safe and happy and do my best for him until he is all grown up'

'And I will be there to help you,' Bett told her as she took the little boy on her knee and held him close.

2

Devon, March 1803

Lucienne looked across the desk at the lawyer and began to feel unsure of herself. She had expected someone older. A mature gentleman with spectacles and perhaps even a powdered wig. Business-like yet kindly. Not this tall, carelessly elegant, darkly handsome person, looking no more than twenty-six or seven. When the clerk showed them into his office, he had risen politely and invited them to sit on the two chairs in front of his desk, but this did not make her feel at ease.

His clever dark eyes flickered over her and Bett, who sat beside her. Both were clad in clothes hurriedly bought from a dealer as soon as they disembarked at Plymouth five days before. At the time, Lucienne had been too glad to be wrapped up against the chill March weather to care that they were other peoples' cast-offs and decidedly old fashioned. Now, under his scrutiny, she found herself wishing there had been money enough to buy something less shabby. Glad to have rehearsed her words beforehand, she took a deep breath, held her head high and spoke in her most formal manner.

'Mr Bazley, I am Miss Lucienne Deverell, and this is my companion, Mademoiselle Moreau. We have come, with my brother, Alain, from Guadeloupe in the West Indies to seek my father's family. I believe they live in Devon and that you are their man of business. I have come to Castlebridge to ask you for their address.'

'Deverell?' He asked sharply, glancing across to where Alain slept on a bench beside the glowing hearth. 'You are related to the Deverells of Ottersbury?'

'I don't know where they live because my father never spoke of England,' she said, not liking his very direct manner. 'He was Mr Richard Deverell and left England because he much preferred the French culture and way of life. In Guadeloupe, after he and my stepmother died, her uncle told us that you, as the agent who sent him money each year, must know where his family are to be found.'

Watching her intently, he asked, 'You say your parents died? I am so sorry to hear that. What happened to them?'

'There was a fire. It was some months ago now.' She heard herself say this calmly, then broke off. A fire. How strange to describe in two short words the terrible inferno that destroyed two people, their home and the life she had known since she was eleven years old. It was as if it had happened to persons she didn't know. Her head began to swim. She glanced down at her hands, saw they were shaking, and felt Bett's comforting arm around her shoulders.

'Monsieur Bazley.' Bett's voice seemed at a distance, 'It is the reaction. To be so tragically orphaned of her father and her dear young stepmother and in a fire deliberately set! We barely escaped with our lives. And our voyage here was not easy.'

'Of course,' Lucienne heard him push back his chair and stand up. 'Let me get something for her. I'll send my clerk out for coffee and something for the child.'

He went out and by the time he came back she had recovered herself enough to listen to Bett telling him about their journey.

'There were such difficulties. Unable to sail from Guadeloupe, we had to first go west to the British possession of Jamaica and wait for a ship to bring us from there to England, so that we could go on to France from here'

'So, you were at sea for how long?'

'Over three months in all. The last weeks were most trying. There were storms and we were not clad for the cold. Then, at Plymouth, it rained constantly and there was talk of flooding while we waited most anxiously for two nights before we could get seats on the coach to reach you here in Castlebridge.'

'A three-day journey along poor roads is less than comfortable at the best of times. You must be weary,' he said and there was sympathy in his voice.

Determined to keep command of the conversation, Lucienne rallied enough to ask, 'Mr Bazlely, can you confirm that the Deverell's of Ottersbury are the people we are looking for?

He nodded. 'I can.'

'And this place where the family live? Is it far from here?'

'Some ten miles, Miss Deverell.'

'Then please direct us to where we can hire a carriage? I think we should go there as soon as we can.'

He leaned back in his chair and studied her for longer than she thought necessary, then said, 'I must tell you that, to my certain knowledge, no one in the Deverell family is aware that Richard Deverell had one child, let alone two.'

Her eyes widened in consternation.

'I knew there was an estrangement, but I thought perhaps my father would have written to our grandfather when Alain was born.'

'It is my understanding that, except to request increases in his allowance, your father never wrote to him until the day the older Mr Deverell died. Two years ago.'

'He is dead?' she gasped, 'You are telling me that our grandfather has also died, and you didn't write to tell my father this?'

'It was not my place to do so. I presumed his older brother Mr Cedrick Deverell, who is now head of the family, would have let him know.'

'So, it is to this Mr Cedrick Deverell I must now go to for help?'

Before he could comment, a young boy brought in a tray with bread and warm milk and set it down on the low table near the fire. At once, Bett went over to Alain, woke him, and sat him beside her. She broke the bread into small pieces, smiling and talking softly as she passed it to him, holding the cup while he drank the milk.

Watching them, the lawyer asked thoughtfully, 'What age is your brother?'

'He's just two and a half years old now. On the sea voyage, we were so afraid for him, but when stronger children fell ill, he remained well.'

'Due to your excellent care, no doubt,' he told her, nodding thanks to the clerk who brought a tray of coffee to his desk. 'It was brave of you to come four thousand miles across the Atlantic, with no exact knowledge of where you were going.' And for the first time, he smiled at her, his long-lashed eyes crinkling at the corners as they gazed into hers.

Her heart seemed to miss a beat and she felt colour rise to her cheeks. For a moment she was light-headed again, then realised she should say something instead of gazing back at him.

She said hastily, 'We planned to sail on from Plymouth to Le Havre in France where we have friends to help us. Unfortunately, the cost of travelling there is more than we expected, so we have to seek my father's family and ask them for help to get to France.'

He got up and poured the coffee, then he asked, 'Tell me, Miss Deverell, have you brought any papers as proof of identity?'

She reached down and took a package from the bag Bett had left lying beside her chair.

'We have them here, she said, 'You wish to see them?'

'If I may.'

While she took Bett her coffee, he sat behind his desk, took an envelope from its protective oilskin wrappings, and withdrew three documents. After studying them at length, he handed them back.

'Mr Cedrick Deverell will certainly find these of great interest. Now, for tonight, I recommend you stay at the Mermaid Inn where the coach set you down.'

She said hesitantly, 'Monsieur, I know your advice is well meant, but we cannot afford to stay there tonight. There is the hire of a carriage to consider'

'All that will be taken care of out of funds I hold for the Deverell family. Tonight, you must stay in Castlebridge and rest.' He hesitated, then went on, 'You say you intend to ask for money to leave England?

'Yes we must get to France. Providing my uncle will help us do that,' she added, hoping he would reassure her

Instead, he leaned forward and said, 'Miss Deverell, for now, if you care to go back to the Mermaid inn, I'll send word with you to the landlord that all your needs will be paid for promptly and in full by myself.'

She rose to go. 'Thank you. That is most kind, Mr Bazley.'

'Not at all. And Miss Deverell, the name Bazley is that of my partner, now largely in retirement. My name is Moncrief.'

After they had left, Jago Moncrief dropped his air of professional calm and strode about his office, running his fingers through his thick, dark hair.

This latest turn of events seemed scarcely possible. Only a week ago he'd listened to his elderly partner's drunken ramblings about a gross irregularity in affairs of the Deverell estate and of a lost document providing proof. It certainly wasn't in his own interest for that document to come to light, but curiosity had prompted him to search through the stacks of dusty old files in the office storeroom. He had been unashamedly relieved not to find it. Now these two young Deverells had turned up and honour warred with self-interest as he considered what to do next. Honour won. If the document existed elsewhere, he must bring it to light, despite knowing this would cause all sorts of difficulties. Meanwhile, he would take steps to keep the existence of Lucienne and Alain Deverell from their relations until matters could be resolved.

He gave a deep sigh, called in his clerk, Joshua Gerrick, and told him that a matter of business would take him away for the next few days.

'Accompanying the two ladies to Ottersbury Manor

then?' Joshua asked him. 'When I walked them over to the Mermaid just now, the older lady told me they wanted a carriage booked for Ottersbury first thing tomorrow morning.'

'That will not be needed. They want to get to France, and I intend to give them the means to do just that. When we've finished here, I'm off to the Mermaid to suggest that the three of them board the coach back to Plymouth tomorrow morning. From there they can take passage to Le Havre.'

'Not possible, sir. Word's come through to the Mermaid that the river's burst its banks. Plymouth road's flooded so deep you can't see where the bridge is. Seems the coach that brought your ladies here will be the last going either way for some time.'

Jago thought for a moment, then gave a shrug of resignation. 'So, to Ottersbury they must go. Now, as I say, I'll be away for a few days, setting off first thing in the morning, so we'd best sort out some matters of business now. And if anyone comes in needing a lawyer as a matter of urgency, Mr Bazley is only half retired, so you can call upon him to deal with it.

'Providing he's sober, sir,' the clerk remarked dispassionately before they settled down to their discussion of other business needing Jago's attention.

Lucky to have a man like Joshua Gerrick to rely on, Jago thought as he locked up his office a couple of hours later and sauntered along the unlit street towards his lodgings. Two years before, he'd left a law firm in Plymouth to come here and discovered his new partner was a soak and the business on the verge of ruin. He'd relied on Gerrick's hard work and honesty to help him pull it back into modest success. And the man was discrete. He must have realised from their name that this shabbily dressed girl and her small brother were related to the wealthy, landowning Deverells, but had made no comment.

The girl, with her sharp intelligence, her courage and long lashed green- blue eyes, intrigued him. Too thin and very pale, she looked younger than her eighteen years. She had, he reflected, the kind of looks that could flare into beauty or fade into insignificance depending on how life treated her.

One thing was certain. Miss Lucienne Deverell would get no warm welcome at Ottersbury manor, and she would learn soon enough that her father's preference for the French way of life was not the only reason he had fled his native land.

Daylight had already begun to fade as they left the lawyer's office walked the short distance to the Mermaid Inn, Bett carrying Alain and chatting comfortably with a dour looking clerk from the lawyer's office. Lucienne, struck by a disquieting thought, didn't join in. Comparing Bett's speech with that of the lawyer, she'd been aware that Bett spoke with a French accent. Her father rarely used his native tongue, but she and Bett had always spoken to each other in English when they were alone. So, did she herself sound like a foreigner here in England? Not that it mattered because, before long they would be on their way to France again.

They reached the Mermaid inn, to be offered a comfortable bed chamber and then shown into a private parlour to wait for their dinner. There was a pleasing fragrance from the pinewood fire burning in the grate, while two oil-lamps hung from the dark beams of the low ceiling and lit the room with a cozy glow.

'They say the English men are awkward and don't know how to converse with a woman, yet I have rarely felt such rapport with a man,' Bett remarked, as she sank thankfully down on a fireside settle in the Mermaid's front parlour 'He was quite disarming! Didn't you think so, Lucienne?'

Lucienne, sitting on a low fireside chair helping Alain dress and undress the rag boy-doll Bett had made for him, shrugged her shoulders.

'I thought he was quite high handed at first, though he did improve. And at least he was able to warn us that my grandfather had already—'

'Lucienne!' Bett broke in, laughing, 'I don't mean the lawyer. I mean his clerk, Mr Gerrick. In those few moments, while he accompanied us over here, there was so much kindness in his eyes. I felt such sympathy, as if he was an old friend. A true, natural gentleman.'

Lucienne, who had barely noticed him, felt obliged to agree.

She paused, then said uneasily, 'Bett, about the lawyer. Didn't you notice? There was something in his manner that made me think that, with our grandfather gone, the family may not be so glad to see us.'

'Well, of course it is unfortunate that you have to ask for money, but I think they will make you welcome. They must be especially pleased with Alain. He is such a little man in his blue velvet suit, already breeched at only two and a half years! And the way he can sing in tune! I think he will be musical like his dear mother'

'I hope so, but all the same—' she was interrupted by the sudden opening of the door by a stout, elderly lady they had never seen before. She bustled in, apologising profusely for disturbing them.

'So unfortunate! They wouldn't send a driver out of

the town so late in case of flooding on the country lanes, so I am unable to return home tonight. But the landlord has told me that a carriage is ordered for tomorrow to take you to Ottersbury! And that is where I live. If we could share the carriage, we can also share the cost, which would be beneficial to both of us, I'm sure.' She paused to catch her breath, then added, 'Oh, how remiss of me. I did not introduce myself. I am a Miss Petty. Miss Regina Petty.' She looked expectantly at Bett.

'I am Elizabeth Moreau, and these are Lucienne and Alain Deverell.'

'We will be only too pleased to take you with us to Ottersbury tomorrow,' Lucienne said eagerly, getting to her feet. 'And you won't have to pay anything because the cost is already being met for us.' As the old lady began a delighted attempt at a protest, she went on, 'How interesting that you live in Ottersbury. We are on our way there to visit our relatives, the Deverell family. Do you know them?'

'I cannot say I am intimate with that family. Mr Deverell is my landlord. Landlord in fact to half the village.' She seemed about to say more when two servants came in with steaming dishes of food and set them out on the white linen cloth that covered the parlour table.

Seeing the fresh crusty bread and pats of butter, roast pork, chicken stew with dumplings, cheese and fruit tart, Lucienne exclaimed, 'Appetites must be hearty here in Devon.' She saw Miss Petty eye the food with longing and added 'Perhaps you would care to join us, Miss Petty?'

Over dinner, Miss Petty needed no prompting to talk of the Deverell family.

'Rich Plymouth merchants a couple of generations ago, they bought the estate from the last of the Aclands. You know how it is with some of these old families. Land held for hundreds of years then mismanaged and lost by one profligate gambler.'

'I can quite imagine,' Lucienne encouraged her. 'And is the present Mr Deverell a good landlord?'

'I think he is, though it is only in the last two years that he has owned my house. Before that, it belonged to me and my dear sister, left to us by our father. We had lived there all our lives.'

'And you sold it to him?'

'There was a terrible winter, the house was flooded, plaster falling off the walls, furniture and carpets ruined. Mud left everywhere when the water went down. We couldn't afford to get things put right and Mr Deverell offered to see to all damage on condition that we sold the house to him. A severe disappointment for my nephew, I'm sorry to say.'

'He was expecting to inherit your house perhaps?' Bett asked sympathetically.

'Indeed, yes. He says the price I was paid was less than it should have been. But, at the time, my poor sister was in her final illness. Her comfort came first, and I did not hesitate. True, my rent is a little more than I expected, but Mr Deverell has had the expense of fortifying the embankment where the river runs through his land behind the village. To prevent further flooding. One has to be grateful.'

That night, as they lay in the comfort of the Mermaid Inn's best bed with Alain snuggled in between them, Lucienne thought about the lawyer. Mr Jago, the clerk had called him when he was talking to Bett. So, he was Jago Moncrief and, though she wasn't going to admit this to the incurably romantic Bett, she had found him handsome. Well, perhaps not so much handsome as very interesting. Presented into Guadeloupe society by her stepmother, just before her eighteenth birthday, she had loved the balls, parties and picnics, the new clothes, the bustle of the capital and the attention of young men. Several made every effort to charm her, but none of them had truly awaked her interest. Her father had not been pleased.

'Not ready for marriage? Are you out of your mind?' he shouted when she returned with her stepmother to Belle Chance. 'Girls out here wed at sixteen, some younger, and I get a letter from Maurice telling me you refused an offer from a personable young fellow with excellent prospects. What is it you want? To fall madly in love? Mark my words, Lucienne, you've only passable looks, and no dowry unless Maurice sees fit to give you something. If you keep ignoring your chances, you'll end up an old maid.'

With that, he stormed out of the house and left her standing in the entrance hall, utterly dejected. Chantelle, seeming unruffled, linked an arm through hers and led her into the salon.

'What a way to be greeted, after our long journey home,' she said serenely as she sank down onto the elegant sofa and patted the seat beside her for Lucienne to join her. 'A few hours out hunting will calm him down. And I think you were wise to refuse the match.'

'Oh, thank you, Chantelle. I felt so sorry for the poor young man at the time. But surely, he deserves better than being married to a person who has no particular feelings for him?'

'The idea is that love will grow, or at least that a healthy respect and consideration for each other's feeling will develop. Though sometimes that does not happen, as I know to my cost.' She took in Lucienne's look of surprise and nodded her head. 'Yes, I was married before when I was very young. A grand, ambitious match arranged by our families. We were

cousins with the same noble name of de Lesseps, but nothing else in common and we made each other completely miserable.' She paused, then said sadly, 'Or I should say that I made him miserable because I never wanted to make love, and nobody had told me that was what marriage involved.'

'What happened to him, Chantelle?'

'He died in the revolution ten years ago. Executed like so many aristocrats. Because we were so much at odds with each other, I had come here alone to visit uncle Maurice and so escaped the guillotine. Now I know what it is to be happy in marriage, I have felt such remorse for my coldness to him.' She gave her sudden, winning smile. 'Anyway, I am glad to have your company for a little while longer.'

Lying in a comfortable bed in the Mermaid inn, gazing into the dark, lost in memories of the past, Lucienne gave little thought to the Deverells of Ottersbury until she heard Bett's voice say softly, 'I wonder what sort of wealthy landowner persuades an old lady to sell her home when disaster strikes, instead of helping her out of Christian charity?'

The light drizzle that washed the streets of Castlebridge when they left the inn the following morning, gave way to heavy rain as they reached the coast road, making their progress slow.

'On a fine spring morning, some drivers can take as little as two hours to cover the ten miles.' Miss Petty told them as the carriage rumbled along at what seemed to Lucienne to be little more than a brisk walking pace, 'But now, with this dreadful weather, I believe we'll be on the road for at least three hours.'

Their journey took much longer than that. The rain never stopped and several times the road had to be dug clear of deep mud. A broken bridge led to a long diversion, and there was a wait of over an hour in a tiny hamlet while the blacksmith replaced a lost horseshoe.

'And what an unusual little boy young master Alain is!' Miss Petty remarked, regarding him with interest as they waited in the carriage and ate a lunch of coarse bread, hard cheese and mugs of hot water that was all they could obtain by way of sustenance in this out of the way place. 'Most children would be shouting and climbing about all over. But there he is. No trouble at all.'

Lucienne, nodded as though she appreciated this as a compliment, though recently she and Bett had begun to worry about Alain's lack of drive. Living on the remote Belle Chance estate, they had seen no other children of the same age, but on the sea voyage there was a little girl some months younger who was full of energy, much given running about and shouting. Alain had watched her with solemn interest, never joining in, and, though he could sing nursery songs in tune, he very rarely said anything. She glanced at Bett, who had begun to talk about something else.

The rain had stopped but it was well into the afternoon and light was already beginning to fade by the time they reached the village of Ottersbury. Tired, hungry, and cold, despite the supply of blankets that came with the carriage, Lucienne wondered if Bett was as worn out as she by Miss Petty's plentiful supply of conversation. Most of what she had to say was interesting, but both Bett and Lucienne were relieved when, just as they entered the village, she called out to the driver to stop at the gate of a small house set well back from the road in its own garden. In the fading light of the early evening, they could see it was one of the few dwellings they had passed that day that had no smoke rising from the chimney.

'Have you no maid living in to keep the place warm while you were away?' Bett asked in concern as Miss Petty flung aside her blankets and prepared to alight.

'No. A girl comes in just twice a week, but I am able to build up the fire for myself and be snug as can be in no time.' Thanking them for bringing her home and hoping they might call in to see her one day, she said goodbye as the driver assisted her down.

From the carriage window Lucienne watched her, buffeted by the cold wind as she opened a wooden gate and hurried down the path. Her stout, lonely figure, pushing open the front door was the last they saw of her as the carriage started to move away

'If we are invited to stay here for more than a few days, I shall certainly visit her. She was such an old chatterbox, but I liked her,' Lucienne said as they started through the village. 'And she never once asked us where we had come from, who paid for everything, or how we might be connected to the Deverell family. Did you notice, Bett?'

'I did, so perhaps Miss Petty is a more discreet person than we might otherwise have thought.'

They drove on, through the village, past an ancient church on its outer edge and started to climb a slow incline, where the road was overhung on either side by massive trees, their branches black against a leaden sky.

'Look, there's a wall alongside the road now. I think we must be nearly there,' Lucienne said eagerly and felt a flutter of excitement as she readied herself to meet her father's family.

3

The carriage trundled between lion topped gate posts, round a circle of grass and came to a halt before a tall, grey-stone mansion. Moments later, after the driver had lifted their trunk on to the gravel drive and made off, they stood shivering before the huge iron-studded door until Lucienne went resolutely forward and pulled on the bell-rope.

They waited. She pulled again, and the door was opened by a liveried man servant who looked unsure about admitting them. Before she could speak, an elderly woman, wearing the plain, dark dress and starched white cap of an upper servant, came from the gloom of the hallway behind him, elbowed him aside and ushered them into the dark interior of the entrance hall. She turned to Bett.

'Good evening, Miss. I am Mrs Dobson, housekeeper here, and I'm to take you and the children straight upstairs to wait. If I'd known beforehand to expect visitors, I'd have had the room properly aired, whereas I was only just given warning,' she said as she picked up a lamp from a hall table.

Instructing the manservant to bring the trunk, she led the way up the wide staircase, along a dark passageway and opened the door to a bedroom. It smelled musty and had little furniture other than an armchair, a small table and a large four-poster bed, but there was a fire burning in the grate and two oil lamps were already lit.

'Mistress only said just now to put you and the children in here so there was no time to get it properly aired, but I'll send a maid up with some more hot bricks to warm the bed. Now, you must excuse me. I'd best be getting back downstairs.' She was about to go when Lucienne, smarting at being described as one of the children, stepped forward.

'Excuse me, Mrs Dobson,' she said firmly, 'Are Mr Deverell and his family all away from home?'

'Why no. He and the mistress are here. And his sister as well.'

'Because I would have thought that one of them would have come out to greet us. After all, we've come all the way from Guadeloupe.'

The housekeeper bridled slightly 'I don't know where that is, I'm sure. And why you should expect—'

'Mrs Dobson,' Bett broke in hastily, 'These are the children of Mr Deverell's brother, Richard. It is only natural that Miss Lucienne is anxious to meet her relations.'

'Mr Richard's children! Well, I never.' She looked hard at Lucienne, then went over to where Bett had set Alain down in the armchair and peered at him closely. 'A lovely little child, I'm sure. Of course, I didn't know Mr Richard, having come into my post here after he left for foreign parts.' She paused, looked again at Lucienne, then said she would let Mr Deverell know they had arrived and hurried away.

'Lucienne,' Bett said as soon as the housekeeper left the room, 'How did they know we were coming here today? Do you suppose that handsome lawyer sent word ahead of us?'

'He must have done, and I suppose we should be thankful. Though I'm not altogether sure I'd call him handsome,' Lucienne told her, determined to keep her thoughts about Jago Moncrief to herself.

Expecting to be kept waiting longer and wondering when they would be offered something to eat, they were relieved when a maidservant came some ten minutes later and said the two of them were to go down to the drawing-room straight away, leaving Alain here in her care.

'Mrs Dobson sent me up to the old nursery for whatever I could find for the little 'un and then I'm to watch him while you're downstairs,' she explained, showing them a faded soft leather ball, a few building bricks, and a small wooden horse. 'She was sending hot water up for you to wash, and a tray with some dinner, but now it'll have to wait 'til after. Best take one of the lamps, to find your way Missis,' she told Bett as they rose to go.

'Surely, someone should have been sent to show us the way to this drawing-room,' Lucienne said crossly as they made their way along the dark passageways and down the stairs. Four doors led off the gloomy entrance hall and, while they were trying to decide which might lead to the drawing-room, a tall, red-haired girl stepped out of the shadows and pointed silently to the one straight ahead. While Bett put down her lamp on the hall table, Lucienne hurried forward, tapped on the door, waited for a voice summoning her to enter then, with Bett at her heels, she pushed open the door and went forward into the presence of her Deverell relations.

There were several people in the room, which was large and well-lit by several elegant lamps. The wooden floors were polished to a high gloss and scattered with luxurious eastern rugs. There were plenty of tapestry upholstered chairs, but nobody spoke, let alone invited them to sit down. A lean, sour-looking man of middle years, who Lucienne took to be her Uncle Cedrick, sat behind a small writing table. Unsmiling, he looked them both up and down, then beckoned for them to stand closer. Ignoring Lucienne, he fixed his cool stare on Bett.

'And you are?'

Startled, Bett replied, 'I am Elizabeth Moreau, Miss Deverell's companion and Alain's nursery governess.'

'Sir. Sir. Hasn't she the manners to address you properly?' a shrill voice demanded. Lucienne turned to look at the two women sitting one on either side of a fire blazing in the huge grate. Both looked so indignant that she wasn't sure which one had spoken. Was it the raddled old thing wrapped in Paisley shawls with her hair piled up and powdered? Or was it the woman of middle years, dressed in a deep red silken gown with a necklace of pearls and rubies around her neck? She glanced about the room. Standing the far end, in the shadows by the drawn curtains of a long window, were two other people. One was a tall, graceful woman who wore an expression of bored amusement. Lucienne decided that it wouldn't have been her, then saw, with a start of surprise, that the other person standing next to her was Jago Moncrief.

Feeling every eye in the room upon her, she turned back to the man at the desk and decided not to address him as uncle.

'Sir,' she said, loud and clear, 'I am Miss Lucienne Deverell, and I am travelling to France with my brother Alain. Our father was Richard Deverell and we—'

'The papers,' he demanded, snapping his fingers irritably, 'Show me what you've brought to support your claim to be related to this family.'

Shocked into silence by the hostility radiating from him, she handed him the papers and saw Jago move across the room to stand beside the desk just as Cedrick Deverell, having glanced at them briefly, threw the papers impatiently down on the writing-table. Remembering that they were written in French, Lucienne was about to offer to translate when Jago picked them up.

'First Uncle, there is a letter to your late father from the Préfet of Guadeloupe, detailing the circumstances of your brother's death. He also introduces your brother's children, Alain and Lucienne Deverell. Then there is a certificate of marriage of your brother, Richard Deverell, to Chantelle de Lesseps, dated 7th July 1796 and taking place in the French possession of Guadeloupe. Last, a certificate of birth for a male child Richard Alain Deverell, dated 3rd November 1800, also in Guadeloupe.'

The older man raised his eyebrows.

'Nothing for the girl!' he asked sharply, then turned to Lucienne. 'Well?'

'My papers were in my father's care. They must have been destroyed with everything else in the terrible fire on the night my father and my stepmother died.'

'How very convenient!'

It was the woman in red with the pearl and ruby necklace who spoke this time, Lucienne was sure of that. She was also sure that the lawyer, who clearly had arrived much earlier in the day to warn the family that she was on her way here, must also have told them about the tragedy at Belle Chance. Did none of them give a fig about what had happened to her father and Chantelle?

She turned to face the woman in red, and said, with

exaggerated politeness, 'No madam. You are mistaken. It was most inconvenient.'

Ignoring an indignant intake of breath from both ladies by the fire, she turned back and heard Cedrick Deverell demanded sharply,

'Then how do you come to be in possession of the certificates you have brought here today?'

'My father married my stepmother in Guadeloupe and Alain was born there. It was all registered there, so we were able to obtain copies.'

Addressing Jago, Cedrick Deverell said sourly, 'Copies! I'm not sure how much, if at all, either of these documents can be relied upon. She could be party to some attempt to legitimise the boy.'

'Uncle, the haphazard arrangements prevalent in this country are not universal,' Jago told him. 'In France and all its territories, births and marriages are registered. These copied certificates are signed by a notary and appear to me to be perfectly in order.'

'Oh, very well. You're the lawyer. So, for the present, we might as well accept them as valid. As for the girl?'

'As for the girl, a foreigner by the way she speaks, I don't consider that letter to be sufficient proof as to who she actually is,' the woman in the pearl and ruby necklace broke in.

Lucienne, losing patience turned on her and said icily, 'Why would I pretend to be somebody I am not, to come to this terrible country, where it never stops raining, to be treated with such rudeness and bad manners? I know who I am, so I don't need proof, thank you, Madam.'

The shocked silence that followed was broken by gasps of outrage from both the ladies and by Cedrick Deverell demanding that she be removed from his sight. Jago came forward, took Lucienne's elbow, and hurried her from the room. Looking over her shoulder, the last thing she saw as he took her through the door was Bett, staring after her in open-mouthed dismay. The last thing she heard was the sound of laughter from the elegant woman by the window.

Out in the hallway, Jago bent his head close to hers, a wing of dark hair falling across his forehead as he said softly, 'Lucienne your position here is, to say the least, precarious. The road back to Plymouth is closed, so here is where you will have to stay, at least for the present. I strongly advise you to hold your tongue.'

She shook herself free, furious when she saw that he seemed to struggle to keep from laughing.

'Tell me, clever Mr Lawyer,' she snapped, 'what is so funny about that woman, who ever she was, insulting me?' But he shrugged, turned and went back into the drawing-room.

'Hateful, hateful man,' she cried after him, loud enough for him to hear before the door closed behind him.

'Mr Jago's, the best of them when you get to know him,' a quiet voice said nearby and she saw the red-haired girl she had noticed earlier, sitting on a bench in the shadows and giving her an encouraging look.

'I think he's dreadful. They're all dreadful. Nobody greeted us or said who they were.' She wiped away angry tears, as the other girl got up and led her gently to sit beside her on the bench.

'Well, for a start, the tall, handsome lady standing by the window curtains is Mr Jago's mother, Lady Isobel Moncrief. She's Mr Deverell's sister and only visiting.'

'That means she must be my aunt. And this Jago Moncrief must be my cousin. Why didn't he tell me that when I saw him in Castlebridge yesterday?'

'That I couldn't say, but the old lady, sitting one side of the fire, is Mrs Belmont. She's the mistress's mother. The mistress herself, Mrs Deverell, is the one dressed up in silks and jewellery, sitting on the other side of the fire.'

'I know the man at the writing-table must be my Uncle Cedrick. Are you their daughter? If so, you must be my cousin too,' she added hopefully.

'Gracious no, Miss.' The other girl looked shocked and drew away from her. 'I'm Beulah Barlow, assistant to the housekeeper. I'm waiting here to help the old lady into the dining room.'

For a moment Lucienne was at a loss for words. How could she have made such a mistake? But then servants she'd met at the inns since coming to England had been an altogether rougher kind than this well-spoken young person.

Recollecting herself she said, 'Oh I see. I'm Lucienne Deverell. I've come here with my little brother, Alain. He's so lovely and I thought everybody would be dying to see him.'

Beulah stood up. 'I'd like to see him, Miss. Let's go upstairs and see him now.'

'But what if they want you to help the old lady?'

'That might be ages yet. Mrs Dobson says all is out of order today since Mr Jago arrived to say you were coming.'

In the bedroom, they sent the maid away and sat on the faded hearth rug, while Alain played with the toys he'd been given earlier. Watching Beulah talking to him about the little horse Lucienne asked quietly, 'Beulah, do you know why the family were so against us coming here? Was it because my father went to live abroad?'

'I don't know Miss. I never heard of mention of a Mr Richard Deverell until we were told to get this room ready for you. Mrs Dobson says that there was a lot of bother between the Master and Mistress when Mr Jago came to let them know you were coming. The mistress was ever so upset, crying and blaming the master, but Mrs Dobson couldn't tell what about.'

'But did Mrs Dobson say anything about my father and why he'd left England?'

'Just that she'd heard there'd been a scandal to do with the master's younger brother, but that was years ago before she came to work here.' She seemed about to say more, checked herself and turned to Alain, who was playing quietly on the rug beside them. She said, 'Most brothers and sisters look at least a bit alike, but you two are entirely different.'

'I don't know who I take after, but Alain is very like his mother. Chantelle had the same sort of very fair hair and such pretty grey eyes.'

'Chantelle was your stepmother?'

'Yes, and not at all motherly, though she was very dear to me. She played the piano and sang beautifully, wore the prettiest dresses you can imagine and had lots of friends to stay, always laughing and talking.' She paused, then 'Chantelle died and my father too. There was a fire.'

'Good heavens, Miss. It must have been awful. How long ago was it? And were you there when it happened?'

Before Lucienne could answer, the door opened and Bett came into the room, looking more strained than Lucienne had ever seen her. When Beulah got up to go, she motioned her to stay.

'Perhaps you will be able to tell us something,' she said wearily. She turned to Lucienne. 'When you left the room, there was so much arguing. The lawyer must have already told them that we wanted money to go to France because your uncle said it was out of the question. There is no hope of his helping us to get to France and he is to claim guardianship of Alain until he is twenty-one years of age.'

'What?' cried Lucienne, jumping to her feet. 'How dare he! Surely, he can't do that?'

'The lawyer said that he can. Your uncle is Alain's closest male relative and so has authority over him until he is one and twenty even without going to law.'

'Oh, Bett, how I wish we'd never come here!'

'But we are here. And that dreadful woman in the red dress, who I took to be your uncle's wife, started to shout that she wouldn't have either of you in the house, with the old lady joining in and making it worse. It was decided that, instead of staying here, you are to go to people who will be paid to take you off their hands. Some distant connection, a clergyman and his wife who will be glad to have the money.'

'Why is my uncle so unkind? He hasn't even seen Alain. Did none of them say they wanted-?

'Just a minute, Miss,' Beulah broke in eagerly. 'I know where he's sending you. It'll be to the Reverend and Mrs Tregarth in Yoxley village, only a few miles from here. I don't think they have any other poor relations. You and the little boy will be made welcome there, I'm sure.'

Lucienne saw doubt in Bett's eyes. To make her feel better, she said, 'That sounds all right, doesn't it? We are certainly not welcome here, and if these people where we are going are sort of relatives, it means we'll still be with our own family. At least until we can somehow escape and make our way to France.'

Bett shook her head in despair and an awkward silence was broken by Beulah saying she'd better go down and help the old lady into the dining room for supper.

'And I'm sure Mrs Dobson will be sending up hot water to wash, and a supper tray now the Master has done with you,' she added and went away. As soon as the door closed behind her, Bett sat down wearily in the armchair.

'At first, after you were taken out, they seemed to have forgotten I was there but afterwards, when it was settled where you should go, I was asked a lot of questions,' she said quietly. 'One was how long had I been in your father's employ. I told them that I came to your parents before you were born.' She paused, then, 'Lucienne, I don't know why they wanted to know, but I think I should admit to you now that what I said was not true. I came to look after you after your mother died. You were just two years old then.'

Lucienne, still sitting on the floor, with Alain falling asleep in her arms, gasped in dismay.

'Bett! All those stories you used to tell me. About my parents. About how happy they were to have a baby daughter. About my christening. None of it true? Why on earth—?'

'Getting angry won't help,' Bett told her firmly. 'Just listen to me, Lucienne. I was younger than you are now when I came to look after you, taken on because I could speak to you in English. You were a frightened little child, crying for your mother and constantly asking for the father who went off on his travels, leaving you with me, a young nursemaid you barely knew at first. Later, when you asked questions, I told you what I thought would make you happy'

'But it wasn't true.'

'The truth would have made you sad. We saw a mother with a new baby, and you wanted to know what kind of a baby you had been. So, I made up a story about that to make you laugh. Putting flowers on your mother's grave, we saw a bride go into the church and you wanted to know what your mother wore on her wedding day. I told you I saw her married in that very church in a dress of pure white silk with white flowers in her hair. Not true, but it made you happy.'

'So, you didn't brush my mother's long golden hair, like you said?'

'Another story, to keep you still while I brushed out your tangles. I knew what kind of hair was because I found golden hairs on her dresses hanging in the wardrobe.'

Lucienne fell silent, remembering the times long ago in Paris, when her father forgot to send money and the dresses, as well as almost everything that had belonged to her mother, were gradually sold by Bett to buy the necessities of life.

'Lucienne,' Bett was saying, 'What I am trying to tell you is that there was something strange about the way your uncle pressed me for details of your parents' marriage. I thought it safest to say that I was present at their wedding in the church of Saint Pierre de Montmartre. I think it best, if you are asked, to tell the same story.'

Downstairs, Cedrick Deverell, scowling, led his wife to the supper table, followed by his mother-in-law, scolding Beulah for no particular reason. Left behind in the drawing-room, Lady Isobel Moncrief, took her son's arm.

'For God's sake, Jago, what are you waiting for? I'm half-starved. I thought my brother would never stop questioning that poor woman.'

'I won't be taking supper here tonight. If the Tregarths

are to collect those two tomorrow, I'd best ride over there now to tell them.'

'Nonsense! It's nearly six already and how long will it take you to get there in this weather? And you know how early these people go to bed. The Reverend Tregarth won't be pleased when you knock on his door and wake the household.'

'Mrs Tregarth won't mind. She'll be too relieved when I give her the money for a carriage to get her here and home again.'

'Yes, I expect she will. Poor Lydia. She and I were such friends as girls and I so wish she could have made a better match. All those children, that dreadful vicarage and her sanctimonious husband. Anyway, let me get to the supper table before I faint with hunger.' She started to move away, but he caught her sleeve.

'One more thing. About the girl. She can go to live with the Tregarths, but I want you to take legal guardianship of her. According to the letter she brought from Préfet in Guadeloupe she was eighteen years old last June so it will be until she comes of age in just over a couple of years from now.' Ignoring her look of astonishment, he went on, 'Tell Uncle Cedrick you feel sorry for her. Tell him what you like to get his agreement to her being your responsibility.'

She shrugged her elegant shoulders, 'Jago, that is quite out of the question, though I do feel a little sorry for her. Pretty eyes, and good teeth, as far as I could see, but painfully thin, straight hair, straight nose, and so very pale. With absolutely no money, I doubt she'll find a suitor.'

'I'm not so sure about that. The last few months have taken their toll, but I think she's rather charming'

'Really? Well, each to his own, but just remember,

Jago, I have my own life to lead. And, if you are so concerned, why don't you apply for guardianship yourself?'

'No judge in the Court of Chancery would put a girl of eighteen into the care of an unmarried man of my age, cousin or no cousin. If we applied jointly, it would be a different matter.'

She gave an impatient shrug of her slender shoulders. 'Well, I suppose I could agree to do it jointly with you, but she must not expect anything more from me.'

'If you'd prefer to have it that way, she needn't even know. Uncle Cedrick most likely won't set eyes on her once she leaves this house, so he isn't likely to tell her. I'll sort out the legalities and, before you ask, I'll reimburse you the expense of her keep.'

He watched her shrug her shoulders again and walk away. How typical of her not to question why her brother Cedrick, with his lack of sympathy for anyone other than his own wife and stepdaughters, should undertake the expense of rearing two-year-old Alain until he came of age at twenty-one. Also it was typical of her to be more concerned about her niece's looks and marriage prospects then about her distress at losing her parents and being kept in England against her will. Personally, the more he saw of Miss Lucienne Deverell, the more she intrigued him. Spirited, brave but too impetuous to hold her tongue, the sooner she left Ottersbury Manor for the safe discomfort of Yoxley Vicarage the better, he decided as he left the drawing room and made his way to the stables.

4

In the lumpy old bed that night, with Alain fast asleep between them, Lucienne lay awake and listened to Bett's soft breathing, like she had long ago when they lived in a tiny apartment in the Pigalle quarter of Paris. Just the two of them, happy, though they were never sure when her father would remember to send them the money to live on. When he did, they hurried to the patisserie to choose eclairs or macarons and then ate them slowly to make them last. Soon, she was peacefully asleep.

It was still dark when she woke, aware that a lamp was lit, and someone was moving stealthily about the room. She sat up and saw Bett taking her belongings out of the travelling trunk and packing them into an old canvas travelling case she hadn't seen before.

'What's happening? Why have you got your coat on?' she asked anxiously.

'I'm keeping off the chill while the fire builds up. And I'm packing this valise the housekeeper found for me last night.' She paused, then, 'Lucienne, I have to leave today and go my separate way.' Her voice was harsh with unshed tears.

It was as if an iron band tightened around Lucienne's chest. 'But how can you be leaving? I thought you were coming with us to the Tregarth's house.'

Bett shook her head, 'I was told last night that I am not needed, and to leave the house this morning. Your uncle was very definite about that.'

'But where will you go?' She slipped out of bed and ran to put her arms about Bett, holding her tight, 'Oh Bett, this is so awful. I can't bear for you to go. And what will happen to you, alone in this strange country? There isn't enough of Uncle Maurice's money even for just you to get back to France.' She started to cry. 'When we left the island, I never thought of this. I thought we would always be together. How can this be happening? We will miss you so much.'

'And I will miss both of you.' Bett was as near to tears as Lucienne had ever seen her. 'To leave you breaks my poor heart when all these years you have been like my own child. But at least you and Alain will be together. And last night, when I went down to see the housekeeper, she told me that this English lady you are going to live with is well known for her kindness.'

'But where will you go? What will happen to you? How will you live?'

'Fortunately, I still have some of your uncle's money, and the housekeeper was very helpful when I spoke with her last night. She advised me to go down to the village as soon as it is light. I must wait at the post office and, when the mail coach comes, pay the driver to take me to Castlebridge. There I must enquire for a road that is clear of flooding to take me some smaller port from where boats go to France. I will go there, write to my brothers for help and find work until they send the money to pay for my passage home.'

'But Bett, France is so far away. If it wasn't for Alain, I'd come with you. I could find work. I wouldn't mind what I did as long as we were together.'

Bett held her tight and spoke softly, 'Lucienne, you are a young lady and perhaps it is best you live with this vicar's family. They are gentlefolk, even if they are not rich. And we need not forget each other. Beulah told us the name of the village where you and Alain will be living. I have taken note of it so that I can write to you at the vicarage there.' When Lucienne didn't answer she added, 'I am so unhappy to leave. To see you so sad does nothing to make me feel better.'

Without speaking, Lucienne dried her eyes on the sleeve of her nightgown, wrapped herself in her cloak and sat down on the hearthstone beside Bett who was silent for a while.

Then she said softly, 'Lucienne, I think something must have happened here that we don't know about, or why are your father's family behaving so badly? For my sake, dearest child, now you are amongst these strangers, take care. Watch what you say, be careful who you trust.' She took Lucienne's hand in hers and they sat together in the fire light's glow and waited for the morning.

After Bett had gone, Lucienne, feeling strangely exhausted, got back into bed beside the sleeping Alain, and stared sadly at the ceiling until she fell asleep. She was woken by Beulah.

'Miss Lucy, do get up, it's nearly eight and your breakfast tray's been brought up a while ago,' she said, then, as Lucienne pulled herself up to sit, 'Are you alright? Your eyes are all puffy and red. Have you been crying, Miss?'

'Of course, I've been crying. Poor Bett's been sent away.'

'I know. Below stairs, they're all saying how hard she was treated.' She frowned as she glanced across at the little boy still lying asleep beside Lucienne. 'Are you sure he's all right, Miss? Most children wake up much earlier than this, running about and wanting things.'

'I expect he is tired after the journey. I am too.' Getting out of bed, she found her legs were shaky and there was a stiffness in the back of her neck.

'Best wrap up while I get the fire built up, Miss,' Beulah told her, holding out her cloak.

'No. It's so warm in here now.' She walked over to the small table by the armchair where fresh bread and butter and a jug of warm milk were laid out on the tray. At the sight of it, her stomach heaved, and she sank down on to the chair. Beulah came over, looked at her more closely, and put a hand on her forehead.

'It's not warm in here at all. It's you, Miss. Your forehead's burning. Let me get you some water.'

Everything seemed to blur. A headache, getting worse, her skin smarting with sweat, then she was cold and shivering, tossing and turning between tormented sleep and troubled wakefulness. From the dark shadows of her mind whirled a mass of insects, stinging her face as she crouched in the small rowing boat; the searing heat of flames all about her as she ran down flight after flight of stairs, her hair on fire; Alain crying out to her as he fell toward the black depth of a raging sea.

She threw out her arms, her fingers scrabbling to grasp his clothing, and found she was clutching bed sheets, but where was Alain? Was that him she could hear, far away, frightened, calling her name? She tried to sit up, fell back on to pillows, her head spinning in a room where the fireplace, the chair, the door were strangely shaped and moving about. And suddenly Beulah Barlow was there, standing well away from the bed.

'I mustn't come too near, Miss Lucy, in case I get ill too.'

'But what about my brother? Where is he?' It was still hard to breathe.

'Mrs Tregarth came for him. And she'll treat him kind and fair, Miss.

'How can you know that?'

'I do know, Miss. I lived with her before I came here. She took me on to help when I was quite a little girl and treated me like one of her own. And young master Alain is settling in well. They sent a message yesterday.'

'Yesterday? How long have I been like this?'

'Over a week, Miss. You've had a bad bout of the ague. The influenza, the doctor says we have to call it now. A woman from the village, who nurses the sick, is here to look after you. I said I'd keep watch while she's stretching her legs.

'Thank you. That's so kind.'

'It's no trouble.

It was easier now to turn her head and she saw raindrops falling on the latticed window. Quite pretty, until she thought of Bett.

'Poor Bett. She won't know where to go. She might be stranded somewhere in the rain and cold.'

'No. Miss. She isn't. We've heard she's living in as housekeeper to Miss Petty in the village. Only Mr Deverell being the old lady's landlord now, and him having got rid of your friend so hasty, it might not suit him. Best not to tell anybody, Miss.'

'I don't think I'm likely to see anybody to tell. My father's family are all against me.'

'It's not you, Miss. Mrs Dobson let slip it's to do with the disgrace over your dad. She's heard the law was after him, so he had to leave England.' She gasped and bit her lip, 'Oh, I shouldn't have said, not while you're so poorly.'

'It doesn't matter, and if you hear any more about him, please tell me. But now I'm so tired,' she heard herself say, as she drifted back to sleep.

Two days later she was well enough for the nurse to leave, could dress herself and walk about the room, but for most of the time, she sat in the big armchair, gazed into the fire, and worried about Alain, alone with strange people.

'It's no wonder you're feeling low on your own in this dreary room all day,' Beulah said when she came to see her. 'Mr and Mrs Deverell have gone out visiting, so while they're out I can take you for a walk about the house. We can go downstairs if you can manage.'

Weak at first, Lucienne felt her spirits lift and her legs get stronger as they made their way along the gloomy passageways to the newer, brighter part of the house though, when they reached the main staircase, she had to hold tight to Beulah's arm as they went down. As they reached the bottom, the drawing-room door opened and a harassed looking maid of mature years hurried out. She brightened when she saw them.

'Good morning, Miss, and thank goodness you're here, Beulah Barlow. Mrs Belmont 's rheumatism is playing havoc with her temper this morning and she's sent me looking for you.'

Beulah rolled her eyes. 'Tell her I'll be there in a little while. I have to take Miss Lucy upstairs to her room.'

The maid scuttled back to where she'd come from,

then returned at once to say that Mrs Belmont wanted to see them both.

As they followed the maid into her mistress's presence, Beulah asked, 'You don't happen to play the piano, do you Miss?'

'Yes, I do. My stepmother taught me.'

'Then please offer to play for her. It's the one thing that keeps her quiet,' Beulah said and led her into the drawing-room where the raddled old lady with powdered hair reclined on a chaise-longue in front of a blazing fire.

'I've already seen her,' she snapped, when Beulah began to introduce Lucienne, 'Came here claiming to be some sort of needy relative.' Pausing to complain about her rheumatics and the way her maid attempted to adjust the shawl that had slipped off her shoulders, she dismissed her and turned to scrutinise Lucienne through a lorgnette, held close to her eyes by a scrawny hand.

'Well?' she snapped.

'I have come to play the piano for you.'

'Then don't just stand there. Get on with it.'

Spurred on by a reassuring look from Beulah, Lucienne made her way to the piano at the far end of the room. She sat down and strummed a few notes to get the feel of it and knew at once that this was a better instrument than the one her stepmother had so treasured in Guadeloupe. A thrill of half-forgotten happiness ran through her as she remembered how Chantelle, usually so light-hearted and frivolous, was serious and patient during their lessons. She started to play pieces she knew by heart, so absorbed that it was some minutes before she was aware that the muttered grumbling from the old lady had subsided. Beulah came and stood beside her.

'She's dozed off, Miss, so you can stop now if you like.' She leaned forward and gently trailed her fingers over a few of the piano keys. 'You play so lovely, I'm sure she'll want you to play for her again, Miss, but you do look tired. Would you like me to take you back upstairs?'

'Yes please,' Lucienne said faintly, a wave of fatigue sweeping over her as she stood up. There was a shriek from the chaise-longue, and they turned to see the old woman glaring at them.

'Be off with you and get on with whatever it is you're paid for,' she snapped irritably. 'Not you,' she added sharply to Lucienne as both girls started for the door. With a helpless look, Beulah left them. When they were alone, the old lady motioned toward the piano.

Lucienne said faintly, 'I am sorry, but I've been ill. I'm too tired to play anymore.'

'Really?' The old woman raised her very dark eyebrows in mock astonishment. Were they painted on Lucienne wondered? Her cheeks were certainly rouged. 'Well then, sit down where I can get a closer look at you.'

Wondering what was coming next, Lucienne sat on one of the tapestry covered chairs while Mrs Belmont subjected her to close scrutiny, then declared, 'No resemblance to any known member of the family.' She threw down her lorgnette and added, with an unpleasant cackle, 'And that's a compliment by the way.' She paused, then asked sharply, 'Now, what do you make of Jago? Handsome rogue, isn't he?'

'If you say so', Lucienne replied, still smarting at the memory of how he'd bundled her out of this very room the first day she'd arrived.

'Oh, like that is it? So, what's your idea of a good-looking fellow then? No, don't bother telling me.' She snapped. 'Jago's a dammed handsome man with no money. So why hasn't he got himself an heiress instead of wasting his time with the law? He's here now looking for something or other in the library. His mother is to blame, of course. Didn't think of his future prospects, when she married his father, did she?'

Lucienne was wondering what to say when Mrs Belmont went on, 'There never was such a fuss as over Isobel Deverell's coming out. A fortune spent on dresses. Parties, balls, picnics. London at her feet and what did she do? Ran off with a Scotsman, useless title, and married him at Gretna green. On the way up to his useless estates in Scotland.' She fell back on to the brocaded cushions of her couch and reached for her smelling salts.

Remembering how Chantelle and her father had lived for each other, Lucienne ventured, 'Perhaps they were in love. They might have been very happy in Scotland.'

The old lady sat up and gave a derisive snort. 'They went off around Europe. Spain, Italy that sort of place, taking their infant with them. We never set eyes on Jago until he was ten years old, and Lady Isobel brought him back and left him here when her husband died. He ran wild, out with the fishermen in all weathers.' She paused and took such a deep sniff at the smelling salts that her eyes watered.

'Do you know what they have decided to do with you?' she demanded.

'I'm to go to live with a lady called Mrs Tregarth.'

'Lydia Tregarth! When she was a girl, she came each summer to stay with a relative here in the village. And you know how it is. A bold young beauty like Isobel takes up with a shy, pretty girl like Lydia and yet their fates were to be so different.' She leaned back on her cushions, gazed at the ceiling and sighed. 'Such happy times. Isobel and Lydia, and my own charming daughter. She had married so well at eighteen to a fine man who passed and left her a rich woman, and then she made another splendid match to your uncle Cedrick Deverell. Of course,' she added acidly, 'That was before his brother Richard brought shame and disgrace to the family. Cleared out of the country quick enough, but his having done murder was not something that could be hushed up.'

She turned her beady stare on Lucienne. 'Yes, you may well look amazed, but you'll get no more from me about it. The less said the better. And if you're not going to play again, you may as well be off. Away you go.'

Trembling with shock at what she had heard, Lucienne left the room and got no further than the staircase before her legs gave way. She sat down on the bottom step, too weak and lightheaded to go further. That her father could be harsh and unfeeling at times she knew, but murder! No wonder his children were not welcome here. She was too overcome to make her way back to her room and stayed where she was until Beulah came hurrying down the stairs.

'You look worn out, Miss. Mrs Dobson had me check the linen cupboard for damp or I'd have come back for you before now,' she explained as she helped Lucienne onto her feet and up the stairs.

Back, in her room, wrapped in her cloak, she sank into the armchair, feeling shaky. She never wanted to see that terrible old woman again and must try her hardest to be well enough to get away from here to join Alain at Yoxley.

She couldn't rest. While Beulah knelt in the hearth building up the fire, she got up and paced about the room, her growing agitation giving her strength. She tried to tell herself that Mrs Belmont, very old and probably muddled in the head, had made a mistake, confusing her father with someone else. This didn't work. She had to know the truth. Beulah and Mrs Dobson might know more than they would say for fear of upsetting her, but there must be someone who would tell her. Suddenly the old woman's words came back to her. *He's here now, in the library, on some business or other.* Jago Moncrief. He was sure to know what had happened and, with his lack of regard for her feelings, he might be persuaded to tell her.

'Beulah,' she asked, as the girl got up to go, 'I should like to have a book to read. Where is the library?

It was a long room with a vaulted ceiling, a darkly polished floor and the strange, papery smell of old books. Tall shelves, lined with these, covered the walls on three sides, while the arched, stone framed windows on the fourth side let in enough light for her to see that the main piece of furniture was a long narrow table. It was piled high with ancient leather-bound volumes and an earnest-looking youth examined one of these, page by page.

She was about to ask where Jago was, when she heard him say her name, turned and saw him, at the top of a ladder in the dark corner of the room. Before she could speak, he jumped down and landed beside her. His dark eyes crinkled in a smile of welcome and she felt the colour rise in her cheeks.

'I came to look for a book to read,' she found herself saying hastily, 'I wonder why it's so gloomy in here. Not good for reading I should have thought.'

'Perhaps the Deverells are not great readers. The entire collection appears to have come with this house when they bought it from the Acland family. Nearly a century ago, and with what looks like a century's worth of dust on some of them. Still, if you are looking for a book—'

'It's not just that. I want to ask you something.' She glanced at the young man at the table and Jago nodded at him to go. When they were alone, he looked at her expectantly.

'This morning I spent some time in the drawing-room with Mrs Belmont.' She hesitated, unsure how to go on.

'You have my sympathy. She's a difficult woman.'

'What I mean to say is that she spoke about my father.' The words tumbled out. 'She said he'd killed someone, had to flee the country because it was murder. And I want to know if it's true. She's a very old person, perhaps she's confused, she might have made a mistake—'

'It's true,' He was watching her intently.

'But who did he kill? And why did he do such a dreadful thing?'

He gave a non-committal shrug of his broad shoulders. 'When I first came here, I heard talk in the village of how my uncle, Richard Deverell, had knifed a man and killed him. I asked the family and was told that your father's name was never to be mentioned again.'

'Why didn't you ask somebody else? A lot of people must have known about it then.'

He turned and walked over to the table, picked a large book up from the pile and started to leaf through it.

Without looking at her, he said, 'I was a boy of ten, left here with my mother's family. I was told by them to leave the subject alone, so I did just that because I wanted to get on well with people I hardly knew.'

At least you were welcome to stay here, instead of being bundled off to poor relations, she thought bitterly, barely managing to stop herself from saying it out loud.

She felt sad for him all the same. It was hard to imagine this self-assured, confident person as a vulnerable child, his father dead and his mother abandoning him.

Determined not to give up, she asked, 'This man who my father was supposed to have murdered, surely his family will know what happened. If I could find out where they live—'

'No chance of that.' He was still leafing through the book. She saw him start with sudden interest as he drew a sheet of paper from between the pages, folded it and slipped it into his jacket pocket as he went on, 'The family of the murdered man, the Widdons, were stonemasons. Like many Devon tradesmen they took their skills to the New World some years ago.'

Another setback, Lucienne thought in despair. Her strength seemed to drain away. She shook her head, trembling and unsteady as she turned to go. Immediately he was at her side, his arm about her. He led her to a chair by the window, had taken off his jacket and was placing it about her shoulders when the door opened and Cedrick Deverell strode into the room. Even more sour-looking than when she'd last seen him, Lucienne thought as he came towards them.

Ignoring her, he asked Jago, 'Any sign of that land title you were looking for?'

'We've searched through nearly every volume, and found absolutely nothing as yet,' Jago told him, with every sign of sincerity, and they went on to discuss how some other estate business could be managed.

Surely, he's just told a lie, Lucienne thought, remembering the paper he'd taken from between the pages of the book? Feeling weak and miserable, she wished she had never left her room that morning, never heard the old lady say such dreadful things about her father. But then, if she had not come to the library to find him, Jago would not have given her his jacket to keep her warm and she wouldn't have known he could be so kind and gentle.

Whatever else he had to say seemed to satisfy her uncle, who was turning to leave when his eyes fell upon her. He stopped and spoke to her quite civilly.

'Now, about this sugar plantation in Guadeloupe. That French woman who brought you here either didn't know or wouldn't say how my brother came by it. His wife's dowry, was it?' He gave Jago a conspiratorial glance, 'If so, the boy has an inheritance out there and it needs to be reclaimed.'

'The plantation was owned by my stepmother's uncle,' Lucienne told him quietly.

'And she was his heir perhaps?'

'He has sons and grandchildren in France so I shouldn't think so.'

Cedrick Deverell turned to Jago with a bitter laugh. 'How like my brother. No provision for either of them. Another mess he's left for the family to clear up,' with which he strode from the room

She was smarting with humiliation when Jago came to her side.

'You'd best be back in your room. Can you stand?' he asked and, without waiting for an answer, drew her to her feet. Still limp and unsteady, she was about to sit down again when he picked her up, as easily as though she were a child, and carried her from the library. By the time they reached the passageway leading to her room, her faintness had gone to be replaced by a strangely breathless feeling as she lay clasped in his arms with her head against his broad shoulder. Almost there, she heard Beulah's anxious voice calling her name.

'Oh, Miss Lucy, there you are. And Mr Jago. Good

morning, sir. I've been so worried, wondering where Miss Lucy was when I brought her tray up just now.' She led the way into the bedroom, where Jago took Lucienne to the fireside chair, the lean tanned side of his face almost brushing against hers as he put her gently down. He straightened up, smiled, wished her well and left them before she could say more than a brief thank you to him.

Beulah, straight-faced and respectful until she closed the door behind him, hurried back to Lucienne, giggling, 'My goodness, Miss! I'm sorry if you're not well, but what a thing, to be carried up here by Mr Jago! Whatever happened?'

'Nothing really, I was just a little faint. It was very kind of him to help me.'

She was lying back, her eyes closed, recalling how it felt to be in those strong arms, when Beulah said, 'I don't know what his ladylove would think if she knew Mr Jago was carrying other young ladies about, I'm sure.'

'His ladylove?' Her eyes blinked open. 'Is Mr Jago engaged to be married?'

'No, Miss, but there's talk that he's the admirer of a beautiful, titled lady whose husband's ever so rich.' She stepped back and bit her lip, seeming to recollect herself. 'Oh, sorry Miss, you must excuse me. That's just servants' gossip, as Mrs Dobson would say. And she won't have it. So, I'd better get back to my work.'

After she hurried away, Lucienne gazed into the leaping flames of the fire, not even pretending that the knowledge of her father's crime was the only thing that disturbed her. The few moments she'd spent in Jago's arms had brought on feelings that she had never known before. But her head was clearing now. Did Beulah mean this married person was Jago's mistress? Her cheeks reddened at the thought. Dear Chantelle, determined to fulfil her motherly duties, had told her what that meant. Or rather she had hinted at it, in such a way as to leave little doubt. So, what sort of a dishonorable person must Jago be to enter into such an arrangement. And what sort of a woman could this ladylove be? To break the marriage vow was a sin, everybody knew that, but there was something about Jago.

She made herself stop. Nervous to think any more about a quality in him that was beginning to disturb her, she got up and went to the window to look at the grey skies. Did the sun never shine here in Devon?

5

Two days after Lucienne learned the dreadful truth about her father, Mrs Dobson brought her a note that had been delivered to the house. It was from Bett and the contents surprised her.

'I thought to see Bett at Miss Petty's house, but this says to meet her at the church tomorrow, at one o'clock in the afternoon.'

'It's too far for you to walk there and back to Miss Petty's so soon after you've been ill,' Mrs Dobson told her, 'I'd be only too pleased to have Miss Bett come up to my parlour, but for the master telling her not to come back here.'

'I understand.'

She was wondering how to fill in the long hours until one o'clock when the housekeeper said, 'The truth is, Miss Lucy, that Mrs Belmont's been demanding that you go and play the piano for her again this morning. That poor maid of hers had a very difficult time with her yesterday, and the Mistress says she'll get rid of her if she can't do her job properly.'

Remembering the look of misery on the maid's face

when Mrs Belmont berated her, Lucienne couldn't bring herself to make an excuse. She dreaded the thought of spending any more time with the nasty old woman but, to her relief, Mrs Belmont was in a mellow mood that morning. She hardly spoke, hummed along with the music, then fell asleep. Lucienne played on for a while, wondering if there would be a piano at Yoxley vicarage so she could play to Alain, just as his mother had?

'Mrs Dobson's found you a pair of walking boots belonging to one of the young ladies that's grown out of them,' Beulah explained when she came to escort Lucienne to the church that afternoon.

'Which young ladies?' Lucienne asked as she sat in the armchair pulling the left boot on over her woolly stocking. It fitted quite well.

'The two daughters of the house, Miss Emily and Miss Georgiana. Didn't you know about them, Miss?

'No. I didn't,' Lucienne said crossly as she pulled on the other boot. 'I've been in this room for two weeks now with no idea I had two cousins living in this house.'

'They aren't here, Miss.' She knelt to tie the boot laces. 'They're away at a school for young ladies. Quite handsome young ladies, and they'll be well off too.' She dropped her voice and went on, 'There's talk of how the Master has been bleeding this estate for years, and putting money by for their dowries, even before old Mr Deverell passed away. Olaf Escott says the state of the labourers' cottages is disgraceful.'

'And who is Olaf Escott?'

'A friend of mine. He lives over Yoxley way.' She sat back on her heels and gave a satisfied smile. 'He asked to marry me when I was only sixteen, but I was living with

Mrs Tregarth then, and she was against young marriages. Then I got the chance to come here, to learn housekeeping, but Olaf's been paying me attention again lately. Anyway, Miss, you'd best get your cloak on, so we can start out or your friend will be kept waiting.'

Outside it was warmer than Lucienne had expected. She took deep breaths and marvelled at how she could feel so well today that the walk to the ancient church on the outskirts of the village seemed easy. Soon they were passing under the lynch gate into the churchyard, where the tombstones stood upright like grey sentinels amid the grass. They had waited only a few moments in the shelter of the arched doorway of the church, when they saw Bett's neat figure, along with a short stout one, starting up the path towards them.

'Oh look, Miss. Miss Petty's with her,' Beulah cried as they went forward to greet them. 'She's Mrs Tregarth's auntie and she was ever so lovely to me when I was little. We used to come visiting her when it was her birthday.'

'And I don't know how many more of those I'll see, I'm sure,' Miss Petty remarked as the four of them met halfway along the path. She took Beulah's arm and went ahead, while Lucienne hugged Bett as if she could never let her go.

'I've been so worried about you,' they both said at the same time and started to laugh as they went into the church. While the other two sat talking softly in one of the front pews, Lucienne sat at the back with Bett, who told her that she'd heard Alain was thriving in Yoxley vicarage.

'I knew he'd do well with that Mrs Tregarth. Miss Petty is her aunt and cannot speak too highly of her as a mother. I was more concerned about you, Lucienne. They told me you were very ill indeed.'

'I am over it now and soon I'll be going to join Alain. But Bett, I'm so glad you're still here. How did you come to be with Miss Petty?

'That morning, after I left you and went to the post office, a labourer passing by told me that there would be a long wait before the mail coach came, so I went to see Miss Petty. I told her what had happened, and she said at once that I might stay with her. She has been lonely since her sister passed away and we do get on so well together.' She put her arm about Lucienne's shoulders and asked, 'And how are you up at the manor house? Are they treating you well?'

'Quite well,' Lucienne heard herself say, deciding this happy occasion wasn't the time to tell what she'd found out about her father, or that her uncle had spoken to her only once and her aunt not at all.

Glad to be together, they talked for a while longer, then, as they stood up to go, Bett said, 'What a pretty church this is, a little dark of course but so fresh and clean.'

'And so it should be,' said Miss Petty who had come to join them. 'It has not long been refurbished. Two years ago, the flooding played havoc with it. Of course, the building was put to rights, but beautiful kneelers we ladies of the village had finished embroidering only the year before were ruined and the parish records, going back hundreds of years were soaked with mud beyond rescuing.'

'I see, but it is strange to have a church situated here on the outskirts of the village. In France it would have been in the centre,' Bett remarked as they went outside.

'No doubt it was built near to the manor house for the convenience of the gentry who paid for it, not for the parishioners,' Mis Petty said briskly before she and Bett said their goodbyes, promising to meet again soon.

Standing in the church doorway, Beulah said they must be getting back to the manor because she'd promised to help Mrs Dobson do the ordering, but Lucienne told her, 'I don't feel like going back just yet. I'd like to have a look round the churchyard.'

'Will, you be all right on your own, Miss? You look a bit pale.'

'I'm always like that, Beulah, and I really do feel much better now I'm out in the fresh air.'

After Beulah went away, Lucienne stood on the church steps, took deep breaths, and had a strange sensation of something familiar not too far away. She breathed deeply again and thought she smelled the sea. Could it be so nearby? She took a path that led her round to the back of the church, through the graves and on, beneath ancient yew trees, to the far end of the graveyard where, in the surrounding grey stone wall, she reached a low a wooden gate.

Beyond the gate was a short stretch of grass and then, without any sign of a beach or shoreline, was the grey expanse of the sea. A cliff top, she realised, and the gate was only a few yards from the edge. She was so surprised that it took her a moment to notice that someone had trodden down the stretch of long grass from the gate to a point on the cliff edge. Suddenly she was afraid that whoever had trampled the grass had fallen over. Or even worse, jumped! She was pushing open the gate to go and see, when a young man, wrapped in a heavy grey cloak against the cold, clambered up over the cliff edge where the trodden grass ended.

He must have seen the alarm on her face because, as he trudged towards her, he called out, 'What's the matter,

Miss? Did you think someone had thrown themselves in the briny?' He was tall, fresh-faced, with blue eyes that sparkled with laughter, and she noticed that he had the attractive, softly spoken accent of the local people.

'No, of course not,' she answered lightly, 'I just wonder what you were doing down there?'

'Looking around the caves for signs of smuggling. A trade that's rife in these parts as you must know.' He had come through the gate, and they began to walk together back towards the church.

'I don't know anything about smuggling. I have only just lately come to live here.'

'I did hear say there was a Frenchie living in the village, but I'd not expected her to be a pretty young lady like yourself.'

'I am not a Frenchie, as you call it,' she told him firmly, though she couldn't help laughing up at him as she spoke, 'I am as English as you are. It's just that I've always lived in places where most people speak French.'

'And it sort of rubbed off on you, has it?' She could tell he was teasing and somehow didn't mind.

They had come to the front of the church now and were starting down the path to the lynch gate as she asked, 'Why should you be out looking for signs of smuggling anyway?'

'Because I'm a coast guard, from the station back near Castlebridge. There's been reports hereabouts of these bad gentlemen, who do his majesty out of his dues in taxes, bringing stuff in from foreign parts on the quiet.' They had reached the lynch gate when he said, 'I left my mount at the Holly Tree pub in the village, so I'll walk that way with you if you're agreeable. My name is Mathew Harris. Are you going to tell me yours?'

'I'm Lucy, and I don't live in the village. My path takes

me in the opposite direction.'

She wished him goodbye and set off up the lane to the manor, pleased when she looked back and saw him gazing after her. Perhaps he had been a little forward talking to her. Perhaps she had been a little forward talking to him. She wasn't sure, but he was natural, open and friendly. If she had not been about to leave for Yoxley, she would have liked to see him again.

A few days later, it came to her that if she was going to see Bett before she left for Yoxley, it would have to be soon. She was sitting in the armchair, about to pull on her walking boots, when there was a knock at her bedroom door and Mrs Dobson came in. She looked more hesitant than her usual self but came straight to the point.

'I have to tell you, Miss Lucy, that there's been a change in the arrangements. The family have decided that you are to stay here for the present and not to go to Mrs Tregarth's.' As Lucienne stared up at her in dismay, she went on, 'It's because of the old lady, Miss. She's been so much better tempered since you've spent the mornings with her that they think you'd be more useful here.'

'And what about what I think?' Lucienne cried. She threw the boots onto the floor and jumped to her feet, 'I think that if Mrs Tregarth is prepared to have me, they can't stop me from going there!'

'Begging your pardon Miss, but that good lady has, to my certain knowledge, been beholden to Mr Deverell on more than a few occasions. Whether she wants you there or not, she'll not be wanting to offend him.'

'Beggars can't be choosers. Is that what you mean?' Lucienne snapped, pacing to and fro. 'And I'm another one. Another poor relation to be made use of, am I?'

'I came here to give you a message, Miss Lucy, not to be spoken to like a skivvy,' the housekeeper told her indignantly. 'So, if you'll excuse me, I have work to attend to.' She made to leave and Lucienne, recollecting herself, ran after her.

'Mrs Dobson, I'm very sorry to have spoken rudely, but it is such a disappointment. I've been so worried about my little brother, longing to be with him.'

Slightly mollified, Mrs Dobson sniffed. She paused. 'I'm sure it can be arranged for you to be taken to Yoxley village to visit him,' she said and swept from the room.

Lucienne collected the boots and pulled them on. Her temper had died down and left her feeling ashamed, and even more aware of the helplessness of her situation. Months ago, when she was so determined to escape from Guadeloupe, how could she have imagined that she would find herself, more or less a prisoner in this dreary place? Only the thought of seeing Bett gave her the energy to set off for Miss Petty's house on the other side of the village.

'Well, my dear, I can only say I did wonder where my poor niece, with all those boys of hers, was going to put you if you had gone to her,' Miss Petty said when Lucienne arrived and told them her news. 'Yoxley Vicarage is a poor sort of place, and two of the bedrooms very damp. Poor Reginald Tregarth is a decent man, but not one likely to advance to a better living in the Church. However, I expect the two of you would like time on your own together, so I'll be off to the dressmaker,' and she left Lucienne and Bett alone to talk in her cozy sitting room.

'Things are not so bad, Lucienne,' Bett told her. 'We will be able to go together to visit Alain. Miss Petty says there is a way across the fields, a shortcut we can walk when the weather improves.'

'I suppose so, and at least you and I are not far apart, but I live such a solitary life at the manor. I have never seen my uncle's wife since the day I arrived, and my Aunt Isobel left for London when I was ill. And it's not only that.' She paused, finding it difficult to go on, even to Bett, but it had to be done if she was ever to find out more, so she related everything she had heard about her father.

'Bett, I am so upset. I wonder if you could ask Miss Petty about it. She has been here all her life and—'

'Lucienne, I have already asked her if she knew why he lived abroad, and she said that she did not. Of course, she must have some idea, but she may be afraid of saying anything against the Deverell family. Your uncle is her landlord, and he is not well liked hereabouts.'

'That I can understand,' Lucienne sighed. She glanced about the low-ceilinged room. A fire burned brightly in the burnished grate, the dark wooden furniture glowed with polish, the faded sofa was adorned by prettily embroidered cushions, and the whole place was fresh and sweet smelling.

'It's so nice here Bett and I'm glad you're happy, but I wonder now if we should have stayed in Guadeloupe with Chantelle's uncle Maurice when he offered us a home? At least there we would have all been together.'

'Perhaps, but we could only do what seemed right at the time.' They sat and talked until Miss Petty came bustling back, and Bett went to make them tea.

Left alone with Miss Petty, Lucienne told her, 'I was talking to a coast guard the other day. Did you know that there are smugglers hereabouts?' She saw the old lady stiffen and alarm flickered across her face.

'I know nothing about that, but we do have the measles again,' she said hurriedly. 'Every three or four years there is an outbreak, such a worry for the young mothers,' and she went on to talk about the comings and goings in the village until Bett came back with the tea tray.

There were little scones with honey gathered last autumn from the beehives in the garden, a jug of cream and a bowl of sugar lumps to stir into the fragrant Indian tea. Their talk was bright and cheerful and soon afterwards Lucienne left, glad there was one place in Ottersbury where she was truly welcome. So perhaps things aren't so bad, she thought as she walked up the rise to the manor house. The sun's rays seemed warmer today and she noticed the tiny green leaves, that had appeared last month on the branches arching overhead, were bigger now and cast a light shade as she made her way towards the lion topped gates.

Best of all, when she was back in her room, Mrs Dobson sent a message to say that the following day, she was to be sent by carriage to visit her brother, accompanied by Beulah Barlow.

'Don't mind old Barny, he's stone deaf,' Beulah told her, nodding at the back of the old groom who drove them as they sat behind him, side by side in the carriage. They went through the village, turned right and bowled along the coastal road as she went on, 'I'm that excited to be out for a drive, Miss, but I'll not be coming with you as far as Mrs Tregarth's, though that dear lady was like a mother to me and another time I'd be only too glad to see her.'

'So, what are you going to do?' Lucienne asked her.

'You know that young man I told you about?'

'Olaf Escott?'

'Yes. His family has a farm near Yoxley. I'm going to call in there to see him.'

'If he asks you again, will you marry him?'

'I could do. I'm one and twenty next month and there's no one could stop me, though, as a housekeeper, a woman has more of her independence. To give that up, I'd need to be sure I could care for Olaf as a wife should. That is if he was to ask me again.'

They had gone several miles when she pointed to a huge, stately mansion set well back amid rolling parkland.

'That's where the titled gentleman lives who owns all the land round here, including the farm where the Olaf's family is the tenant.' She gave a muffled giggle, 'And, as I told you before, it is said that his wife, the beautiful Lady Helena, has Mr Jago for her lover.' She glanced at Lucienne, 'You needn't look so shocked, Miss Lucy. A gentleman like Mr Jago is bound to have a ladylove and at least he's not ruining some innocent village girl.'

'But what about the lady's husband? Doesn't he know what's going on?'

'That I can't rightly say, Miss, though perhaps rules in those circles get broken more often than would be tolerated among decent, common people.'

'Even so, I think it's deeply shocking, Beulah,' but perhaps, she thought, the lady was like Chantelle whose first marriage, when she was very young, was to someone she could never love. Even so it wasn't right. 'It is shocking and dishonorable,' she said firmly though, remembering how she'd felt in Jago's arms when he carried her from the library, she thought there was something about him that might tempt any lady. Stop that, she told herself crossly and sat up straight, staring at the passing countryside until, a little further on, Beulah said goodbye and got down at a five-barred gate by the side of the road.

After this there was a further drive of half a mile or so

before the carriage slowed down and turned into a narrow, winding lane. Here, the hedges had been left to grow so tall as to be almost meeting over their heads by the time they arrived at their destination, and she saw that Yoxley village was little more than a hamlet. The tiny houses looked in a poor state of repair, the vicarage not much better, and it was Lydia Tregarth herself who opened the front door when Lucienne knocked.

She was tall, and with the leanness of a woman used to keeping busy. Her hands were reddened through hard work, her dress faded and worn at the cuffs, but there was about her an indefinable something that marked her as a gentlewoman. She smiled a pleasant greeting.

'Miss Lucienne Deverell, I think, come to see Alain,' she said and led her into a large, sparsely furnished living room. And there was Alain, sitting before a fire railed off by an enormous iron fireguard, a jumble of playthings scattered around him. Lucienne went forward smiling, thinking he would come to her. Instead, he got up and ran to hide behind Mrs Tregarth's skirts, peeping out shyly and dodging back again until that lady picked him up. After a few seconds of hiding his face against her shoulder, he turned to Lucienne, reaching his little arms out to her. Taking him, holding him against her chest, she was suffused by a glow of happiness she had almost forgotten. His little hand reached up and patted her cheek, then pointed to the hearthrug where the rag doll Bett had made for him lay.

'Alphonse loves you,' he said quite clearly, and she was delighted because he had hardly spoken before he came here.

'Please to sit down,' Mrs Tregarth said, indicating a well-worn couch, and Lucienne sat with Alain on her knee, so happy to feel his dear little body snuggle down against her.

'I received a letter yesterday to say that you were to stay at Ottersbury Manor,' Mrs Tregarth said when Lucienne began to explain. 'I know how you must miss him, but it's such a joy for us to have little Alain here. He is a small child compared with my youngest, who is much the same age, but just as clever. They play together all day long'

'I was hoping to see your own children, Mrs Tregarth.'

'The two little ones are asleep, and the next three are with the vicar of a neighbouring parish who tutors them. My oldest two are fourteen and fifteen years of age now, both very able boys. They are in Plymouth, gone to live with a relation of their father. He has found occupation for them there.'

From the tone of her voice, Lucienne was thinking that their occupation was not what their mother would have hoped for when Mrs Tregarth started up and said she could hear that her youngest boys had woken from their nap. She went away to get them.

Left alone, Lucienne looked more carefully around the room. There were no carpets here, the furniture was old and well worn, battered even, the window curtains threadbare, but it was warm, clean, and very tidy considering that a large family lived here. A much homelier place for a child than Ottersbury Manor.

Mrs Tregath came back with a robust, cheerful looking child of about two years old and the other, very much the same but a year or so older. Alain slipped off Lucienne's knee and ran, laughing, to greet them.

'I've never seen him play with other children like this before,' she said, watching the three of them chasing about the room, 'I'm so glad he's happy here with you.'

Alain ran back to her, bringing the rag doll for her to hold. He leaned against her knees, smiling up at her and told her about the big tabby cat they'd been chasing, then ran off again.

It was a happy reassuring visit until it was time to leave and Mrs Tregarth picked up Alain and took him to the door to say goodbye. Lucienne kissed him goodbye and told him she would come back soon, but he sobbed and stretched out his little arms, begging her not to go away. The door was firmly closed, and Lucienne hurried down the path, still hearing him cry and call her name. Biting back tears of her own, she climbed into the waiting carriage and drove away.

When they drew up at the five-barred gate, a young boy was looking out for them and ran to fetch Beulah from the farmhouse. She climbed into the carriage looking so serious that Lucienne thought the visit must have been a disappointment.

'No, it's not that.', Beulah told her. 'Everybody was pleased to see me. Olaf could only stop for a bit because of his work, but he was lovely and we're to meet again soon. His mother said she'd forgive me for breaking his heart when I was sixteen, but I could see she was laughing and his sisters as well.'

'What went wrong then?'

'It was just something his old Gran told me. When she heard that you'd brought me there, she started off saying that if it was not for your father, they would never have got the tenancy of their farm.' She broke off, 'Oh Miss Lucy, I'm not sure if I should be saying—'

'I already know he was supposed to have killed someone and old Mrs Belmont said it was murder, so you may as well tell me anything more that you've heard today,' Lucienne said bleakly.

'All right then, Miss. It turned out they all knew about it. They said when your father, Mr Richard, was a young man he was sweet on a school master's daughter who was educated and refined, but not good enough for the Deverells. He went touring abroad, as these young gentlemen do, and when he came back, he found she'd had to marry this man called Widdon who was the tenant of Escott's farm at that time.'

'Why did she have to marry him?'

'Because her father was a gamester and he'd lost so much money playing hazard with Widdon, that her marrying him was the only way of settling the debt.'

'How dreadful. Was she forced into it?'

'I don't know Miss, but when Mr Richard Deverell was back from abroad and came to the farm to see her, there was a fight. I'm sorry to have to tell you, Miss, but it was said that Mr Richard pulled a knife and killed him. He ran off straight after, took her with him, and neither of them was seen or heard of again. Anyway, that left the tenancy of the farm vacant and the Escott's got it.' she paused. 'You look so upset, Miss. Perhaps I shouldn't have said.'

'No, it's all right, Beulah. I'd rather know.' Beulah looked unconvinced, so Lucienne said quickly, 'It's all old history now. Don't let it spoil our day out. Tell me more about the farm. And Olaf. Is he dark or fair, short, or tall, does he make you smile, or is he always serious? Did you let him kiss you, Beulah?'

The rest of their drive back to Ottersbury was full of Beulah's happy talk, but that night Lucienne couldn't sleep. She sat up in the armchair, wrapped in her cloak and going over in her mind what she had learned that day. The school master's daughter must have been her mother and how dreadful for her to have been forced into the intimacy of marriage with farmer Widdon. Bett had told her that, after her mother's death, her father went travelling because he was too distraught to stay in Paris, so they must have really loved each other and been happy, whatever dreadful things had happened to draw them together.

Feeling a little better, she turned down the lamp and climbed into bed.

Next morning, Mrs Belmont was so serene and pleasant in her greetings that Lucienne wondered if the maid had used some kind of medicine to calm her. There was no mention of her rheumatics, and it didn't seem to matter whether she played something she knew from memory and played well, or if she made mistakes attempting new pieces from the pile of sheet music in the piano stool. Mrs Belmont listened with rapt attention, now and then singing in a quavering soprano voice when a tune she particularly liked was played, while to Lucienne the music brought back bittersweet memories of her life in Guadeloupe.

'Stop now and tell me about your life in the tropics,' Mrs Belmont said quite pleasantly halfway through the morning.

Lucienne went to sit beside the old lady, who eagerly devoured every detail about the grand plantation house of Belle Chance, the food, the trees and flowers, the weather, the river, and the beautiful gowns Chantelle had worn, especially when there were parties. Most of all she liked to hear about how her father and her pretty stepmother had lived for each other.

'Love, love, love!' she cried. 'What joy it can bring and what havoc, what torment! Richard Deverell knew that more than any of us. Have you heard what happened to him, so many years ago?'

She's forgotten she told me about the murder, Lucienne realised, but could there be more to tell? She mustn't sound too interested in case the old lady had one of her moods and refused to go on. She said cautiously, 'It seems that he killed a man.'

'But did he?' snapped the old lady, very excited now. 'Or did the young woman, seeing her brute of a husband with his hands around the throat of her childhood sweetheart, strike out with the blade to save him? There was a witness. One of the farm labourers.'

'And did he say that it was the young woman who stabbed her husband?' Lucienne gasped.

'No. At the inquest, he swore on oath that Richard did it, but it was rumoured locally that he bore false witness. There was no trial because the two of them fled the country that very night and were never more heard of.' She fell back on to her silken cushions and went to sleep, leaving Lucienne so upset that she could only pace about the room, wishing there was someone else she could ask to find out what really happened.

6

When her maid came to take Mrs Belmont to her midday meal, Lucienne hastily tidied away the music sheets ready to escape into the cool, fresh air outside. She needed to sort out her thoughts. First the old lady had said that her father had killed her mother's husband. Now, she'd said it was her mother who stabbed him. Of course, this might have been another of Mrs Belmont's flights of fancy, but Lucienne couldn't be sure how much of this was true. Would she ever know for sure? Her mind in a whirl of agitation, she hurried out into the hallway and was almost at the front door when Beulah stopped her.

'Miss Lucy, Mr Deverell said he wanted to see you soon as you'd finished with the old lady, but Mr Jago's just this minute arrived, unexpected, to see him. Best come with me and I'll let them know you're waiting.'

Lucienne's heart sank lower. She hadn't seen her uncle since the day he'd asked her if Alain could expect an inheritance from Chantelle's family and she wasn't looking forward to seeing him again. When Beulah left her in the passageway outside his door, she expected a long wait but was almost immediately called into the study. Then, standing before the desk, she suddenly found herself more aware of Jago's tall, athletic figure leaning against a bookcase than she was of her uncle, sitting opposite to her.

'I have called you here to discuss a matter which, in all fairness to the family, must be addressed,' Cedrick Deverell was saying. She turned her attention to him, noting that he had not asked her to sit down, and was speaking to her as though she were a servant summoned here for a reprimand. He asked her how old she was.

'I will be nineteen on the 7th of June.'

Cedrick Deverell looked at her in triumph. 'Quite so.' He drew a deep breath and went on, 'I am obliged to tell you, with regret as I know this will cause you pain, that perusal of the facts, including the information you yourself have just given, lead only to one conclusion. You are not, cannot be my brother Richard's child.'

Speechless with shock, she sat down in a nearby chair. 'What are you saying? How can that be—' She glanced at Jago, hoping for some kind of support. Her heart fell as he looked back at her, his face expressionless.

'When my younger brother, Richard, reached his majority,' Cedrick Deverell went on forcefully, 'he went abroad for two years on his grand tour, returning in late December 1783 just before his twenty-third birthday. He ran away, with your mother, whose husband he killed in a brawl, three weeks later in January 1784. You have just indicated that you were 18 years of age on 7th June last year, which means that you were born on 7th June 1784. No five-month child survives. Therefore, my brother Richard cannot have fathered you. Hence, you are not a member of the Deverell family and can have no expectation from us.' He spread his hands in a gesture of satisfaction,

'What other conclusion can any intelligent being draw from these facts.'

Lucienne leapt to her feet, all the anger, and resentment of the past weeks welling up.

'I can tell you what conclusion I've come to, Mr Deverell,' she cried,' I conclude that I don't want to belong to a family of such selfish, arrogant people. I came here to ask for help to get to France. It was not my wish to stay here or to be separated from my brother. If I have no right to be here, I'll gladly leave this house. I shall pack my belongings and go,' with which she jumped to her feet and ran from the room.

Outside in the corridor she stopped, only too aware that her declaration of independence was useless, because there was no place she could go to. Certainly not to Miss Petty or to Mrs Tregarth. Neither of them could risk angering her uncle by taking her in. She was about to hurry on, when one of the wooden panels on the wall beside her swung open and Beulah, motioning her to be silent, pulled her into what appeared to be a tall cupboard. She pointed to a small crack in the wooden panelling of one of the walls, then slipped outside and closed the door behind her. Plunged into darkness Lucienne felt for the crack in the woodwork, leaned forward to peer through, could see nothing, then put her ear there and heard their voices.

'What have you got to prove that the date you give for your brother's return to this country is correct.' Jago was saying. 'Twenty years is a long time back. I ask you to consider this again. Might not your brother have returned a year earlier? Say in December 1782?'

'Don't come the lawyers talk with me, Jago,' Cedrick Deverell snapped. 'I'm damned if I'm going to have my word questioned on this or any other family matter. And

God knows the scandal that followed his return to this county was enough to make the date stick in my mind.'

'Still, Uncle, I believe we should find the old family bible and see where Richard's date of birth was recorded because, if he went abroad soon after he was twenty-one and came back two years later, in 1783, he must have been born in 1760. Should the bible entry show that he was born earlier, say in 1759, then he would have returned from his tour abroad in December 1782, well in time to have fathered the girl in question, So, where is it? The Deverell family bible.'

'I have no idea. It was very old and in poor condition. On the occasion of our marriage, my late father-in-law presented your aunt and I with a revised edition. Since that girl arrived here, I've had this place gone through, attic to cellar, looking for the old one and no sign of it. Did you have any luck with your searches in Plymouth?'

'Unfortunately, I did not. The newspaper reports at the time of Widdon's murder would have given us the date of his death to compare with the date of her birth, but it seems the backdated copies were destroyed in a fire. I applied to the coroner's office for the record of the inquest, but it couldn't be found. Unsurprising. The place looked a shambles to me.'

'Pity. Either could have settled the matter once and for all.' His tone softened slightly, 'The thing is, Jago, I believe I made a wrong decision when the three of them turned up here a couple of months ago. I should have done what they wanted. Given them the money and got rid of them. And that is what I intend to do now. You just heard the girl say she wants to leave, and that French woman is living in the village. The sooner the pair of them are packed off to France the better.'

'And the boy?'

'As it appears that he is my brother's child, the boy must stay here.'

'The problem is, Uncle,' Jago said reasonably, 'The problem is that news came through this morning that we are now again at war with France. I came here to let you know. Our ships are blockading their ports, so travel between England and France is now impossible.'

'War! My God man, why the hell didn't you tell me that as soon as you got here.' There was the scraping sound of a chair being pushed back as Cedrick Deverell got to his feet. 'I must get into town and speak to my banker about what can best be done to protect my interests.'

In the dark, stuffy, cupboard, Lucienne drew away from the woodwork, miserable and disappointed. It had been bad enough to be told she wasn't her father's child, but somehow it felt even worse to find that Jago had been seeking proof that she couldn't be. For some foolish reason she would have hoped he would stand up for her. Disappointed in herself for caring about this, she waited until the sound of footsteps hurrying past the cupboard died away, then fumbled in the dark for the door latch. Just as she found it, the door was pulled open, and Jago stood outside. He eyed her with what looked like amusement.

'I grew up in this house and every possible hiding place is known to me.' he told her as she stepped out into the passageway. 'And before you ask, I guessed you were in there because I picked up the sound of the cupboard door closing just after you ran away in such a frenzy.'

'Can you blame me?' She hesitated, feeling foolish as she added, 'I've said I was leaving, but there is nowhere for me to go.'

He grinned. 'Lucienne, my uncle has two spoilt stepdaughters and a hysterical wife. He is used to females shrieking threats and rushing out of rooms. Just keep out of his way and carry on as if it never happened. Most likely the effect of war on his investments overseas will keep him too occupied to worry about you still being here. And now I must get down to the village to let the men know that we are at war before they take the boats into the channel.'

Leaving, he gave her one of his devastating smiles, but it didn't work. How dare he try to charm her when she had just overheard him scheming with his uncle to prove she was not her father's child! And did that terrible man, Cedrick Deverell, really believe she could ever have been persuaded to go to France and leave Alain behind? Seething with hurt and indignation, determined to escape from this dreadful place at least for a few hours, she hurried to the front door. She was about to leave when an inner voice brought her to a halt.

Was the old Deverell family bible really lost? She felt a rush of excitement. Only a few days before, while she was searching for a piece by Scarlatti that Mrs Belmont demanded, she felt something at the very bottom of the piano stool beneath the big pile of sheet music. She hadn't taken much notice at the time but now she hurried back to the drawing room.

It took her only moments to find the bible and unwrap the black cloth that covered it. An old, leather-bound bible with a metal clasp. She took a deep breath of sheer and utter relief. In here would be her father's true date of birth, the evidence she needed to disprove everything they had said about her. Her fingers clumsy with anxiety, turned the thin, yellowing pages, searching for where the Deverell births and deaths were recorded. At last, she found the page she wanted.

Isobel Anne Deverell born 3rd January in the year of Our Lord 1755

Cedrick Edward Deverell, born 6th January in the year of Our Lord 1757

Richard Henry Deverell born 20th December in the year of Our Lord 1760

For a moment the shock seemed to paralyse her. She had been certain her uncle's insistence that she was not his brother's child was another sign of his hateful disposition. A lie, to prove her illegitimate for some strange purpose of his own, but this meant what he had said was true. Born in 1760, returning from his tour abroad just before his 23rd birthday, at the end of December 1783, Richard Deverell had eloped with her mother late in the following January. He could not have fathered a live, healthy child born to her only five months later.

She'd shouted in anger that she had no wish to belong to this family, but what would happen to her if Cedrick Deverell found this evidence to prove him right? He would throw her out of the house. Get rid of her just as he had got rid of Bett. Where would she go? Not to France now that war was declared. Bett would try to help her somehow, she knew that. But Alain! Her heart missed a beat. She loved him, had vowed to his dead mother to look after him, but now, if it became known that they did not share the same father, the world could say she had no claim to him. No one, she decided passionately, must ever know they were not of one blood. But what if someone else were to find the bible and read this? Cedrick Deverell's searchers missed it, but Mrs Belmont had said that her granddaughters played the piano for her during their school holidays. They might stumble across the bible if she left it in the piano stool.

In that instant, her mind was made up. It was useless just to tear out the incriminating page, the whole thing must be got rid of. Made to disappear without trace. She was about to put it back, to come for it after dark, when she caught sight of one of Mrs Belmont's paisley shawls lying on the floor beneath the chaise-longue. If she put it on and held the bible under her arm, she could take it now and throw it into the sea.

She met no one as she left the house. The summer sky was overcast and there was a sudden down pour of rain as she hurried towards the manor gates, but once out in the lane she faltered. Was it a step too far to destroy the bible? There must be some other way. It could be hidden somehow. Bett would help her, she thought as she turned and walked quickly beneath the sheltering boughs of the beech trees towards the village. A little way along, she stopped. It wasn't fair to involve Bett. She must do this alone. For a moment she considered going back to the manor and hiding it somewhere in the attics. No, it had to be got rid of forever.

The rain was heavier now, breaking through the canopy of leaves as she turned back, then took a narrow, overgrown path into the woods that she thought must lead her to the sea. Through the trees and out in the open again, she smelled salt water, heard the roar of waves crashing against a rock face and knew she was nearing the cliff top. The wind from the sea drove the rain so hard into her face that it was difficult to see very far, but there seemed to be nobody about as she clasped the bible firmly under her arm and went towards the cliff edge. Halfway there, the waves sounded so near that she knew she had come at high tide, and memories of the relentless, terrifying power of the sea came flooding back. She stopped and stood with her eyes closed, frozen with fear. Yet it must be done. If she was somehow to get Alain back and fulfill her promise to care for him, no one must ever know she was not his sister.

Miraculously, as she opened her eyes, she felt the wind from the sea drop. She walked to the cliff edge, said goodbye to the ancient Deverell bible and hurled it into the black, churning depth below.

Much lighter of heart, she made her way back on to the lane. The rain had stopped, and she was out of the wind so that her wet clothes didn't bother her. No need to hurry inside yet. She paused to lean back against the silver-grey trunk of an ancient beech tree that overhung the lane, closed her eyes, and breathed in the crisp, cool air, knowing she was safe.

Her mind went to Richard Deverell. He must have known he wasn't her father. Small wonder he had left her to go on his travels when she was a little girl, but he at least employed Bett to look after her and sent for them when he was settled in Guadeloupe. He seemed happy to have her there until she was old enough to quarrel with the way he accepted, without question, the merciless treatment of the slaves who toiled on the plantation. Remembering their suffering, she felt it was better that she was not his child, though to the world she must still be known as Lucienne Deverell. Sister to Alain.

Incredibly it seemed to her, life at Ottersbury Manor continued as before. Her humiliation by the dreadful man who she must still call uncle, and her discovery that his suspicions were fully justified, might never have happened she thought a few days later.

She was free that afternoon, light of heart and glad to be out walking along the lane in the sunshine, when she saw, among the wayside grass, clusters of pale blue flowers like tiny, delicate bells. She'd never seen them before and picked some to take back to her room, then saw the narrow, overgrown path through the woods and decided to go that way again.

Out on the sunlit strip of grass that topped the cliffs, everything seemed different, almost as though the scene she had played out here a few days before, when she got rid of the bible, had been enacted by some other person. A light breeze stirred the air and, looking over the cliff edge, she saw a broad stretch of silvery-white sand gleaming in the sunshine. The tide was a long way out so, if she went down to the beach, she might find the smugglers' caves. Remembering that there was a way down near the gate at the back of the churchyard, and she was setting off in that direction when someone called out to her

Looking back, she saw the coast guard, Mathew Harris, striding towards her, so she stopped and waited for him.

'Been picking hair bells have you, Miss Lucy?' he said, looking at the blue flowers she'd gathered.

'Is that what they are called? They are so pretty.' There was a pause while he gazed at her with frank admiration.

'There's no other houses this side of the village,' he surprised her by saying, 'so I reckoned you must be from that grand house beyond the trees. I'd have come calling anywhere else, but I reckon your Pa wouldn't have the likes of me paying attention to his daughter.'

'Oh, I'm not the daughter of the house.' She couldn't bear to tell him her true situation. Beulah's words from the day she arrived came back to her and, on impulse, she said, 'I am assistant to the housekeeper.'

'Then can I call on you, Miss Lucy?

She smiled and shook her head, 'No followers allowed,' she told him, more words she'd heard from Beulah.

As if by some unspoken agreement, they turned and walked, side by side, along the cliff top to where they had first met at the churchyard gate. Thinking of the caves, she asked him to show her the way down the cliff.

'Steps cut into the rocks face, years ago,' he told her as they peered down rough-hewn steps to the beach, over a hundred feet below. 'You'll be safe enough going down if I take your hand,' he told her.

'I'll be safe enough if you go first and I follow,' she laughed and started after him as he made his way down to a rock-strewn, sandy beach.

The pungent smell of seaweed, the calling of the gulls, and the pleasant, never-ending sound of the distant waves all added to her delight. The faraway sea, rippling in the sunshine was very different from the dark, swirling mass of savage water that had snatched the Deverell family bible and devoured it only days ago.

'On a day like this,' she told him, as they sat beside a pretty rockpool where little crabs scuttled, 'When it is all so calm and beautiful you can't imagine how frightening rough seas can be.'

'That I can. I was at sea from fourteen years of age to twenty-one, and I'd be there still if family concerns hadn't brought me back on land.'

'And do you like being a coast guard? Is it interesting?

'Very interesting indeed, when I'm sitting in the sunshine with a pretty young maid like yourself, Miss Lucy,' he laughed. 'And exciting when we get word of smugglers bringing their stuff in from France and must go after them. At other times, it's a trying business. Like when I'm sent to get to know local people, in the hopes of finding one who'll take a bribe to help the law bring smugglers in.'

'And do they? Take bribes I mean.'

'Not if they've any sense. A desperate lot, those smuggling gentlemen. Splitting on them isn't worth the risk. And it's not just low life that's involved. Tis said there's many a member of the gentry hereabouts getting a good return from investing money in the goods taken to France in exchange for what's brought back.'

'You told me there were smugglers' caves down here. Can we look at one?'

'The caves are further on along the beach. I'd take you to see them, but the tide's coming in now and we'd best not risk being cut off.'

They talked for a little while longer, then climbed back up the steps to the clifftop.

'Mathew,' she said, suddenly remembering the news Jago had brought, 'Will it make a difference to your work now war with France has been declared?'

'That it will. Been pending for some time and now it's started, I reckon we'll have even more to do .'

'Why is that?'

'When goods can't be brought in legal anyways, there's even more profit bringing them in illegal,' he told her, 'More reason for the wicked gentlemen to be cheating His Majesty of his rightful custom dues.' They walked on through the churchyard towards the lane.

As they stood beneath the lynch gate, he said, 'I have to come this way from time to time. If I was to be here in the afternoon, same day next week, might you be out walking on the clifftop again, Miss Lucy?'

She said she might, feeling happy and carefree when he took one of the blue hair bells from her hand and put it in the buttonhole of his jacket, then gazed into her eyes for a long moment as they said goodbye.

What relief it was to have met someone who was young and friendly and who knew nothing about her, she thought, as she made her way back. Someone who didn't know that the people in the grand house were trying to disown her. In the grand house where in truth she had no right to be. Determined not to dwell on that, she went to her room and thought of every safe, friendly moment she had spent with Mathew Harris.

She wanted to talk about him when Beulah brought up the supper tray, though she was unsure how much to say. After all, she had only met him twice. Best to bring him into the conversation in a roundabout way.

'Beulah,' she began, 'Did you know smuggling goes on near here? Someone I met today told me about caves where they hide—' She stopped. When she mentioned smugglers, the same expression of alarm she had seen on Miss Petty's wrinkled old face appeared on Beulah's smooth, young one as she put the tray down and bent so that her lips were just by Lucienne's ear.

'Miss Lucy,' she said softly, 'best not to listen to that sort of talk. Smugglers could be hung for bringing stuff in from France, illegal. Anyone gets too interested in their doings has been known to disappear.'

7

'You can't come with me dressed like that,' Mrs Belmont snapped some weeks later when she announced her intention of taking a cure for her rheumatism. 'The city of Exeter is a fine, fashionable sort of place. We must look our best.'

There followed a week or so of frantic preparation of her wardrobe. For Lucienne, some pretty muslins cast off by the absent daughters of the house were found and sent to the village dressmaker to be let down and taken in to fit her, along with a pale blue woollen pelisse more suitable for spring wear than her heavy cloak.

The two-day journey to Exeter went well but the inferior quality of the lodgings at the Eagle Inn, where they had arranged to stay, so infuriated the old lady that, after less than a week, they moved to an elegant apartment in an hotel that lay within the city walls and boasted a magnificent view of the ancient cathedral.

After this, Mrs Belmont hardly mentioned her rheumatics. Whether this was due to the skill of the physician she had come to see or to the excitement of being in Exeter, Lucienne couldn't be sure. Much enlivened by theatre visits, afternoon tea and card parties in the Assembly rooms with patrons of her own age and social standing, she scarcely napped but was much sweeter tempered than at home. Even so, Lucienne's days were arduous. After mornings spent wheeling the old lady's Bath chair round the fashionable areas of the city and afternoons of playing the piano in one of the small parlours of the hotel, she was frequently required to push Mrs Belmont along the well paved, gaslit streets to attend musical evenings.

One morning, some weeks into the visit, it was a relief to be told by the lady's maid that her mistress wished to lie in bed late that day. For a few precious hours, she went out alone to explore the fine selection of shops only a few minutes' walk from the hotel. Since living at Ottersbury Manor, she had received a small monthly allowance that she had saved and now spent some of it on a pretty scarf for Bett and a set of tiny wooden farm animals for Alain, then went from shop to shop, examining the lovely merchandise. All too soon it was time to retrace her steps and get on with entertaining the old lady.

When she got back to the hotel, Jago was waiting for her. Despite all her resolutions not to let him affect her, her heart missed a beat when she saw him, standing in the hotel lobby, tall, lean and handsome. But when he greeted her, he didn't smile and the sombre expression in his dark eyes told her that something was very wrong.

'What is it? Is it Bett? Please tell me nothing has happened to her,' she begged as he took her arm and led her into a small parlour. 'Has there been an accident?'

'Lucienne, I am so sorry, but it is your brother,' he said gently. 'There was an outbreak of the measles at Yoxley. The little boy fell ill and passed away.'

She felt as if he had struck her, was speechless for a

long moment, gasping for breath, then cried, 'Oh, how can this have happened? I was meant to look after him. To keep him safe. I should never have brought him here. Never!' She clung to him as he supported her to a sofa, then sat beside her, his arm around her, her head against his shoulder as she wept. After a few moments, still trembling with grief and shock, she managed to suppress her tears, sat up and said quietly, 'I must go back at once. Bett will be so distressed and there is the funeral to arrange.'

'Lucienne,' he interrupted quietly, 'Alain is already buried. Miss Petty was not sure of the date, but she thinks he passed away just over three weeks ago.'

'Three weeks ago!' She heard herself cry as she jumped up and faced him. 'How could that be? Surely Bett would have written to say he was ill. And you Jago. It is very good of you to have come to tell me, but why have you left it so long?'

He got up and went to her, 'I was away in Castlebridge and only learned what had happened when Miss Petty flagged me down in the late evening as I rode into Ottersbury village a couple of days ago. I set off early next day to come to you. And Bett did write, but she addressed her letters to the Eagle Inn, where she believed you to be staying.'

'But I wrote to let her know that we had moved to this hotel.'

He shrugged his shoulders 'Your letter must have gone astray. When I reached the Eagle this morning, they gave me two letters addressed to you there and not forwarded because they said they didn't know where you'd gone. It has taken me until now to find you.'

His eyes were full of tenderness as he took her trembling hand into his strong warm one and seemed about to say something more when they heard Mrs Belmont's shrill voice from outside in the lobby. She was asking one of the hotel servants if they had seen Miss Deverell idling about.

He looked at her earnestly. 'Would you like me to tell her what has happened?'

'Please don't. I'm not ready to talk about it to anyone. I just need some time to myself.'

'Then I'll distract her, say I'm in Exeter to do with Assizes and called to pay my respects, offer to join her for lunch. That should give you an hour or so of grace.'

She nodded, letting her hand slide from his, then stood still with her eyes shut tight as the door closed behind him, knowing she should have stayed in Guadeloupe. Alain might have got ill there, but she could have looked after him herself, willing him to get well and knowing that if she ever had a child of her own it could never be more precious to her.

With a sigh, she opened her eyes and saw that Jago had left the two letters on a small table near the sofa. Both were in Bett's hand and addressed to her at The Eagle Inn, and she thought of poor Bett, waiting for the replies that never came. She broke the seal on the first letter, then couldn't bring herself to read it. Not now, she thought bleakly. Tonight, when everybody is asleep, I will read them and write back to her.

When they met again that afternoon, Mrs Belmont was so full of delighted chatter about her luncheon with gallant and handsome Mr Jago Moncrief that she didn't bother to ask Lucienne why she had been absent so long.

Lucienne was desperate to be with those who shared her grief but, though expressing sympathy for the loss of Alain, Mrs Belmont's own enjoyment of her stay in Exeter was such that she extended the visit for an extra two weeks so that June was nearly over when they returned to Ottersbury. By sheer good fortune, Mrs Belmont had nodded off to sleep when they drove into the village, so Lucienne asked to be put down at Miss Petty's gate.

She ran up the path, rang the bell and almost immediately Bett opened the door. They fell into each other's arms, silent for a long, sad moment, before Bett took her into the sitting room, and sat beside her on the sofa.

Still holding Lucienne's hand, she began, hesitantly, 'Shortly after you left, I saw Alain again at Yoxley, so happy with his playmates that he hardly cried when I had to say goodbye. I promised to go back, but then I had an accident and hurt my knee so that I couldn't manage the walk. I wrote to Mrs Tregarth to explain. When there was no reply, I took it to be because she was busy with her large family. You cannot imagine how I felt later on when Miss Petty received a letter from her, telling us that Alain was dead and buried a more than a week before and no one here knew anything about it.'

'But Bett how could that be? Surely, even if Mrs Tregarth didn't think to tell you, she must have let my uncle know what had happened.'

Miss Petty, coming into the room just then, told her, 'My dear, I don't suppose for one moment that Mr Deverell would have let Bett know even if he'd been here but, as it happens, he and Mrs Deverell were away, taking their daughters for a visit somewhere beyond London. And as for my poor niece, it seems her husband had got his long-awaited move to a more prosperous parish just at that time. They had to pack up and go straight away. Everything seemed to have happened at once. It was all so unexpected.'

'And we mustn't blame poor Mrs Tregarth, 'Bett put in

sadly. 'She had her own boys down with measles too, though of course, they're strong country lads, whereas our little Alain— Oh dear, I thought I had no more tears to shed.' She bent her head and wept silently onto Lucienne's shoulder.

Miss Petty said, 'One could tell from the disjointed state of her letter to me that my poor niece was almost out of her mind with it all. Half her life was spent in Yoxley village, and her first child, her baby girl, rests there in the churchyard too.'

'Even so, I can't just leave it like this,' Lucienne said firmly, 'I must see her. She must tell me more about how it happened. This new parish the Tregarths have moved to, is it far away?'

'It is miles away. And even if you went there, what else could she tell you? Perhaps a letter would be more appropriate now my niece has had time to recover herself.' Miss Petty paused as if uncertain how to go on, then said in a rallying tone, 'Bett, my dear, I think we all need a cup of tea. Such a comfort I always find. So, if you could make one for us?' As soon as Bett left the room she hurried over and took her place on the sofa.

'Lucienne,' she said in a tone of quiet urgency, 'I am sorry to burden you with this, and Bett asked me not to say, but the fact is that she did not have an accident to her knee, as she may have told you. She was attacked in the dark by an unknown assailant.'

Lucienne looked at her in horror. 'But when did this happen? And where was she?'

'Here in my own back garden, late one night not long after you went to Exeter. She'd gone out to the privy and she was set upon by a rough brute of a man, beaten and thrown to the ground. God knows what might have happened if I hadn't agreed to look after the neighbour's dog while they were away at a wedding. It's a yappy little thing and it ran out, making a terrible row. I rushed straight out and just made out the man getting away over the back fence.'

'How dreadful! What did you do?'

'Got her inside and put to bed. The next day I sent for the doctor. She had a broken rib as well as a sprained knee and some frightful bruises.'

'Poor Bett. Why on earth would anyone do such a thing?'

'I believe it is to do with her being a French woman.'

'Surely not! Nobody could blame Bett for the war with France.'

'My dear, there are hotheads even in a quiet place like Ottersbury. All they need is a cause and, no sooner than war was declared than a recruiting sergeant was in the alehouse with a lot of talk about how the French would be over here murdering us in our beds if they weren't put down.'

She broke off as Bett came back with the tea, which they drank with appreciation, then talked quietly for a while until they heard the doorbell ring. Lucienne went to answer it and found Beulah waiting on the doorstep.

'It's starting to rain quite heavy, Miss. The Master's still away, so Mrs Dobson got old Barny to bring me down here in the trap to get you. And, Miss Lucy, we're all so sorry about your loss.'

Lucienne nodded her thanks, went back into the parlour to say goodbye, then climbed into the trap, thankful to sit in silence as they drove through the village. When they alighted at the front door of the manor house, she couldn't bear to go in. Ignoring Beulah's protests, she turned and walked quickly across the lawn and out of the grounds, only stopping when she reached the lane outside. With a sadness too deep for tears, she stood there, letting the rain soak through her clothes and drench her hair so that it clung to her wet chest like snakes while she looked back at the grey walls of Ottersbury manor, rueing the day she brought Alain to a place where neither of them was wanted.

So why had help to leave been denied them? '*Something must have happened here that we don't know about*,' Bett had said on the first day they arrived here, and it seemed to Lucienne ever more likely that this was true. Whatever that truth might be, one day she would find a way to leave here, but for now she had no choice but to spend the next few hours with Mrs Belmont. Her hands felt too shaky to play the piano, though perhaps it could be avoided. Lately, Mrs Belmont wanted to talk about when she was a carefree young girl, coming out into society and waiting to fall in love.

When Cedrick Deverell and his wife returned, Lucienne took care to keep out of their way. She received a formal note in which they offered their condolences, but that was all.

There was no sign of Jago and she told herself to be glad of that, though his kindness to her in Exeter had meant so much. She couldn't have withstood her feelings of grief and desperation if she had heard of Alain's death from anybody else, but she must remember that kindness was all she could ever expect from Jago. She was nineteen now, old enough to understand that a man who had a beautiful mistress was lost to anybody else.

'*Don't ever waste your time or your thoughts on such a man*,' Chantelle had warned her and she must remember that, but found it was easier said than done.

Life went sadly on until, one afternoon a few days later, one of the downstairs maids stopped her as she was leaving the drawing-room.

'Miss, a nice fair-haired young man came up to me this morning when I was coming back from an errand in the village.' She giggled. 'He said to tell you he'd been looking out for you and wondered if you were back yet.'

Mathew Harris! She'd told him she'd be away for four weeks and now it was nearer eight, but today was Thursday, the day that they used to meet, so he might be looking out for her that afternoon. She'd almost forgotten him, but what a relief it would be to talk to someone who didn't know what had happened to Alain or to Bett. Someone who thought she was in service at the manor, not a still unwelcome guest.

That afternoon, when she left the shelter of the woods and reached the cliff top, her heart lifted as Mathew came striding towards her through the rough grass, smiling his broad, engaging smile.

'Miss Lucy, I thought you were never coming back. Exeter must be a fine place if your old lady kept you there so long.'

'It's a very fine place', she told him. 'Shall we go down and sit by the rock pool while I tell you about it?'

'Tides coming in too fast for that. Best we go to the old church yard. There's a bench it would be nice to make use of.'

They walked, side by side in the sunshine, to the church yard, then sat on the stone bench in the shade of the ancient yew trees behind the church while she told him about the sights of Exeter.

He listened with rapt attention, then suddenly asked, 'How many folks are in service up at the manor, Miss Lucy?'

The question was unexpected, and one she wasn't sure how to answer. 'Why do you want to know?

He grinned. 'Just it seems strange, rich folk having so many servants to look after so few of them. So, who's working up there and what are they doing all day long?'

'Well, there's me and Mrs Dobson, that's the housekeeper,' Lucienne began, finding it strange that she had been living there for months without considering this. ' Three housemaids, two ladies' maids, the cook and a girl in the scullery. Then Mr Deverell has a manservant who is his valet, and there's the footman and the butler, but he's getting on in years and there's talk of him retiring.'

'Locals are they, the two younger men?'

'No, I believe I was told one's from London and the other from Plymouth way. The two grooms and the stable boy are locals, of course. And the gardener and his two boys are from the village as well,' she finished, so relieved at having worked out what to say that she didn't stop to wonder why he wanted to know.

'That's seventeen people tending the needs of how many?'

'Three at present, but the two Miss Deverells come back from school now and then. And it is a big house to be looked after.'

'Lot of dusting to be done, no doubt,' he laughed.

'So, I'd better get back and see that it's all done properly,' she said as she got to her feet, deciding to go down to the lane and return to the manor house that way.

Mathew came with her, and each was so interested in what the other had to say that they came to where the path ended at the lynch gate before she saw the white flowers scattered on the ground. Anybody entering the church yard must tread on them.

'Must be something troubling the locals,' Mathew told her.

'Why? What are the flowers supposed to do?'

'Ward off evil. One of those old beliefs that country folks have,' he told her. 'See, there's yarrow, garlic and elder, all white for purity and goodness. Usually put round houses when there's sickness or some harm done. Strange though, leaving them here.'

'Very strange,' Lucienne agreed, glancing back towards the church. Something caught her eye. 'Mathew, one or two— no, three of the gravestones have fallen over. I'm sure they weren't like that when I came to church on Sunday morning. And look, there's another one just by the wall.'

He followed her gaze, then walked over to the nearest of the fallen stones.

'You're right,' he called back, 'And there was a wild storm a couple of nights ago.'

'It can't have been bad enough to knock gravestones over.'

'No, but it will have been loud enough to stop anyone hearing stones being dug up and chipped away at. Come and look at this.'

She went to where he stood and saw that the old, mossy gravestone lying at their feet had been defaced. The name, the date and part of the message of remembrance had been hacked away. They went to look at the other fallen stones and found they were in much the same state, then noticed that one of those still standing had been damaged as well.

'Sandstone, from the look of them, and easy enough to damage with a mason's chisel, or some such,' Mathew told her, then added, 'Look, Miss Lucy, I'd best be off. I'll ask round in the village to find out what's going. But don't worry about the flowers,' he called out as he went away, 'That's just a lot of old nonsense.'

Even so, Lucienne felt uneasy and pushed the flowers aside so as not to tread on them as she went out into the lane. Walking back to the house, she couldn't help thinking how much at ease she was with a friend like Mathew Harris, whereas thinking about Jago made her very uneasy at times.

There was a hush about the place when she returned to the manor house and made her way to the housekeeper's parlour in search of Beulah, but found only the housekeeper. Looking stricken, she started up when Lucienne went in.

'Mrs Dobson, what is the matter?'

'Miss Lucy where have you been? I'm so put out. There's been ructions here.'

'Ructions?'

'A lot of shouting. Mr Deverell was very angry, and now the Mistress is upstairs crying her eyes out. I had to send Beulah to help the maid calm her down, poor lady and I am sure it's not her fault.'

'I don't understand. What started all this?'

'It was Mr Jago. He came here, unexpected, earlier on and went straight into the study to see Mr Deverell. Then there was words between them, arguing to and fro, even before the master got so worked up. Beulah went to listen, but she couldn't make out what it was about, though your name came up more than once. Then Mr Deverell came rushing out of the study, white in the face and calling for that man of his to go to the stables and see that his horse was saddled. Then he went upstairs. After that, Mr Jago came strolling out of the study, cool as a cucumber.'

'Where is he now? Mr Jago I mean.'

'He went off again and said he'd be back in a day or two. And if I was you, Miss, I'd keep out of the way in your room until we know what's going on and things have settled down. Best go up by the back way in case you meet Mr Deverell coming down.'

Next morning, Beulah looked flustered when she brought up the breakfast tray.

'You may well ask me what's the matter, Miss Lucy. The fact is, I'm leaving.'

'Whatever's happened? Have you been dismissed?'

'No, Miss, it's my own doing. At half-past eight this morning, Mrs Deverell, who's never been seen 'til near midday until now, called me into the breakfast room and told me that they're going to live at Heverton village. I already knew the Master rode off over to a place they have over there yesterday evening, and he told Mrs Dobson that Mrs Deverell was to follow him there in the next few days with the old lady. She wanted me to go with them to start as housekeeper.'

'And it's not what you want?'

'No, it is not. It's been hard enough to see my young man as it is, let alone if I was to go miles away. Mind if it wasn't for him, I'd be only too glad because of having dear Mrs Tregarth at the vicarage nearby.'

'So, Heverton is where the Tregarths moved to so suddenly when they left Yoxley ?'

'It is, but it's too far away for me now.'

'So, what are you going to do?'

'I'm going to Escott's farm, to tell Olaf I'll marry him. I wasn't sure if that's what I wanted, but this has made my mind up for me.'

'I'll miss you, Beulah.'

'And I'll miss you, Miss, but I have go now, so it's goodbye for the present and good luck, Miss' She turned to go, then turned back and said hesitantly, 'Miss, there is one thing I'd like to ask. It's for Mrs Dobson. She's been so good to me. Taught me so much I could have run that house at Heverton if I'd wanted to, but her sight's going. Even with her strong glasses, she can't read well, and I know she's frightened she'll lose her post. Do you think you could help her, just now and then with the shopping lists and that?'

'Of course, I will, Beulah, if you'll promise to invite me to your wedding. And I'm so glad you have found your true love with Olaf,' Lucienne told her, smiling though inside she felt a little wistful.

When she went down to the drawing-room, she found Mrs Belmont distraught and held the old lady's thin, wrinkled hand while she railed against at being moved to Heverton Manor, a house she didn't like.

'And worse', she sobbed, 'that unfeeling brute Jago won't let you come with me, so I will lose the companionship that you, my dearest young friend, have given to me in our few happy months together.

Mrs Belmont had been better tempered since the visit to Exeter, but, remembering the scoldings she'd sometimes endured before that time, Lucienne was at a loss for words. It occurred to her then that, when the old lady left, her own role in the household would be at an end. Somehow, she must find a new one.

The following morning, Mrs Belmont was equally distressed, and Lucienne had barely managed to lull her to sleep with some gentle music when she heard Jago's voice calling for Mrs Dobson as he came through the front door. She waited, remembering her resolve to distance her emotions from him, then, determinedly calm, she rose from the piano stool and went out into the entrance hall.

More sun-bronzed than she remembered and slightly dishevelled, Jago watched her with his dark, heavily lidded stare for a long moment. He took a deep breath, then turned to Mrs Dobson and gave her a pleasant nod of dismissal.

He turned to Lucienne and gave her an appraising glance. 'You're looking well today.'

'Thank you.' She paused, then went on, 'I understand that Mrs Belmont is to leave in a few days. She is very upset. Could she not stay here, at least until they're settled at Heverton?'

'Yes, she can stay for a while. If her daughter cares to leave her behind.'

'Thank you. I'll let her know. I am sure she will be most relieved.' As she turned to go, he stepped forward and stood between her and the drawing-room door.

'Lucienne, have you given any thought to the conversation you overheard a couple months ago between myself and Uncle Cedrick?'

'You mean about whether or not I'm a Deverell? Of course, I have.'

'Well, remember he has found no proof.' She held her breath as he went on, 'The parish records of baptisms that would have shown the date of your father's birth, were destroyed a couple of years ago by flood, and the old bible can't be found. There is no evidence that his doubts about your parentage are justified.'

Relief swept over her. Relief mingled with a certain amount of guilt, which she brushed aside and asked, 'Do you think he will leave the subject alone from now on'

'We can only hope so.'

She wanted to ask what they had quarrelled about. Why her name had been mentioned and why were Cedrick Deverell and his wife leaving.

Deciding it was best not to appear too interested, she said, 'I must get back to Mrs Belmont. Entertaining her is, I believe, the only reason I have been kept here.'

Silently, he reached forward and opened the drawing-room. Avoiding his gaze, she went through and found the old lady struggling to her feet.

'Do we have to go now, Daughter? I am not ready,' her frightened voice called as Lucienne hurried to her side and helped her back onto her chaise- longue.

'It is me, Lucienne, come back to look after you,' she said softly. The old lady was trembling and her wig had fallen down over one eye. Lucienne straightened it and handed her the smelling salts. 'Don't be afraid. Mr Jago says you can stay until the house at Heverton is properly set up.'

'Then I'll be here for a good long while unless m'daughter's given up the drink,' she sighed as she sank back amongst her silken cushions. 'I never liked that place. It was my dowry, then my daughter's. Now her husband owns it and he's welcome, I'm sure.'

Lucienne had told no one, not even Bett, what she had found out about her parentage, though, on her next visit to Miss Petty's cottage she told them about the other changes taking place at the manor. She kept Beulah's request that she assist Mrs Dobson until last.

'And what I intend to do,' she explained, 'Is to gradually learn her skills so that one day in the future I'll be able to seek employment as a housekeeper, though not in such a grand house, of course.' She half expected disapproval, but Bett nodded her agreement.

'You were prepared to do anything you could to earn a living if only we could go back to France together. Now we must stay here, and it would be a respectable situation.'

'And a more fortunate situation than others open to a young lady without any fortune, as I understand you to be,' Miss Petty put in. 'Perhaps not what you were brought up to expect but a better position than that of a governess, I'm sure.' She paused, then asked, 'And you say that the Deverells are leaving the manor for their place at Heverton? Mr Deverell recently gifted the living at the vicarage there to the Reverend Tregarth, my niece's husband.'

'So, it was through Mr Deverell's influence that he moved there?' Lucienne asked in surprise.

'Yes. As the owner of the estate that paid for the church to be built, he can choose who is appointed vicar, subject to the approval of the bishop. I'm surprised that Beulah Barlow doesn't want to go to work there, her being so close with my niece. Whatever's got into the silly girl?'

'She's in love with a young farmer who lives near Yoxley, and she's gone to tell him she'll marry him.'

Miss Petty's eyes lit up. She asked for details, and the conversation turned to romance in general.

'Believe it or not,' she told them, 'When they were young, Cedrick Deverell greatly admired my niece, Lydia. That didn't hold him back from marrying a rich young widow with a considerable fortune, but it's likely why he's helped her over money problems, despite being otherwise tight-fisted.'

It wasn't until Bett, whose leg was much improved, offered to walk part of the way home with Lucienne that they spoke about Alain.

'Perhaps it's as well we have to stay in England,' Bett sighed, 'because I could not bear to go and leave him here with no one to tend his poor little grave.'

'We'll go there soon, with flowers and a stone jar to put them in,' Lucienne told her, trying to sound positive. 'And remember, he is with Chantelle in heaven now. Though we are sad, he will always be safe and happy.'

Not wanting to give Bett any more distress, she had held back her grief until they parted at the village green but, hurrying on alone, she shed bitter tears at the thought of Alain's dear little body, lying stiff and cold under the ground. In the lane outside the manor, she stopped for a moment to calm herself before walking between the lion topped gate posts.

Jago was standing directly in front of her, in discussion with the old gardener about what should be done with the overgrown tangle of pale pink roses and lilac coloured wisteria, that tumbled over a long section of the grey stone wall. His smile made her heart lurch, but she merely nodded her greeting and walked on, her head held high.

8

Jago caught up with her when she was halfway to the front door.

'Not speaking to me today, Lucienne? Have I offended you? Is that why you look so severe?' He sounded amused by the idea.

'No of course not. It's just that, I was talking to Bett about Alain. It made me so sad. And Yoxley seems so far away. Perhaps I'd feel better if he were in the churchyard here.'

He was silent for a moment, then said quietly, 'Sometimes we just have to accept things as they are, Lucienne. But, you have only to ask, and the groom will take you over there to visit his grave as often as you like.'

The gentle kindness in his voice making her feel tearful again, Lucienne swallowed hard and murmured her thanks as they walked in silence to the door of the manor house. Once inside she was surprised by him coming with her to the housekeeper's parlour where Mrs Dobson had her accounts accounts laid out on a table.

Pleased to see them she rose, took off her pebble lensed spectacles and was smiling graciously until Jago stated, 'Like much of the garden, this house is neglected and needs a great deal of attention.'

Alarmed indignation wiping the smile from her face, Mrs Dobson said sharply, 'I'm sure I've done my best, Mr Jago, but with the master so tight with what could be spent, and the mistress so often indisposed with the wine she took at dinner, it's not been easy to keep things as I would have wished.'

'I'm sure it hasn't, and from now on you have my permission to order whatever materials are needed, and make sure all repairs are attended to. Also, I want an inventory made of the contents of all rooms. Starting with the drawing room.'

Seeing the housekeeper's startled expression, Lucienne said quickly, 'I can help you with the inventory, Mrs Dobson. I think it would be most interesting.'

'Good,' Jago said, approvingly, 'So, before I go, are there any questions.'

Mrs Dobson, recovering herself, said pointedly, 'I've been given to understand that the master and mistress are moving to their estate at Heverton and I have to ask, on behalf of myself and such as the staff not going with them, if this house will be kept open?'

'Indeed, it will, and I shall be living here for the foreseeable future. Now, have you any more requests?'

They couldn't think of any, so he left them.

'What the foreseeable future means I do not know,' Mrs Dobson said as soon as he was out of earshot. 'But if he's living here as well as the old lady, and wanting all this work done, I'll not have to let any of the maids go, which I was dreading.' She paused, then went on in a business-like tone, 'Now, did Beulah mention about my needing a little assistance with the accounts now and then.'

'She did, and I'll be only too pleased to help you,' Lucienne told her, glad of the opportunity to go on and discuss her own plans to learn household management. The housekeeper listened, at first surprised, then accepting the idea.

'I'd be only too pleased to teach you all I can along those lines, Miss, but it must be made clear that you are still a young lady who is part of the Deverell family. Keep your distance from the staff, or you'll have no authority when it's needed.'

'Speaking of authority, Mrs Dobson,' Lucienne said thoughtfully,' I wonder by what authority does Mr Jago Moncrief decide to come to live here and start telling everybody what to do?'

'I'm sure it's not for me to question the ways of the gentry,' the housekeeper told her primly, 'Though I do myself wonder what it was he had to say that got Mr Deverell out of here in such a hurry but, as long as this place is kept open and wages are paid, I'm just grateful.'

Even before Mrs Deverell and her maid left at the end of that week, changes were taking place at Ottersbury Manor. The elderly butler and the valet had already gone to Heverton, but the footman was left behind and promoted to butler. Spurred on by Mrs Dobson, he busied himself with duties that the older man had begun to neglect. About the housekeeper herself, as she supervised the maids and inspected their work, there was a new briskness. Together, she and Lucienne worked on the inventory and, in little over a week, the contents of all the downstairs rooms had been noted down.

'These attic rooms are full of rubbish, which has been getting on my nerves for years,' she told Lucienne as they went round a part of the house that she had never seen before. 'In my opinion, it can only point to one thing.

You'll have heard from Beulah that Sir Humphrey passed away last month.'

'Sir Humphrey?' Lucienne frowned. 'No. I don't know who you mean.'

'Sir Humphrey Riverton. He had that big estate where Olaf Escott's family are tenants. Lady Helena Riverton will be wearing widow's weeds for a year yet, but after that she may well leave her Dower house to find herself a married lady again, and I wouldn't be surprised if Mr Jago is wanting this place put to rights before he brings her here,' she said as she opened the door to an attic room and led the way inside.

With a sinking heart, Lucienne, wearing what she hoped looked like a disinterested expression, glanced about at broken chairs, a legless sofa, and several cracked mirrors, and said, 'A lot of these things look as if they should be thrown away.'

'Before we get on with that, we must find some likenesses of the old Acland family that lived here long ago. Mr Jago says he remembers seeing them somewhere in the attics when he was a boy. He wants some of them brought down to put up in the hallway.'

'I'll have a look in the other rooms up here to see if I can find them,' Lucienne said with a brightness she didn't feel and hurried away to spend a few minutes alone with her thoughts. Until now, she had kept up with her resolve to be sensible about Jago, admitting to herself that he'd had never shown anything more than a kindly interest in her, but living here in this house with him married to Lady Helena didn't bear to thinking of. And now, standing alone among the cast-off relics of bye-gone ages, she resolved that, in the next year, she must learn all she could about housekeeping, find a post elsewhere and leave before the marriage took place.

. . .

Between attending to Mrs Belmont and her new responsibilities about the house, Lucienne was kept busy, but, on the next Thursday afternoon, she managed to slip away to the sun-drenched clifftop to meet Mathew Harris.

'I hear there's been a few changes up at the manor, with folks coming and going,' he said as they sat together on the seat under the yew tree in the churchyard. 'What happens up there is the talk of the village. It's said the master and his lady left in a bit of a hurry. Why was that then?'

'I've no idea. They didn't give the staff their reasons for leaving, Mathew.'

'What about this lawyer gentlemen that's moved in? How is it the locals are so pleased, saying it's his place to be there?'

'Are they?'

'The old fellows down the pub are,' he paused, smiling 'And why am I wasting time asking about that when I could be asking a pretty young girl for a favour?' He suddenly leaned forward and tried to kiss her, but she pulled away from him and jumped to her feet.

He smiled up at her. 'What's the matter, don't you like kissing?'

She felt herself blushing. 'Mathew, I just wanted to be friends. I hope you don't think I've been leading you on '

'A fellow doesn't need any leading on Miss Lucy.' His blue eyes sparkled and he was laughing. 'More especially when a girl gets prettier everytime he sees her and he's a single man looking to settle down. So, you can't blame me for trying. But friends it is for now. And you can always change your mind.'

That night she lay in the old four-poster bed and

thought about Mathew. A little while ago, when she had believed herself to the daughter of a gentleman of good family, she might have thought a coast guard not a suitable young man for her to marry, because that was what he'd meant by settling down. Now, aware that her real father had been merely a tenant farmer, she could have no such reservations, except that she didn't love Mathew. She liked him, felt more at ease with him than almost anybody else but never could love him in the way she knew, from what her stepmother had told her, men needed to be loved.

For the next week, there was so much to be done in the house that Lucienne couldn't be spared to visit Bett. Longing to spend even a short time with her, she got up very early one morning and went to Miss Petty's house to only hear shocking news. Bett was going away.

Several weeks before, she explained, there had been an advertisement in the Plymouth journal. A family, sailing to a government post in Port Royal, Jamaica, wanted a lady's companion, preferably one familiar with that part of the world. She applied, had been accepted and, in a few days' time, she was to travel to Plymouth to join them.

'But Bett,' Lucienne cried, 'How could you have done all this without telling me? And to go so far away! I know you were attacked in the garden that night, but this war with France may soon be over and then it will be safe for French people to live here.'

'We can have no certainty of that. Lucienne, and I fear for my life. Only last week a French man, a saddle-maker in Castlebridge for many years, was severely beaten and his shop robbed of everything he owned. And there have been other such incidents reported in the newspapers. I must get away from here, and a chance like this may not come again. Of course, it breaks my heart to leave you, but you are grown up now, and in a situation where you are safe. One day we will meet again, I am sure of that.'

They sat in silence for a while until Lucienne felt able to say, 'I hope they are a good family and that you are happy and have a safe journey. Will you have time to come to visit Alain's grave before you go? I have asked for a carriage and as soon as I—'

'Lucienne,' Bett interrupted, 'Listen to me. I hadn't heard from you, and a neighbour was kind enough to take Miss Petty and me to Yoxley. I have to tell you that we couldn't find the grave.'

'But how can that be?' Her heart missed a beat. 'Mrs Tregarth wrote to Beulah Barlow that Alain was buried there before they left for their new parish. His grave must be there. Didn't you ask anybody?'

'We couldn't find the sexton or the new vicar. The churchyard was very neglected, overgrown with weeds at this time of year, but we searched everywhere. Of course, it is too soon for a stone to have been erected, but there should have been a small wooden cross with his name burned into it. Other recent burials were marked like that.'

I must have the carriage to take me there at once, Lucienne told herself as she hurried back to the manor house. The thought of poor little Alain lost somewhere under the dark earth, as well knowing Bett was going away, was almost too much to bear. By the time she reached the manor house her heart was beating so fast she could hardly breath.

Once inside, she called Mrs Dobson's name, heard her own voice rising in agitation as she hurried to the housekeeper's parlour, found it empty then dashed through to the main part of the house. Thankfully, Mrs Dobson was coming down the stairs as she reached the hallway. She was gasping out what had happened when Jago, frowning and looking preoccupied, came from the direction of the study.

'Lucienne, all that shouting was most unseemly. Need you get so worked up?

'You don't understand,' she protested, wiping her eyes on her sleeve. 'And you don't need to be so pompous. Bett said they couldn't find—'

'I heard you the first time,' he said firmly. 'Now listen to me. Either the child was laid to rest somewhere else, or he is buried at Yoxley. The way forward is for us to go there and find out. Join me in the stable yard when you've composed yourself,' with which he turned on his heel and left them.

'Is he completely unnatural?' she gasped as Mrs Dobson led her to the housekeeper's room 'Can't he see how awful it is that they couldn't find my poor little brother's grave?'

'Gentlemen have more control of their feelings, Miss Lucy, and at least he's taking you to look into it,' the housekeeper told her, but it took a small glass of Spanish sherry, cold water splashed on her face and many reassurances that Jago was not an unfeeling brute, to calm her.

In less than ten minutes, she was able to walk into the stable yard with her head held high, but she avoided his eye and neither of them spoke as he handed her into an elegant two-wheeled chaise. He swung himself up into the seat beside her, picked up the reins and drove them out into the lane, through the sunlit village and on to the coastal road.

Travelling at a much faster pace than when she had come this way to visit Mrs Tregarth, she was still smarting at the way he'd spoken to her. Yet, sitting so close, she thought of the day he carried her from the library to her room. Feelings she had pushed to the back of her mind came seeping through again. Did he remember? Probably not. She glanced sideways at his dark aquiline profile, wishing he would say something.

He didn't, so when they came alongside the five barred gate that led to the Escott's farm, she said, 'Beulah, who used to work with Mrs Dobson, lives there now. She's to be married to the farmer.'

Jago nodded and drove on.

At Yoxley a young boy, scything away long grass in the churchyard, told them that the new vicar and his sexton were out on church business, then led them to the site of the more recent graves. There was none for any small child, let alone one with Alain's name on it, so they separated to search among the older graves. Lucienne, finding nothing and losing heart, was almost in despair when she heard Jago calling her name. She ran to where he stood beside a small, white marble headstone, then saw that the name carved into the surface was not Alain's name.

'This is for Mrs Tregarth's little girl, Elizabeth,' she said, disappointed until he knelt and drew the long grass away from the lower part of the stone. And there it was. Alain's name, the dates of his birth and his death, freshly carved into the stone erected for a child who had died nearly twenty years before.

She sank down and pressed her hand to his name as she said, 'I brought him away from Guadeloupe, I thought we would be safe, but everything went wrong. It's my fault he died—'

She stopped as he said gently, 'No, it is not your fault.

Most people would have made the same decision.' He stood up. 'Stay here while I find that boy. I'll give him something to keep the grave clear of weeds.'

He turned away and left her alone with her thoughts and gradually it seemed right that her brother had been put to lie beside another greatly loved child. Much better for him not to be alone. True, she would always have regrets that he was lying in this tiny grave, but Jago's words of kindness had helped so much. And soon she would come again, with flowers and a stone jar to put them in.

Afterwards, as they climbed into the chaise to drive away, she thanked Jago for bringing her there.

He shrugged. 'The least I could do. The child was my cousin, though sadly I never set eyes on him. And I'm sorry if I appeared unkind earlier when you were talking to Mrs Dobson. I had a lot on my mind just then. Now, as we've come so far, you might like to pay a visit to your friend, the farmer's wife to be. I'll leave you there for a couple of hours while I go to make a call of my own.'

She got down when they reached the five barred gate and he drove away. Then, about to start up the path, she was suddenly afraid, remembering that this path led to the farmhouse was where either her mother or Richard Deverell had killed Luke Widdon, the man she now knew to be her real father. Could she bear to enter the house where it had happened? Couldn't she just hide somewhere out of sight, wait until Jago came back, then drive away and never come here again? No, she could not because Beulah, who was so happy to be her friend, lived here now. She forced herself to walk on up to the farmhouse.

Her anxiety faded when she was greeted with delight by Beulah, Olaf's two younger sisters, as well as his grandma and his mother, who lost no time in mentioning that Beulah slept across the bottom of her bed at present to preserve her virtue until her wedding day. This was a happy home, with much joyful talk of preparations, of what the bride would wear and who was to be invited, so that the two hours passed quickly. Only for a few seconds did Lucienne remember Beulah telling her that Jago's lady love lived nearby. She didn't doubt that was where he was now.

Bett was to leave a few days later, catching the mail coach as it passed through the village at six o'clock in the morning. On the night before she was to leave Lucienne barely slept, instead sitting up in bed and remembering how, less than a year before she had been on the other side of the world with family that she thought was hers forever. Tomorrow, when the person who was dearest in all in the world to her boarded the coach and drove away, she would be alone. Where would life lead her? Would she ever marry? Or would she go from here to another house to work as a housekeeper until she was old and short-sighted like Mrs Dobson?

Chantelle's plans for her future in Guadeloupe came drifting back. Had she been stupid to undervalue her introduction into society there? Memories of the lovely dresses she had worn, the parties, balls and picnics she had enjoyed. The proposal of marriage she had refused. A husband, a beautiful sunlit house, and a band of servants, all these could have been hers, instead of which, she seemed destined to become a servant herself. An upper servant to be sure, but a servant still. For hours she was awake, then fell asleep at daybreak and woke up later than she'd meant to. Scrambling out of bed, she threw on her clothes and hurried out into the cold September morning.

She was spared the agony of long goodbyes because, by the time she reached Mis Petty's house, it was almost time to set off again for the post office. The mail coach was already waiting there and, after a loving hug and kisses that Lucienne knew she must treasure forever, Bett climbed on board and set off for Castlebridge on the first leg of her journey. Lucienne and Miss Petty waved her farewell until the coach was out of sight.

'A dish of tea at my house?' Miss Petty suggested anxiously as Lucienne walked silently away, too sad for tears.

'Thank you, but no. I must get back. Mrs Dobson will be wondering where I am, and I'm so miserable. I never thought Bett and I would ever be separated.'

Walking along beside her, the old lady surprised her by asking, 'Lucienne, how old is Bett?'

'She's thirty-five, thirty-six in December. Why do you ask?'

'Because at that age, a woman may still have dreams for her own future. I know I did, though unfortunately they came to nothing. Besides, much though I valued her company, I could afford to pay Bett only a pittance. Now she will have a proper wage and the chance to travel. And who knows,' she added wistfully, 'Out there in the wide world, she might find a good husband.'

A little ashamed that such a possibility had not occurred to her, Lucienne said she hoped so too, and Miss Petty went on, 'It certainly wouldn't surprise me. Even here in the village, an admirer called to see her more than once. He's the dressmaker's brother and a very good sort of person.

'I had no idea, that is Bett never told me about it.'

'Possibly the interest was more on his side than hers, but it goes to show she has a few good years yet. Love may still find its way into her heart.'

And if that happens while she is so far away, she will never come back again, Lucienne thought sadly, and they walked on in silence for a while.

'What a joy to see repairs being started that should have been done years ago,' Miss Petty remarked as they passed some labourers' cottages, where the roofs were being mended. 'Jago Moncrief has a sense of duty to the poor. So very different from his uncle Cedrick. Years ago, that man persuaded old Mr Deverell to sell the mine, still rich in tin. The new owner used his own men to work it, depriving many of our villagers of their living. But now things will improve, I am sure. There is even talk of the morning school being set up again.'

She chatted on, mainly about village affairs, explaining as they neared the church.

'Some of us older ladies undertake to tend the more neglected graves and I sometimes think I know the graveyard as well as I know my own garden.'

Listening, a sudden memory stirred in Lucienne's mind. Though he died miles away at Escott's farm, her real father's family had lived in Ottersbury village, so he might be buried in the church yard here. Buried with a headstone telling anyone who came looking the date when he died. A date that could prove she was not one of the Deverell family.

Stifling the panic that rose within her, she turned to her companion and asked, as calmly as she could, 'I wonder if there are graves here for a family called Widdon?' Then, as the old lady looked wary, she went on, 'You've lived here all your life, Miss Petty, and you must realise why I want to know. Luke Widdon was my mother's first husband. The man my father killed in a fight.'

'Some things are best left in the past my dear.' The old lady patted her arm, thought for a moment, then said, 'But yes, there is just the one grave. The Widdon family were incomers here and they didn't stay long after he died, so that Luke Widdon is the only one of that name buried here. He lies on the left, at the rear of the church, well back towards the wall. His brothers were stonemasons and gave him a fine black marble tombstone with gold letters.'

They parted at the church gate, Lucienne trembling with anxiety as she walked on alone. Why hadn't she realised that the date of his death would be on his gravestone, showing that he died in January 1784, so that he and not Richard Deverell must have been her father. Cedrick Deverell was living far away from here now, but that did not mean she was safe. He could easily locate Luke Widdon's grave if he realised that the evidence he had been searching for would be there, carved in stone.

There wasn't time now, but as soon as she could, she would find the grave and come here with something to chip away the dangerous inscription.

She was back in the Manor before breakfast, dismayed to think of the long day ahead, though luckily Mrs Belmont was in a good mood that morning.

'Now Jago Moncrief is master here, I expect the best families will come visiting. There will be luncheon parties, dinners, musical evenings. That sort of thing, more especially after he' s married,' she told Lucienne later that morning. 'My poor daughter did her best, but these old families can't be fooled. Snobs and proud of it, most of them.'

Lucienne, miserable about Bett, worried about Luke Widdon's grave and struggling at the piano with another difficult passage of Scarlatti the old lady had demanded, said crossly, 'So why is Jago so well in with all these snobbish old families? He's been earning his living as a lawyer.'

'Don't be pert with me,' the old lady snapped. 'He's also the son of a Scottish aristocrat of ancient lineage. The County recognise their own kind.

Still playing, Lucienne said thoughtfully, 'What I don't understand is how Jago comes to be master here, anyway. I'm glad Mr Deverell has gone, but why should he leave just because he quarrelled with Jago?'

The old lady 's painted eyebrows shot up. Briefly, she looked at a loss, then said sharply, 'None of your business, I'm sure. We are where we are, and soon there will be music and laughter, though of course, Jago cannot claim his bride until she is out if her widow's weeds.'

Hearing yet again that Jago would eventually be married to Lady Helena so disturbed Lucienne that she left Scarlatti for another time and began to strum a Scottish air.

But she had to know more and said casually, 'One day last week, Jago very kindly took me to visit my brother's grave at Yoxley and I believe he called on Lady Helena then.'

'Glad to hear it. He was wasting his time with her as a married woman. A rich widow is quite another story. Of course, at eighteen they were very much in love, until her father pushed her into an ambitious marriage. That must have been eight or nine years ago now, but lately he's been back in her arms and in her bed, if gossip is to be believed.' Yawning she added, 'So I'm warning you, don't lose your heart to your cousin Jago. He's not for the likes of you. Better take up with a nice young curate. Should you be so fortunate as to get the chance,' she murmured as she drifted off to sleep.

Lucienne stood up and walked restlessly about the room. Wondering what lady Helena looked like, she went to see her own reflection in the huge, gilt-framed looking glass over the fireplace, glad to notice that she was not so thin. Otherwise, though with more colour than before, she was just an ordinary sort of person, her mass of dark brown hair pulled back tidily in a bun and dressed in a sombre dark blue dress suitable for a housekeeper.

Still, some people admired her. The last time she met with Mathew Harris in the old church yard he'd told her, 'Miss Lucy, you have the prettiest eyes of any girl I've ever known, which is unsurprising, you being the most charming of all the girls I ever met anyway.' Before she could thank him for the compliment he went on, 'I greatly admire you, Miss Lucy, in fact I'm in a fair way of falling in love with you. So, I'm asking you again to be my girl, with a view to us being wed next year when I get my promotion?'

And, before she could reply, he had taken her hand and kissed the palm in a gentle respectful sort of way. Realising that she must put a stop to this as kindly as she could, she drew her hand away said firmly, 'Mathew It is a great compliment to be asked, but I have no plans at present to marry you or anybody else.'

For a few seconds disappointment flickered in his eyes, then he gave her his cheerful grin and said, 'We'll have to see about that. I'm posted down the coast, temporary for the next couple of months, but I'll write to you letters, and come to see you when I get back, hoping you'll have changed your mind, given time to think it over.'

About to leave, he'd turned back and said, 'Remember that time I asked you who lived up at the big house? It was because we think there's somebody clever that masterminds the smuggling going on here abouts. Most likely an outsider but someone known and trusted by the locals who take the risks involved in bringing goods illegal.'

'It can't have been my Uncle Cedrick because he wasn't like or trusted in the village.'

'So, I understand, but if you should ever hear anything that gives you a clue, keep it to yourself for safety's sake and let me know when I come back here.'

She turned away from the mirror, knowing she wouldn't change her mind about Mathew, who might forget about her now he'd been posted away. I do hope so, she thought as she walked past Mrs Belmont's sleeping form and sat down at the piano. I hope some sweet girl has captured his heart and returns his love, so he can marry her and be happy.

She gave a deep sigh as she began another attempt to master the Scarletti.

9

Tomorrow morning, Lucienne promised herself as she climbed into bed that night, she would take a small hammer and chisel she'd found in a toolbox in one of the storerooms, go out very early, find Luke Widdon's grave and chip away the date of death on his tombstone. After this last piece of evidence to prove her an imposter was gone, she would be safe.

She stared at the ceiling. Why was she so anxious to stay here when Alain and Bett were gone? To master housekeeping skills needed to make her way in the world? Or was it something else? The look of concern in Jago's dark eyes, the feel of his strong arms about her when he'd carried her from the library soon after she'd arrived here was always there at the back of her mind.

Next morning it was barely light when she slipped out of the manor, too early for even the villagers to be about, she reassured herself as she hurried down the lane to the church. At the lynch gate she stopped, suddenly nervous. A low-lying mist from the sea curled low about the gravestones so that they looked as if they were eerily detached from the ground. Everything seemed strange and for a moment she didn't want to go any further. But there could be no giving up now. Shivering in the cold morning air, wishing she had brought her cloak instead of just a shawl, she took a deep breath and made herself go up the path to the church, then round the side of the building to the back.

And there it was. A black marble tombstone behind the stones of more recent graves so that she hadn't noticed it before. She moved closer and saw that the faded gold letters spelled out the name 'Luke Widdon' just as Miss Petty had said. What she hadn't said was that the date of his death had been chipped away.

So, she was safe. But surely there was something odd about this. The other damaged gravestones were made of sandstone, much softer and easier to cut away than marble. It was said in the village that the damage had been done by a wondering madman, randomly attacking any stone that took his fancy, but why include a marble stone, so much harder to deface?

And then, out of nowhere, a feeling of sadness crept over her. Sadness tinged with remorse because there, beneath the ground at her feet, lay the man who had been her real father and she'd never given him so much as one kind thought. Everybody who mentioned him claimed he was cruel and brutish, almost as if he had deserved to die, but had any of them known him? Could it all have been malicious gossip, put about by—. She stopped short. Was that the sound of men's voices? And the distant sound of feet on a gravel path? Yes. She was sure now. It was coming from the direction of the graveyard nearest the sea. And to get out on to the lane, whoever it was must pass where she was standing.

Suddenly, the sound came closer, too close for her to run away without being seen. Frightened now, aware that she was alone and defenceless, she turned and darted behind the tall black marble headstone on Luke Widdon's grave. Crouched down out of sight, she felt her heart pounding.

Perhaps they were just villagers, back from night fishing and would do her no harm. But the fishermen brought their boats into the harbour near the village, not to where they had to carry their catch up steep, rocky steps from a deserted beach A beach where Mathew Harris said dangerous and violent smugglers were known to bring their contraband ashore.

The tramp of feet drew closer. She held her breath as she heard them pass but couldn't resist peering out. Three men, each carrying some sort of load on his shoulder, disappeared round the side of the church. Then there was silence. A sudden silence, not the fading sound of footsteps on the path. So where had they gone?

She waited a bit longer, but rain was soaking through her shawl now and it was getting light, so she stood up, crept softly to the back of the church and looked around the corner of the building.

She saw no one and decided it was safe to get away but, as she passed some moss-covered steps leading to the crypt beneath the church, she glanced down and noticed that the ancient wooden door at the bottom of the steps looked to be slightly ajar. She stopped and, listening against the sound of the wind from the sea and falling rain, heard muffled voices and knew they were coming from down there in the crypt. So, these men were not fishermen on their way to the village. They were smugglers, hiding their booty among the lead coffins down there below the church and it was up to her to get away and raise the alarm.

Suddenly some instinct warned her, and she turned to see a big, rough man a few feet away. He lunged at her, seized the end of her shawl, dragging her towards him. As she fought to get loose, the pin holding the shawl together at her neck broke and it was jerked from her shoulders. Freed, she ran for her life, leaving the path, dodging between gravestones with him coming after her so close she could hear him panting for breath.

Just before she reached the lynch gate, he slipped on the wet grass and fell, giving her time to be out on the lane and running for home before she heard him again, pounding along behind her. She ran harder, felt as though her lungs would burst, knew he was gaining on her when she saw a horse galloping towards her. Her heart leapt with relief. The rider was Jago! Then he was beside her and she was gasping that she needed help. She saw him look the way she had come, then frown as he looked down at her. She glanced back and saw the man had vanished.

'Jago,' she cried, 'He was after me. One of the smugglers! I saw them. They're hiding stuff in the crypt under the church.'

Without a word, he leaned down, caught her, swung her up into the saddle before him, turned the horse and rode back to the manor house gates. He put her gently down.

'Go inside, Lucienne. Make up any story you like about the state you're in but tell no one what you've just told me. Do you understand? Tell no one.' Gazing up at him, she nodded. 'Quick now,' he told her, 'Into the house. I'll go back the church to see what I can find. And I'll speak to you later today.'

She leaned against one of the tall, grey stone gate posts as he rode away, feeling the strength drain out of her now she was out of danger. But was she? Would she ever be safe now one of the smugglers knew she had seen them? She glanced down the lane, afraid that he would reappear now she was alone. He wasn't there, but Jago's urgent words drove her to find the energy to run back to the house.

Relieved to meet no one, she reached the safety of her room and barely had time to wash and tidy her hair before it was time for breakfast. She went downstairs again, doing her best to behave as if nothing untoward had happened as she sat down to eat with Mrs Dobson and the rest of the staff. Inside she was so shaken that she wondered how she was going to get through the day.

Mercifully, Mrs Belmont stayed in bed with a sick headache and didn't need to be entertained that morning. Instead, Lucienne was sorting through the silver cutlery in the dining room, when Jago sent for her.

He was sitting at the long table in the library looking at some papers but brushed these aside as he stood up to greet her, then asked gently, 'Have you recovered from this morning's ordeal?'

'Yes, I think so. But Jago were the men still there? Did you see them?'

He shook his head. 'The door of the crypt was locked, so I went over to the sexton's cottage for the key.'

'But I was sure the door was slightly open.'

He shrugged. 'It was very dark at the bottom of those steps. You could easily have been mistaken.'

'Or perhaps that man who chased me went back to warn them to get away."

He looked doubtful. 'That's possible but when I got the key and a lantern from the sexton and went inside, I found no bales of French silk, no lace, no kegs of brandy, chests of tea, or anything else to suggest it was being used as a smuggler's lair. A bit of spilt candle wax that could have been there for years was all I found.'

'But Jago, it was so strange. I could still hear their footsteps on the gravel path when they went around the corner of the church. Then they suddenly stopped. If they didn't go into the crypt, where did they go? And if they weren't smugglers, who were they?'

He gave her a reassuring grin, 'I'm pretty sure they must have been fishermen, dropped off from the boat that takes lobsters along the coast to Castlebridge market. They probably left the gravel path and took a short cut to the village through a break in the wall. Once they got onto the grass between the gravestones, you wouldn't hear them.'

'But that man who chased me, I was certain he was one of them or why did he go for me like that?'

He raised his eyebrows. 'There are other reasons why men chase after young girls in lonely places. I strongly advise you to be more careful about your safety in future.'

Not entirely convinced, she didn't reply, and he asked, 'What were you doing there alone, at that time of the morning?'

She was at a loss for a moment, then realised that there was no harm in telling him the truth so long as he didn't know she had gone there to erase the evidence.

Even so, she felt a touch reckless as she explained, 'If I'd found the date of his death, it could have proved whose child I was. I didn't expect his stone to have been defaced.'

'Like several others. There was panic in the village until it was realised that only the graves of families that have no kin still living here were damaged.' He gave her a reassuring smile. 'Now, let's turn to something better. That, day we met here in the library, I was searching for some land titles when I found a letter, written to our grandfather by our great grandmother Deverell, shortly before she died.'

'You mean our grandfather's mother?'

'I do. She informed him that, for some unexplained reason, she had willed the Ottersbury estate to your father, his second son. Finding her actual will took longer, but recently it did come to light and it proves that she did exactly as she promised. She left the Ottersbury estate, in its entirety, to your father, Richard Deverell who was four years old when she died.'

'But why would she overlook her own son and his other two children in favour of his youngest child?'

'That we will never know. It was hers to give and that was what she decided to do, though when I came here as a boy and until the day he died, it was generally believed that our grandfather had inherited Ottersbury.'

'Do you suppose my father ever knew it really belonged to him?'

'He will have certainly been told that by a lawyer when he reached twenty-one, and that was immediately before he went on his tour of Europe. As you know, shortly after he got back, he had to flee the country again, so he must have allowed his father to continue here for his lifetime, most likely intending to sell when the old man passed away.'

'And that's why Uncle Cedrick didn't tell him their father had died?'

'It must have been. How long this could have continued I have no idea, but clearly your father never knew that the old man had died.'

'But surely your mother must have known it wasn't legal? '

'Lucienne, I truly believe that my mother grew up

completely unaware of the true situation. Like everybody else, apart from Cedrick, she thought the old man owned the estate. She was living abroad when our grandfather died would simply have accepted that he'd left the estate equally between her and uncle Cedaric.'

'But I don't understand how your uncle got away with it. Surely there must have been papers, deeds or something to say who owns what?'

'Of course, there were. What lies were told, bribes were taken, or forgeries made to deal with the legalities, I've yet to discover, but what my uncle did not expect was for Richard Deverell's orphaned children to appear out of nowhere.'

'But we didn't know anything about all this, so why didn't he help us to go to France. Get us out of his way?'

'Probably because there was always a chance that the truth would somehow come out. By keeping your brother here and claiming guardianship, he ensured that, come what may, he would have charge of this estate for nearly twenty years until the boy came of age. Your brother's death should make you the sole heir, coming into your inheritance at twenty-one years of age. That is in less than two years' time.'

Lucienne stared at him across the table, speechless with shock. Now is the time, she thought desperately. Now I should tell him about finding the bible, seeing what it proved and throwing it into the sea. But somehow the words wouldn't come.

'You look horrified.' He was watching her, his smile showing that he suspected nothing. 'I thought you would be delighted.'

She couldn't meet his steady gaze, looked away, then got up and went over to one of the arched windows and looked across the green lawn to the massive trees that lined the lane outside. Beyond were the cliff tops and the rocky shore below. Then, just down the lane was the church, the village, the home farm, and goodness knew what else. This enormous house, the furniture, gardens, carriages, stables, the horses in the stables. Could all of this really be hers if she kept up the pretence that she was Richard Deverell's daughter?

She couldn't do it. When she had believed herself to be a penniless orphan, it didn't seem dishonest to pretend that she was Richard Deverell's child. Now, to pass herself off as his rightful heiress would be nothing less than theft. To tell the truth would be hard, but it must be done. She took a deep breath and turned to find Jago standing a little way behind her.

'No need to look so overwhelmed, Lucienne. I said you should be Richard Deverell's heir, but that depends on whether he was married to your mother.' She tried to interrupt, but he went on, 'Your friend Bett may have convinced our uncle that she witnessed their wedding ceremony in Paris, but I've seen too much false evidence given in court not to recognise a lie when I see one.'

'She was trying to help me. And they must have loved each other, so why shouldn't they have been married?'

'They probably were, but until the conflict with France is over, we can't get the documents we need to prove the marriage and with it your entitlement to inherit Ottersbury.' He paused, then added quietly, 'When and if you live to reach your majority.'

'Why shouldn't I live that long? It's only two years away.'

'Your life may be in jeopardy now. Lucienne. My uncle, Cedrick Deverell is your nearest relative. He and my mother stand to inherit legally if you die before them.

Until you are of age, and can sell the estate or gift it elsewhere, you can do little about that.'

Shocked into silence for a moment, she shook her head. 'I can't believe he would try to have me murdered!'

He shrugged, turned away and sat down at the long table. Leaning back, his hands linked behind his head, he said, 'I'm not so sure. He was mad with rage when I confronted him with all this and threw him out of here. And consider that attack on Bett Moreau. Did she tell you her assailant carried a knife?'

'No! She told me she'd been beaten because of the war with France.'

'Lucienne, some drunken oaf, fired up against anything French, might throw stones, call insults, even beat a defenceless woman. They wouldn't attempt to stab her. By some miracle of chance, the knife only slashed the back of the coat she'd put on to go outside.'

'Are you saying Uncle Cedrick sent someone to kill her so that she couldn't swear she'd seen my parents married?'

'I'm saying that it's possible, so mind how you go.' He stood up and picked up the sheaf of papers. 'I need to get down to the village to see about some extra work needed to stabilise the river embankment, so I'll let you go now, Lucienne.' He smiled down at her. 'Perhaps we can meet again when you've had time to think about your situation? This library is my favourite room, so meet me here at eight o'clock this evening.'

She nodded and left without another word. Could her life really be in danger? Perhaps the man who chased her this morning wasn't a smuggler. Perhaps he'd been sent to follow her to the churchyard, and watch her, waiting for the moment to overpower her, perhaps strangle her and throw her over the cliff into the sea.

Half-way up the stairs she stopped and took a few deep breaths, trying not to let her imagination get out of hand. Upstairs in her room she paced about, sorting out her thoughts, then stopped and stared through the window. Jago confronting Uncle Cedarick about his wrong doings had got rid of him, but why was he so keen to prove she was the rightful heir? Why, when his mother was supposed to have inherited half the estate from old Mr Deverell, was he so keen to change things and forfeit his own inheritance from her? Of course, it could be that he wanted to see justice done at whatever cost, but was that likely? Whatever the meaning of all this was, she knew, in her heart of hearts, that she should have told him that she was not Richard Deverell's child. But, if she let it be known that she had no right to be here, what would happen to her then?

If only she could talk things over with dear Bett, who by now must have left Castlebridge and be travelling by coach across the Devonshire moors to Plymouth to start a new life with strangers. She had promised to send a letter before she crossed the ocean to the far away island of Jamaica, Lucienne thought wistfully, but what would she think of me, masquerading as the rightful owner of this great house where we were made so unwelcome?

She sat on the edge of her bed, her mind restless with so much that had happened. She could have sworn she heard voices when she listened outside the crypt that morning, but Jago had found it locked and with no sign of anyone having been there. So, was coming back to the village through the churchyard usual for harvesters of lobsters? She didn't know. She knew very little about the estate Jago believed she should own.

Hardly able to credit it was so early in the day when so much had happened, she went down to the midday meal and felt better after eating, even resigned to playing the piano when Mrs Belmont's maid announced that she was well enough to come down to the drawing-room that afternoon to be entertained.

Today the old lady was in a mood to reminisce about the heyday of her youth and beauty. While Lucienne strummed quietly in the background, she spoke at length of how, at a ball in Grosvenor square, the Prince Regent kissed the hem of her gown and begged her, an innocent girl, to become his mistress. As she must be at least thirty years older than the prince, Lucienne didn't believe her, but such daydreams made Mrs Belmont happy and better tempered.

It also gave her time to think about the meeting that evening with Jago and, after thinking, doubting and reconsidering, her mind was made up. It would harm no-one if she let things be for now. In which case, perhaps she should think of questions a person might ask if they really were an heiress waiting to inherit an estate.

Feeling better, she decided she must look the part, but it was too chilly to wear any of her pretty summer dresses. Up in her room, she opened the travelling trunk and took the blue velvet dress bought in Plymouth the day she arrived in England. She had been so pleased with it then, but now it looked crumpled and shabby. She threw it back into the trunk, closed the lid, straightened her ordinary, housekeeper's frock and rehearsed what she'd decided to ask Jago when they met at eight o'clock.

Late that afternoon, Jago met with Joshua Gerrick, his clerk from the law firm in Castlebridge. Born in Ottersbury he had come to visit relatives and friends who still lived here.

'Or at least what's left of them,' Joshua said as they trudged through the village together. 'It was different when I was a boy, but with the mine gone, there's nothing to keep the men here apart from the fishing and farm labour, both seasonal. All right for gentlefolk with money coming in, but working families, here for generations, can be half starved in winter.'

'There's a chance now to remedy that,' Jago assured him. 'I'll never recover what my uncle sold off, but the engineer I got in to look for copper found huge deposits of china clay. Setting up a pottery being cheaper than starting a copper mine, we'll do that first. Meanwhile, there is enough work repairing the roads, re-roofing cottages and strengthening the river embankment to get most families through the winter.'

They had reached the road where Joshua turned off to reach his sister's house and he said quietly, 'Mr Jago, about that delivery you asked me to arrange. There's been a bit of a delay but I'm hoping to get it over there in the next few days. We have to be careful when there's moonlight, but the lads are willing and it will be safely landed soon as maybe.'

'Good man, Joshua. A lot depends on that particular delivery getting through,' Jago told him as they shook hands and went their separate ways.

The library looked very different at night. A huge fire in the grate at the far end cast flickering lights and shadows about that end the room and candles shone in a silver candelabra on the table close by. The rest of the room was so dark that Lucienne could hardly see the bookcases as she made her way to where Jago stood beside the fire, leaning with one arm on the mantle shelf. She tried not to notice how darkly handsome he looked in the firelight's flickering glow as he motioned her to sit down on one of the leather fire side chairs.

He said gravely, 'Good evening, Lucienne. Now you've had time to think about your ownership of the estate what do you have to say? Is there anything you would like me to explain?'

Still standing, she clenched her hands to keep herself steady and took a deep breath.

'Yes, Jago there is. I would like to know, what is your position in all this?'

He raised his eyebrows. 'Meaning?'

'Meaning that you got rid of Uncle Cedrick because he was living here as if he owned the place when he knew it wasn't his. And now you are doing the same thing.' He took his arm off the mantle shelf and stood up straight. Feeling nervous, she pressed on, 'This estate now being mine, by what right do you do that?' In the pause that followed, his look of surprise was followed by one of amusement.

'Perhaps the possibility of becoming a landowner has gone to your head, Lucienne, but the position is this. If your parents were not married, so that you are not the rightful owner of this estate, I am here because my mother owns half of it. If you are the rightful owner I am here as your legal guardian until you reach the age of one and twenty.'

'My legal guardian?' she gasped, 'How can you be? Nobody ever told me that.'

'Wards are not generally consulted when these things are arranged, but I assure you that I do have that responsibility, jointly with my mother. She has empowered me to act on her behalf as well as my own.'

'But I only saw my Aunt Isobel once and she never spoke a single word to me. Besides, who said —'

'We applied jointly to the courts shortly after you got here. Obtaining guardianship of what appeared to be a penniless orphan was not difficult.'

Completely taken aback now, Lucienne sank into one of the fireside chairs, then looked up at him for a long moment before asking, 'Why? Why did the two of you care to do that?'

'Quite apart from the fact that an under-age girl should have some form of guardianship, I'd heard a rumour that your father was the real owner of the Ottersbury estate, so that his children should inherit. Whereas Uncle Cedrick would never have agreed to us getting control of Alain's affairs, believing him to be the only legitimate heir, he agreed to you becoming our ward without a second thought. The point is that, until you come of age, this gives me control of the Ottersbury estate.'

'And that's what you want?'

He gave a non-committal shrug. 'Let's talk about what you want, Lucienne.'

'I want to go back to Paris.' Somehow the words came out without her even thinking about it but what else should she say, knowing that her secret admiration for him was not returned? 'France is where I meant to go when I left Guadeloupe. I'll wait until the war with France is over and I'll send for Bett to come with me. Of course, she may have got married by then, but I would still go to France, even without her.'

'I see.' He strolled over to the second armchair and sat down. 'Perhaps you would require money from this estate to set you up in Paris?'

She wasn't sure what to say, then, remembering her

role as the rightful owner, said, 'Yes. I suppose I would need some money.'

'Then I must warn you that, since our grandfather's death, the Ottersbury estate has been mortgaged to the hilt by our uncle, the lenders he borrowed from believing him to have inherited ownership. All that money he has taken for his own family, but the debt falls upon the estate. Interest on what he borrowed, as well as the original sum, could only be repaid if the estate was sold. There would be very little left.'

She stared at him in dismay. 'I don't understand. If Uncle Cedrick took that money, shouldn't he be made to pay it back?'

'If we were sure of that your parents were married, putting your position as the rightful owner beyond dispute, I could take him to law on behalf of you and you late father. As things stand, with no evidence of your legitimacy, that would not be wise.'

At a loss for words at the injustice of it all, Lucienne stared into the fire, then back at Jago.

Their eyes met in a long moment of hesitation, then he asked, 'Do you trust me, Lucienne?' She thought for a moment, then nodded, and he went on, 'I am prepared to put what capital I have into payment of the most pressing debts. It will not be enough to cover all that is owed, but it will satisfy the main creditors for the present. With careful management and development of certain assets, I can pay off enough over the next two years to avoid disaster. But there is a condition.' He paused. 'I want ownership of Ottersbury. And don't look so surprised. You have just told me that Paris is your place of choice. Ottersbury is mine.'

Thinking she understood, she demanded, 'You want me to sell the estate to you when I come of age?'

'I want it now. As a minor, you can't sell or transfer property and it must be legally mine before I risk what money I have to save the place from ruin. The only way is for us to marry. By the law of this country, Ottersbury will then be mine.'

Speechless with shock, she gazed at him open-mouthed, while he calmly got up and, from a crystal decanter standing on a small table that stood between them, poured two glasses of deep red wine. She shook her head when he offered one to her.

'I never expected to own the estate, and as for marriage—' she began.

'Lucienne, I propose a marriage in name only, and for less than two years. After that you will be free to leave, provided with a healthy income from the estate. If we do nothing, you stand to go bankrupt and lose everything.'

'But what if I want to marry somebody else?'

'And give your estate to him?' he put their two glasses firmly down on the table, 'Not while you are my ward, Lucienne. And remember a marriage in name only, that is an unconsummated marriage, can be annulled after two years, leaving you to do as you please.'

'But what if we do marry, then the war ends, and my uncle makes searches in France and proves that my parents were never married. I wouldn't be heir to this estate then.'

'I think we can take a chance on that. Bonaparte, the First Consul of France, is intent upon increasing the prosperity of his country. If he starts wars to expand into Europe, it will take many years to put him down. Meanwhile, we don't have to prove anything at all. Are you prepared to trust me in this, Lucienne?'

'I don't know. Surely marriage cannot be the proper way to solve—'

'Lucienne, if the creditors are given nothing, they can claim possession through the courts and sell the place off to anyone who'll have it. The estate could be broken up and sold off piecemeal. It has happened in other places. But, if I carry out my plans for the future of Ottersbury, I can bring new prosperity to everyone who lives here. If I do nothing, families that have worked this land for generations could be turned out. Some might find work elsewhere, many could be left wandering the countryside, begging or starving.'

She got up, moved away from him and stared into the fire. Was it really up to her to save the villagers from this fate? Knowing she was not Richard Deverell's child, could she bear to take her deception as far as marriage and then live out a charade until it was time to go?

Still not looking at him, she said, 'But to marry you, carry out the role of mistress of this house, to go on your arm to be entertained in the homes of neighbouring gentry, to entertain them here in return! I don't think I could do that.'

'Lucienne, you are very young, but you have a charming appearance and manner. I am sure, with my help you would easily learn what society requires.'

Indignantly, she turned to face him. 'I don't need to be told what is required in the way of social correctness. What I learned from my nobly bred stepmother would suffice here in the wilds of Devon, I'm quite sure of that. What I cannot do is to join you in some pretence of being one of a happily married pair. Or should we tell people the truth and have them speculate as to how you are to get rid of me if it turns out the estate belongs to Uncle Cedrick and your mother after all?' Slightly out of breath, aware that she had never spoken like this to anyone since quarrelling with her father, she was relieved to see it was Jago's turn to seem unsure how to answer.

He looked at her intently for a long moment, then said, 'Lucienne, if I had asked yesterday how you intended to spend the next two years, what would you have answered?'

Surprised, she said, 'I suppose I'd say I expected to stay here and help Mrs Dobson run the house.'

'Exactly. You would have stayed here, a young person living in the family home of your nearest relatives. So, if you were content with that role yesterday, why not continue to play it? We can be married in secret.' Seeing her still unsure, he went on 'No need for pretence, no social embarrassment, but a legally binding contract whereby I get Ottersbury and, on reaching one and twenty you get enough to make you independent.'

For a moment she wavered. Would marrying Jago to save the poorest tenants from lives as homeless vagabonds outweigh the deception involved? She decided that it would, took a deep breath and gave her agreement.

'So, let's drink to that,' Jago said, adding, as he bent to pick up their two glasses, 'I promise you that our secret marriage needs be known only to a very few people.'

And will the beautiful lady Helena be one of them, Lucienne thought as she took the glass he offered and sipped the finest French wine she had ever tasted.

Later, sitting upstairs in the old armchair, exhausted after a long day of such varied events, she gazed at the dying embers of the bedroom fire and wondered if she had made a terrible mistake. She wanted to help the village people, save them from homelessness and dire poverty, but marriage, even in name only! Would she have agreed to such an arrangement if anyone other than Jago had suggested it? Jago, who didn't give a fig for her.

But had she really agreed? Could she change her mind? Explain that, after everything that had happened that day, weariness had muddled her head? Did she dare tell Jago she wouldn't marry him? Did she really want to tell him that?

Downstairs, gazing into the dying embers of the library fire, Jago leaned back in his chair and stretched his legs, grinning as he thought of how she'd challenged his right to be running the estate almost as soon as she'd entered the room. She was courageous, clever and a good deal prettier than when she first arrived, and what more could any thinking man require in a wife?

He got up and began to pace restlessly about. Must their arrangement last only for the next twenty or so months until Lucienne reached her majority? Marriage had never been high on his agenda, and for the last few years his liaison with Helena Riverton had met certain needs in both of them. But now that was at an end, and there was a growing awareness in his heart and mind that a deeper, more meaningful kind of love might be within his reach. Lucienne was very young, but she was brave, intelligent and increasingly desirable.

His pacing came to an abrupt halt. The girl was his ward, put under his protection by the law of the land. It would be legal for him to marry her, but he was a man of twenty- eight, experienced in the ways of love and she was an innocent girl of nineteen. To think of deliberately seducing her should be unthinkable when what they had agreed to amounted to a business arrangement and nothing more.

He picked up his glass of wine and drained it in one swallow, telling himself that, in all decency, any intimacy between them could only come about if and when Lucienne let him know that it was what she wanted. Meanwhile the marriage ceremony had to be arranged before she changed her mind, but applying for a special licence was not the best to ensure complete secrecy, so there would be an unavoidable delay.

10

A few days later, when Mrs Belmont's maid had taken her away for lunch and Lucienne was sorting out the music sheets from the piano stool, she glanced up and saw Jago watching her from the doorway. Her heart gave a sickening lurch. Now she'd agreed to marry him, the more she'd thought about keeping the secret of her true parentage from him, the worse it seemed. Should she tell him now and risk ruining everything?

'From the look of you, I take it that the old lady was more than usually demanding today,' he was saying, smiling as he came toward her.

Hoping he hadn't come to tell her a wedding date had had been set, she managed, ' No, she in a good mood today. In fact, she's been a lot calmer since her treatment in Exeter.

'I'm, glad to hear that, but what I've come to tell you is that the old meeting house by the Holly Tree Inn, is ready for use as a village school. Miss Petty has taken it on, but she'll need help. I volunteered your services.'

'I'd love to help her, but what about Mrs Belmont?'

'Our uncle's wife has at last seen fit to have her mother join the household at Heverton Manor. She can go there as soon as her possessions can be packed by that long-suffering maid of hers. Later today can you meet up with Miss Petty? She needs to talk about running the school.'

Jago had been one of Mrs Belmont's favourites, but the following morning, she was venomous in her condemnation of him.

'He's getting rid of me because I know too much,' she screeched as Lucienne went to sit down at the piano. 'Leave that thing alone, will you? There's never any peace with you hammering away all the time. Come over here and find my smelling salts.'

'You are holding them, Mrs Belmont,' Lucienne told her as she came over to the chaise longue. The old lady took a sniff, then motioned her to sit on a nearby chair.

'I'll tell you something,' she muttered darkly, 'I'm old enough to remember what went on, what's still going on, and that's why he wants me out of here.'

'Mrs Belmont, I'm sure that's not true, it's just that your daughter has—'

'There's bad blood in Jago Moncrief, I tell you, and it's from his mother's side. His grandmother was the last of the old Acton family that owned this place years ago. They'd gone down in the world, living in some miserable little farm,' the old lady declared venomously. 'Of course, she was a beauty, which is why your fool of a grandfather married her, but I know about it. And I have my sources. I've heard other things about what goes on in Ottersbury village, things that could see certain persons on the gallows and that's why he wants me out of here.'

'I really don't think so, Mrs Belmont.' Lucienne told her gently, 'I believe that your daughter has put her new home in order and naturally wants you with her,' but the old lady had taken another deep sniff at the smelling salts and fallen back on her pillows in a daze.

Poor thing, Lucienne thought. She seemed to be getting more confused lately, recalling such alarming details about her struggles to escape the attentions of the Prince of Wales that anything she said about other events seem less credible.

The old lady left and Lucienne was free to spend her mornings in the stone-floored, white-washed schoolroom beside the village inn. This proved even more enjoyable than she expected.

On her first morning there, Miss Petty, having recruited such children as were willing to attend the morning school explained, 'We have only eight pupils to start with, all little things from here in the village, so we can divide them between us for now, but more will come when word gets around that bread and cheese are to be sent in from the Holly Tree first thing each morning. The older children are having a rest now they are back from the harvesting but, soon enough, we'll likely be overrun with them.'

'But Miss Petty, these little children's clothes are hardly adequate. Some are running barefoot. They must have shoes when there's snow on the ground.'

'We will do what we can for them, Lucienne, but the life of the poor has ever been hard. Mr Jago assures me that we'll always have a good blaze in the grate to warm the room and they're to have a cup of broth before they go at the end of the morning. Better than some of them would get at home, I believe.'

One of the ragged little children had brought her

brother, a child of three, with her. While the class learned to chalk their letters on little slate boards, he played about the place quite nicely. Grief pierced Lucienne's heart as she watched him. Alain should have been his age now. How strange that she could kneel by the grave and feel nothing, whereas the sight of this little fair-haired boy brought back the same love and sorrow she had felt when Jago first came to tell her he had died.

One of the children, needing help with his letters, brought her back to the reality of the classroom where Miss Petty started to tell the children that, at Christmas time, there would be a party here in the schoolhouse for all the children of the village. '

'Not for some weeks yet,' she said cheerfully when their pupils had gone home, 'but arranging a party, with little gifts for each of them, will give us plenty to think about.' Glad of anything that would take her mind off her proposed marriage, Lucienne heartily agreed with her.

When her wedding day came, Barny, the old groom, drove Lucienne to the gate of the Escott's farm, as he always did when she went to visit Beulah. Then, as soon as he was out of sight, Jago picked her up in the chaise and took her to an ancient church in a distant parish where they were not known.

This was what she had agreed to. A clandestine ceremony, witnesses sworn to secrecy. So why, she asked herself as she alighted from the chaise and went to wait at the lynch gate, why did she feel so disappointed? Immediately she knew the answer.

Today, despite her felt bonnet and the woollen dress beneath her cloak, she shivered in the November cold but, in her dreams, the wedding day would have been sunny and bright, her dress and veil of pure white silk and on her head a wreath of silken flowers. Bett and Alain would both be there, and, best of all, it would be a of marriage of true love. Not this cold-hearted, ordinary arrangement.

The day was darkened by clouds threatening rain and she drew her cloak about her. Surely Jago should be back by from tethering the horse by now. He'd told her to wait here, but the wedding was to take place at midday and the fingers of the church clock were already almost at twelve.

There was a sound behind her, and she turned to see Joshua Gerrick, the lawyer's clerk. With one of his rare smiles, he said gruffly, 'For you, Miss Deverell,' as he handed her a bunch of flowers. 'I do believe 'tis the fashion for young ladies to carry a bouquet on their wedding day. '

She gasped with delight as she took in the pristine beauty of white flowers, delicately flushed with pink and tied together with a green silk ribbon, and suddenly the day seemed brighter.

'Why, thank you, Mr Gerrick! How kind of you. I didn't know there were flowers to be had so late in the year, let alone anything so very pretty.'

'Hellebore, Miss, called the Christmas rose hereabouts because they'll show themselves well into January. I thought to bring them as I'm to take you to the altar where Mr Jago 's waiting.' He motioned her to take his arm and, feeling better now, she walked beside him up the path.

The church was very ancient, and the narrow, stained-glass windows high on grey stone walls let in so little light that the candles on the altar shone like beacons to guide them up the aisle. At the altar rail, Jago stood waiting. He looked down at her, a long unfathomable glance, turning away as an aged clergyman came from the shadows and began to conduct the ceremony.

Suddenly she was nervous. What if, in the next few months, the war with France ended and—?

She dragged her mind back to the present, trying to concentrate on the words that would bind them together. Words that seemed to make her deception worse. And what did they mean to Jago? He was at her side, but where were his thoughts? Where was his heart?

It was almost done. They had made their responses, his ring was on her finger when she heard the words, "you may kiss the bride." Then Jago's arms were about her, his lips on hers, lightly at first in a kiss that seemed to deepen into the briefest moment of passion. Response leaped within her, her heart beating so fast as he let her go that she barely took in the clergyman's final blessing. When she glanced up at Jago, his expression was as calmly impassive as ever.

Had she imagined those precious seconds of intimacy, she wondered moments later, feeling strangely disturbed as they left the church and said goodbye to clergyman and witnesses.

He's behaving as if nothing unusual has happened, she thought when he handed her into the chaise. So, I must try to do the same. But, as Jago climbed into the seat beside her, his face showed concern.

'Lucienne, what's the matter? are you not well?'

'No, it's not that.' She couldn't admit the truth, must try to sound matter of fact. 'It's just that the reality of actually being married has suddenly dawned on me '

He bent towards her, his eyes gazing earnestly into hers, 'There is no need be afraid. Nothing is going to alter. I swear to you now that I will honour our plan and that, in less than two years' time, you will be free to leave. Please believe me that nothing between us will be in anyway different from how it was yesterday.'

He was watching her intently, waiting for her to say that she was reassured, so she forced a smile and a nod of agreement. As if this was what she really wanted and knowing all the time that it was not.

Then, while he took the chaise skillfully through the narrow, winding lanes, she sat quietly by his side looking down at the wedding bouquet in her lap. Some brides threw their bouquets to eager young bridesmaids. Some pressed the flowers to keep for ever, but this afternoon, when Jago left her at Escott's farm, she would give them to Beulah who would never guess how she had come by them.

She returned to her usual life. And Jago to his, Lucienne thought sadly a few weeks later as she unwrapped her silk handkerchief and took out the bright gold ring. She slipped it onto her finger, remembering when he had put it there and how her heart had beaten faster at the touch of his lips on hers, but since then he behaved exactly as he had before. In a good mood, he was as pleasant to herself as he was to Mrs Dobson. At other times he seemed pre-occupied and distant, and every few weeks he was away from the manor for two or three days.

'Visiting his lady love, I shouldn't wonder,' Mrs Dobson had remarked knowingly. Lucienne was dismayed, but what had she expected? That the simple words of the marriage ceremony would make him look at her with new eyes and forget his mistress? Impatient with herself, she took off the ring, wrapped it carefully in the handkerchief and hid it at the bottom of the travelling trunk, remembering that this afternoon Beulah Escott was to call.

She came in her own carriage. 'Olaf got it cheap because it was so neglected when this big house the other side of Castlebridge was selling up,' she explained as she stepped down into the stable yard from the newly painted horse-drawn trap driven by one of her young brothers-in-law. 'It's a nice ride now, except there's no springs to speak of.'

They went inside to drink tea in the housekeeper's parlour where Mrs Dobson was eager to know how Beulah was faring as a married woman.

'I'm getting on nicely, Mrs Dobson, thanks to you training me in household management and my dear mother-in law being not too well and needing me to take over most of the time. And,' she added, smiling sweetly, 'I do believe I'm to have a baby in the new year. Me and Olaf are so very pleased and surprised at finding ourselves even happier than we were already.'

Afterwards, when Mrs Dobson left them alone to chat, she asked eagerly, 'And what about you, Miss Lucy? Haven't you met some handsome young man that takes your fancy?'

Needing to say something to account for the pause when she couldn't think how to answer, Lucienne told her, 'Someone did ask me to marry him. A coast guard, who thought I was in service at the manor. I refused, though he was very nice. He was posted to a station further down the coast and promised to write. He never did, so perhaps he met another girl and forgot about me. His name was Mathew Harris.' She stopped. 'What's the matter? Are you not well?'

Beulah had turned pale. Her hand on her breast, she gasped, 'I know that name, Miss, it was in the newspaper, and I have to tell you the reason he's not written to you is because he was very badly hurt. It was during a night raid on wicked smugglers further along the coast. Mortally wounded, it said in the newspaper weeks ago, so he must be with our good lord by now.'

So shocked that she had to force herself to speak, Lucienne managed, 'Oh, how very dreadful. I don't often see the newspapers. I had no idea.' She bit her lip to hold back tears. Tears as much of anger as of sorrow for his strong young life snuffed out by vile men who broke the law.

'Oh dear, now you're crying. Did you love him, Miss Lucy?'

'No. Not really. I mean he was just a good, kind friend, but it's so dreadful to think of his dying like that,' Lucienne told her, thinking of Mathew's sparkling blue eyes, and of the way they'd talked and laughed together as they walked along the cliff top. And his declaration of love. A love wasted on her.

She brushed away her tears with the sleeve of her dress, swallowed hard to compose herself, took a deep breath and asked, 'Have you visited Mrs Tregarth in your new carriage?'

'No, I have not. Aside from the distance, she wrote to say the Reverend won't have me in the house because Olaf's staunch Chapel and it seems the Reverend has turned against all but the Church of England. Since he moved to his new parish. I have to make do with Mrs Tregarth's lovely letters, that I keep and read over and over. They mean so much to me, Miss Lucy.'

She rose to leave soon afterwards and, as they walked back to her carriage in the stable yard together, Lucienne said,' Beulah, there is no need to call me Miss now. We are friends, so just Lucy will do. Or Lucienne on special occasions.'

'Well then, it shall be Lucienne when you are God Mother to my baby,' Beulah said, very pleased, 'That is if they have godparents in the Chapel.'

'If not, I shall be a special sort of aunt,' Lucienne called out as she waved goodbye, thinking of Beulah's talk of life at Escott's farm, so full of love and happiness. Olaf's sisters baked cakes and pies to sell at the market in Castlebridge, there were games and sing-songs in the evenings and her mother-in-law was delighted that her eldest son had married such a superior sort of girl as Beulah.

Glad for her, though a little wistful because of her own very different and often lonely situation, Lucienne walked slowly into the echoing quiet of the manor, remembering Mathew Harris, with the anger she felt about his death burning deep in her heart.

Next day, some portraits of the old Acland family were brought down from the attics and laid out to be cleaned on trestle tables set up in one of the storerooms near the kitchen. Out of more than a dozen, Jago had chosen these four. All were so dusty and discoloured that at first Lucienne could barely make out that they were of men in different styles of olden day costumes, suggesting that they had lived at different times. None were dated, though she could only think that the two painted on wood must be older than those painted on canvas.

The instructions she found in Mrs Dobson's housekeeping manual recommended olive oil soap and soft cotton cloths to clean them, and she set about the smallest one, rubbing very gently at first, then realising more effort was needed to remove the grime of ages. Even so, it took three weeks for the four men of the Acland family to emerge. When hung on dark panelled wall of the entrance hall, they looked more at home than the flattering portraits of Cedrick Deverell and his family had ever done, though the clever dark eyes that now looked down on her were something short of friendly. She went up to the attic to look again at the remaining paintings and picked out one of a young woman who looked less forbidding. She took this down to the storeroom and was starting work on it, when Jago came in.

Lately there was a guarded, more formal way in which they spoke to each other, as if the reality of the marriage had begun to affect them in ways they had not expected. Still, she needed to ask him about something that had been troubling her.

'Jago,' she said carefully, 'When we made our arrangement for the estate to become yours, you told me that you would use what money you had to pay off some of what was owing?'

'And I have done that.'

'But so much is happening on the estate. Apart from the work on the cottages, the pottery is under construction and yesterday I learned that a new mine is to be sunk for copper. All of this must take money.'

He smiled and shrugged his shoulders. 'My credit is good. Being seen to pay off so much debt made it better.'

'Do you mean you have borrowed more money?'

'What else? So, let us hope the new ventures will bring the affluence needed to see the estate prosper, if you are to be to set on your way to independence in two years' time. Less than two years. You must trust me to make it work Lucienne, because you haven't any other means of achieving your goal of escaping from here.'

She was about to protest, to say she was happier since her uncle had left when he said, 'Not that I blame you. It is the land outside and the people who live on it that I have always cared about, not so much the house.' He paused, caught her gaze, smiled and added, 'Though it seems better since you've been here.'

As the end of November drew near, a trip to the market at Castlebridge for the purchase of special household items for Christmas was on Mrs Dobson's mind.

'Old Barney is to drive us into Castlebridge, and it will make a nice outing for you and me,' she told Lucienne. 'And we can get everything we need without worrying this year because Mr Jago won't be quibbling about what's been spent.'

The day was bright with winter sunshine as they drove along the coast road to Castlebridge and alighted at a large, bustling market set up on the Broadway. Amid crowds of good-natured country folk, they went down the lanes between the many stalls, Mrs Dobson leading the way until they found the one that sold cloth.

'We want five yards each for the maids to have made up into their dress for next summer,' She told Lucienne, 'And you'd better choose, being a young person yourself with more of an idea of what suits.'

After this it was a pair of boots for the youngest gardener's boy, second hand but very serviceable, a new milk pan and a baking tin the cook had asked for, and several pounds of dried fruits and sugar for the Christmas cakes as well as sundry other items Mrs Dobson decided they had need of. The large canvas bags they'd brought with them were soon overflowing as they wandered happily among stalls selling fresh meat and fish, dried food, metal pans and hardware, fine leather goods and heavy boots for winter wear. All were doing a brisk trade, but it was the one selling clothes that caught Lucienne's attention.

There were a good many garments for sale, but a coat hanging to one side of the stall was what she particularly noticed. A woman's coat, very like the one Bett had bought when they first arrived at in Plymouth, light grey with darker grey bone buttons. The style was not uncommon, so she was about to walk on when she caught sight of a black bag, embroidered with coloured flowers. It was hanging up at the back of the stall, half hidden by purses and satchels, and looked so like the one that Bett always carried that Lucienne's heart skipped a beat. But it couldn't really be Bett's bag. Common sense told her that. Even so, she knew she wouldn't rest until she'd asked the stall holder to get it down for her to see, but there was a queue of customers waiting to be served and Mrs Dobson was tiring under the weight of her share of the packages.

Lucienne took her to wait in the parlour of a nearby hostelry, then hurried back only to find that bag had been sold. The coat was still there and so like Bett's that she asked the stall holder how she had come by it, but the woman said she only worked there and didn't know where the goods came from.

When she told Mrs Dobson that she thought Bett might have come to harm, her things stolen and now for sale on the market stall, the housekeeper was not convinced.

'How can they have been hers? She sent you that nice letter from Plymouth just before she sailed. She was hardly likely to have gone there with no coat and no bag, was she? You want to cheer up a bit, Miss Lucy. I don't know what's come over you lately.'

Remembering all that had happened to her, about most of which the housekeeper could have no idea, Lucienne tried to look cheerful as they sat down to a meal of pasties and ale to fortify themselves for the journey back to Ottersbury. Thinking things over on the way, she remembered Jago telling her that Bett's coat it had been slashed when she was attacked by an unknown assailant. The repair would have been easy to find, but she hadn't thought to look. Still, coats in that style and colour were not uncommon. So, Mrs Dobson must be right, and she most likely mistaken.

11

A few days later a letter came from Beulah to say that her dear Mrs Tregarth had died after a long illness. She begged Lucienne to come to Escott's farm to visit her.

'I was so sorry to get your sad news, Beulah. Were you allowed to see her before she passed away?' Lucienne asked as she sat beside her friend in the warmth of the farmhouse kitchen.

'Yes, and I was so glad to be invited because, since the day I married Olaf, I'd never been allowed to set eyes on her or her boys that were like brothers to me growing up. It was a long way to Heverton, but I so looked forward to going to see them as well as my sweet, kind lady.'

'I expect they were glad to see you again.'

'They weren't there. The two oldest are training in Plymouth now and the housekeeper, taken on when Mrs Tregarth was so ill, told me the other five were sent miles away to live with a relative of their father's. To keep the house quiet for their mother.'

'Surely, being separated from them wasn't what she would have wanted!'

'I thought it must be the Reverend's doing. He was out preaching somewhere, and I was glad about that. And my poor lady was very ill, lying in her bed, pale and weak. She was so pleased to see me, glad that I'm happy in my marriage and said how she longed to hold my baby in her arms. I think we both knew that she wouldn't—' She broke off, her lips trembling with grief. 'Anyway, we talked about when I was little and laughed at things we remembered. I'd always loved her coral necklace from when she was a young girl going out to dances. That and a cameo brooch were the only pieces of finery she ever owned, and she had them there on the bedside table ready to give to me.

And, suddenly, she was crying, begging me to pray that she'd be forgiven for a bad thing she'd done. I had no idea what she meant, so I said that, if she'd done wrong, it must have been for some good reason. She smiled then, squeezed my hand, and thanked me. In a little while, she drifted off to sleep while I sat beside her, knowing it must be our last time together. Then Olaf came in and said we should go to be safely home before dark because there'd be no moon that night.'

'It must have been very hard to leave her.'

'Yes, and to make things worse, when we were a little way out of the village, I realised I'd forgotten the things she'd given me. Olaf left me there in the carriage by the side of the road and took a short cut back through the fields to fetch them. He didn't tell me until we were home, but the way he went brought him out behind the vicarage. He got over the wall and looked through the kitchen window, and there were the five boys, sitting around the table eating their supper! They'd been kept out of the way somewhere nearby and let home as soon as I'd left.'

'But why would that be?'

'Olaf says it was the Reverend punishing me for marrying into a family that's Chapel.' She stifled a sob. 'Lucy, I am so fortunate in my loving husband and his family, but Mrs Tregarth was like a mother to me. And it is so hard to know she is gone, as you yourself must know.'

'I think I do,' Lucienne said, remembering Bett, far away in Jamaica and longing for news of her. Soon afterwards she said goodbye and left, promising to come back before too long.

Beulah's tall fair-haired husband stopped her as she started down the path. With his usual lack of preamble he said, 'Morning, Miss Lucy I've a favour to ask of you.'

'Of course, Olaf. What can I do for you?'

' 'Tis Mrs Tregarth's funeral tomorrow. Beulah can't go, because the midwife says to rest herself. If you could go to get sight of the Tregarth boys and bring back to her how they're getting on, it would be a great comfort.'

'I'd willingly go, Olaf, but I scarcely knew Mrs Tregarth. Wouldn't it seem odd for me to go so far? And how would I get there?'

'Miss Petty's going. She was the lady's godmother and I'm letting her have the carriage with one of the lads to drive her, leaving her house prompt at seven o'clock in the morning. I took the liberty of telling her you might be glad of an outing.'

'Such a comfort to have you with me', Miss Petty told her as they set off next day, wrapped in rough woollen travelling rugs Olaf had given them against the bitter chill of the morning. 'I'll swear these are horse blankets, but they're clean enough and he's a dear man to have thought to provide them.' She took out a kerchief and dabbed at her eyes. 'Many are the tears I've shed this week for my dear Lydia, taken with an inflammation of the lungs after surviving childbirth with such lamentable frequency.'

'Is it usual for ladies to be at the graveside in England?'

'No, we attend only the wake, but I hope to find somewhere I can stand well back and watch my dear girl lowered into the grave from a safe distance. I was awake half the night thinking about it,' Miss Petty told her, then subsided into an intermittent doze for the rest of the journey, which lasted nearly four hours.

Despite cold air pinching her face and being tossed about on rough country lanes where the carriage's lack of springs was very noticeable, Lucienne enjoyed the journey to their sad destination.

'Such a distance,' Miss Petty exclaimed, waking up as the road took them through the prosperous looking village of Heverton to the lynch gate of the parish church. 'I so missed Lydia and her boys once they moved, though I was glad their fortune had taken such an encouraging turn. This parish provides a much better living than Yoxley.'

As they reached the church and got down from the carriage, Lucienne glanced up the path and saw the end of the funeral procession disappearing around the side of the building.

'Only just in time,' Miss Petty whispered moments later as they hid behind the huge trunk of an ancient yew tree and peered at the backs of the black-coated men assembled around the open grave, some twenty yards away across the frozen grass. Two figures on the opposite side of the grave drew Lucienne's attention. They looked to be little more than boys.

'My niece's two older sons, David and Daniel,' Miss Petty whispered. 'Sixteen and seventeen years of age now and such fine young men. Lydia worried so much about what life would offer them until, just after the family came to live here, an inheritance on their father's side paid for premium apprenticeships. The older boy is with an apothecary and the younger with an architect, no less.'

After that, they stood in silence, Miss Petty weeping as the coffin was lowered into the ground. Lucienne put her arms around the old lady and gave her a comforting hug, then kept well out of sight as Miss Petty watched the mourners leave the graveside. They came in slow procession down the path, out onto the lane and set off in the direction of the vicarage.

Lucienne and Miss Petty started to follow, then saw a little troop of village women coming up the path towards them.

'To pay their last respects,' Miss Petty sighed. 'My niece was always good to the poor, even in the days when she had little enough of her own to manage on. I'd best have a word, perhaps go with them to the grave to watch as it's filled with earth and say a prayer or two. Why don't you have a look round the church? I believe it is very ancient.'

Better to walk about outside and try to get warm, Lucienne thought as she set off towards the rear of the church along a lonely, overhung path. Beside her ran a high stone wall that she thought must separate the churchyard from the vicarage garden and, a little way along, she came across a wooden gate allowing access from one to the other. About to walk on, she heard a boy's voice calling and another answering.

On impulse, she lifted the latch, pulled open the gate, went through and saw three young boys kicking a football about on a piece of rough land near to where she stood. Further away, at the other end of the very long garden, she glimpsed two much younger boys chasing a puppy dog in and out of some laurel bushes. These must be the five younger Tregarths, and now was her chance to talk with them and have something to tell Beulah on her next visit to the farm.

Almost at once, the ball came towards her. She ran forwards and snatched it up, was about to throw it back when the two smaller of the three boys came towards her, smiling.

'Do you want to play, Miss?' one of them asked. He looked to be about eight years old, the other about six.

'Not today thank you.' Smiling, she tossed the ball to him, 'My name is Lucy and I think you must be two of the Tregarth boys.'

'I'm George and he's Edward,' the smaller of them volunteered He was about to say more when the third boy, who was perhaps thirteen or fourteen years old, came to join them. When Edward introduced him as Robert Tregarth, he bowed politely.

'You're very welcome, Miss, though it is a sad day for all of us.' He glanced back to the other end of the garden where the two youngest boys were throwing sticks for the puppy. 'They're too little to understand what Mama's passing really means.'

The two beside him stopped smiling and Edward asked, 'What's your other name, Miss Lucy? And, come to think of it, how did you know who we are?'

'I am Lucy Deverell and I am a friend of Beulah's. She couldn't come so asked me to look out for you today.'

Robert's open expression changed to wariness. He said, stiffly, 'You must excuse us, Miss. We have to go now,' with which he took hold of both the younger boys and marched them away. The three of them rounded up two smaller boys and ran with them to the house. Strong, sturdy boys. She swallowed hard, thinking of Alain, so small and easily swept away. For a few moments she was half crippled by the pain awakened in her heart, then turned and made her way back into the churchyard.

'As soon as I mentioned Beulah, they hurried away,' she told Miss Petty when they met at the lynch gate. 'It was as if they'd been forbidden even to talk about her.'

'Knowing the Reverend Tregath and his peculiar ways, that wouldn't surprise me,' Miss Petty remarked, giving Lucienne's arm a comforting pat as they reached the vicarage gate. 'After our long journey, Lucienne, you must be as famished as I am, so I hope there will a good spread at the wake, though the people here today will be local and unknown to either of us. Except for your uncle.'

'Uncle Cedrick? Are you sure? You didn't say he was here when you were watching just now.'

'Didn't I? Well, of course, he and Lydia were distant cousins of some sort and your uncle is ever mindful of the proprieties,' she said as they linked arms and set off for the vicarage.

Cedrick Deverell met them at the door, almost as if he had been waiting for them. His expression hostile, he ignored Lucienne's greeting and addressed himself to Miss Petty.

'What,' he said sharply, 'has possessed you to bring with you a person, unknown to the Reverend Tregarth, to what is a private, family occasion?'

'I thought to give Lucienne a ride out.' For once, Miss Petty looked flustered. 'Young people do so enjoy an outing,' she added with a smile he didn't return.

He shrugged impatiently, 'It is inappropriate for her to be here. I suggest that she takes herself to the village hostelry and waits for you there. In fact, I insist upon it.' He turned on his heel and left.

Miss Petty looked most uncomfortable. 'I'm so sorry, my dear,' she said, fumbling in her purse. 'You'd best go and wait at the inn. Take this two- shilling piece and get yourself a warm drink and something to eat. I won't stay long, an hour at the most,' She paused. 'So unexpected. Your Uncle has his faults, but at least he is usually polite.'

Not to me, thought Lucienne, smarting at the way he hadn't even addressed her directly. She went briskly back to the village, walking tall though the afternoon was chilly, and she was glad to reach the warm, smoky parlour of the Barley Mow Inn.

'A sad though heart-warming occasion, and the refreshments were quite wholesome,' Miss Petty told her afterwards as they set off on the long journey home. 'And such a lovely family my poor niece has left, though even before I arrived the youngest two had become over excited and had to be taken out by the housekeeper, so I didn't see them and, being so young, they might not have remembered me. But there was quite a crowd of very pleasant folk, though none I knew, apart from a physician from Castlebridge and his wife.

'So, the wake wasn't such a very private, family affair after all,' Lucienne remarked.

Miss Petty patted her arm and changed the subject.

'As I said before, weakness in her lungs was something poor Lydia had to bear even as a young girl. I must get in touch with your aunt, Isobel, and let her know about Lydia's passing. They were such friends as girls, though their stations in life were different, especially when Isobel was presented at court and became Lady Moncrief. Oh, I do go on so. You must be exhausted by my ramblings.'

'No, Miss Petty. I enjoy them. And what about the older Tregarth boys? Did you get to talk to them?' she asked hopefully, and, over the next few miles, she got all the news she needed to satisfy Beulah.

It was so late when she got back to the manor house that she went straight to bed. Next day she discovered that Jago had not slept in the house that night, and a message had come from the village to tell Mrs Dobson that he was out with the fishing boats. The housekeeper didn't seem surprised.

'That's the way with these bachelor gentlemen. Restless. The sooner he's married to and settled the better.'

'Not much chance of that, I should think,' Lucienne said lightly, thinking of her ring hidden at the bottom of the travelling trunk. She turned their talk to restocking the larder and realised that the running of the house had become very important to her. Reluctantly she admitted that was because Jago was concerned with improving things at Ottersbury Manor and she wanted to impress him in any way she could.

Still, over the next few weeks, she maintained a reserved decorum in her dealings with Jago, though she saw more of him, sometimes helping him categorise the books in the library, or meeting him when he called in at the schoolhouse. Most often, they were together when she played the piano and he listened to the music while he sat at the writing table in the drawing room, poring over plans for the development of the estate. This did not escape Mrs Dobson, who drew her aside.

'I'll speak no ill of the Master,' she said carefully, 'but I think it wiser not to be spending too much time on your own with him. We don't want the maids talking, do we?

To which Lucienne could only reply that she did not.

12

After they found where Alain was buried, Lucienne went there each month to tend his grave, and at the beginning of December she invited Miss Petty to go with her to Yoxley on a day when the school was closed. Miss Petty, invigorated by her role of headmistress, suggested that they went across country on foot, as she had always done when visiting her niece at Yoxley vicarage.

'The weather is fair for the time of year,' she said, 'And I long to tread those country ways again. You will hardly credit the pleasure of walking there, though it is several miles distant, so best I make up a picnic.'

They set off early in the bright winter sunlight, Miss Petty leading the way through a network of narrow paths used by labourers to reach the fields and to make their way between villages. The hedgerows were bare, the leaves fallen from the trees and ice on frozen puddles crackled beneath their feet, but walking kept them warm as they went through the fields to a long stretch of open countryside.

They had been walking for over an hour when they

reached a bridge and crossed a river, which Miss Petty said meant they were nearly halfway there. The land hereabouts had become undulating and wooded, more interesting, but they had gone only a few yards beyond the bridge when Miss Petty stood still. She looked surprised.

'How strange,' she said, 'I understood that old place to be deserted.'

Lucienne followed her gaze to where smoke coming from the chimney of a house almost completely hidden by fir trees and some distance away on their left. Miss Petty, now quite uneasy, quickened the pace until they were well beyond it, then glanced behind them and gave a startled cry.

'There are horsemen coming after us. This was a lawless place in days gone by and we are two women, alone and unprotected.'

Alarmed, because Miss Petty was usually fearless, Lucienne looked back and saw two figures on horseback racing along the path towards them. Instinctively, she turned and dashed after Miss Petty into the shelter of the trees alongside the path.

Peering out, from between the trunks of two young beech trees, she saw them quite clearly as they galloped passed. First, on a fine chestnut mare and with her own chestnut hair streaming out from beneath her plumed riding hat, was a beautiful woman in a black riding habit. And behind her was the lean, tall figure of a man, pursuing her on his black stallion.

'Well, I never,' declared Miss Petty, who had been watching from behind another tree. 'Jago Moncrief and the recently widowed Lady Helena Riverton! Of course, their friendship has been the source of great speculation for some time now, as you may well have heard.'

Lucienne, with a sinking heart, admitted that she had heard, while Miss Petty declared that the excitement had sharpened her appetite, making it time for lunch. Setting out her picnic cloth on the fallen leaves beneath the bare branches of the trees, she was inclined to speculate.

'It is halfway through the morning, but lovers lie late abed, and I do believe they came from that lonely house we just passed just now. I'm not sure who it belongs to, probably part of the Riverton estate, but I can see why they would meet in such a secluded place. Lady Helena's reputation must be safeguarded, and it would not do for them to openly spend the night together at either of their houses.' She drew herself up sharp, 'Though perhaps I should not say such things to a young, unmarried girl. Still, I'm an old unmarried one, so perhaps it doesn't matter,' she ended, cheerfully unaware that her young friend's bite of cherry cake seemed like ashes in her mouth.

When they reached Yoxley just after midday, the church yard was bleak and lonely place, and the grave seemed smaller and sadder than ever.

Seeing her young friend's look of desolation, Miss Petty said bracingly, 'To be sure, things are never at their best in the cold, but we'll soon have it looking a tad more tidy,'

Lucienne, kneeling to arrange sprigs of red berried holly, orange rose hips and misty green spruce in the stone jar she had first brought there for summer roses, said gratefully,

'I am so glad you came with me. But you know, it's very strange. Every day, I miss Alain so much yet, when I come here to say a prayer where he lies buried, I feel no closeness to him.'

Miss Petty, brushing away fallen leaves from around the grave, told her, 'My dear, whatever the clergy have to say about the resurrection of the body, your brother's little soul was the most important part of him. And that has gone to heaven, to be with his dear mama, safe and sound. She stood up and shook the creases out of her skirt. 'Now, I have an old friend living here who will surely give us something warm to drink before we set off for home, but we mustn't stay long. We have a two hour walk home to Ottersbury and it will be dark by four o'clock.' '

When she returned to the manor house that evening, Mrs Dobson met her in the front hall and told her that Jago had been asking for her.

'He's in the library and says you're to join him there as soon as you get in.'

With the memory of seeing him ride by with the strikingly handsome Lady Helena still smarting in her mind, Lucienne decided she just couldn't face him.

'Mrs Dobson, I'm tired from walking so far today and I need to rest,' she said firmly, 'So please give my apologies to Mr Jago,' and she went away up the stairs.

Once inside her room, she paced about, so disturbed, by the memory of Jago and lady Helana riding out together, that she even considered demanding an explanation from Jago when she met him next morning. Then, recollecting sadly that in their marriage of convenience it should be no concern of hers how her husband spent his time, she changed into her nightclothes and climbed into her lonely bed.

. . .

Next day, just after half passed eleven o'clock in the morning, the household was thrown into confusion by the arrival of Jago's mother, Lady Isobel Moncrief, who swept into the front hall in a flurry of luxurious furs and bad temper. She demanded to see her son.

'She'd not been here five minutes before there was raised voices behind closed doors,' Mrs Dobson told Lucienne about an hour later, when she came back from her morning at the village school. 'At least hers was raised. Master Jago kept his voice down but they're still in the study now, still arguing.'

'Did you know she was coming to stay, Mrs Dobson?

'No and I don't think the Master did either or he'd have warned me, so we'll just have to do the best we can'

'Is there anything I can do to help?'

'Yes, there is. Lady Isobel always liked the Chinese room, so I sent the maids up to get it ready for her. Could you go up and see everything's straight? She's very exacting.'

Upstairs in the Chinese room, where the walls were papered with faded scenes of strangely beautiful landscapes, the bed hung with dark blue silken curtains and the floor scattered with luxurious eastern rugs, everything seemed to be in order. A lady's maid who Lucienne had never seen before was busy unpacking the contents of several valises into open drawers but, at the command of Lady Isobel who strode into the room a moment later, she hurried away to order hot water to be brought up for a bath.

'And you are?' Lady Isobel, her handsome face still flushed red with bad temper, demanded with an imperious glance at Lucienne. Her manner softened. 'Of course, my niece! My brother Richard's girl and so much improved in looks and manner that I didn't recognise you for a moment. Now forgive me, my dear, but I must refresh myself after my journey. And later today, perhaps we can get to know each other a little better.'

'And about time too,' Mrs Dobson remarked when Lucienne went downstairs to relay the conversation to her. 'You've been here for best part of a year and not a bit of notice taken. While she's staying, which won't be for long if I know her, the master says you're to have dinner with them.'

That evening, in an antique gown of rose-pink silk velvet she had found in the attic, her hair put up and wearing the crystal earrings that were Mrs Dobson's most precious possession, Lucienne sat down to dine with Jago and his mother at the long, darkly polished dining table. Creamy beeswax candles in each of three silver candelabra cast a flickering light over white linen napkins, gleaming silver cutlery and sparkling crystal wine glasses on what was to be an uncomfortable occasion.

Jago, wearing his most enigmatic expression, sat at one end of the table. Lady Isobel, haughty and condescending, at the other. Whatever they had been quarreling about must still be unresolved, Lucienne decided, as they barely spoke and there was an atmosphere between them of scarcely veiled hostility. Seated alone to one side of the table, with two empty chairs on either side of her, she wondered uneasily what had caused them to quarrel.

At the end of the meal, when the servants had removed their dishes and left the room, her thoughts were interrupted by Lady Isobel addressing her.

'My dear niece,' she said pleasantly, 'You must believe that until today I had no inkling that my grandmother had willed the Ottersbury estate to my brother Richard, making you the rightful heiress. I fear I have not fulfilled my duty to you as an aunt, nor yet as a legal guardian. That shall be remedied, but first tell me how you have filled your time, tucked away here at the back of beyond?'

'I have been assisting the housekeeper with her duties,' Lucienne told her, irritated by the smirk that crossed Jago's handsome features, but rewarded by a startled gasp from her aunt who recovered herself and gave an understanding smile.

'How wise. Unusual, though sensible to acquire such knowledge. So many young girls are totally in the hands of the servants when they have their own establishment. However, I'm sure you will have had enough of it by now. It is my intention to take you with me to open up a house I have in Plymouth, where there is much congenial society. That will be for the first month or so and then, when the season begins, we will go up to London for you to be presented at Court, as was I as a girl. And then, out into the marriage market with you.'

'But Aunt Isobel, really, I can't possibly—'

'Of course, you can. You must. As heiress to an estate on the verge of ruin, as my son has so helpfully told me today, your best plan is to find a husband with plenty of money.'

'No Aunt Isobel, I really couldn't do that—'

'Why ever not? Even the son and heir of some vastly rich merchant, educated to be a gentleman and needing the prestige of marrying into a county family, would do. There are plenty of them about. With my help, you could become quite a beauty and to take your pick.'

'Truly, it isn't possible for me to do that.' Lucienne insisted, glancing for support at Jago. He appeared to be studying his fingernails.

'My dear, of course, you can. You have style, so don't undervalue yourself. Confidence is everything in these things—'

'But I may not be an heiress. It's not at all certain that Ottersbury will be mine when I come of age.' Lucienne told her in desperation. Out of the corner of her eye, she saw Jago give an almost imperceptible nod. 'Because of the war, we can't go to France to find out, but my parents may not have been married.'

'Why should they not have been? My brother Richard, the soul of honour, was madly in love with Barbara Widdon. He must have married her at the first opportunity,' Lady Isobel declared masterfully. 'As for yourself, at nearly twenty when the season begins next year, you will be older than many of your fellow debutants. Some are barely seventeen so, in your first season out, you simply must secure a suitable husband.'

Lucienne, at a loss as to what to say next, turned to Jago for support. This time he shrugged, and she felt her temper rising. He'd sworn her to silence about their marriage pact, so surely it was up to him to provide her with a way out of this. Trembling with apprehension, she waited and when he said nothing, she made up her mind and turned back to her aunt.

'I can't go looking for a husband, Aunt Isobel, because I am already married.' Out of the corner of her eye, she saw Jago start forward in his chair, but didn't care. Lady Isobel gave a startled gasp.

'Are you telling me that you were married in whatever God forsaken place it was you came from before you got here? Why on earth was this not made clear from the start?'

'I was not married in Guadeloupe, Aunt Isobel. I was married here in Devon. I am married to Jago.' There, I've said it, she thought defiantly, feeling less sure of herself when her aunt seemed about to faint with shock, then rallied, pushed back her chair, and jumped to her feet. Her face contorted with rage and indignation she confronted Jago.

'How dare you make any decision about my ward without consulting me? Let alone marry her. Did you choose to forget I too am her legal guardian? The marriage can't be valid. I shall take steps to have it dissolved.'

Gazing at her with a provocative grin, Jago shrugged again.

'You agreed to apply to the court for joint guardianship only if all responsibility and decisions regarding Lucienne were to be mine. So, take whatever steps you like, Mama, but I can assure you that the marriage is legal.'

'We'll see about that. You've enticed my niece into this travesty of a union to get your hands on her property. And tell me Jago, do still carry on your affair with that redheaded trollop?'

'I've made no comment on your various liaisons over the years,' Jago told her with irritating composure, 'So I'll thank you not to concern yourself with mine.'

'How dare you! While your father lived, I was a faithful, loving wife, whereas you, the vile seducer of this innocent young girl, are no doubt defiling her marriage bed with your adultery.'

Lucienne, unable to bear it a moment longer, cried, 'Stop! Stop at once. There is no need for all this. I agreed to marry Jago in name only so he would use his own money to save the estate from ruin. There was no other way.'

'You, poor, silly girl!' Lady Isobel cried. 'As your

guardian, he was bound to look after your interests anyway. And he'll be lucky if his wonderful plans will come to anything with the little capital he has to pay for them. Any fool could have told you that your way forward was a marriage bringing in enough money to save this estate twice over.'

'But I don't want to be married' Lucienne heard herself cry as she scrambled to her feet. 'I just want to go back to live in France with my darling Bett.' Hot tears of anger and frustration rolled down her cheeks as she pushed aside her chair and ran to the door.

'Who is this person, Bett?' she heard her aunt demand as she left the room.

Upstairs, still trembling with agitation, Lucienne paced about her room. Had she done the right thing in admitting to the marriage? At least she could have made a more dignified exit. She stopped pacing, threw herself down on her bed, stared at the ceiling and wondered what to do. Over the last weeks, she had almost dismissed the fact that she was not Richard Deverell's child. Now, being an imposter made everything seem so much worse.

But what would it have been like to experience the fashionable London season? If she hadn't been married to Jago, would she have agreed to go there? She could hardly have refused. There would have been lovely dresses, dances, parties, and perhaps some nice young man to fall in love with her. Much nicer than arrogant, clever Jago, who didn't love anything about her except her inheritance. And as for the beautiful, red-headed Lady Helena—

There was a rapping on her door. She sat up, expecting it to be Jago and wishing she'd thought to turn the key, but the door opened and Lady Isobel walked into her room. Dignified and unruffled, she sank gracefully into the armchair and motioned to Lucienne to stay where she was when she sat up and started to get off the bed.

'Jago and I often have opposing views, my dear,' she explained calmly. 'I hope you weren't too disturbed just now by our little skirmish.'

Little skirmish, Lucienne thought in amazement, then remembered to ask, 'Aunt Isobel, why are you so determined that Ottersbury should be mine? If it turns out that my parents were not married and I am not the heir, then it would rightfully belong to you and Uncle Cedrick.'

Lady Isobel gave a snort of contempt. 'I simply detest my brother Cedrick and it seems he's had more than his fair share out of this estate already. I myself don't wish to be encumbered with a large property. All I want is a sufficient income to live as I like to do.' She paused. 'I think I must have been travelling abroad when little Alain died. I heard about it only this morning. I am so sorry for your loss, my dear,' and before Lucienne could thank her, she changed the subject.

'Of course, I don't begrudge Ottersbury to Jago. I just don't see how, with the best will in the world, he can drag this place out of the mess left by my brother Cedrick. Dreadful man! Even as a child I much preferred your father. As did our grandmother, or she wouldn't have left him the estate. And, after all, it was hers to leave it wherever she wanted to.'

Lucienne broke in, 'Why do you think she did that? Why ignore her own son in favour of his youngest child?'

'That we will never know, though I expect you 've heard that your grandfather was married twice. She couldn't stand my mother, who was the first wife, so she left me nothing. Cedrick and your father were by the second wife, of who she approved, but Richard always was her favourite, so he got everything.'

She rose, stretched, smoothed the creases from the skirt of her emerald silk gown and added, 'I told Jago I'd bring you down to join us for a glass of wine in the library. Do come along, or he'll think we've abandoned him.'

Exhausted by the events of the evening, it took Lucienne some time to convince her aunt that she was going to stay where she was. Eventually, wearing an expression that suggested she couldn't understand why this might be, her aunt went away.

How much had the servants heard of last night's events in the dining room, Lucienne wondered when she went downstairs next morning? Nothing important she decided, judging by their lack of reaction when she met them going about their tasks.

Facing Jago was what she dreaded most. Still, it had to be done, but when she asked after his whereabouts, Mrs Dobson told her he had just left the house.

'He's in a bad humour this morning,' she added, 'Said he'd be away a few days but, if you need to speak to him, you might just catch him in the stable yard before he rides off.'

Hurrying through the house, trying to decide what to say about the scene in the dining room, Lucienne reached the stable yard where the black stallion was held ready by Barney, the old deaf groom. About to mount, Jago greeted her with an unsmiling nod of the head.

'Good morning, Lucienne. In a calmer frame of mind today, I hope?'

Ignoring the sarcasm in his voice, she said, 'I'm surprised that you're going away when Lady Isobel has come to stay.'

'I think you'll find she'll soon be gone because she didn't get what she came for.'

'Which was?'

'Money,' he said brusquely. 'Since wrongfully inheriting half this estate, she's been drawing income from it. My writing to inform her that this must now stop was what brought her down here, though she has an adequate income from my late father's estate in Scotland,'

And before Lucienne could think of anything to say, he swung himself into the saddle, took the reins, bid her a curt goodbye, and rode away.

A lump came to her throat. How could he make her feel so miserable, just by leaving in a bad mood? And where was he going this time? To his Mistress? She couldn't bear the thought. She was wondering what to do with herself when she realised someone was speaking to her.

'Will you be riding out, Miss? We have the little grey mare, name of Starlight, safe as a rocking horse if you was to try.'

It was the old groom, trying to cheer her up. She smiled and shook her head, remembering how, in Guadeloupe, she had ridden so well that her father said she should have been a boy, which from him was praise indeed. With a sigh, she went back into the house and made her way to one of the storerooms beside the kitchen, glad she had something nice to do to cheer herself up.

In the summer she had stored the petals of scented

plants from the garden, preserving them with thin layers of coarse sea salt as they dried. Lavender, rosemary, Jasmine flowers, rose petals, mint, marjoram, with shredded orange and lemon peel, all mixed in with cinnamon bark and cloves from the larder. Lastly, she'd stirred in Orris root powder to fix the perfume and sure enough, when she lifted the lid from a large white enamel bowl, though the colours were faded, the delicate scents of last summer rose to meet her. She plunged both hands into the mixture, stirring up the petals and taking in the fragrance. Then, hearing a sound, she withdrew her hands and glanced up.

Jago was standing at the open door watching her. Before she could say anything, he stepped forward.

'Lucienne,' he said earnestly, 'I am sorry to have spoken to you as I did just now. I came back to apologise.' Before she could answer he came closer, inhaled deeply, and said in a different tone, 'What a lovely scent. You made that?'

'Yes, it's potpourri of last summer's flowers from the garden. I learned to do it when I was a little girl in France,' she said as he bent forward. She thought he was going to smell the bowl of dried flowers. Instead, he took her hand and breathed in the scent of the skin on the front of her wrist. A shiver of delight ran through her as he turned her hand over and pressed one soft, lingering kiss into her palm and another, longer and more intense, then closed her fingers over the kisses as if to keep them safe. He stood up and looked into her eyes.

'Lucienne,' he said softly, 'I know I'm not the easiest person to understand and I know you are very young. But, since we have spent time together, I have come to hold you in high regard, to admire your spirit. We get on well, I think we have common interests. I must go now, but while I'm away, I want you to think of how our life together could be if we reconsidered our plans and became truly man and wife.'

She had not expected this. Nothing in the way he had behaved towards her until now had led her to expect it, but her heart leapt with joy. She almost cried out that he didn't need to wait so long for her answer when a glimmer of inner resolve held her back. Should she risk spoiling this precious moment and all it promised for the future by asking the question that must otherwise always be there at the back of her mind? Yes, she decided, she should.

She closed her eyes for a few seconds, steeling herself, then opened them as she stared into his eyes and said, 'Jago, before we can go forward with this, I must know about Lady Helena. If you cannot agree to give her up, then I cannot enter into a true marriage with you. It would not be right, and I couldn't bear it.'

He held her gaze. 'I can say to you in all honesty that my relationship with her is at an end. Do you remember that day we went to Yoxley to find Alain's grave and afterwards I left you at Escott's farm?'

'Yes, of course I do.'

'It was then I went to see Helena, intending to ask her to release me from what had been between us. Before I could do that, she told me that she herself had plans for a future far away from here, so there was goodwill on both sides, and we have not been together for many months now.'

It was as if a chill engulfed her. 'Two days ago,' she said stiffly, 'I was out walking when I saw you ride past with her. And you now tell me that you have not been with her for some weeks!'

He shook his head and smiled. 'Lucienne, you are

such an innocent. Saying that she and I have not been together is a polite way of saying we have not been together as lovers. Do you understand me?'

She bit her lip as she felt her colour rise. 'Yes. Yes, I understand that now.' She hesitated 'So why then did you meet with her?'

'She wanted to sell some of her late husband's property that was not included in the entail before the Riverton heir comes back from abroad to claim the estate. I went to see it and a price was agreed. That was all. We must have been going there or coming away when you happened to see us ride past. 'He paused. 'You do believe me, Lucienne?'

Relief sweeping over her, she nodded, 'Yes, I think I do.'

'And do you appreciate that most men, who have reached my age of twenty- seven, generally have had some such involvement?'

'I hadn't thought about it. But yes, I imagine so.'

'Then I must tell you that a man with any decency will always have some kindness in his heart for a woman who has lovingly granted him her favours. More especially if they were sweethearts when very young.'

'I understand. But it is different for me Jago. There has never been anybody who I could truly call a sweetheart.'

He grinned. 'We'll talk about this later, but now I must go.'

'Where to this time? And will you soon be back?

'I'm going to Plymouth to recruit some eager young lawyer to work in the firm in Castlebridge now that I am occupied here on the estate. It might take time to find the right man, so I'll be away for a week at the very least.'

He leaned forward and kissed her again. This time, the firm pressure of his lips just below her ear where her neck met her jaw, sent a shivering sensation through her entire body. Like nothing she had ever experienced before, she thought as he bowed and bid her a smiling goodbye.

When he was gone, Lucienne leaned against her worktable, amazed that in so little time he had made a grey winter morning seem as lovely as any summer afternoon. Still a little out of breath, she wondered what she should say when he asked again if she would become his true wife. Smiling to herself, she decided there and then what her answer would be.

Recollecting what she had come here to do, she took six small Chinese porcelain bowls she had found in the attic and filled each of them with the potpourri of flowers, then left the storeroom and went to place them here and there about the downstairs rooms. Whenever she passed one of them, the perfume would remind her of the wonderful thing that had happened to her this morning.

As she put the last dish down on the hall table, she glanced at the silver letter tray and saw an envelope addressed simply to Miss Lucy. Opening it, she found a person called Alice Narramore had written to her, explaining that she was Mathew Harris's sister and that she would be in the church yard the following day at 2 o'clock in the afternoon and would Miss Lucy would please be so kind as to meet her there?

Next day, the woman Lucienne found waiting for her looked to be a few years older than Mathew but otherwise so like him that, even if they had met somewhere else and quite by chance, she could have guessed they were from the same family.

'I hope you will not take it amiss, me asking to see

you, Miss Lucy, but my husband was coming this way and I came with him. I wanted to let you know that, when my poor brother lay in bed at my house, so dreadfully wounded, he often spoke of you,' she said, her voice heavy with emotion as they sat together on the stone bench beneath the yew tree in the churchyard. 'In his last days he was concerned that you might have thought he had some bad intentions when he was so familiar with you before he went away.'

'Of course, I didn't think that.' Lucienne told her. 'He was a dear, kind, respectful young man and I was glad to know him. He was my dear friend.'

'But to him, I believe you were more than that,' the older woman said earnestly. 'I believe he loved you with all his heart. He told me so and would have come back here and asked you to be his bride if things had worked out different.' Her eyes held an unspoken question, and Lucienne knew her answer must bring this poor woman no more pain.

She said carefully, 'Mrs Narramore, any young woman with the good fortune to win his love would have been proud to be your brother's bride, if she was free to do so.'

For a few seconds she feared this might not be enough, then was relieved to see the other woman smile.

'That puts my mind to rest, knowing his feelings were not wasted. A very great comfort indeed, for it was me that persuaded him to leave his life at sea, believing he'd be safer at home with the family, uncle to my little boys, never thinking he'd fall victim to smugglers. Those wicked men, depriving our noble King of his rightful custom dues, and not hesitating to shoot a coast guard dead if he tries to stop them.'

She spoke with such feeling that Lucienne could only

take her hand and hold it for a while until the older woman brushed away her tears and spoke again.

'Our meeting has been a great help to me. I can remind myself of what a fine young woman he gave his love to and how glad I would have been to see the pair of you happy and content together.' She smiled and stood up, 'I am so pleased to have met you, Miss Lucy, but that's the church clock striking three and I'm to be picked in the village in just a few minutes, so I must say goodbye. But one thing. I understand that you are well placed here, in service at the big house, but if you should ever be in need of help and shelter, you'd find that in my home. Narramore, Sail Makers are easy enough to find in Falmouth.'

She tried to smile as she rose to go, but there were tears in her eyes so Lucienne took her arm and walked with her as far as the Holly Tree Inn, where her husband was waiting for her.

Left alone, Lucienne stood shivering in the winter afternoon, then turned to walk back towards the manor house, the sadness of Mathew's death all the more poignant now she was alone. But no, she thought resolutely, she wouldn't think of that. She would remember him on those sunny afternoons, striding along the cliff tops to meet her, strong and carefree and wreathed in smiles. He was a good and decent man, in his company she felt light- hearted and happy. Could she have made him happy and been content with a man she liked and admired, but who didn't have the power to make her heart race like Jago could without even noticing? Mathew had said he loved her. Would she soon hear those words from Jago?

13

Lucienne longed for Jago's return, to be in his arms, to whisper words of love, but meeting Mathew Harris's sister had unsettled her. That night, she hardly slept, was wide awake next morning when it was barely light. Determined not to lie in bed thinking sad thoughts, she was considering how to fill the long hours until the rest of the household stirred when she remembered the old groom telling her that Starlight, the grey mare, was there for her should she want to ride out. On horseback, could she get to Yoxley village to visit Alain's grave one last time before the year ended and still be back in time to start the day? She could try, she thought, as she slipped out of bed shivering as she pulled on her cloak, but cheered at the prospect of being on horseback again

Long ago in Guadeloupe, when her father taught her to ride, there had been no lady's saddle in the stables at Belle Chance. Until one could be bought, she'd learned to sit astride the horse like a boy which she much preferred. If she went out early enough, who would notice if she rode like a boy today? And she knew where to find a pair of breeches. She turned up the wick of the oil lamp and by its light made her way along the dark, silent passageways and down the stairs in search of some old clothes Mrs Dobson brought down from the attic to give to the needy at Christmas.

They were in one of the storerooms beside the kitchen and, searching through them, she found a tweed suit of boys' clothes, a cap and a short cape, and took them up to her room. They smelled of something used to keep away the moths, were a shade too big, but much warmer than the heaviest of her dresses.. She slipped on the suit over her nightdress and tightened a leather belt around her waist to hold up the trousers, then, with her hair tucked up into the cap, she put on the cape, boots and gloves and made her way through the silent, gloomy house.

Out in the stable yard, where it was very cold, still barely light and too early for the grooms to be about, she found the grey mare's stall and spent a few moments getting to know the gentle creature, patting her flank and talking to her softly, before she saddled up. Soon she was mounted, out into the lane and riding through the village. Sensing the mare was as pleased to be out in the open as she was herself, she decided to leave the road and ride to Yoxley by the way she'd walked with Miss Petty.

The ground was firm with morning frost and, with no styles to cross, she rode the paths through the fields and out onto the long stretch of open grassland beyond. There was an icy sharpness in the air, but it was getting lighter, and her spirits lifted as she revelled in the freedom of riding out alone, urging Starlight into a canter until they reached the river. They had crossed the bridge at a brisk trot when she caught a glimpse of the hidden house further along and over to the left. No smoke rose above the trees from the chimney so, if some caretaker lived there, they must still be asleep. Curiosity overcame her. No one would know if she went to look at this place where Miss Petty had told her Jago met with his beautiful mistress.

She rode on until she was level with the house, turned off and rode up a rough track for about two hundred yards. There she dismounted, left Starlight tethered to the branch of a fallen tree, then followed the track through fir trees to the back of a low, grey stone-built house that fronted towards a long narrow creek where the river made its way out to the sea. Aware that she was trespassing, she trod softly on the mossy path along the side of the house and, near the front, came to a window. She hesitated, then moved forward to peer inside and saw a glow of light. Instinctively, she dodged back. The inhabitants must be awake, so she should leave, but curiosity got the better of her and she found herself leaning forward again.

The small panes of glass were dirty, but she could see that the light was from a storm lantern atop a small barrel. She had begun to make out a pile of dark shapes that looked like boxes or packages when she heard a man's voice calling from somewhere nearby. Instinctively, she drew back, turned to go, then stood stock still as she saw them.

About fifty yards away, among the fir trees and shrouded by the morning midst, were the figures of two men. The shorter of them had his back to her, but the other, taller man was facing in her direction and had only to look up from their conversation to catch sight of her. Her heart thumped in her chest. What she had just seen through the window, boxes, barrels, packages, could be contraband and, if the two men she was looking at were smugglers, they were dangerous, would stop at nothing to silence anyone who could betray them to the coast guard.

Her first instinct was to flee, but any sudden movement might attract their attention. Swallowing hard, she pressed herself back against the rough stone wall and edged slowly away until she guessed she was out of their line of vision, then turned and ran.

Her hands shook as she undid the tether, mounted the grey mare, spurred her into a gallop, heading for home. Still very frightened, she neared the river and looked back. No one was following her. Slowing her mount to a trot as they crossed the bridge, she began to feel less certain about what she had seen at the lonely house just now.

A light atop a barrel and some dark shapes on a floor, seen through a window so dirty as to be barely transparent. Two men seen through a morning mist. That was all. Though her instinct warned her there was wrong-doing afoot, common sense told her something more was needed to prove that whoever lived there was involved in smuggling.

Once on the other side of the river, she felt safe and ashamed of the way she'd panicked. After all, there'd been no sign that the men in the wood had noticed her, and no one had come after her. Wishing she'd seen more, she brought the mare to a halt when she noticed a track running along the riverbank. If she turned off here and followed it, she might get a view of the house from this side.

It was easy at first, but when the path grew steep and too overgrown for the mare to tread safely, she dismounted and went ahead alone on foot. By the time she drew level with the grey stone house on the opposite side, the river had entered a deep, narrow creek that led out to the sea.

It was less misty now and, from where she stood, the house looked to be little more than a neglected cottage and there was no sign of the men. She was about to come away when she glanced down into the water far below. There, safely hidden in this remote place, she made out a boat, and it was not the sort of craft a poor man might use to catch a few fish to feed his family. The sails were down, but it looked to be a strong, seagoing vessel, moored where no one would pass by and chance to see it. A place from where it could slip out into the open sea and, even now with the two countries at war, reach some lonely place on the coast of France to pick up contraband and bring it back to England. Was this proof enough to send for the coast guards? She still wasn't sure.

The first snow of winter was falling when she reached the stable yard and led Starlight to her stall. She heard the stable boy at work with the other horses, called out to him come and attend to the mare, then slipped away through the swirling snowflakes, sure he must have heard her voice but had not seen enough to notice how she was dressed.

Moments later, up in her room, she stripped off the borrowed clothes, damp with snow and hid them in a cupboard. So cold that her teeth chattered, she wrapped herself in her heavy woollen cloak over her nightdress and climbed back into bed. Sinking back on her pillows she stared at the ceiling, at first reliving the events of the morning then, feeling drowsy and much warmer, she closed her eyes and gave herself to sleep.

Smugglers were the first thing that came into her mind when Mrs Dobson, worried by her not coming down to breakfast, sent a maid up to wake her. Deciding it was best to keep what she'd seen to herself it to herself until Jago came back, she got up and dressed, glad it was a school day so that she'd have something else to occupy her mind.

Learning their letters, writing their names and counting to ten, came more easily to some of the little children than others, but all of them were keen to draw pictures, listen to stories and ask questions, so that it was easy to keep them occupied. At the other end of the room, Miss Petty found the older children more of a challenge.

'After working in the fields for half the year, some of them find it hard to sit down long enough to learn anything at all and, though most of them are adept at counting, reading and writing is much harder for them. Two of the boys just cannot grasp the written word,' Miss Petty told her when the children had gone home, and they were collecting pieces of chalk and wiping the slates clean for the next day's class. 'Fortunately,' she went on, 'There's no disgrace in illiteracy among the poor, though it's a cause of shame and humiliation elsewhere in society. I have one such unfortunate who I'm helping in the evenings. A boy, run away from a better sort of family, working as a labourer in the gang brought in to build the potting sheds. Apart from this particular difficulty, he is a very sensible young fellow, so keen to learn that I think we are at last making progress.. It seems unfair that some of the youngsters in my class here are sharp as two needles but can't see the reason for book learning as they call it.'

'Even so, I think you enjoy teaching them,' Lucienne told her, thinking that Miss Petty looked years younger since she had taken over the school.

'True and I only wish I'd come to it earlier. Now, before we go, please tell me how the little ones are getting on.'

They talked on for another half hour or so and when Lucienne returned to the manor house she found Lady Isobel waiting impatiently in the drawing room.

'You are late, Lucienne, but I have stayed to say goodbye to you,' she said as she rose to go, 'I wish you well, my dear, and I promise you that my lips are sealed about your unfortunate marriage to my son. I blame myself for not taking you in hand earlier, but regrets are useless, and things might yet turn out for the best. Who knows?' she ended, sounding doubtful but with a charming smile.

She was standing in front of the portrait of the lady of the Acton family that Lucienne had brought down from the attic and the likeness between them was inescapable. She saw Lucienne staring and shrugged her shoulders in much the same dismissive way that Jago sometimes did.

'That must have been painted a century ago, but I know the similarity is inescapable. It was even more so when I was a girl, and the story went that my mother was the last of the ancient Acton family that once owned Ottersbury. Whether or not that was true I really couldn't say. It was all a long time ago, so what does it matter now?'

It matters to Jago, Lucienne thought after Lady Isobel had donned her furs, kissed her farewell, climbed into the waiting carriage and departed. It must matter to Jago, or he wouldn't have had the portraits of the four grim faced Acton men of old hung in the entrance hall for all the world to see. Believing he was descended from the ancient family that held the land for centuries was most likely one reason for him going to such lengths to regain what had once been theirs.

That evening, reminding herself wistfully that there would be at least four more long days to wait until Jago came back from Plymouth, Lucienne went early to bed. She had changed into her nightdress and was kneeling at the hearth, building up the dying embers of the fire, when suddenly the door opened, and Jago walked into the room.

Feeling her colour rise she got slowly to her feet and swallowed hard. Memory of their last encounter over the potpourri of summer flowers made her suddenly shy and so pleased to see him that she couldn't speak.

When she didn't greet him, he asked, 'Lucienne, Is there something wrong?'

She shook her head. 'It's just that I wasn't expecting you back so soon. Did you find a new lawyer to work in Castlebridge?'

'Yes, there were two excellent candidates, so I left my partner, John Bazely, to decide between them. After all, he'll be working with the new man, not me.'

'I thought Mr Bazely was mainly retired?'

'He was, but his new wife turned out to be something of a scold. He's glad to get out of the house.'

'I hope all goes well for Mr Bazely—' she began.

Laughing, he shook his head, and said impatiently, 'Lucienne, why on earth are we talking about John Bazely? After what happened between us before I went away, I thought you would be as eager to see me as I am to see you. Perhaps I offended or distressed you—'

'No of course not. What happened made me happy, so very happy' she told him, her voice a little breathless.

'But, Jago, I wonder, I can't help wondering, when our marriage was for no other reason than to give you Ottersbury, why did you suddenly change your mind and ask me to stay and become truly your wife?'

He smiled down at her. 'I could say it was because I value your courage and intelligence, your caring nature. I could say it was because the closeness growing between us is something I never before realised was lacking. All of this would be true, but it is the way you look at me so seriously from beneath your lashes, the sweetness of your lips, the curve of your slender neck, turning away from me as your colour rises. That is what stirs my blood. I want you. I want to possess every last little bit of you. And I promise to be your true and gentle husband and lover. Do you understand me, Lucienne?'

Faint with need for him, she could only murmur that she did.

He drew closer and asked softly. 'So, you are glad that I am back?'

She nodded again, in bliss as he bent to kiss her, gently just beside one corner of her mouth and, when she didn't resist, moved to her lips, which seemed to swell to a new fullness as the tip of his tongue trailed across them. Instinctively, her body moved to his, his arms encircled her, and his lips met hers in a melting kiss as they sank together into the wide armchair.

Breathlessly, they drew apart and he murmured softly, 'Where did you get the boy's clothes from, Lucienne?'

Her eyes jerked open, the magic of the moment fading as she turned to meet his dark, searching gaze. She drew away from him and sat up.

'From the attic. We brought a lot of old clothes down to give away at Christmas time and I wore them yesterday because of the cold. But how did you know—?'

'I was there, in the woods alongside the house. At first, when you were peering in at the window, I wasn't sure. Then, when you suddenly ran away, I followed you down to the edge of the woods, recognised Starlight and knew for certain it was you. What on earth were you doing there?'

'I was on my way to the churchyard at Yoxley when I remembered Miss Petty telling me about a house hidden there. I just went to have a look,' she said weakly, thinking it sounded a lame excuse.

'Lucienne, I'm asking you again not to go out alone to lonely places. Apart from anything else, our uncle doesn't know that we are married. He still believes that, if anything happens to you, he has a lot to gain.'

'You mean he could harm me so as to claim back his inheritance. But why should he? You've said yourself that he took everything he could and left the estate crippled with a mountain of debt.'

'The rich seams of copper we've discovered here change all that. He'd be back if he got the chance. So, no more exploring lonely places, like you did yesterday.'

She slipped from his knee, stood facing him and asked quietly, 'Why were you there, Jago?'

'I was visiting my tenant. A sheep farmer, recently moved in. I was talking to him when I saw you creeping round the side of the house.'

'Your tenant? I thought all that land belonged to the Riverton estate.'

'It did but years ago, when the last of the old Acton family were reduced to poverty, they rented it. I believe my own grandmother lived there as a girl and sentiment prompted me to raise the money to buy it. There's not much land, and I called in to tell the tenant I've secured permission for his sheep to graze on to some Riverton land nearby.'

His eyes crinkled at the corners as he gazed up at her at her and said, 'So what next for us, Lucienne? Do we shake the household by telling them we are man and wife, or shall we wait a while?'

'I'm not sure, Jago,' she heard herself say uncertainly. 'Perhaps we could wait?' Her voice died away.

He stood up, the dark eyes that fixed on hers unreadable. There was a long, awkward pause and, when she didn't speak, he shrugged. 'So be it, If that is what you truly want, Lucienne,' he said quietly as he left the room.

She paced about, knowing that it wasn't what she really wanted. Her joy at his appearing so unexpectedly had dashed everything else from her mind, until he told her that he was one of the men she'd had seen at the hidden house. Then, all her fears and suspicions had risen up because, as the owner, Jago must know what kind of boat lay in the creek just below his property. Did this mean he was one of those gentry who invested in illegally trade with France and made a handsome profit? Could that be where the money he was spending to rescue the Otterbury estate came from, and not from borrowing from the banks as he had told her?

The magic of the time spent in his arms faded as she thought of Mathew Harris, Killed by smugglers in the course of his duty, but still she wept silent tears of disappointment before she went to sleep that night.

The next day was the last at school before the Christmas holiday and, after a few hours in the lively buzz of the classroom, Lucienne thought again about Jago and found she'd begun to doubt herself. Had she simply jumped to a wrong conclusion? She'd never even asked him about the boat in the creek. Perhaps there was no need for everything to be spoiled between them. Wasn't it only fair to tell him what she'd seen and give him a chance to explain? She wasn't sure how to broach this, but it had to be done, she decided as she hurried home that afternoon.

Nearing the manor gates, she stepped on to the grassy verge to avoid a covered cart coming out into the lane and, though the driver didn't appear to notice her, she had a good view of him. Her heart missed a beat. She would have known him anywhere as the man who chased her from the church yard all those months ago. And suddenly all her old uncertainty about what exactly she had seen that morning started to come back. Jago had persuaded her then that his search of the church crypt found no evidence of smugglers and that the men she had seen were honest fishermen. Should she have believed him?

Her heart fluttering with agitation, she hurried on in search of Mrs Dobson, to find out what the driver she'd just seen had been doing at the manor house.

'He was delivering from a wine merchant in Castlebridge,' the housekeeper told her moments later. 'Seems Mr Jago put in the order the other day when he went through on his way to Plymouth. Fine wine from France, both red and white and very welcome, I'm sure, because it's hard to come by, us being at odds with that country now.'

'I should think there will always be plenty more where that came from,' Lucienne, muttered beneath her breath as she made her way to the library where Jago was working on some ledgers to do with estate business. He gave her his charming smile as he rose to greet her.

'Lucienne, I'm so glad to see you. I'm so sorry to have

spoiled a precious moment for both of us last night when I asked you about the boy's clothes. The question suddenly came into my head, but I should have kept it for another time. Forgive me?'

He was so disarming that, at any other time, she might have forgotten what she had come about, but now she pressed on.

'Jago, just now I saw the driver who brought an order of French wine to the house and I know it was the man who chased me in the churchyard. In spite of what you told me at the time, I still believe he was involved in smuggling.'

The smile faded a little as he said, 'If it was, he must have mended his ways because he's employed by a respectable dealer in fine wine and spirits now.'

'So where does a respectable dealer get French wines from, when we've been at war with France for nearly ten months?'

He sat down, leaned back in his chair and watched her. 'Yes, even the biggest warehouse must be empty by now, so perhaps the wine merchant buys his stock from smugglers. Is that what's bothering you?'

'Yes, of course it is. How can it be right to have dealings with those wicked men?'

He sighed. 'Lucienne, listen to me. The currency smugglers use in their transactions with the French is not English pounds. It is woollen cloth. High quality, finely woven cloth, made in the Castlebridge wool mill, dependant for years on exporting to France. The war brought an end to legitimate trade, pushing them to the verge of ruin. If smugglers buying their cloth to barter with the French helps to keep the mill going even on short time, I've no quarrel with that. Would you prefer to see the mill workers begging on the streets?'

'Of course, not', she snapped, 'but what about the coast guards, maimed or shot dead by smugglers in the course of their duty.'

'Our government having decreed smuggling a crime punishable by death, smugglers don't go looking for the coast guards. They strive to avoid detection. But, if the guards come after them, what can they do but fight for survival?'

'So, you are taking their side!'

He paused, then, 'That's putting it a bit too strong. Let's just say that I think we, with our comfortable lives, should be glad that poverty hasn't driven us to break the law.' He gave what looked to Lucienne like a dismissive shrug of his shoulders as he reached for one of the papers on the table in front of him and started to read it.

Fuming, she heard herself say, 'It isn't only poverty that drives people, Jago. I've heard that some landed gentlemen invest in such crimes and make a handsome profit.'

There was a long pause, then without looking up he said, 'And, if such gentlemen happen to be married, it's worth remembering that, under the law of the country, their wives cannot give evidence against them.'

It seemed not only an admission of guilt, but as if the death of blameless young men like Mathew Harris didn't trouble him. Too shocked to say any more, she turned on her heel and left. Out in the passageway, she stopped and tried to calm herself. The thought of how she might have given herself to him in love, eager to be completely his, shamed her now. Did he think she was just a silly young girl with no convictions or principles of her own? Was she married to a criminal?

She waited until her breath was slower and more even, then went to the kitchen where the Christmas cakes had been taken out of the oven and left on racks to cool. She joined Mrs Dobson in complimenting the cook and accepted a slice of the smallest cake, especially made so they could taste it and be sure the recipe had worked as well as the year before. It looked delicious but, too upset to eat anything, she wrapped her slice in a linen napkin, then, to calm herself, decided to walk back into the village while it was still light and give the cake to Miss Petty.

Even a brief chat with her old friend could make her feel much better so she was disappointed to get there and find her busy teaching the young labourer she had mentioned earlier that day how to read.

A tall, pleasant looking young lad with a shock of dark brown hair, he stood up as they came into the sitting room and said, 'I can leave now, and come back another time if you've come about something important, Miss.'

The old lady looked as if she might let him go, but Lucienne gave her the Christmas and told her firmly, 'No, I've just dropped in with this for you, Miss Petty. I can always call in for a chat another time when I'm passing by,' and she left, thinking as she went away, that she might have seen the young labourer somewhere before.

Christmas came, with a party in the schoolhouse, all the more joyful because it was the first that most of the children had ever attended. The front hall of the manor was decked with boughs of holly, carol singers came to the door, a Christmas dinner was held for the servants with gifts for all of them. Everything went well but, beneath her smiles, Lucienne was sad and lonely. Since her last exchange with Jago, a distance had come between them, almost as though their brief intimacy had never taken place. He was faultlessly polite in his dealings with her, but she had the feeling of being managed like a child that had disgraced itself, whereas it was he who tolerated criminal behaviour. And possibly even took part in it.

In the freezing January days, the joy of the children at finding themselves back in the warm schoolroom cheered her when she was with them, though at other times she felt herself growing more and more unhappy. There was almost a year and a half to go with Jago as her guardian. A year and a half before she came of age and could escape from here and from the thoughts of a happiness lost for ever.

14

Towards the end of February, Mrs Dobson said anxiously, 'We'd best be getting on with the spring cleaning early this year. The month of May will see Lady Helena Riverton out of her widow's weeds and, from what I've heard, she'll be wed again and mistress of this house shortly afterwards.

'I don't think that's very likely,' Lucienne told her, knowing it could never happen, but wondering if the rift between Jago and herself had driven him back into Lady Helena's arms.

Checking through the list of foodstuffs, cleaning materials, sewing notions and everything else to be ordered for the month ahead, she pretended she wasn't interested enough to care. Pretended her heart didn't ache with loneliness and disappointment. She swallowed hard, almost wishing she had never gone to look at the lonely house beside the creek, never seen what looked like evidence of smuggling, never found out that Jago himself was involved in whatever was going on there, never confronted him. They could be lovers now instead of people who lived like strangers.

But could that be what she really wanted? To be an adoring wife who lived in unsuspecting ignorance of her husband's involvement in crime and his indifference the fate of decent young men like Mathew Harris? No, it was not. To live like that would be a travesty of a marriage, she told herself firmly, all the time knowing, deep in her heart, that it was Jago's unfeeling indifference to her that hurt more than any threat to the noble principles of right or wrong.

But did she have to stay here and put up with him treating her with the cool disregard that had persisted since she confronted him about the smugglers? In less than year and a half, she would be one and twenty and free to leave, but she needed go sooner than that.

Suddenly, determined to find a way, she went into the library to look at the newspaper where she'd seen notices from respectable families looking for housekeepers. Had she learned enough from Mrs Dobson to run a gentleman's residence? Perhaps, at nineteen, it would be better to apply to be an assistant housekeeper. Or a nursery governess. There seemed to be quite a need for those, but it wasn't necessary stay here to apply for a post. Much better to get away, then start her search.

Knowing that Beulah, happily awaiting her baby's birth, would make her welcome at Escott's farm was reassuring, but it was the first place that Jago would go to look for her. If he cared to look for her. Perhaps he'd be glad she was gone. She pushed the thought away, reminding herself that she had money enough, saved from her allowance, to pay for respectable lodgings if only she could decide where to go. It was then she remembered Mathew Harris's sister, Mrs Narramore, who had offered a welcome to her home in Falmouth should she ever be in need. Mrs Narramore, believing her to be in service here at Ottersbury manor, would think it quite natural for her to be applying for a similar post elsewhere. Mrs Narramore, who no one here but herself had ever heard of.

Within hours, the idea had become a plan and she knew that, unless she acted soon, the determination she needed to carry it out might ebb away. That afternoon, when Jago was out on estate business, she slipped into his office to write two brief notes. The first, thanking Mrs Dobson for all her kindness and wishing her well, was easy to compose. The one to Jago was much harder. She made several attempts, tore them up, then wrote simply that she could not bear to remain here any longer in the house of a person who had no respect for her. To tell him now that she wasn't Richard Deverell's daughter would only complicate matters, so she merely said that she would contact him when she came of age so that he could take steps to end their marriage of convenience. She found her hand was shaking as she signed it, almost tore it up to start again, then made up her mind and let it be.

What about Miss Petty? A note wouldn't do. She couldn't leave such a good friend without saying a proper goodbye and offering some explanation of why she was going. So, at seven o'clock that evening, she slipped away and hurried through the dark February night to the cottage.

Miss Petty opened the door and welcomed her into the cosy sitting room. Seeing the books, paper and writing materials laid out on the table, Lucienne began to apologise for interrupting another lesson and was promptly reassured.

'That young labourer I teach has only just arrived. He's in the kitchen having a bite to eat before we begin, so do sit down for a few minutes.' She paused, then asked, 'What is it, dear? You look so troubled.'

'I can't say why or where I will go, but I must get away from here. In fact, I'm leaving first thing tomorrow, on the mail coach. I haven't told anybody else, but I've come to say goodbye to you, Miss Petty because you have been such a good friend to me. And there is the school. I'm so sorry to let you down. I've loved teaching the children, but I just can't' stay here because—'

Her voice seemed to fade away and the old lady asked quietly, 'Lucienne, is this about Jago? I've often wondered if you might have fallen a little in love—'

'Please stop, Miss Petty.' Lucienne said quickly, getting to her feet. 'I'll write to you when I am settled, but I must go now.' She stooped to kiss the old lady's cheek and hurried away to pack her bag for tomorrow.

Don't think too much or you won't go through with it. Just get on and decide what you need to take, she told herself as she packed some of her belongings into a stout canvas bag she had found in the attic. Reaching into the bottom of the travelling trunk for a shawl she had brought from Guadeloupe, she saw something small, wrapped in a silk handkerchief.

The wedding ring. What should she do with it? Somehow, and she didn't know why, she couldn't bring herself to slip it into the letter she had written to Jago. Best let it lie at the bottom of the travelling trunk where it had been for so long. Someone might find it and give it to him. She squeezed back tears, brought the lid of the trunk firmly down and got on with packing the few belongings she had decided to take with her.

Lying in bed that night, uncertain what her own future might be, she felt more guilty than ever at having married Jago under false pretenses. There was nothing could be done about it now, but he had spent all he had, even involved himself in crime, to save an estate that might still somehow be discovered to rightfully belong to his extravagant mother and his ruthless, grasping uncle.

Waking next morning in time to catch the mail coach presented no difficulty because she hardly slept from worrying about what the future might hold. By five o'clock she was up and dressed, had left the two notes on the silver letter tray on the hall table, and hurried in the half light of early morning across the frozen grass to the gates of Ottersbury manor. For the last time, she thought sadly, remembering how Jago had once rescued her as she fled from her attacker in the graveyard and carried her to safety here. She glanced back at the house, thinking of that first time when he had carried her from the library to her room, holding her close enough for her to feel the beating of his heart. And, for a fleeting moment, she longed to go back.

Sharply, she pushed such useless thoughts aside, shouldered her canvas bag and set off through the cold February morning towards the village, telling herself she was ready to face whatever her new life might bring.

A boy in workman's clothes was waiting for her outside the post office. He came forward, smiling nervously and said, 'That time when you brought Aunt Regina a piece of cake during my lesson, you didn't recognize me, did you, Miss?'

She saw it was the labourer's boy Miss Petty was teaching to read. Looking more closely, though he was very much grown, she remembered where she had seen him long before that.

'Are you one of the Tregarth boys?'

'That's right Miss. I'm Robert Tregarth. I knew you from that sad day when you came to my dear Ma's funeral, and last night I was in the kitchen when you came, and I heard you say that you were going away. But there's something I have to tell you.' He hesitated, looking worried as he went on, 'Just lately I found out about a wrong that's been done to you.'

'What wrong has been done to me Robert? And who is it that wronged me?'

'My Pa and my dear Ma. She wouldn't have, only we were so poor when we lived at Yoxley. She was very upset afterwards, even though we were so much better off at Heverton. At first, I thought it was because we had come away and left my little sister buried in Yoxley churchyard.'

'I'm so sorry, Robert, but what has this to do with me?'

'I'm getting the hang of reading now.' He paused as if unsure how to go on, then, 'Sunday last, I went across to Yoxley to visit my little sister's grave, knowing my young brother John, who'd died just before we left, was buried there with her. But it wasn't his name I could read on her stone. It was the name of the orphan child my parents took in to bring up as their own. He's called Arthur Tregarth now, but Alain Deverell was his name when he first came to us and that's what's been added to my sister's gravestone.'

The mail coach had rumbled to a halt on the road in front of them, but Lucienne ignored it and said breathlessly, 'You are sure of this, Robert?'

'Course I'm sure, Miss. I was there when my little brother John died of the measles. Arthur got over it and he's still alive.' He paused, then said anxiously, 'After we moved to Heverton, and my Ma got ill, I heard her saying it was a punishment because they had done a bad thing for money, and my Pa saying they were doing Arthur a favour, bringing him up in a true Christian home. And he most likely believes that. Pa won't get into trouble, will he, if it all comes out?'

'I don't know, but I'll have to go to Heverton and bring Alain back with me to where he belongs.'

'I suppose so, Miss, though he's happy and a great favourite with our housekeeper, Mrs Lamb. She's a good woman. If my Pa was to be turned out of his parish because of what he did, I don't know what would happen to Mrs Lamb and my brothers still at home.'

'Listen Robert. I promise to make no complaints to the church authorities or anyone else. I just want to get my brother back. Your father will have to sort out what is written on the gravestone as best he can,' she added.

There was no question now of seeking shelter with Mrs Narromore, she told herself as the boy left her to go to work. She must get back to the manor and tell Jago what had happened, then go with him to Helverton and rescue Alain.

Ignoring the post master's warning that the coach was about to leave, she had picked up her belongings, meaning to head back to the manor house, when it started to rain. She waited a little while, sheltering in the doorway of the post office but, when the downpour got heavier, she pulled the hood of her cloak well down over her head and started in the direction of Miss Petty's house, just a few hundred yards away, to ask if she could borrow an umbrella.

An early riser, Miss Petty opened the door to let her in and wouldn't hear of her leaving again until the rain stopped.

'Off with that wet thing and I'll hang it over the clothes rack to dry in front of the kitchen range,' she said firmly as she took Lucienne's cloak and cast an interested eye over the canvas bag she was carrying. 'Put that down out here in the hallway, then you can tell me why you are still here when the mail coach must have left these twenty minutes gone,' she added as she led the way into her comfortable sitting room. She went away to make some tea while Lucienne sat on the sofa and stared into the flames leaping in the grate. Their warmth embraced her and somehow, despite her what she'd heard from Robert Tregarth, the weariness of her wakeful night overtook her and she fell asleep. She woke up to find Miss Petty in her armchair, busy with her knitting.

'Over an hour you've slept. I expect you'd like me to heat up your tea now you're awake?' she said as Lucienne struggled to her feet. 'And perhaps a little toast and honey for breakfast?

'No thank you, Miss Petty,' she said as the memory of Alain, stolen and robbed of his true identity, came flooding back to her. 'I just need to borrow an umbrella and get back to the manor at once.'

This was no time to be thinking of the disappointments that, only a few hours before, had driven her to leave, she thought as she hurried through the village. Alain had to be rescued and Jago, once he learned the truth, was sure to come with her to get him back, she told herself as she started up the lane to the manor house.

Once there, she slipped in by the side door, dashed through to the front hall and was snatching up the notes she'd left there just as the housekeeper appeared.

Hearing herself a little breathless, Lucienne wished her good morning and asked, 'Is Mr Jago still here, Mrs Dobson?'

'No, he is not, Miss. Word came from Castlebridge last night to say that old lawyer, Mr Bazley, was taken ill. With an important case going to court today, the new young lawyer wasn't sure how to proceed, so Mr Jago went straight off first thing this morning to see to it.'

Lucienne's heart fell. The court case could go on for days and she couldn't wait that long. Alain must be found and brought back at once. Ignoring Mrs Dobson's enquires about why she had gone out so early, she asked her to order the carriage and half an hour later was on her way to the vicarage at Heverton.

Gazing out of the carriage window in a state of mounting indignation, she detected Cedrick Deverell's hand in this. The Tregarth's terrible act of deception must have been done at his behest so as to get rid of Alain, who he believed to be the sole heir to the Ottersbury estate. She wanted to be angry, ready for a confrontation with Vicar Tregarth but, as the long journey drew to an end, all she could think of was the joy of being reunited with her darling little brother. Of course, it was months since he had seen her, but she felt sure he would remember her. Would he remember Bett? Ask where she was? How could she explain to a little boy of three that Bett had gone away and never wrote to her?

When the carriage reached the vicarage, she alighted and hurried to the front door. Trembling with anticipation, hoping to hear the sound of children's voices and then to see Alain, she rang the doorbell, remembering that they called him Arthur now. The door was opened by a well-built, rosy, cheeked country woman of middle age, who identified herself as the housekeeper, Mrs Lamb. She invited Lucienne into a large, comfortably furnished living room and offered her a seat, having been quite overcome when she introduced herself as Miss Deverell.

'From the big house? I understood the family had gone away.'

'No, though I am a relative of Mr Deverell. I live some distance from here and I've come to see the vicar.'

'He's not here just now, Miss Deverell. He's been out all night, sitting up with a labourer whose wife is dying. There's no family and the poor man is afraid to be alone with her when the end comes,' she explained. 'Not every clergyman puts the needs of the poor and humble first, but the Reverend Tregarth never spares himself. He will not leave until that poor woman has passed away and, no doubt he'll refuse the payment he'll be due for the burial, as is his way when there's poverty enough.'

'How long have you been with the family, Mrs Lamb,' Lucienne asked quietly, thinking perhaps the vicar wasn't the self-seeking, dishonest sort of person she been imagining on her journey here.

'I've been with the family since his poor wife was struck down with her illness soon after they came to live here in July last year. A dear lady, very troubled to be leaving her lovely boys. She begged me to stay here and look after them for her and it's been a joy to me, a widow never blessed with children, to have the four young ones still at home, all so well and happy despite their loss.'

'I understand that one of them is an adopted child,' Lucienne ventured, watching the other woman carefully, wondering how much she knew.

'A little orphan boy they took in out of Christian charity, but I can truly say that no differences are ever made.' She smiled fondly. 'In fact, young Arthur is something of a favourite with all of us. Ever so clever and funny, and very musical even at such an early young age. I'd ask him to sing something for you but he and Nicholas start larking about very early in the morning and they're having a nap just now, so as to keep going until bedtime.' She seemed to recollect herself. 'What was it you wanted to see the vicar about, Miss Deverell? Perhaps you'd like to leave a message—'

'No,' Lucienne broke in quickly. 'Thank, you but it was really Mrs Tregarth I knew when she lived at Yoxley. Mrs Tregath and her smallest boys. I'd love just to look at them while they are sleeping. I promise not to wake them.'

'They are having their nap down here so as I can keep an eye on them,' Mrs Lamb said fondly as she led the way into a small parlour where they lay on a sofa, fast asleep, the youngest Tregarth, dark and stocky, head to toe with Alain. Still very fair and slender though well grown now, he really was there, alive and well, her own darling little brother. Lucienne felt the urge to take hold of him and never let him go, wanted to claim him and take him away with her, then saw the look of motherly devotion in the housekeeper's eyes as she gazed down at him.

It came to her then that, though she had known him and loved him for much longer, she had no more claim of blood on Alain than did this good woman, who said kindly, 'My dear, you've tears in your eyes. I could weep myself sometimes, thinking how these two lost their dear mother, but you can rest assured that, while I live, these little mites and their brothers shall have a mother in me. I was never blessed with children until now and they mean all the world to me, as did their brother Robert, that ran away from home because he couldn't do his lessons. I worry so much about what might have happened to him.'

Lucienne, realising with a sinking heart now that her plan to take Alain home with her must be delayed until the vicar could be confronted, swallowed hard.

'Mrs Lamb, I happen to know that Robert is safe and well in Ottersbury, the village where I live. He is earning his living and his aunt, Miss Petty, is teaching him to read and write. I 'm sure she will help him write a letter to you,' she added before she said goodbye and left without revealing anything that could worry this sweet, kind person whose love for Alain was plain to see.

Even so, he couldn't be allowed to stay here with her, she told herself as she walked away. He was not a poor orphan child. He was the rightful heir to half the Ottersbury estate, to the whole of it were the truth about her own parentage be known, and he must be taken back to live there. She sighed deeply, only too aware that, though the thought of this this brought joy to her heart, to Mrs Lamb it could only bring sadness and disappointment.

Sadness and disappointment, almost certainly caused by the wickedness of Cedrick Deverell, Lucienne thought indignantly as she walked towards the waiting carriage. He must have rewarded the Tregaths to do what they did by giving them an escape from the poverty of Yoxley vicarage to a comfortable living in this prosperous village, and goodness knew what other bribes as well.

She was about to ask the groom to drive her back to Otterbury when she remembered old Mrs Belmont, taken unwillingly to live with her daughter at here at Heverton. Mrs Lamb had said the Deverells were away from home, but most likely the old lady would have been left behind and this would be a good opportunity to visit her. She had seen Heverton Manor signposted on the way here, so she left the groom at the village inn and, to stretch her legs before the long journey home, set off to walk there.

When she reached Cedrick Deverell's house, she saw that, though it was smaller than huge, rambling Ottersbury manor, it was still an impressive gentleman's residence, surrounded by smoothly cut lawns and with not a shrub or flower bed in sight. Well maintained, but somehow without character. Unloved, she thought.

She was about to approach the front door when a groom came round from the back of the house, leading a steady looking cob horse to the mounting steps by the gate. Almost immediately the front door opened, and Cedrick Deverell strode purposefully out. All the anger that had been gathering in Lucienne since her encounter that morning with Robert Tregarth welled up as she confronted him.

'Good morning to you, Sir,' she cried furiously, 'I have just been to the vicarage, and I found my brother Alain there. He is alive and well.'

For a brief instant, she saw shock and apprehension flicker in Cedrick Deverell's pale eyes, then he snapped, 'Why would he not be there? You will remember that I put him into the Tregarth's excellent care when you first brought him to this country. I have no reason to believe he does not thrive.'

'That is a lie, a barefaced lie. Last summer, while I was away in Exeter, I was told that he had died. When I came back, you sent me a note of sympathy—'

'You still have it in your possession perhaps?' he snapped. 'No, I thought not. This disgraceful accusation is a figment of a hysterical, not to say deluded, mind.' He took a step nearer and spoke in such a tone of menace that she backed away, 'Let me remind you that I am my nephew's legal guardian and any attempt at interference by you, an imposter leaching off a respectable family, will be severely dealt with. So, get off my land. And mind how you go, Miss Widdon.'

With a sneer of contemptuous satisfaction, he strode over to where the groom held his horse, mounted and rode away, leaving Lucienne cold with shock at the use of the name that should have been hers. She was about to turn and go when the door opened again and an elderly woman she recognised as Mrs Belmonts's maid beckoned her inside.

'The butler saw it was you, Miss, when he opened the door for Mr Deverell. He came at once to get me because we've been so worried about my poor mistress. She is very much gone down since we came here, often recalling her happy days with you at Ottersbury. You will come to spend a few moments with her, please Miss Deverell?'

Still badly shaken, Lucienne managed a smile. 'Of course, I will. That's why I came here. But I was surprised to meet with Mr Deverell just now. I'd heard that the family were away from home.'

'Mrs Deverell and the young ladies went ahead to prepare for the London season,' the elderly maid told her as she led the way upstairs to Mrs Belmont's room. 'And my mistress is annoyed at being left behind, though to tell the truth, she didn't get on too well with her grand-daughters.'

'Silly pair of fliberty gibbits, both of them,' Mrs Belmont snapped as soon as Lucienne asked after them. 'Pretty enough in a vapid sort of way. Accomplished at this and that and each with a sizable fortune behind her, so my daughter should get at least one of them off her hands this season without too much bother.'

In her gloomy room at the back of the house, she was sitting up in bed, well propped with pillows, very wrinkled and deathly pale without her rouge but still wearing her high, powdered wig.

'And what about you my dear?' she asked with unexpected sweetness. 'Still wasting your life as an unpaid domestic for the dashing Mr Jago Moncrief? He's off his head if he still tangles with that red-headed she-devil when he should be married with a family on the way.'

'I really don't know about that, Mrs Belmont. I try not to listen to gossip, 'Lucienne said carefully.'

'In that case you'll miss most of what's going on. I've always kept an ear to the ground myself and there's been plenty to pick up over the years.' She turned to the maid who had been hovering nearby and snapped, 'Don't just stand there. Go and get hot chocolate for me and the young lady. And don't forget the sugar this time.' The maid left the room, but the old lady still dropped her voice as she told Lucienne. 'The Deverells are a bad lot. Though, to be fair, your father Richard was more just a young nuisance.'

She paused dramatically and Lucienne asked, 'How so? I mean, what kind of a nuisance?'

'For one thing, he'd no sooner got back from abroad than he started chasing after that school master's daughter again when she was safely married off to a good and decent man. A farmer named Luke Widdon.'

'I heard Luke Widdon was a cruel man. People said he treated her badly, that she married him to pay off her father's gambling debts.'

'Lies, put around afterwards. It was her father who knocked her about and Luke Widdon that took her away to safety respectability as his wife. He paid off her father's debts to get his permission to marry her because she was but twenty years of age at the time, but it was well was known that they were happy and content together.

Lucienne, though engulfed in relief to learn something good about her true father, was still anxious about her mother's part in what happened. She said, 'You told me rumour had it that the young woman struck Luke Widdon down.'

'Only by unlucky chance. Widdon came into the farmhouse kitchen and caught young Deverell pestering her. He went to give him a thrashing and Deverell picked up a knife. She went to pull it out of his hand and somehow her husband fell on it.'

'But Mrs Belmont why would she have agreed to run away with Richard Deverell when he was the cause of all the trouble?'

'Doubtless she was afraid for her own life, the law always blaming the woman in such cases. Then, afterwards, a man came forward at the inquest and gave false witness against Richard Deverell. Why I do not know.'

But I think I know, Lucienne thought, with mounting conviction. After Richard Deverell had taken her mother to safety in France, someone in his family must have bribed the witness to get him branded as a murderer so that he couldn't return to claim his estate. But how did Mrs Belmont know all this? She started to ask, then saw that the old lady had lapsed into a deep sleep just as the maid returned with the hot chocolate.

'My mistress does that more and more these days,' she remarked sadly, as she handed Lucienne a delicate china cup. 'I hope she wasn't spinning you one of her far-fetched tales.'

'I'm not sure,' Lucienne told her, 'Because she's told me several versions of the same story.' She sipped her hot chocolate, then smiled and added, 'But this last version is the one I'd like to believe is true.

15

On the journey home, Lucienne's mind was a mishmash of emotions. Joy, that she had seen Alain alive and well. Pity, for the grief poor Mrs Lamb must feel when he was removed from her loving care. Anger, at Cedrick Deverell for his lies and the contempt he'd shown for her. Guilt because, hateful though he was, Cedrick Deverell was right, had always been right, in insisting that she was not his brother's child and therefore had no claim to the estate, or anything else for that matter. More guilt, because she had let Jago believe she was the rightful heir to Ottersbury. Apprehension because she knew that now must be the time to tell him the truth.

The weather changed to bleak and rainy, and it was dark by the time the carriage arrived back at Ottersbury Manor. She alighted, stiff with cold and exhausted with worry, as the front door opened and Jago stood on the threshold. She had never seen him look so angry as he stepped aside for her to enter.

'Good of you to come back,' he snapped, 'How dare

you take yourself off without a word to anyone? And is it too much to ask where the hell have you been?' He nodded toward her canvas bag standing by the doorway. 'Or should I be enquiring where you'd been hoping to go this morning when you left your luggage at Miss Petty's house.'

Ignoring the sarcasm in his voice, she cried, 'Jago, stop. Please listen to what I have to tell you.'

Waving away Mrs Dobson, who stood to one side her face agog with curiosity, he took Lucienne by her elbow and hurried her into the comforting warmth of the library. All she had learned that day came tumbling out.

'You must go with me first thing tomorrow to bring Alain back,' she ended as she sank into a fireside chair, watching him anxiously. He stood, leaning with one arm on the mantle shelf, the glow of the fire flickering over his guarded expression.

'And you are sure that the child you saw was your brother?'

'Of course, I am. He's so like his mother, totally different from the Tregarth boys. I'd know him anywhere.'

'And you didn't see Vicar Tregarth to ask him what happened? Why he, a man of the cloth, preaching to the poor and humble how to behave, came to do such a despicable, indeed criminal thing?'

'No, and the housekeeper had only worked for them since they moved to Heverton, so she couldn't have known anything about it.' She paused and when he remained silent, went on, 'And I must tell you something else that happened. I went to see Mrs Belmont and met Uncle Cedrick. He tried to pretend he didn't know anything about my being told that Alain had died.' She paused, suddenly too upset to go on and his expression softened.

'He probably said whatever came into his head to get rid of you, but he won't try that with me. When Alain was supposed to have died, we talked about it at length. If I know my uncle, he'll be on the road at the crack of dawn tomorrow, trying to escape the mess he's got himself and Vicar Tregarth into.'

'Jago, let's just go there and bring Alain back,' she said anxiously. 'I promised Robert Tregarth that his father wouldn't get into trouble,'

He looked at her as if he could scarcely credit what she'd said. 'Lucienne,' he told her firmly, 'The man is guilty of a crime, carried out for personal gain and, as far as I am concerned, both he and Cedrick Deverell must take the consequences.'

She wanted to beg him to spare the whole Tregarth family the misery of disgrace, to tell him nothing mattered except having Alain safely here with her but knew, from the look on his face, that it was no use. Her mind worked one way, she thought sadly, and his hard, lawyer's mind worked in another.

That night she went to bed so affected by the day's events that she was sure she'd lie awake worrying, but fell into an exhausted sleep and woke after eight o'clock next morning.

Remembering she was to go back to the vicarage at Heverton with Jago, she dressed and hurried downstairs only to be told that he had ridden away in the early hours of the morning.

Surprised and disappointed, she went to the village school and told a surprised and pleased Miss Petty only that she was still available to teach the youngest pupils. It was a busy day like any other and, as the morning wore on, she could scarcely believe that such momentous events had happened only the day before.

That afternoon, Mrs Dobson seemed to be in a strangely distracted mood and unwilling to give her any instructions about what needed her attention. Wondering what had happened to cause this, Lucienne decided to get on with spring-cleaning the larder, then went upstairs to look at the empty room next to hers to see if it was suitable to be made into a nursery for Alain. It was, but to begin with he wouldn't need a bed in there because she would have him sleep with her in the big bed in her room until he got used to being at Ottersbury.

The afternoon seemed to go on forever and it was five o'clock before she heard the sounds of activity in front of the house. She looked down into the gathering dark and made out Jago on his black stallion, and also a carriage she had never seen before. Her heart leapt with joy. He must have hired the carriage to bring Alain back, probably in the care of Mrs Lamb, who would want to stay to see him safely settled here before she let him go.

Down in the hallway she went quickly to the open front door and, to her amazement, saw Mrs Dobson and Mrs Belmont's maid assisting old Mrs Belmont out of the carriage. She hurried forward to look for Alain but, to her utter dismay, there was no sign of him. Jago, his face impassive, handed his mount to the groom who had come round from the stable yard. He avoided Lucienne's eye until he was beside her, then hurried her into the house and on to the privacy of the library.

'What has happened?' she cried, pulling herself free of him. 'Where is Alain? You said you would go to bring him back.'

'No, Lucienne, I didn't promise you that,' he told her as he poured himself a glass of wine, then turned to face her. 'I said I would go to see him at the vicarage and that is what I did. I found him happy and secure there in the care of a warm, loving woman and with the playmates he thinks are his brothers. He has been with them for nearly a year now and I knew, when I watched them playing, fighting and hugging each other, that it would be cruel to take him away from a home where he is so happy.'

'But I love Alain. I want to look after him,' she cried, horrified, 'And remember, he is my father's child and owns half of the Ottersbury estate. What right have you to decide he shouldn't live here?

'As from today, I claim every right to decide where he lives. I went to Heverton manor first, early enough to see my uncle before he left for London. I threatened to have the law on him for his part in Alain being declared dead unless he signed a statement renouncing all claim to the boy's guardianship. Needless to say, he immediately complied.'

'But can he do that? Wouldn't you have to go to court to get everything altered?'

'No, I would not, because his application for guardianship never got as far as the court. My uncle asked me to deal with it but, having heard rumours that made me suspect his motives, I made sure there were delays. Then, when the child was supposed to have died, the application was dropped' He paused, the said decisively, 'And now, as Alain's next closest male relative, duty of care falls to me. I shall apply for legal guardianship and meanwhile I shall decide where he lives.'

Hardly able to believe what he was saying, she couldn't speak for a moment, then heard the break in her own voice as she asked, 'But what about me? You can have no idea what it is like to have a little brother you love more than anyone else in the world and then to lose him.'

'No, I can't imagine that. I was an only child, moved about Europe constantly at the whim of my parents. My distress at breaking with the few childhood friends I made is something I wouldn't inflict on any child.' He paused and, when she turned her head away, went on more gently, 'Lucienne, you can visit Alain at Heverton. Mrs Lamb promised me that she'll welcome you there to stay, and when he is old enough to understand his situation, Alain can come to us for at least part of the time. Until then he must stay where he is happy and secure.'

Lucienne sank back into her chair, at war with a feeling, deep in her heart of hearts, that Jago could be right. Her love had been enough for Alain when she shared his care with dear Bett, but now perhaps Mrs Lamb and the Tregarth boys were better for him than she alone could ever be.

Squeezing back tears, she managed, 'Whatever we decide, it isn't fair that Uncle Cedrick can get away with all he's done just by signing a piece of paper, especially if you mean to get Vicar Tregarth into trouble.'

With a shrug of his shoulders, he told her, 'That was a threat made in a fit of fury when I heard what he'd done. But when I saw him today, comforting a poor villager whose wife had just passed away, he seemed almost glad to confess to what had happened and why. And God only knows what I might have tried myself if I had to support a wife and six children on his miserable pittance as vicar of Yoxley. To persuade him to do what he did, my uncle offered him a much better living at Heverton as well as the money to buy premium apprenticeships for his two oldest boys. The temptation was too much for him.'

'I see.' She paused 'And Mrs Belmont? What made you bring her back here?'

'After my uncle rode away, I went upstairs to see her. That place is cold as a tomb, and he's let most of the servants go. She was lonely and afraid, so I offered to bring her here, at least until her daughter claims her.'

He took a deep swallow of his wine, stared silently down at her for a long moment, then said quietly, 'Lucienne, you must understand that finding Alain alters the future for all of us.'

'I realise that you married me to get possession of the Ottersbury estate and now you will be entitled to only half of it.'

He shook his head and said carefully, 'There is something more I must tell you. Something I hoped you need never know.' He paused as if he wasn't sure how to go on, then sat down in the chair beside hers as he went on, 'Do you remember the day my uncle called you into his study and claimed that you couldn't possibly be Richard Deverell's child?' Avoiding his eye she nodded, and he said, 'He'd already discussed his suspicions with me, and I'd agreed to go to Plymouth to get proof of the date of Luke Widdon's death from the Coroners' office.'

'I remember you said you couldn't find it.'

'A deliberate lie, because I did find it, and the date of Luke Widdon's death, as recorded at the inquest, proved my uncle's suspicions justified. Richard Deverell came back from his Grand Tour less than a month before he stabbed your mother's husband and ran away with her. You were born barely five months after that, so you could not possibly have been Richard's child.' He waited, as if expecting some sort of horrified reaction. When she stared down at her hands and said nothing, he went on, 'The coroners' clerk was an elderly man, on the verge of retirement. He was only too glad to take a healthy bribe to hide the report somewhere so deep in the archives that it is never likely to be seen again. Then my clerk, Joshua Gerrick, found a stone mason he could trust to keep silent and brought him secretly at night to destroy the inscription of the date of Luke Widdon's death on his gravestone here in Ottersbury church yard.'

She stared at him in amazement, 'Joshua Gerrick had that done? As well as to all the other gravestones that were damaged?'

'Exactly, the intention being that it should look like the work of some wandering madman, defacing anything that took his fancy. With the parish records destroyed in a flood a couple of years ago and the old family bible nowhere to be found, there was nothing left to prove you were not Richard Deverell's child.'

For a moment she hesitated, knowing this was the time to confess how she had taken the bible and thrown it into the sea, but instead she asked, 'Why did you do all that, Jago? Why go to so much trouble.? '

'To prevent my uncle keeping control of Ottersbury, but also to keep you safe, Lucienne. You were just a young girl, alone in the world. Being declared illegitimate would not have helped you in anyway. My uncle would have turned you out of here, my mother would have refused to go through with her application to the courts for guardianship, and the outbreak of war made a return to France impossible. Your situation here was far from ideal, but at least you were safe.'

'That was kind of you Jago, but there are things I don't understand —'

'Lucienne,' he interrupted firmly, 'Let me finish. The searches I made elsewhere discovered a will that left the Ottersbury estate to Richard Deverell and therefore it must be inherited by his children. When we believed Alain to be dead, I was happy to pretend that you were the rightful heiress in order to marry you and take possession of the estate before my uncle Cedrick brought the place to complete ruin. But in truth Alain is Richard Deverell's only child, and I am honour bound to admit that the Ottersbury estate belongs entirely to him.'

'Yes, I suppose it does,' she said slowly. 'Of course, I see that now. You must be very disappointed.'

He nodded, 'I admit that I am though, as Alain's guardian, I will have control over what happens here for the eighteen years until he comes of age. When the pottery and the mine are up and running, I can reclaim the money I invested, find a good estate manager and go back into the law firm in Castlebridge.' He paused and when she didn't speak went on, 'The real problem is yours, Lucienne. When you agreed to marry me, I promised you would leave here with an income for life. The money was to come from the estate, but that revenue is no longer legally mine, which means I have no right to give it to you. If you leave here it will not be as a rich woman.'

He stopped speaking, watching her with his steady, dark-eyed gaze. Her heart beating fast, she raised her eyes to his and said quickly, 'Jago, I don't want to leave here now.'

'You mean you've discovered that Alain is alive, and you want to stay here to be near him.' He stood up, took his glass from the mantle shelf and drained it. 'Not a flattering thing to tell a husband you were running away from only yesterday morning. Nobody likes to be rejected, Lucienne, and months ago you made it very clear that you don't want the attentions of a husband from me.'

'Jago, you said something that made me think you were one of the smugglers, or at least sympathised with them and I knew someone who was killed—'

'If you knew the meaning of desire and needed me as I needed you that night, nothing would have held you back from letting me come to your bed.'

She gazed at him, too confused to speak until he added, 'But the fault was mine. I should have realised that you are too young for that kind of love.'

She started to protest, but he interrupted, 'It's not so much a matter of years, Lucienne. More to do with a state of mind, the change from girl to woman that comes to some later than to others.' He turned away, looking into the fire as he added, 'And, of course, we married out of convenience to both of us, rather than any inclination on your part. That night I came to your room, after my return from Plymouth, it was wrong of me to take advantage of the situation.'

Indignantly she jumped to her feet, 'It was you suddenly asking me where I'd got boy's clothes that spoilt everything,' she cried, 'So don't try to tell me that I'm some sort of silly child. I'm nearly twenty and I know what I felt. The reason I was leaving yesterday was because we've been living like strangers for months and I just couldn't bear it any longer.'

He turned away from her, ran his fingers through his hair, then turned back so that they were facing each other as he said softly, 'Neither could I, Lucienne. It was the last thing I wanted. But there has been something on my mind, something I am not at liberty to explain. A promise I made that even now I cannot break.'

Her heart sank a little as she asked, 'Was it a promise to lady Helena?'

'Of course not,' he told her with a short laugh. 'Lucienne, that entanglement ended months ago, on the day I took you to find Alain's grave. Ended amicably and by mutual consent as it happens. But Lucienne in spite of what I said just now, all through the months of coldness between us I was hoping that something would happen to bring us together. Hoping your feelings could have changed.'

'My feelings didn't need to change,' she cried passionately. 'I've always wanted you, I've always cared for you, it's just that I was so frightened and upset at what I saw, or thought I saw, things that made me think— I mean there was that boat, hidden away in the creek near that cottage.' She saw him grinning down at her and stopped.

'You thought it was a smuggler's vessel? Lucienne, that boat belonged to the late Sir Humphrey Riverton. He owned the coast land for miles around and could moor his craft wherever he chose. I very much doubt that he was involved in anything illegal'.

'I see. I suppose I've been rather foolish,' she was saying as she turned away, but he caught her wrist and pulled her to him.

'You are anything but foolish, Lucienne, and the only thing that matters to me is you saying you'd always cared for me. How did you always care for me Lucienne,' he said softly? 'As a cousin? A husband? As a lover?' And before she could answer, his lips descended on hers in a tender caress, deepening into a long, searching kiss that took her breath away.

'As a lover,' she whispered as they drew apart, gasping for air, only to reunite, seconds later in a long moment of desire. Her senses swam and need seemed to meld them together in a way she had longed for as she clung to him, wishing this moment could go on forever.

The sound of the library door opening and then

quickly closing again brought her down to earth. They drew apart and Jago went over to the door to let Mrs Dobson into the room. She stepped cautiously over the threshold, looking flustered as she told them that supper was laid out and waiting for them in the small parlour.

'Mrs Belmont has been settled into her old room and her supper's gone up to her on a tray,' she added, then stood for a moment as if deciding whether or not to leave.

'Was there something more you wanted to say, Mrs Dobson?' Jago enquired politely.

Bridling a little she told him firmly, 'Yes, Mr Jago, there is. This morning, while both yourself and Miss Lucy were away from the house, a carriage drew up and a lady got out and said she'd come to call on young Mrs Moncrief. She was a talkative lady and, seeing me so surprised, she said she was a friend of Lady Isobel's who had told her that yourself and Miss Lucy were wed some months ago.'

'And, in view of what you witnessed when you opened the door just now, it will have been a relief to know us to be safely within the bonds of matrimony,' Jago said with one of his inconsequential shrugs. Lucienne brushed him aside and hurried forward.

'Mrs Dobson, it must have been very awkward for you to be told something so important by a complete stranger. Lady Isobel particularly promised not to tell anybody about the marriage until certain problems within the family were sorted out.'

'And happily, those problems are now settled,' Jago broke in, 'So ask the maids to collect Mrs Moncrief's belongings and transfer them to the bedroom next to mine. Immediately.'

Blushing to the roots of her hair, but mollified by

further reassurances from Lucienne, the housekeeper withdrew.

'She's off to tell the maids and the house will be buzzing with it,' Jago said as he sank into the armchair and pulled Lucienne on to his knee. 'By lunch time tomorrow, it will be all round the village.' His lips close to her ear, he murmured, 'So tonight, you must truly be my wife, and tomorrow take your place as lady of the manor.

16

In the soft morning light, she lay against the warmth of Jago's strong, lean body and sighed with utter contentment. Today, the first month of their true marriage was at an end and she had never been so happy.

'I thought you were still asleep,' she murmured as he kissed the back of her neck and whisper softly that he loved her.

'No. I was lying here and thinking that, now that we are together like this, things that once were so very important don't seem to matter nearly so much as they did before.'

She turned to face him. 'What sort of things?'

'Ownership of the Ottersbury estate for one. After all my plotting and scheming to get possession, I was dismayed when you told me that Alain was alive because I knew that it rightfully belongs to him. Now that we are together as man and wife, I can accept what has happened. We'll have to stay here for a few years yet but, after that, will you be happy as the wife of a country lawyer?'

'Blissfully happy, but what about your father's estate in Scotland?'

'After his death, I allowed my mother to draw the income from there and that must continue, otherwise she might have come to live with us. When I thought Ottersbury was mine I intended, after her death, to make the Scottish estate over to a distant cousin whose hard work keeps it afloat. Now I'm not so sure.'

'I see,' she whispered as she slipped her arms about his neck and whispered, 'But, Jago, tell me what you really do, every few weeks, when you say you are going out with the fishing boats?'

'I do precisely that. The fisher folk befriended me when I came here, a lonely, fatherless child. But I grew up and spent years away and came back almost a stranger to them. To regain their trust and friendship, I sometimes join them in their arduous life at sea.'

'I understand now.' She sighed. Her face close to his, she said softly 'It's early yet, Jago. What shall we do to pass the time?'

At first Mrs Dobson, perturbed by Lucienne's change of status, seemed to expect some alteration to take place in the way the house was run.

'No,' Lucienne told her, 'There is still a lot I can learn from you, so best we continue to manage everything between us.'

'Very well, if that is how you wish to proceed, Madam.' She pronounced the last word awkwardly.

'Mrs Dobson, 'you call my husband Mr Jago, so for the present I think we will both be more comfortable if you continue to call me Miss Lucy. Or Mrs Lucy if you prefer.'

That first month was full of things that had to be done, like astonishing Miss Petty with the fact that she and Jago were married. Then there was Beulah, radiant in new motherhood, to visit and share her news, and, best of all, to spend a few days at Heverton vicarage with dear Alain. Not so shy as she had feared he might be, he asked her where she'd been and, when she left, he kissed her goodbye, and stood at the gate, waving and calling out that she must come back soon.

As spring wakened the world outside, the ancient manor house seemed to grow light and cheerful. Mrs Belmont, seeming chastened by her exile in Heverton, was calm and pleasant for much of the time, graciously welcoming the morning visitors who called to meet young Mrs Moncrief when Lucienne was at the village school as she saw fit. To play the piano for her was a now pleasure and Lucienne's afternoons were filled with music, her nights with all the rapture of newly married love. Perfect happiness except that, six long months after she had gone away, there was still no word from Bett.

She and Jago were out picking the snow drops that grew in profusion by the surrounding wall just by the gate, when she said, 'I just can't get Bett out of my thoughts. I'm sure something bad must have happened to her. I don't even know if the ship she sailed on crossed the Atlantic safely. Surely there must be a way of finding out if —'

'Lucienne, there is something I must tell you. It is what I wanted to tell you long ago, but I had vowed to keep silent.' He stopped and looked away as if not sure how to go on, then made up his mind. He said abruptly, 'Bett didn't go to Jamaica. She went to France.'

She stood stock still and gazed at him, bewildered.

'But that letter she sent to me from Plymouth before she sailed?'

'Written by her and taken to Plymouth to be posted by somebody else while Bett was on her way to France. She was afraid here after the war began and told me she was desperate to get back to her own country. And it was possible, for a price, to get her there.'

'But why was I told such lies about where she was going. I can't believe that Bett would do that to me.'

'Lucienne, she couldn't tell you. Nothing goes unnoticed in a place like this and, for weeks in the spring last year, you were seen out on the cliff tops meeting a coast guard. The men who could put her ashore in Normandy make a dangerous living, smuggling goods in and out of France, and they didn't trust you. They agreed to take her only if I swore you knew nothing about it. And remember, what I am telling you now must go no further.'

'Of course, I won't tell anyone, but poor Bett, I suppose it was selfish of me to want her to stay. And she must be happy in France with her brothers. They used to write to her when we were in Guardeloupe and they always asked her to come home.'

Jago ran his hands through his hair, as if still undecided, then said, 'There is something else you should know. In return for my paying her way across the channel, she agreed to go to Paris and find proof that Richard Deverell married your mother, so that your claim to the Ottersbury estate couldn't be disputed.'

'Even though you already knew that he wasn't my real father?' she began, but he interrupted her.

'Nobody else knew that. Remember, at that time we thought Alain was dead, so his rights didn't come into it. Evidence of their marriage would have put your claim beyond doubt.'

'And was I supposed to go on forever, believing that Bett was in the West Indies but couldn't be bothered to write to me.'

'No. Regardless of my promise of secrecy to the men who took her to France, I intended to tell you the truth as soon as they came back and told me she was safely ashore in Normandy. But they never came back. They could have been caught by French coast guards, English men landing on French soil in time of war, and if they were, was Bett arrested with them? Or was the boat lost at sea? If so, was this before she reached French soil? Or on the way back, in which case she might have been already landed safely and gone on her way? There was no way of knowing and I thought it best to wait, in the hope of hearing from her before telling you anything.'

He reached out to put his hand on her arm, but she shook her head and pulled away, pacing to and fro, her mind awash with hopes and fears.

At last, she managed to say, 'And if she did land safely, got to Paris found evidence of the marriage or didn't find it, how was she to let you know?

'She was to return to Normandy and leave a message with the French traders in Normandy to pass on to whichever of our men next took a consignment of goods over there. Precarious, but there was no other way.'

She stared down at the snowdrops, pretty, delicate things with snow-white petals tipped with green, then said, 'Perhaps, even if we never hear from her, she might still be safe. And she meant to stay in France?'

'Yes. She meant to settle with her family in Le Havre, though she promised to come back to visit you after this war in Europe is over.' He slipped a comforting arm about her waist to draw her to him. This time she didn't resist.

Laying her head against his chest, she said sadly, 'In

that case, I think it will be many years until she comes to Ottersbury again.'

A few weeks later, as she came down the stairs, Lucienne heard a carriage draw up in front of the house, footsteps on the path, and, through the open front door, saw an elegant figure silhouetted against the bright April sunshine.

A neighbour, paying a morning visit, Lucienne thought, going forward to greet her, then felt her heart miss a beat as she heard her name called out in the voice she had so longed to hear. It was Bett.

Next moment they were embracing, laughing, crying, asking questions, interrupting, then just hugging each other in the sheer joy at being together again.

'Bett, I can't believe it's really you. Jago told me that you meant to stay in France,' Lucienne said as she led the way to the drawing room.

'And that was what I so longed to do when he first offered to get me there, but—' and here Bett hesitated, dropped her gaze for a moment, then smiled as she looked up and said, 'Oh, Lucienne I have so much to tell that I don't know where to start. And so many things have happened here while I was gone. You have married Mr Jago, which I was not too surprised to hear that because I always thought he liked you. But best of all our darling Alain has been discovered, safe and well. I could scarcely believe it when Joshua told me.'

'Joshua? Who is Joshua, Bett?'

'The lawyer's clerk, of course. Joshua Gerrick!' Her eyes shone as she said his name. 'And, though I missed you so, I confess it for him I that came back.'

'Bett, I never knew there was anything between you!'

'Lucienne, for both of us, it was secretly in our hearts from that very first day we came to Castlebridge to find Mr Jago. Do you remember how Joshua escorted us to the Mermaid inn? Neither he nor I knew then how much the other was affected, though both of us felt such instant rapport. And by sheer good fortune he has family in Ottersbury village and he came to see me there.'

'And you never said a word to me about it!

'Joshua is a very discreet person, and I wasn't sure what he felt until just before I left for France. It was Joshua who knew how to arrange to get me across the channel but then, only days before I went, he declared his love, and begged me to stay and marry him. He said he wanted to protect me from all harm and that, as his wife, I would not be so much persecuted because of the war. I very was torn because I knew I loved him, that perhaps this was my chance for the happiness that every woman dreams of.'

'So why did you go?'

'I longed to see my brothers again, to meet their children, my nephews and nieces. To see the land of my birth once more, but also to find proof of your parents' marriage, to make you safe forever. But I promised Joshua that I would return, and the longer I was away, the more I missed him and the more I knew that my true place was here in England, at the side of the only man I have ever truly loved.'

Lucienne, secretly surprised that the dour looking lawyer's clerk could feel or inspire such devotion, remembered how he gave her the bouquet of exquisite white flowers on her wedding day and understood.

She said, 'Whatever your reason for coming back, I am so pleased. And how elegant you look. That deep red is so flattering to you. Did you buy those clothes in France?'

'No. I went to France disguised as a peasant woman, so I had to leave my ordinary clothes behind. Joshua took my dull grey coat to a tailor in Castlebridge and had this beautiful new one made in finest English wool to fit me. This elegant hat I believe was chosen by his sister, as were the gloves and this charming purse. It is a little too small for my taste, but he had given away that one I always carried. It was rather old.'

'One day I was sure I saw your coat on a market stall!' Lucienne exclaimed, 'Your bag too. I couldn't understand how they could have got there, because you were wearing the coat and carrying the bag that day you were supposed to be on your way to the West Indies.'

'My dear, forgive me. I felt so bad to tell you such lies, but it was the only way at the time. I did not expect to be away so long, but France is a big country and so much of my time was spent on getting from one place to another.'

'Bett, travel is so expensive in this country, surely it must be much the same in France, so how on earth did you pay for it?'

'Dear Joshua got money for me before I left.' Lucienne noticed how her eyes sparkled with love and pride when she mentioned his name. 'He knows so much of what goes on in Castlebridge as well as here in Ottersbury. He knew that, in peace time, the wool merchants selling in France took payment for their goods in French francs that a bank in Plymouth exchanged for English pounds. When the war began so suddenly this stopped and the merchants were left with French money on their hands. One of them was only too pleased to sell him as much as he wanted. It was all done in secret, and Mr Jago paid of course, but it was dear, clever Joshua who knew how things could be managed. '

At the back of her mind, while they were talking and laughing together Lucienne found herself remembering what Mathew Harris had told her so long ago. '*We think someone clever is master minding the smuggling that goes on from hereabouts. Someone the locals know and trust*', was what he'd said. Could Joshua Gerrick, who was able to arrange so many secret goings on, be that person? She looked at Bett's glowing countenance, felt a rush of gratitude at her return and decided to keep her thoughts about smugglers to herself for now.

She was telling Bett about her secret wedding, when Jago joined them. He took Bett's hand and clasped it warmly.

'Welcome back. I met Miss Petty in the village, and she told me you stopped off to see her on your way up here. She thinks you've come back from Jamaica to marry Joshua Gerrick! I'd say he's a very lucky man but, in all the months you've been away, he's never said a word to me about it.'

'It is his way to be discreet,' she smiled and went on, 'And now there is so much I have to tell you both. Most important is that I at last found proof that a marriage did take place between Richard Deverell and Barbara Widdon.'

'I' m so glad,' Lucienne said, though now it scarcely seemed to matter whether they had been married or not. 'But was it difficult? You were away so long that we almost gave up hope.'

'You must remember that, when I was put ashore in France, I first had to travel to Le Havre to visit my brothers. They were very pleased to see me, expecting me to stay with them but, when I told of the mission I had undertaken for you, they understood, so I went on to Paris and began my search. It proved difficult. Marriages made since the revolution are easy to trace because of the excellent public records, but your parents were married before that. I searched in every church, every place where a marriage could have taken place and I found nothing.

'Then, when I had almost given up hope, I came upon an old friend of your father's. He told me he believed they married soon after they arrived in France and were staying with a young nobleman who your father knew from his travels in Europe some time before. He remembered only that the place was near St Lô, in the Manche department of Normandy, though he had the family name. It was De Lesseps.'

Lucienne started forward in astonishment. 'But how strange! That was my stepmother's name, taken from her first husband,' she explained to Jago. 'She told me that he perished with so many aristocrats in the time of the revolution, but her name was Chantelle de Lesseps before she married my father.'

'I will not burden you with the details how I found the small town near to where, before the revolution, the De Lesseps family once owned vast estates' Bett continued, 'but it was there that I met an old priest who had been chaplain to the De Lesseps family. He told me that he had married your parents when they stayed at the chateau with Count Guy de Lesseps and his beautiful young Countess, Chantelle.'

'So that was how my father first met her. I remember Chantelle telling me about how, after she was widowed, they met again in Paris when she was on a visit from Guadeloupe, ' Lucienne exclaimed, then fell silent when she saw Bett's serious expression.

'The priest was only too pleased to provide me with a

signed and witnessed statement that your parents' marriage had taken place, but when I told him about Chantelle's marriage to your father he was horrified. He told me that her first husband did not die in the revolution. He escaped and secretly made his way to Italy where he joined a religious order and where he still lives to this day.' She paused and then added sadly, 'So, though the thing was done in all innocence, theirs was a bigamous marriage and our poor darling Alain is a bastard child.'

'Another secret never to be told' Jago said thoughtfully later that evening when they were alone together, and he leaned back in his armchair in the glowing warmth of the library fire.

'I'm sure we can rely upon Bett's silence on the subject,' he added as he stretched out his arms for Lucienne to come to him.

She slipped on to his knee and snuggled down against his chest as he added thoughtfully, 'You realise that Alain, being proved illegitimate, is not entitled to inherit the estate.'

'If the truth be known, neither should I,' Lucienne told him firmly, 'So, who exactly would own Ottersbury, if neither Alain nor I did?'

'In law, everything should go to Richard Deverell's nearest relatives. That is my mother and his brother Cedrick. Uncle Cedrick has already taken enough out of the estate to bring it to the verge of ruin and my mother has only to marry one of her admirers and her share would be his.'

'We can't let that happen,' Lucienne said, sitting up in alarm.

'It won't. All is safe unless the family bible turns up

and Uncle Cedrick gets hold of it,' he told her and shook with laughter when she confessed how she had thrown it into the sea.

Gently pulling her close again he said softly, 'So, for the good of the people whose forebearers toiled on this land, and whose safe livelihood depends on how it is managed now, let's tell ourselves that half of the estate was yours and therefore is now rightfully mine. Legitimate or not, Alain is Richard Deverell's child and, to my mind a rightful heir, so his half I shall manage until he comes of age, though the life of a country squire may not be what he chooses.'

'Possibly not,' she agreed, thinking of her last visit to the vicarage at Heverton when the cheerful little three-year-old boy, sitting on a pile of cushions so that he could reach the keys, played Mrs Lamb's harpsicord as well as a child three times his age.

She leaned back in Jago's arms, knowing that the vow she had made long ago in Guadeloupe, to keep Alain safe and happy until he grew up, would never now be broken. And later in the year she was almost sure there would be another child to love and cherish, though Jago didn't know that yet.

ACKNOWLEDGMENTS

I take this opportunity to express my gratitude to all family and friends who have helped and encouraged me in writing this novel.

My particular thanks must go to Julie Roberts, of the Romantic Novelist Association for her ongoing support and for so skillfully editing the final draft.

Also I take this opportunity to thank my publisher, Lynn Burke of Lily Dale Press for preparing this novel for publication and for her charming cover design.

ALSO BY ALISON BURKE

CHARITY OF STRANGERS

You can find almost anything in a charity shop, but can you find love?

You can certainly find friendship, and there is both laughter and tears ahead when 19-year-old Zaffron, lonely, anxious, and without direction, meets Blaire Daintry, good-looking, charming, and gay.

Both volunteers in the charity shop, he has a hidden agenda, she has secrets, but they are friends from the start, despite Blaire's constant sparring with Ida, the stern, good-hearted older volunteer who Zaffron admires. And perhaps Ida has secrets too.

Together with other victims of the city's housing crisis, Blaire and Zaffron set up a safe and happy home. Secure at last, she tells him of the dreadful incident in her childhood that has marred her life, but not even his total acceptance gives her the confidence to start a relationship with an attractive and decent young army sergeant who falls in love with her.

Is it fear of the truth coming out that holds her back? Or is there some other reason, buried too deep in her heart for her to recognise?

ALSO BY ALISON BURKE

SEARCH FOR THE HOUSE OF DREAMS

City of Bath, 1847

'A lovely young woman on the threshold of life,' is how a stranger sees 18 yr old Genevre Stratton but, in a household where debts pile up while her feckless parents throw lavish parties, her concern is to care for her three much loved younger siblings.

When they are suddenly orphaned, poverty forces her to give them up to their wealthy, charismatic half-brother. Bitterly resenting this, she is led by fate to London's world of musical theatre. Here, her beautiful singing voice promises an independent career, but should she instead surrender herself completely to the rich and powerful enemy who has become her lover?

The need to choose is delayed when an errand of mercy takes her to Paris, where dark secrets from the past emerge that must change the course of Genevre's life forever.

Recommended for readers of Kay Seely and Ella Cornish.

Printed in Great Britain
by Amazon

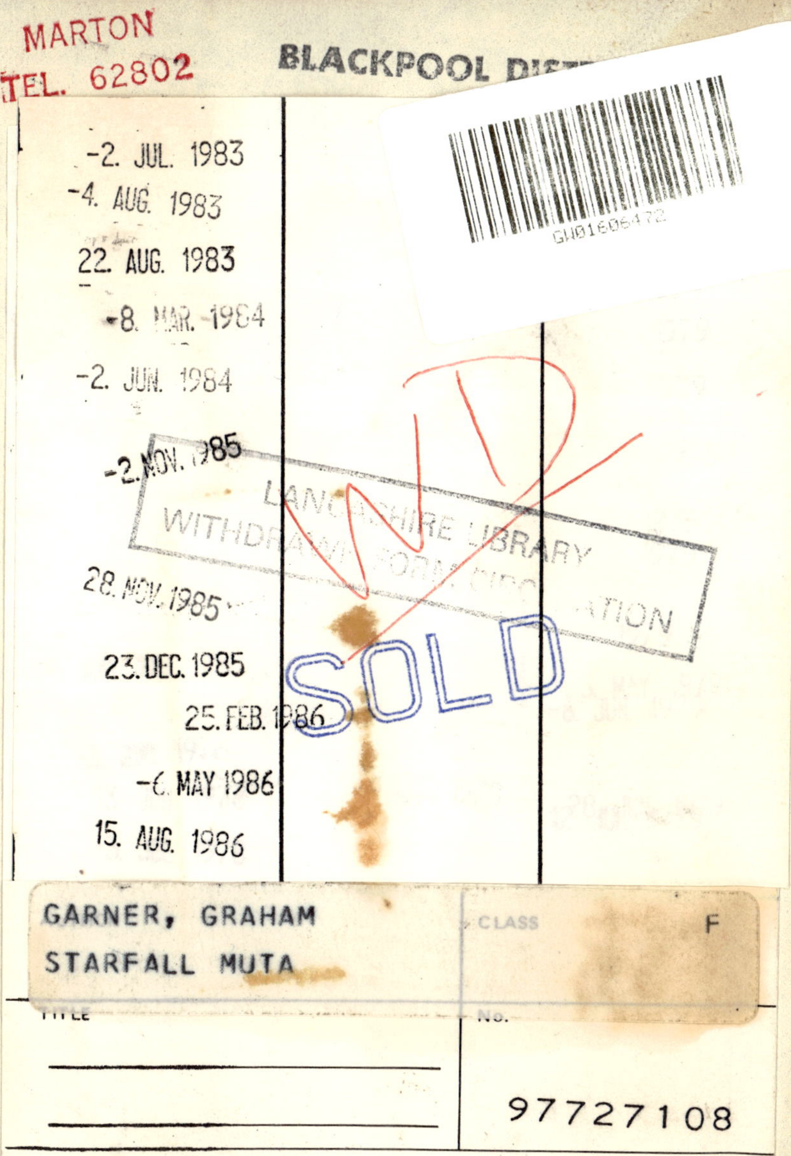

STARFALL MUTA

The shuttlecraft detached from *Probe* 2 when Muta orbit was reached, carrying Commander Theron Clark and three crew members down to the mysterious surface of the planet. But trouble struck them before they reached the ground, enveloping them in a horror-filled nightmare that seemed to have no ending. From that moment they faced the inhospitable planet and its terrible inhabitants. There were Avics—half-man, half-bird; Ogrins—fifteen feet tall and purely savage; Brutans—more sophisticated but equally dangerous; and last but not least the Merscs—Marshmen no taller than an average schoolboy but as deadly as all the other aliens put together. Clark was faced with prohibitive odds, but he was not a man to give up. He kept on until the climax overwhelmed them.

By the same author

Space Probe

STARFALL MUTA

by

GRAHAM GARNER

ROBERT HALE & COMPANY
63 Old Brompton Road, London, S.W.7

First published in Great Britain 1975

ISBN 0 7091 4541 1

PRINTED IN GREAT BRITAIN BY
WILLMER BROTHERS LIMITED, BIRKENHEAD

Chapter One

The atmosphere in the control cabin of *Probe* 2 was tense, and had been for days. In addition to the normal duty watch the first landing party was assembled for final briefing, and they were staring at the planet of Muta that was looming now on the forward scanner screen. Captain Hurn looked at the four members of the landing party—three men and a woman—and as his gaze took in the tall, athletic figure of Commander Clark he knew this vital mission could not have been placed in better hands.

'We'll be swinging into an orbit around Muta in thirty minutes,' Hurn said. 'Be ready to detach from the ship in precisely thirty-one minutes. I guess we've covered everything possible in this briefing, but you will be expected to act upon your own initiative as soon as you detach. You know your mission, and all I want are your reports. Don't try to exceed your orders. Once we've satisfied ourselves as to the suitability of Muta for general landing we'll expand the foothold you'll gain for us.'

Commander Clark, aged 30, tall and dark, glanced at the globe of the planet they had come two hundred light years to check out. *Probe* 1, sister-ship of *Probe* 2, had disappeared after reaching orbit around this planet. The last recorded message from *Probe* 1 had been the report that the ship had gone into orbit.

'I won't take any chances, Captain,' Clark said tightly. He glanced at his Number Two, Major Balfin, who caught his eye and smiled. 'I think we'll do a good job.'

'You won't have to worry about security,' Balfin retorted. 'I'll handle it.' He glanced at Lieutenant Rip Mallory, and tightened his lips. He wished Mallory wasn't going along. Mallory was reliable, except where women were concerned, and the fourth member of the party was Magenta Sabir, a scientific observer; a beautiful woman not yet thirty.

'Just establish your base and set up your screens,' the Captain said. 'Soon as you report that you are established and have checked your surroundings I'll start sending the main party down. But you'll be on the planet's surface at least two hours before any help could possibly reach you, should an emergency arise, and you'd better remember that and make allowances for it.'

Clark nodded. He glanced at the scanner screen once more. The planet of Muta was somewhat larger than Earth, with a pair of small moons in orbital attendance. The yellow sun that gave light and life to Muta appeared to be two thirds its way to burning out, but had enough life left in it for this present survey to go ahead without worry. But there was something to worry about, Clark reminded himself. *Probe* 1 had signalled arrival in Muta orbit, then nothing!

'We'd better start preparing for detachment, Captain,' Clark said, and he forced his concern into the background. His younger brother Vernon was Communications Engineer aboard *Probe* 1. He tried not to think of his brother's fate.

'Good luck,' Hurn responded, and they turned and departed quickly from the control cabin. . . .

The shuttlecraft was forty feet long, a miniature spaceship that was cradled in the underside of the parent ship. Clark found his tension mounting as he entered and sat down in the pilot's seat. He belted himself in the seat and then ran through the sequence of checks that were necessary before they could detach. In the background he could hear the sharp voice of Rip Mallory checking the communications systems, and when he had ended his checks, Clark looked around to check on his crew.

Balfin was strapped in the observer's seat, handling the controls of the shuttlecraft's armament. He grinned boyishly at Clark as he glanced up. At forty-five, Balfin was unusually youthful, the fittest man on the ship.

Clark let his gaze slide left to the small figure of Magenta Sabir, the scientist. The woman's dark eyes were watching him, he discovered, and she smiled, her full lips curving gently, as he met her gaze. He smiled in return, and for a moment his attention was diverted from his duty. She was a woman beautiful enough to turn the head of the most ardent duty-lover, he told himself, and compressed his lips and took a deep breath as he glanced at the chronometer.

'Ten minutes to detachment,' he called, and tension hit him once again. He pressed a button on the console in front of him and a red light came on as the *Airlock Open* sign glowed. His right index finger moved rapidly, depressing various buttons that activated red and green lights, and labels became illuminated as mechanical orders were passed through the computer. 'Drive Ready!' he reported.

'Five minutes to detachment,' Mallory reported.

Magenta Sabir strapped herself into an observation seat and took up a scanscope, peering with it through a viewport, looking at the planet, and Clark found his attention being drawn to the woman once more. He set his teeth into his bottom lip and checked the time. The minutes seemed to be fleeting by swiftly now.

Mallory sealed the hatch, and Clark glanced at the warning light, waiting for it to change from red to green. It flickered and changed, and Clark nodded to himself. He took a deep breath as he stretched out his right hand and let his index finger hover over the detach-button. He stared at the clock, waiting stolidly for the countdown. The next instant Mallory's voice started counting down from ten. At zero, Clark pressed the detach-button, and they eased away from the massive black hull of the parent ship.

Clark felt a strange sense of vulnerability as they sped away from the larger ship. He glanced through the viewport at his right shoulder, saw the outline of the mother ship dropping back, and glimpsed the black backcloth of Space beyond, stretching away illimitably, knowing that no matter how far they travelled through Space, they would never reach its edge.

Clark was filled with a sense of wonder as they flicked into orbit. He forced himself to concentrate upon his job, and heard Mallory's voice in the background, in contact with *Probe* 2. He glanced sideways at Balfin, and felt safe in the big man's company. The Major had a reputation that was hard to beat.

Mallory was talking into the communicator, reporting that all systems were fine, but suddenly the Lieutenant broke off and began pressing buttons on his console. Clark frowned and turned his head to look at Mallory, and at that moment the interior of the small shuttlecraft was briefly illuminated by a sudden purple-white flash. Almost simultaneously the shuttlecraft lurched sickeningly and wrenched out of its smooth course. It almost stood on its tail, and whirled out of control.

Clark instinctively thumbed down the stabilizer button, leaning heavily against his straps. There was no undue sound to account for the unexpected gyrations, and he clenched his teeth as he looked at the rows upon rows of dials and meters, looking for an explanation.

'Oh, my God!' There was almost a note of hysteria in Magenta Sabir's harsh voice.

Clark glanced at the woman, saw she was holding a scan-scope to her eyes, staring through a port at *Probe* 2, and

Magenta let the scanscope drop from her hands. Clark saw her face was chalky white, her eyes wide with shock, and a sudden cold fear clutched at his heart.

'What's wrong?' he snapped.

She turned shocked eyes wearily towards him. Her lips were stiff, her mouth gasping as if she were in the last throes of oxygen starvation.

'The ship!' she cried. 'It's gone! There was an explosion!'

Clark felt disbelief seeping into his mind. He struggled to keep his thoughts steady. The shuttlecraft was beginning to return to its smooth flight, and he flicked a switch that let the auto-pilot take over, cutting in the computer control that would take the craft down to within landing distance, when he would again resume control. He got out of his seat, his hands trembling as he moved to Magenta's side. He took up the scanscope and moved to the rear observation panel, peering out with the scope, trying to pick up *Probe* 2.

He had trouble finding it! At first he couldn't believe the evidence of his eyes. Instead of the massive space ship with its smooth, unbroken lines, there was merely a shattered hulk, with the pale light of the nearby yellow sun slanting through the shredded metal.

Clark caught his breath, unable to take in the terrible vision, and before he could take a second look there was another gigantic flash which almost blinded him. He blinked and lowered his face into the crook of his right elbow, and when he was able to take another look at *Probe* 2 he discovered that there was nothing but a whirling group of particles riding the spot where the giant spaceship and four hundred humans had been!

'What the hell happened?' Balfin demanded. He was at Clark's shoulder, his voice taut and filled with shock. 'Is the ship all right?'

'Its gone,' Clark retorted, and his voice was harsh and bitter. 'Disintegrated—blown to pieces.'

There was a short silence, and Mallory, at his console, was still trying to regain communication with *Probe* 2. Clark turned on him.

'You can quit trying, Mallory,' he retorted in low tones. 'The ship is gone.'

Mallory turned a pale face towards him, his mouth slack, his eyes wide with unnatural shock.

'I heard a voice in the background, just before the lines went dead,' he said jerkily. 'It reported picking up missiles on the scanners.'

'So the ship was attacked!' Balfin turned and went back to his seat, prepared to fight.

Clark returned to the pilot's seat, switching on the scanners. He was thinking of *Probe* 1, trying to impress upon himself that his brother might still be alive. But after what had happened to *Probe* 2 he knew it couldn't be possible.

'If *Probe* 2 has been destroyed, how do we get away from this planet?' Mallory demanded.

Clark's lips pulled tight as he considered. If alien action was responsible for the loss of the vast spaceship then there was more trouble to come! Balfin was obviously thinking along the same lines.

'What makes you think we've got any kind of a chance of getting away?' the Major demanded roughly. 'Whoever destroyed *Probe* 2 used a very sophisticated weapon, and no doubt we're being tracked right now. It'll be our turn next.'

'Cut that out, Kester!' Clark's voice cracked in the tense atmosphere. 'Let's get this ship down on the ground as fast as we can.'

'But what about when we want to get away?' Mallory demanded. 'We're gonna be stranded down there.'

'We'll be safer on the ground than up here. With the kind of weapons being used, we'd be sitting ducks up here in orbit.' There was a harsh note in Kester Balfin's voice. 'Get us down on the ground as quickly as you can, Commander.'

'We're going down all right,' Clark said through his teeth. He was checking the control console, and quickly saw that the ship was being forced out of its present orbital descent. 'Someone is using a tractor beam on us. We're being controlled.'

'We established before we reached Muta orbit that the planet is inhabited,' Magenta said thinly.

Clark strapped himself once more into his seat, and peered through the view port at the grey and brown planet. The shuttle-craft was on an even keel once more, functioning normally after the terrific shock wave that had overpowered her.

'We'd better prepare ourselves for a fight,' Balfin said grimly. 'The planet is habited all right, and the natives are not friendly. They fired on the ship without warning.'

'It's what must have happened to *Probe* 1,' Mallory said. 'For Heaven's sake, Commander, let's keep off the ground. There are four of us. We can't hope to win any fight, and we certainly won't be able to parley with the natives.'

'We're too far from home, or any friendly planet, to hope to make safety in this craft,' Clark said, and he fought down the tremor of panic that threatened to engulf him. In the back of his mind was the knowledge that without *Probe* 2 there was no way of returning to Earth. They were stranded out here on this alien planet.

'Try and take manual control of the craft,' Balfin said. 'Perhaps we've got a computer malfunction. We did take a heavy knock back there.'

Clark switched out the computer and took over the controls. For a few moments he was unable to get any response, and his supposition that they were under the control of alien forces was strengthened, but suddenly the craft jarred slightly, then the instruments began registering, and he found control in his hands.

'I've got it,' he said, and there was hope in his tones.

'Are we landing?' Mallory demanded.

'We have no alternative.' Clark pulled his lips tight. 'I calculate we have two hours before we touch down.'

'And if we're being tracked on some kind of radar?' Mallory demanded. 'Then what?'

'I don't even want to guess,' Clark retorted. He switched on sensors and radar, half afraid to look at the screens, but there were no tell-tale dots of light showing anywhere to warn of approaching warheads.

'Do you think anyone got off *Probe* 1?' Balfin demanded.

Clark didn't want to think about that. He dared not let his mind dwell upon the four hundred personnel aboard *Probe* 2. Captain Hurn and all his colleagues—all gone, wiped out in that blinding flash!

Suddenly the dials and indicator lights blinked and ceased functioning, and Clark jabbed anxiously at the testers.

'We're in trouble,' he reported at length. 'The ship's controls are dead. Nothing seems to be functioning.'

'Are we gonna crash?' Mallory demanded.

'Unless I can find out what the trouble is!' Clark was already checking circuits. He had an idea where the trouble might lay, thanks to the interminable months of training. He quickly decided that the main circuits were not damaged, but there was no life at all in any of the power units. While panic tried to invade his mind he reasoned it out coldly, his hands steady as he searched for faults. The testers worked, and he was frowning when he saw that none of the circuits had been damaged.

'Found anything?' Balfin demanded anxiously.

'Nothing yet!' Clark's voice was steady, but his forehead was beaded with sweat. 'Everything seems to be in order.'

'Then it must be the main drive,' Balfin retorted.

'No!' Clark shook his head. 'All indicators are working. There's nothing wrong with main drive.'

'Except that it's dead!' There was a grim note in Balfin's voice. 'It looks as if the rest of our crew had it lucky. I don't suppose any of them knew what hit them. But we're going to burn up in that atmosphere down there if you can't get a spark out of our motors.'

'The computer!' Clark compressed his lips as he considered. 'If the computer is damaged then it would kill all power.'

He reached out and switched off computer control. The craft was still behaving erratically, but with less alarming antics. Tension gripped the interior, and the silence was throat-clutching. Clark cut out the feeder and switched off the impulse regulator. He took a deep breath as he pressed the ignition button. A spark of hope spurted through him when the main drive turned over, but it didn't catch, and he moistened his lips as he prepared to try again. At his side, Balfin was breathing heavily.

But this time the main drive picked up, and Clark fed power to it and turned to grin at Balfin.

'It must have been the computer,' he said. 'I think it will be all right now. But I shan't be happy until we get down on the ground.'

'It won't be too long at this rate,' Balfin retorted.

Clark watched the small scanner screens, and saw the surface of the planet in more detail. He worried about the tractor beam that had been holding them, and used the controls to check if they were still being held. He found the craft veering to the right, and hope began to raise its head once more in his mind. The tractor beam had been switched off or had lost them.

But reality was hard to face, Clark found. His mind was laced with the shock of what had happened, and he seemed to be living in a nightmare. He stared at the planet they were approaching, wondering what lay ahead of them. There was hostility for certain, for *Probe* 2 had been destroyed without warning. He found himself tingling with anticipation and apprehension.

'We're getting pretty close to the planet now,' Balfin commented. 'What can we do for the best, Commander? Have we got sufficient fuel to take us anywhere? This course might drop us straight into trouble. That tractor beam held us, so someone knows we're alive and on this approach.'

'We're on manual, and as soon as our speed decreases I'll turn away from our present course.' Clark found his mind beginning to work freely once more, his shock at the destruction of their ship being pushed into the background by his discipline and training. This was the kind of emergency his training had been slanted to cover.

'To the right!' Balfin's voice quivered with suppressed emotion. 'It looks like habitations to me—a town maybe.'

Clark took his gaze from the screen and peered out the viewport. He saw grey patches on the horizon, and nodded slowly.

'You're right, Kester,' he retorted. 'Looks like a town to me. They'll be watching us, I've no doubt.'

'Let's get out of here completely,' Mallory said, his tones rising. 'This craft will take us out of this area. We can make for the nearest friendly planet. We've got supplies aboard, sufficient to save our lives.'

'We might be able to get clear, if these aliens don't have us tracked,' Clark said through his teeth. 'Perhaps we're not being fired at because we are landing. It might be another matter if we try to get away.'

'I say our best chance is to land,' Balfin cut in. 'Apart from any other consideration, we've got to try and find out what happened to *Probe* 1.'

'I figure we know well enough what's happened to that.' Mallory retorted. 'It was destroyed, like our own ship.'

Clark threw a cautious glance over his shoulder at Magenta, wondering how the woman was taking the turn of events. He saw her face was white and drawn, showing shock quite plainly, but she nodded slowly as she met his gaze.

'I have perfect confidence in you, Commander,' she said, as if reading his mind.

Clark took a deep breath and returned his attention to the console. He glanced at the screen and studied the grey spots that looked like townships, and he swung the craft away from them, heading for the interior of the planet over which they were speeding.

'Looks like we're going into the wilderness,' Balfin commented. 'It might not be such a good idea, Commander. If we hit trouble on the ground we'll be lost in the wilds, and that could cost us our lives.'

'And if we come down close to habited areas we could find those hostile aliens and get ourselves killed that way.' Clark shook his head. 'We got ourselves the hell of a choice, huh?'

'Try that area over there!' Balfin was pointing to the screen. 'That looks like a forest. The vegetation will conceal us.'

Clark nodded and changed course. They were very low now, skimming in towards the surface, and he held the craft purposely low to throw off any tracking stations that might have followed their descent. He changed course again, to get away from any plot which the aliens might make after losing contact with them. His mind was alert to all possibilities as they swept on. The craft slanted down, and they swooped over a cluster of buildings. Clark merely caught a glimpse of them, intent as he was at the controls, but Balfin whistled through his teeth.

'Hell, did you get a look at those buildings?' the Major demanded.

'What was wrong with them?' Clark clenched his teeth as he stared through the forward viewport, the screens forgotten now. He could see the vegetation of a dank black forest below, and he intended setting down in the first available clearing.

'I only got a glimpse,' Balfin said, turning to stare out the rear viewport, 'and I guess our height and speed distorted my vision somewhat, but I'd swear those buildings were houses of some kind, and they stood around sixty feet high!'

'They've got housing problems, same as on Earth,' Clark retorted, slitting his eyes. He figured a clearing was coming up, and there was the glint of water at one side. He could not see dwellings of any kind, and reached out to the controls. 'We're going down there,' he said thinly. 'Brace yourselves in case it gets rough.'

It was a clearing, small and irregular, but there was water in it, glinting dully in the sunlight. Clark felt the push of gravity as he brought the craft around in a tight turn, and then they were dropping in to land, the retro-rockets firing automatically to slow their descent. Clark concentrated upon getting in under the fringe of the trees for cover, and the dust rose in black clouds as they steadied, then dropped heavily over the last four feet. He cut the power instantly and slumped in his seat for a moment, and in the ensuing dead silence he fancied he could hear his heart thudding.

'We made it,' Balfin said, and there was a strange note of relief in his hard tones.

'Let's get out of here and away from the ship in case it was tracked down,' Mallory said curtly. He reached out to break the seal on the hatch, but a scream of horror from Magenta made him freeze.

Clark swung around in his seat, to find the woman staring out the rear viewport. He got out of his seat and went to her side, aware that she was unable to speak, shocked immeasurably by something she had seen. He stared through the thick glass, frowning when he could see nothing at first. The woman was pointing a tremoring finger, but he couldn't see anything to get alarmed about.

Then he spotted movement, and a cold sweat broke out on his rugged forehead. A man eased forward momentarily from the cover of a tree—a man such as Clark had never seen before. He had black leathery wings, a bat-like face, and ostrich-like legs. Two humanoid arms showed below the wings, and one of the clawed hands was holding a weapon that looked suspiciously like some kind of a Laser gun.

'Don't open that hatch!' Clark tried to keep his tones level, but there was a ragged quality in his voice. 'We've got company already.'

The others came crowding at his shoulder for a look, and they stared in silence, while two other birdmen appeared to study the shuttlecraft. Clark discovered that he was holding his breath, and he sighed heavily, then inhaled quickly. He was wondering what kind of a nightmare they had dropped into. . . .

Chapter Two

'What the hell are they?' Balfin demanded.

'Let's get back into the air before they attack,' Mallory cut in.

'Don't let's panic,' Clark retorted. 'Just take it easy. They're not making any hostile moves.'

'But they're armed with some kind of a weapon.' Balfin's tones were shaky, and Clark frowned as he glanced at the big man. He had never known Balfin show any kind of emotion in a tight corner. But after what had happened to their parent ship he was not surprised that their nerves were ruffled.

'You're the scientist amongst us, Magenta,' Clark said. 'Have you ever come across anything like these creatures?'

'No!' The woman was striving to remain outwardly calm. 'They're semi-humanoid. Those features are not far removed from Man, and they are not at all birdlike.'

'More like a bat,' Balfin said.

Clark silently agreed. 'I'm going to try and make contact with them,' he said.

'Don't leave the craft,' Mallory warned.

Clark went back to his seat and opened a communication line, switching it to audio, and he paused as he considered what to say. He plugged in a semantics transmuter to the computer, then twisted in his seat as he began to talk.

'We mean you no harm,' he said. 'We are friendly.'

They could not hear Clark's voice sounding outside the craft, but it echoed through the clearing and scared the bird-men. Clark saw two of the creatures run out from the trees and flap their massive leathery wings. They took off and went circling the clearing, looking grotesque and unreal.

'There are a couple who haven't taken off,' Balfin said. 'Better put up our deflector screens, Commander. They're beginning to look hostile.'

Clark jabbed a finger at the button controlling their power screens, and when the green light came on he turned once more to peer through the rear viewport. He saw two of the winged men standing together, and this time he examined them in more detail.

They were around six feet in height, with head and shoulders like a man. But there all resemblance ended. They had curious features; a beaklike mouth and a stubby nose, and their ears were like leathery tufts towards the top of their heads. Their chests were powerfully developed to cope with their wings, and their hands were humanoid, although Clark could not count digits. He saw the weapons they were holding, and narrowed his brown eyes. He continued to study the creatures, and shook his head when he saw that the lower part of their body was birdlike. He likened their legs to that of an ostrich, and wondered what strange vagary of Nature had evolved this species. They had to be intelligent, he knew, and wondered if he could make contact with them. For some instinctive reason he suspected that they were not responsible for what had happened to *Probe* 2.

He called them again on the audio, but they merely faded into cover, although furtive movements of branches warned him that they had not retreated far.

'We're wasting time,' Balfin said slowly. 'They could be bringing in help. If they attack us there's likely to be little chance for us in this clearing. Maybe we ought to get into the air and move on, Commander.'

Clark was tempted to do just that, but he knew they had to make contact with these aliens, and the sooner the better. He needed to let them know they were friends.

'I'm gonna take a chance and go out there to try and talk with them,' he said sharply, and tension hit him as he spoke, although he did not show it.

'That could be the mistake of the year,' Balfin retorted, shaking his head. 'If someone has got to go out there then it better be me.'

Clark started to protest, but Balfin was their security man, and a good all-round fighter. He nodded slowly, holding Balfin's pale gaze for a moment.

'Okay, you'd better handle it, Kester,' he said. 'Take a transmuter with you and try and make contact with them. But don't take any chances. Someone destroyed *Probe* 2. I somehow don't think it was these creatures, but we can't be too careful.'

'One thing is certain,' Balfin said as he prepared to leave the craft. 'These creatures don't live in those tall buildings I spotted before we came over the forest. If you ask me, there are several kinds of creatures on Muta.'

'You could be right.' Clark moved to his seat and switched on the scanners. He looked around the clearing, spotting more than a score of the birdlike creatures, all waiting in cover and staring at the craft with beady eyes. They were all holding weapons. 'I don't like it, Kester,' he said reluctantly. 'I'm not gonna let you make it out there.'

'Let's lift off and head somewhere else,' Mallory said. 'This place gives me the creeps.'

'You're the boss,' Balfin said. 'I'll give it a whirl if you reckon it's the right thing for me to do. I'm not afraid of those creatures.'

'It's not a matter of being afraid,' Clark retorted. 'I can't afford to lose your support, Kester.'

He prepared to switch on the main drive, but Mallory called a warning, and when he looked at the screens in response to Mallory's cry, Clark saw an aircraft approaching, skimming the trees. It was more like a skyraft than any kind of craft that Clark had ever seen, and they stared at it intently as it wavered through the air.

Clark was thankful he had put the shuttlecraft down almost under the trees, but he fancied they would be spotted. He saw Balfin out of the corner of his eye, dropping back into his seat and preparing to use the Phasers. It was in Clark to stop the Major, but he knew this newcomer was a different proposition.

The next instant the flying raft was in action, hosing long streams of purple light at the clearing. Clark realized at once that the birdmen were being attacked, and he reached out and placed a heavy hand upon Balfin's arm.

'Hold your fire, Kester,' he said curtly. 'Our screens will protect us. Let's see if they spot us. They're not shooting at us.'

'They're killing the birdmen,' Magenta reported in quivering tones.

'The birdmen are fighting back,' Mallory cut in. 'Those weapons they're carrying. They're powerful. They're knocking lumps off that flying machine.'

Clark was watching the fight on the screen, and saw the cupola on the skyraft taking streams of tremoring light that distorted its smooth shape. The next instant the craft had gone from sight beyond the trees, and the birdmen disappeared once more into the forest, leaving a number of their dead on the soft ground.

'What do you make of that?' Balfin demanded. 'Those birdmen are no push-over. We'd better not tangle with them if there is any other way of handling them.'

'I'm wondering if that skyraft was here for us,' Clark said.

'If they were responsible for the loss of *Probe* 2 then I'm on the side of the birdmen,' Balfin said, and Clark nodded.

'We'll have to try and make contact with those birdmen,' he acknowledged. 'We've got to try and find out what the deal is.'

'They didn't attack us instantly, like they did when the skyraft showed up,' Mallory said, and for the first time since they had left *Probe* 2 there was hope in his tones.

'I didn't get a look at the people on that skyraft,' Magenta put in. 'Did anyone see them?'

Clark shook his head. The others agreed with him.

'It happened too quickly,' Balfin said. 'But you can bet they'll be back. Are we getting out of here, Commander?'

'We don't know that they spotted us,' Clark pointed out. 'If we pull out we might land in worse trouble. I'm for trying to contact those birdmen. If we can learn what the situation is on this planet it'll help a great deal.'

'Looks like we're being approached,' Mallory said sharply. 'A couple of those batmen are coming this way.'

They peered from the starboard viewport, and Balfin spoke quickly.

'Commander, if they walk into our force field they'll think we're being hostile.'

'I'll cut the power. We'll have to take that chance,' Clark retorted. He depressed a button and a red light came on in place of the green. The next moment two birdmen were moving in towards them, cautious and ready to flee, their weapons in their hands.

'I'll go out and talk to them,' Balfin said. 'You can listen in, Commander.'

'Okay, but don't take any chances. Use the transmuter and try and get their language. The computer will soon break it down. Mallory, you stand by the hatch. Keep it open to let the

Major get back in quickly if necessary.' Clark paused. 'I'll cover you from in here with one of the main phasers, Kester.'

'I hope you won't have to use it,' Balfin retorted. 'It would make a mess of me too.'

He went to the hatch and Mallory opened it. Clark sat down in the observer's seat, arming the weapon bank and swinging one of the phasers on the manual control. He covered the two birdmen, frowning as he stared at them through the forward port. They looked like something out of a nightmare.

Balfin departed quickly and Mallory closed the hatch. The next moment Clark saw the Major appearing in front of the viewport, and he heard Balfin's voice as he spoke to the aliens. The computer clicked as Clark set it into action to take samples of the aliens's speech.

'We are friends,' Balfin said, wanting a response from the birdmen.

Clark watched the aliens closely, ready for trickery. But one of them twittered in reply, waving the arms that came out of the shoulders below the roots of the leathery wings. The computer clicked as the alien spoke at great length, and Balfin remained silent, waiting for translation to come through. The transmuter he was carrying was reporting the alien language to the computer, where it would be broken down and analysed. In a matter of moments they would be able to understand what the birdman was saying.

The twittering continued, a musical gibberish that could not be understood in any degree by humans. Clark waited tensely, ready to back up Balfin should trouble start, but then the transmuter began operating, and the computer programmed the strange language, analysing and relaying in English. Clark turned up the volume on the audio, and heard the twittering suddenly change into English.

'We know you are aliens,' the birdman was saying. 'We have some of your species living with us deep in the rain forests where the Brutans cannot find them. We have waged eternal war against the Brutans. We welcome you and invite you to come with us.'

Balfin heard the English translation and turned to gaze up at Clark, who had moved forward to peer down through the viewport. Clark lifted a hand and signalled that he would alight, and he turned to the hatch.

'Be on your guard, Mallory,' he warned as he passed through the small airlock. 'Just in case.'

Mallory nodded tensely and Clark dropped through the hatch to the ground. He took a quick breath, instinctively testing the air, and found it similar to the quality they were used to on Earth. He went forward to stand beside Balfin and regarded the birdmen intently.

'We welcome you,' the foremost birdman said, its beaklike mouth opening and snapping shut very rapidly. A twittering was coming from the creature, but the transmuter was relaying its words in English. 'I am Pacian, leader of the Avics. We have some of your species living with us in the forest.'

'Your words are cheering,' Clark replied, and paused to listen to the transmuter changing his English into the twittering language. 'We are friendly, but there are hostiles on this planet. Our ship was destroyed in orbit.'

'The Brutans,' Pacian replied. 'If you will trust us we shall conduct you to our secret places deep in the forest where the Brutans cannot penetrate. Take what you need from this craft and we shall destroy it before leaving. It would otherwise fall into the hands of the Brutans.'

'This ship is our only link with Space!' There was protest in Clark's voice. 'Can we hide it?'

'Impossible.' There was no emotion present in the reedy voice that came out of the transmuter speaker, but Clark fancied he detected a note of impatience. 'Please hurry. The Brutans will return. We are no match for them, but we fight them at every opportunity. If we are to survive then we must leave immediately.'

'One more question,' Clark said. 'You have some of our species with you. Who are they?'

'Men like yourselves, who came to ground from a spaceship. Their parent ship was destroyed by the Brutans when it entered Muta orbit.'

'Do you have any names?' Clark was thinking of his brother, aware that the Avic was talking about *Probe* 1 survivors.

'Later is the time for talking. Now we must leave. If you fail to accompany us the Brutans will get you, or worse still you may be captured by the Ogrins.'

'What about it, Commander?' Balfin demanded. 'We'll be taking a big chance by trusting them, but we can't argue about the trouble we'll find if that skyraft comes back with reinforcements. We've got to get out of here.'

Clark gazed into the beady eyes of the Avic, and took in the expressionless face. He inhaled slowly, held his breath for an interminable moment while his mental processes sought for a decision, and then he nodded.

'We'll go along with them,' he said. 'Let's take as much of the survival gear as possible, and destroy the shuttle before moving out.'

'That's kind of burning our boats behind us, isn't it?' Balfin asked quietly.

'We can leave it intact, but if the Brutans find it they will probably set a trap in the hope of catching anyone who is tempted to come back to it,' Clark said. 'Okay, I guess it would be good sense to leave it. I'll time-lock it, and with any luck it will remain intact in case we need it later.'

'Please hurry!' Pacian was hopping from one scaly leg to the other, and the feathers covering the lower part of his body were rustling in agitation. 'We have extremely well developed ears, and already I detect the note of a Brutan aircraft. If we are not clear of this place by the time they return we shall be unable to escape.'

Clark turned to the hatch and called to Mallory.

'Pass out four survival kits,' he ordered. 'Kill all power and circuits and bring extra weapons. We're leaving the shuttle here.'

There was an immediate protest from Rip Mallory, and his pale face appeared in the hatchway.

'You're crazy if you're planning on leaving the ship,' the Lieutenant retorted.

'You've been given a direct order, Mister!' Clark rapped. 'Get on with it.'

Four survival packs came tumbling through the hatch, and a moment later Magenta came dropping through to earth. The woman straightened, her face still pale, although she was beginning to recover from the shock she had received. She came scrambling away from the hatch.

'Look out!' she cried, and as Clark started forward the hatch was slammed and sealed.

'Get back!' Balfin snapped. 'Mallory is gonna take off.'

They hurriedly retreated as the power was switched on in the shuttlecraft, but even so they were lashed by the blast that came from the rockets as they ignited. Clark managed to get an arm around Magenta's slim shoulders as they went staggering, and they rolled on the soft ground together as the force of the rising craft struck them. By the time they regained their feet the shuttlecraft was forty feet above the tree tops and racing away.

'The fool!' Clark clenched his hands in sharp anger.

'Quickly,' Pacian said in his reedy tones. 'The Brutans are returning.'

Balfin ran back to the spot where their survival kits lay and snatched them up, tossing one of the packs at Clark. They hurried after the Avics, who were retreating among the trees, and as they reached cover Clark glanced back and saw two skyrafts sweeping into view across the clearing.

'I hope the shuttle is a match for those rafts,' Balfin said as they followed the swiftly moving Avics.

'The shuttle should be, but is Mallory?' Clark said . . .

They soon found that travelling through the forest was a nightmare. The fronds and undergrowth of the dark black forest made travelling difficult. There was little light amongst the trees when they got away from the clearing, and the ground was boggy under their feet. The air was heavy, oppressive, aromatic with heady perfumes and the scent of strange resins and oils. The boles of the twisted trees were more black than brown, and the foliage was brittle, thorny.

The Avics travelled easily on the ground, their ostrich-like feet taking their light weight whenever they found soft ground, and they were not heavily laden. A group of a dozen of the creatures accompanied Clark and his two companions, and they were deployed to give protection.

Clark found himself wondering about these creatures. They appeared friendly, and this was exactly what was needed at this particular time. But Clark could not dwell upon his personal aspects of the situation. He was concerned about Rip Mallory. The fool should never have been selected to join the advance landing party. He was not mentally equipped to face the shocks and rigours of alien confrontation.

But in the background of Clark's mind was the hope that his brother Vern was one of the survivors that had been mentioned. Impatience filled his mind and he made stronger efforts to move faster. The Avics could travel twice the rate of their present progress, and it was the Earth party holding them back.

Magenta was the first to crack under the strain of the fast pace. She was following Clark, with Balfin bringing up the rear, and Balfin suddenly called to Clark, who turned and saw the woman leaning against a tree in a half fainting condition. He in turn called to Pacian, the Avic, and went back to Magenta.

Pacian came back, looking like something out of delirium. His beady eyes were blinking furiously, his bat-like face working.

'We cannot stop here,' Pacian declared, his tones coming through reedy on the transmuter. 'We are in the area where the Ogrins hunt.'

'What are Ogrins?' Balfin demanded.

Before Pacian could reply there was a commotion nearby, a chaotic twittering and an immense roaring like an animal in pain. Pacian turned away instantly, producing a hand gun, and Clark looked swiftly at Balfin, who was staring in the direction the sounds were emanating.

'This is what I feared,' Pacian called thinly. 'We have made contact with an Ogrin hunting party.' He did not stop, and Clark dropped his gear and glanced once more at Balfin.

'Stay put with Magenta,' he ordered. 'I'll go take a look and find out what's doing.'

Balfin nodded, shaking his phaser from its holster, and his heavy face was set in grim lines as he crouched at the woman's side.

Veering right, Clark hurried after the fast moving Avic, and it struck him that this was the most incongruous situation he had ever encountered. He was acting in concert with strange aliens that looked more bird-like than human, and he was in the midst of a hostile environment. He dared not let his thoughts rest upon their ultimate fate. In the back of his mind was the certain knowledge that he wanted to get off this planet and return to his own kind, but that really was in the background. There seemed to be a great deal to be done before that eventuality took precedence over all considerations.

The next moment he was startled out of his thoughts,

coming to a halt behind the crouching Pacian. There was a small clearing ahead, and standing in it were two of the biggest creatures he had ever set eyes upon.

Clark stared at the monsters, and that was the only way to describe them. They were roughly anthropoid, standing around twelve feet tall, with bodies roughly proportionate—two-armed with tremendous hands. Their limbs were long and thick, and apart from a rough skirt around their loins they were naked, their flesh dark, mainly covered with a mahogany fur rather than hair. In a broad leather belt they carried a variety of weapons, including sophisticated energy guns, Clark noted instantly. But he let his gaze sweep upwards to their heads, and he felt a pang of wonder at the bestial expressions on the bearded faces. Their heads were blocky, looking as if they'd been carved from rock, and they had pendulous ears. The face was jutting, with long jaws, and sharp teeth showed plainly in the midst of the hair that covered the lower part of the features, while the nose was porcine, flat at the end with breathing apertures dilating rapidly and contracting to mere slits.

Pacian turned and spoke quietly to Clark, his beady eyes blinking. Clark fancied that he had awakened to some kind of a nightmare, but he took a grip of his faltering nerve.

'Our weapons are next to useless against the Ogrins,' the birdman twittered. 'They hunt us for food.'

Clark shook his head in disbelief, but there was movement in the small clearing and his glance was quickly attracted to it. He saw one of the Ogrins lumber sideways surprisingly fast, then reach into the undergrowth with a long, powerful arm. When the arm was withdrawn Clark saw an Avic clutched in the cruel fingers, and before he could move the Ogrin had bitten off the head of the birdman!

Pacian uttered a shrill twitter of anger and despair, and began using his weapon. Clark saw the Ogrins struck by the beams, and although they staggered under the impact, neither giant was seriously hurt. The one nearest them turned swiftly and came in to attack, and Clark unlimbered the Laser on his hip. He was being drawn into the fight whether he wanted it or not. . . .

Chapter Three

Mallory blasted up out of the clearing in a blind panic, his nerves strained to breaking point. He looked around wildly as he cleared the trees, and realized he'd made a mistake the instant he spotted four dots in the sky, rapidly approaching and taking the shape of skyrafts. He glanced back at the clearing, but it was dropping back out of sight, and he compressed his lips as he boosted the drive, intent upon escaping the trap into which they seemed to have fallen. He checked instruments and dials, and erected the deflector screens, wondering what type of weapons would be turned against him. It was useless now to try and hunt cover, and when he glanced backwards to check the position of the skyrafts he was shocked to find them effortlessly closing the distance.

He gunned the motor and shot ahead, but the rafts followed him as if joined to the shuttlecraft by invisible wires. His teeth clicked together when he saw he couldn't outrun them, and he clicked in the auto-pilot and moved into the observer's seat, depressing buttons, arming the ship's weapons, and tension began to fill him as he tried to prod himself into fighting.

There seemed to be no alternative, he thought remotely. He was unable to gain height for fear that the type of weapon that had destroyed *Probe* 2 might be used against him. He figured it would be useless trying to make a run for it. These strange craft had the edge on him for speed. He began to wonder what kind of a situation Clark had landed them in.

When he thought of his companions his lips tightened and a harsh expression settled upon his boyish features. He had begged Clark not to land anywhere near the habitations. He had warned of trouble, but Clark had been intent upon finding out what he could about the destruction of *Probe* 2, as if it would make any difference to the crew that had died aboard it.

He glanced out of the rear viewport and saw three of the rafts gaining on him. There was little to see aboard the alien craft. It was not frightening to stare at seemingly deserted ships, but suddenly beams of light winked at him from the cupolas on the craft, and the shuttlecraft juddered under the impact of the attack. He checked dials and satisfied himself that the screens were taking it, but he knew constant use of them would drain his power quickly, and when the screens became useless he would be at the mercy of these aliens.

Flight seemed to be the only answer and he channelled the power into the drive. He moved back to the pilot's seat and gave the shuttlecraft everything it could take. When he glanced out the rear viewport once more he was gratified to see that the skycraft had fallen back, and for the first time since he'd left *Probe* 2 he could smile.

His smile faded, however, when he checked his radar screens and discovered that other craft were in the sky ahead of him. He stared ahead, unable to spot anything, and tried to work out what next to do. A bleeper sounded then, warning him of attack, and he peered upwards through the astral viewport and saw a skyraft dropping down at him at incredible speed.

Mallory gave the computer control of the armament, and the next instant the Phaser banks were blasting at the intruder. He stared upwards, fascinated by the streaks of brilliance that cleaved the air, and the skyraft exploded in a mass of disintegrated molecules.

The shuttlecraft juddered again, but the screens held, and Mallory looked around. The ship's weapons were being controlled by the computer, and a battle was raging without his help. For the moment he seemed to be winning, and he clenched his hands and half wished he had remained with Clark and the others. His eyes glinted when he thought of Magenta, and a pang of frustration stabbed through him. But it was too late to think of going back.

He realized that the shuttlecraft was gaining height, and when he looked through the various viewports to check on his position he was astounded to see no less than a score of skyrafts after him. He was approaching a coastline, and he figured that once he was over the sea the skyrafts would close in to try and finish him off. He took over control of the ship, dived to get closer to the ground and make his target area more difficult to hit, and slammed the controls for as much power as possible. He sped across a large township, and could see figures running along the wide streets, many of them looking up at him. But everything passed by in a blur of speed, and he was trying to work out what to do. It was obvious he could not shake the skyrafts, and no matter how many he destroyed, there would be more to replace them.

A remote desperation seized hold of him. He was afraid to die. He had fled from Clark and the others because his nerve had been upset by the shock of what had happened to *Probe* 2. He had not recovered his mental poise, and now he seemed to be in a worse situation than before.

He wondered if he could get back to Clark. This was a matter of survival! If he could lose contact with these persistent aliens he might be able to locate Clark later.

He increased speed and swung in an arc, keeping as close to the ground as he dared. He used maximum-plus in his effort to evade the trap that was closing in about him. Sweat stood out on his brow and his hands shook as he handled the craft. His handling was a little rusty, because there had been few opportunities for practice during the long flight they'd made from Earth.

But the aliens were reluctant to shoot at him over the land he soon discovered, and for several minutes he began to figure he was pulling away from them. But he saw more and more of them arriving to join in the hunt and he fought off his despair. He kept the shuttlecraft moving at maximum while he considered what to do.

It was slowly coming home to him that by taking off as he had done he'd jeapordized the lives of the others by depriving them of their only means of escape from the surface of the planet. He narrowed his dark eyes and clenched his teeth. He had to get back to them. If he was meant to die on this expedition then he didn't want to die alone.

He swept back over the jungle in which Clark and the others had disappeared, but he had no way of knowing what clearing they had landed in. When he checked from the viewports he saw more than fifty skyrafts around him, all at a great distance, but appearing from all directions, and he could see that he was boxed in and completely trapped.

His one chance seemed to be in the jungle. If he could lose himself amongst the trees then he would stand a better chance of survival down there than obviously apparent in the sky. He began to watch for a suitable landing area, his mind filled with intolerable tension.

He swept over a clearing that looked at first glance as if it might be suitable, and he prepared to swing around in a tight arc to attempt a reckless landing. He dared not slacken speed until the last possible moment, and if he misjudged distance and speed he would crack up and probably kill himself.

Sweat beaded his forehead as he came around, and he saw

some of the skyrafts closing in on him like angry bees disturbed from their hive. He swept lower, braced in his seat, nerve summoned for a last desperate effort, and he fired the retractor rockets at precisely the right moment. He sagged against his straps as deceleration hit him.

Too late he realized that he would overshoot. He clenched his teeth and opened up the booster once more, straining the craft in every inch of its frame with the powerful surge. The craft tremored violently, began to lift in answer to the controls, then sideslipped, and Mallory caught his breath as he realized what was coming. But before he was fully aware of the situation the underside of the shuttlecraft hit the tree tops and upended. Mallory saw the dark foliage rushing up towards him, and then a black curtain fell before his eyes, blotting out sight and sound. . . .

Clark realized he was in dire danger as the nearer of the two Ogrins lumbered towards him. He lifted the Laser and prepared to fight, and his attention was almost distracted by the familiar sound of the shuttlecraft roaring overhead, invisible beyond the tree tops. Pacian was squawking angrily, but ready to retreat as the Ogrin came on despite the impact of the energy bolts the Avic was firing. Clark stepped around Pacian and levelled the Laser, and when he fired the deadly beam struck the giant and blasted him off his feet. Pacian twittered with delight, and Clark pressed forward to get a clear shot at the second of the two monsters.

In the background of his mind, Clark heard the sound of a terrific crash, and his teeth clenched together on his bottom lip as he fancied that Mallory had brought down the shuttlecraft. He stopped his concentration faltering and fired at the second Ogrin, knocking it down instantly.

Pacian flapped his wings and reached out a large, claw-like

hand to grasp at Clark's shoulder. The Avic was in a ferment of excitement.

'We have never possessed weapons powerful enough to harm the Ogrins,' he cried in his reedy voice. 'None of your friends had this weapon along with them when they landed. You will do well against the Ogrins. They will no longer be a threat to us.'

'I haven't come prepared to fight a whole species of aliens,' Clark said. 'Are there many Ogrins in this area?'

'They do not live here. They only come into the forest to hunt us. They live to the south, beyond the trees. But we must go on quickly. There will be more in this hunting party, and they will come for us.'

Clark was considering the crash he'd heard, and his eyes narrowed as he looked around. Balfin was coming forward once more, helping Magenta, almost lifting the slight feminine figure off the ground in his haste.

'I heard the fight,' the Major retorted, 'but there's more trouble coming up from the rear, I fancy. I can hear sounds of someone coming through the trees, and they don't have any care for stealth' He caught sight of the fallen Ogrins then, and Clark saw his face pale as he took in the monstrous proportions of the aliens.

'What the hell are they?' Balfin gasped.

'Ogrins!' Clark moved back. 'Follow Pacian and make as much speed as you can. I'll drop back to give cover. The Ogrins can't stand up to the Laser. Did you hear the shuttle-craft going over? I figure it crashed a couple of miles from here.'

'It's in the general direction we're heading,' Balfin said. 'We'll check it out on the way.'

Clark nodded and dropped back, ensuring he knew which direction the Avics were taking, and a strange silence fell quickly as soon as the familiar figures of Balfin and Magenta were lost among the trees. Clark remained behind a tree, listening intently, watching carefully, and now there were none of the heavy sounds Balfin had reported.

He glanced over his shoulder at the two dead Ogrins, and shook his head slowly as he tried to hold his shock in check. This was a nightmare that seemed to be getting more horrible as time went on. He glanced around again, keeping himself under tight control, and when he was satisfied that he was not being approached he prepared to slip away and follow his party.

He skirted the clearing and followed the faint trail that had been left. Now Mallory was very much in his thoughts, and he tried to judge the direction the crash had sounded. If Mallory had come down and was not dead he might be needing help.

The silence in the jungle was eerie now, and Clark kept looking around apprehensively. There was a brooding quality to the atmosphere, and none of the natural sounds that one normally associated with a jungle were now apparent. There were no signs of Balfin and the others, and Clark increased his pace to come up with them.

When he spotted another clearing he paused and lay in the undergrowth, staring at the small patch of blue sky that showed among the trees. A skyraft went silently overhead, and it was low. He could see dark figures aboard, and wondered at the Brutans, as Pacian had called them. If the Avics themselves and the Ogrins were anything to go by then the Brutans would also be horrific.

He moved on and was careful to remain under cover. He followed the faint tracks that had been left by his party, and hurried to gain on them. He knew they could be followed by the signs that were left, but he could not worry about probabilities while there was so much definite trouble to face.

Soon he caught sight of a couple of Avics acting as a rear-guard for the party, and they halted when they spotted him, testifying to their alertness. He spoke to them, reassuring them, then went on to where Balfin and Magenta were sitting down with their backs to a tree. There was no sign of Pacian and the other Avics.

'Pacian's gone on ahead with some of his men to check for Mallory,' Balfin said. 'They figure he came down around here, and they know the area better than we do.'

'I'd better go take a look.' Clark did not pause. 'You keep a sharp eye open, Kester. We don't want any more nasty surprises.'

'You can say that again,' Balfin said, and took hold of his Laser.

Clark hurried on, soon disappearing in the dense undergrowth, and he found it difficult to track the Avics, but he came eventually to sure signs that a craft had crashed. The tops of the trees were mown down in a swathe that stretched for many yards, and foliage was strewn on the ground, but soon the trees themselves were down, some of them uprooted at the impact with the shuttlecraft, and Clark pushed on until he came to the craft itself, lying in a twisted mass of broken trees, upended with its nose buried in the soft ground.

Pacian and four Avics were staring at the silent craft, and they did not move when Clark came up with them. Clark paused for a moment, his eyes narrowed as he took in the obvious signs of irreparable damage. Then he clipped the Laser to his belt and went forward to try and discover the whereabouts of Mallory.

He could not get at the hatch, and in any case it was sealed and would resist all efforts to be forced open. He clambered on the dented forward section and peered through a viewport, his lips thinning against his teeth when he saw the limp figure of Mallory hanging against the seat straps. He could see blood on

Mallory's face, but could not tell whether the man was dead or not.

Pacian trilled at him, and Clark turned enquiringly. He saw the leader of the Avics pointing upwards at the hole torn in the treetops by the descending craft, and framed there in the opening was the motionless shape of a skyraft, its very silence more ominous than if it had opened fire without warning.

Clark dropped to one knee on the front section of the shuttlecraft and reached for the Laser. He crouched a little as a beam stabbed down from the skyraft, and a number of trees to his left disintegrated instantly. Without waiting for more trouble, Clark fingered the mechanism of the Laser and subjected the alien craft to a shot. Immediately there was an explosion and the skyraft sideslipped to the ground, erupting in a white glare of brilliance.

Pacian came to the side of the craft. His beady eyes were bright, his bat-like face unable to show expression.

'Please, we must leave this area. It is too dangerous. The Brutans will be landing very soon now to check this craft. We cannot delay.'

'I'll be right with you,' Clark said. 'But first I must check on the man inside. I don't know if he's dead or alive.'

He turned to the shuttlecraft, lifting the Laser. The viewports were the most vulnerable to fire, and he was thankful Mallory had not erected the deflector screens. He chose a side viewport and hoped to avoid Mallory with the Laser beam. He fired the weapon and cut the viewport out completely, then leaned in through the aperture he had created and reached for one of Mallory's limp arms. He was surprised and relieved to feel a pulse beating weakly, and he turned to Pacian.

'Mallory is still alive. We can't leave him.'

'Can you lift him out? We will carry him if you get him to the ground.'

Clark climbed in through the opening and unstrapped the

unconscious man. He carried out a swift examination before attempting to move Mallory, and suspected the man had sustained broken ribs. Mallory had somehow struck his head at the moment of impact, and there was a nasty swelling on his left temple. Clark could not tell if the skull had been fractured, and he grunted with the effort as he tried to ease the limp body out through the shattered viewport.

The Avics came to help him and Mallory was borne swiftly away. Clark alighted and hurried after them, noting as he left the area that two more skyrafts had appeared over the broken area of jungle, and he knew they were not a moment too soon in departing.

Magenta had somewhat recovered by the time they returned to the spot where Balfin awaited Clark's return. They pressed on once more, the Avics struggling to carry Mallory, and Clark became increasingly uneasy as they went deeper and deeper into the forest. He was aware that he had placed to much trust in these strange aliens who had apparently befriended them, and all his training had been pointed to the fact that one could not trust aliens in any circumstance. But he appeared to have no choice in this particular situation, and he carried the Laser ready for action just in case his hunch proved to be correct.

They went on and on, and it was obvious to Clark that he would never be able to find his way back to the spot where they had landed. The shuttlecraft was gone, and with it their only means of escape from the planet. He did not want to dwell upon useless thoughts of what might happen. He could only go on with the hope that disaster was not waiting to overwhelm them. But he noted that the Avics began to lose their tension, and he assumed that they had left the danger area.

'How much farther to your camp, Pacian?' Clark demanded when they rested once more.

'We are almost there. In a short time now you will meet the survivors of the other spaceship.'

'Do these survivors have names?' Clark pressed. He could not but hope that his brother would be among them. 'How many are there?'

'Four, and they arrived in a ship such as the one you landed in.' The Avic spoke in his reedy tones, his bat-like face giving no expression.

Clark shook his head, feeling that it was hopeless that his brother might have been one of the four from four hundred. But Vern had been Communications Engineer on *Probe* 1, and it was possible that he had been selected to go with the advance landing party, as Mallory had been chosen for his own party.

They went on as soon as possible, and Balfin edged towards Clark as shadows began to grow densely around them. Clark looked at the tough Major, and saw uncertainty on the big man's face.

'What's on your mind, Kester?' he demanded softly.

'I'm wondering if we're making a mistake, going into the interior like this,' Balfin retorted. 'How far can we trust these aliens, do you suppose?'

'We're trusting them all the way,' Clark replied, and tried to kill his own uneasiness. 'Our lives are practically in their hands. We've got to go along with them, but just be ready for anything. That's all I can advise.'

'I'll feel a lot easier when we meet up with the survivors from *Probe* 1. When we've compared notes with them we'll know exactly where we stand.' Balfin tried to conceal his uneasiness, but Clark could see it in the background, and because this big man was uneasy, Clark found his own outlook deteriorating.

'It's getting near sundown,' Clark observed.

'It's been a long day,' Balfin retorted.

Presently the undergrowth began to thin out, and Clark

soon saw the sky in places through gaps over their heads. There were some dark clouds drifting quickly, and night seemed imminent. Clark felt strands of weariness wending their way through his consciousness, and as the shadows increased he became more acutely aware of his depression. They were a long way from home and all the indications were that they would never be able to return.

His thoughts were shattered by a sudden commotion ahead. The Avics were twittering like a flock of starlings, and somewhere an Earthman's voice was calling a sharp challenge. Clark caught his breath. Had they arrived? Were they amongst friends at last?

Chapter Four

Their surroundings were now too shadowed for Clark to make out any details as they moved slowly forward after the challenge, but presently figures appeared ahead, and the next instant two men were confronting Pacian and the two Avics carrying Mallory. Clark, with the semantics transmuter in operation, heard one of the men demand to know what had happened, and he was talking in the Avic language.

'Hello there!' Clark could not keep a tremor from his tones. 'Are you men from *Probe* 1?'

'Who the heck are you?' came the startled reply, and Clark grinned despite his sombre mood.

'We're the survivors from *Probe* 2!' he retorted. 'We fell into the same kind of trap that wiped out your craft.' He paused, unable to bring himself to ask the vital question about his brother. But it had to come, and he stiffened his lips as he went on. 'I understand there were four survivors from *Probe* 1. Who are they?'

'There were four of us,' came the reply. 'One was caught by the Ogrins a couple of weeks ago. We figure he's dead by now.'

'I'm Commander Theron Clark. My brother Vern was Communications Engineer aboard *Probe* 1. What happened to him?'

'I'm sorry, Commander, but your brother was not among us

who survived. There were only four of us in the advance landing party, and Commander Wragge was taken by the Ogrins a fortnight past. The three of us left are Lieutenant Paine, who's ill with some kind of poisoning, and two crew members. I'm Gunner Hanton and this is Mr Searby, a scientist. We're all that's left of *Probe* 1.'

Clark was silent for a moment, recalling the explosion that had claimed *Probe* 2, and he could imagine the explosion that had taken his brother's life. There was an image of Vern's face on the screen of his mind as he took a deep breath, then exhaled sharply to rid himself of the accumulated tension.

'How are you situated here, Hanton?' he demanded.

'Comfortable, but in a parlous position. The aliens on this planet, with the exception of the Avics, are terrifying.'

'We've met the Ogrins,' Balfin said, standing at Clark's side. 'What are the Brutans like?'

'They're more like our species than either the Avics or the Ogrins,' Hanton replied. 'But they're cold blooded. They kill at the least excuse. You have only to be an alien to give them the excuse.'

'They appear to be more advanced technologically than us,' Clark commented.

'They are, Sir,' Hanton agreed. 'But so far we've managed to hold our own against them. They don't penetrate this far into the jungle, which is fortunate for us. Do you have any weapons along heavier than the general issue sidearms, Commander?'

'We're equipped with a couple of Lasers,' Balfin said. 'We've already had a run-in with some Ogrins, and tangled with Brutans, although we haven't seen the Brutans personally.'

'We'll put you in the picture more fully after you've rested up, Commander,' Hanton said. 'If you'll follow us we'll take you into the camp and see you get some food and drink. I guess you've had a long trip, huh?'

'It's been a bad day,' Clark agreed.

They went on, and came eventually to a spot where the trees had thinned out but still gave good cover to the ground. There were several huts built under the trees, and small huts set among the lower branches of some of the sturdier ones, with here and there an Avic male, or female, squatting in the branches.

Clark sighed with relief when they entered one of the huts, and he got the chance to look at Hanton and Searby. Hanton was an oldish man, around forty, which was old for Space, and he looked into Clark's eyes as he turned up the wick of a lamp set on a heavy table.

'All the comforts of home, sir! Hanton said, grinning. 'We've settled in quite well. It may take you a time to get used to the surroundings, but it'll come to you eventually.'

'Are there any chances of getting off this planet?' Balfin demanded.

'We haven't found the means in the months we've been here,' came the pessimistic reply. 'The Ogrins aren't advanced enough to possess such craft, and we haven't dared venture into those areas where we might contact the Brutans. They would kill us on sight. There have been three determined efforts made to get us, but thanks to the Avics we've eluded trouble each time.'

'Sounds as if it isn't an uneventful place,' Clark commented. 'Where is Lieutenant Paine? I'd like to see him. Is he seriously ill?'

'The Avics says he will die. He's picked up some kind of poison. I don't like the look of him, sir, but I'm not a doctor, and there's been little I could do for him.'

'I've had medical training,' Magenta said, her dark eyes dull and showing shock. 'Perhaps I'd better take a look at him.'

'This way then.' Hanton sounded cheerful, and Clark

wondered if he would ever become as resigned to his fate as this man had evidently become.

They went to the next hut, and Hanton lit a lamp. Clark looked around and saw a figure lying on a pallet in one corner. He went across with Magenta at his side, and they both stared down at the pallid face of the unconscious man confronting them. Clark remained silent while the woman examined the man, and when she glanced at him her dark eyes were practically concealed by her curving black lashes.

'He's far gone, Commander,' she reported. 'How did he get poisoned, Hanton?'

'Something he ate, ma'am,' the Gunner replied. 'We've been very careful, and the Avics have been most helpful, but the poor Lieutenant ate some orange berries he found before checking with our friends the birds. The Avics reckon the Lieutenant won't pull out of it. It's a lingering death, they say.'

'You've got a couple of medical bags with you, Magenta,' Clark said. 'See what you can do for him, will you?'

The woman nodded and departed to fetch her equipment. Clark remained staring down at the Lieutenant's face for a moment, then turned to the watching Hanton.

'Is there any danger at this camp?' he asked.

'Not usually, Commander, unless the Brutans make a push to try and catch us. Normally they won't bother, but if they know they got *Probe* 2 then they'll be stirred up by another invasion by aliens. I think they might make a sweep to try and pick us all up.'

'We'll need to rest up a couple of days. I doubt if an attack could be mounted within that time.' Clark narrowed his eyes as he spoke. 'Then we'd better move into a safer area while we plan what should be done.'

'What can be done, apart from ensuring that we don't fall into alien hands, sir?' Hanton watched Clark with steady gaze.

'We'll have to see about getting off the planet!'

'Lieutenant Paine was always talking about that, but with respect, sir, it seems to me that it's only a hope we can hold on to for the sake of our confidence. There's no reality to it, as I see it. We'll be wasting a lot of time and effort that could be employed more usefully in other ways. I think we have to concern ourselves with survival.'

'That is the first priority, of course.' Clark nodded thoughtfully. 'But I was given a specific job to do. I've discovered now what happened to *Probe* 1. My task is to get that information back to Earth, and to prevent a second follow-up disaster. You know what will happen if they send a *Prob*e 3, don't you?'

'That goes without saying, sir, but what can we do about returning to Earth? Lieutenant Paine checked out the local situation as best he could, and came to the conclusion that it was not feasible to lay our hands upon an alien craft that might be capable of lifting us off this planet.'

'We'll go into details later, Hanton,' Clark said. 'I think any discussion will go all the better if I've rested and eaten.'

'Certainly, sir. I'll attend to the details. If you'd return to the other hut I'll see about some food.' Hanton turned to leave, but paused and lifted his steady gaze to Clark's face. 'I'd like to think there was a chance we could get off this nightmare of a planet, sir! We've been here a matter of months now, and I still can't believe that we're stranded here, amongst birdmen and giants and murdering monsters who have no pity. They wage a constant war, one against another, except the Avics merely fight for survival. They've been real friends to us, sir.'

Clark nodded. He could understand Hanton's feelings. It was beginning to get through to him that he was stranded for the rest of his life upon a monstrous planet that held nothing but danger and sudden death at every turn. But he could not afford to lose hope. That was the one quality they needed to help them try to get out of their difficulties. Without hope they were finished, and he accepted that.

They ate food, and afterwards Clark settled down on a pallet and slept, to awaken next morning feeling refreshed in mind and body and filled with a deadly resolve to get clear of danger. After breakfast he called a meeting, and faced his companions across the table. He looked into Kester Balfin's face, saw determination and resolve in the Major's eyes, and felt heartened. While he had Balfin at his side he could not be beaten.

But Magenta Sabir was looking strained and uneasy, and Clark felt a momentary pang as he studied her finely etched face. He half wished that she hadn't come along, for this was intolerable for a strongman, but she was here and he had to ensure that her chances of survival did not lessen because she was a woman.

Gunner Hanton and Frank Searby were silent and watchful, and Clark wondered if both men resented the appearance of newcomers. They had settled into a kind of existence that was not built on hope, and perhaps they did not have the strength of mind necessary for a change of outlook.

'How are Lieutenants Mallory and Paine this morning?' Clark demanded.

'Mallory has four broken ribs and concussion, Commander,' Magenta reported. He won't be fit to be moved for a week at least. Lieutenant Paine is still in a deteriorating condition. I don't think he'll live many more days. I'm going to have a talk with the Avic doctors this morning in the hope that there might be an antidote, but from what I've learned already from Gunner Hanton I fear there's little hope.'

'Hope is the one thing we must cling to,' Clark said, and tightened his lips when he saw Hanton smile softly and shake his head. 'I can understand how you can feel about the situation, Hanton,' he went on. 'I'm a new boy here, and you're thinking that I'll soon come to grips with the real situation and accept that we're lost for good, with no chance of getting away from Muta. Well I'm telling you the moment I lose hope we shall be lost completely. These Brutans have some pretty efficient craft.'

'Those skyrafts they dart around in aren't built to leave the atmosphere, Commander,' Hanton said. 'We got hold of one once and tested it.'

'If the Brutans are capable of building such craft then they have the technical know-how to build something better.' Clark could feel his eagerness striking upwards through his mind. 'I think we'll find a few chances left to us. But first I want a good briefing in the local situation. Until I know exactly what is what I won't know how or where to direct our efforts. Professor Searby, what can you tell me about the species of life on Muta?'

Searby shook his head slowly. He was medium-sized, with heavy features and unblinking brown eyes. He shrugged his thick shoulders and clasped his strong hands together, interlacing his fingers, and he leaned forward in his seat and stared straight into Clark's eyes.

'Commander, if you're thinking of trying to parley with the Brutans then you're making a big mistake. They have only one emotion, as far as I can ascertain, and that is a penchant for murder. They're a savage race with the skills of a well developed civilization to give their thirst for blood-letting a certain amount of sophisticated methods of achieving their aims. I had thought we might communicate with them and try to arrange for some fair treatment. We are, after all, aliens and intruders on their planet, and we ought, by all rules of conduct laid down by Space Law, throw ourselves upon their mercy. But I'm afraid we would be committing suicide by making any kind of approach to them.'

'What are they like, physically?' Balfin demanded.

'They're very like us in build, standing on average around two metres, and are humanoid in appearance. They must be the true product of this planet, the Ogrins and the Avics being some kind of deviation from normal evolution, and I believe this is the reason why the Brutans are so bloodthirsty. They're trying to rid the planet of these other species.'

'I can understand any race wanting to be rid of the Ogrins,' Clark said. 'But the Avics have proved themselves friendly and non-aggressive.'

'We have always found them so. They had no need to be disposed to friendship towards us, but they saved our lives in those first days of our being on this planet, and we have tried to repay their kindness by helping them in every way possible.' Searby glanced at Hanton, who nodded slowly. 'We have a debt to pay, and even if the chance to return to Earth arrived, I should feel reluctant to leave until I had done all that is possible to secure the Avics against their worst enemeies, the Ogrins.'

'The Ogrins eat the Avics, sir,' Hanton said, his face showing revulsion. 'I certainly agree that such a species should be exterminated without compunction.'

'I'm inclined to agree with you, after meeting two Ogrins,' Clark said softly. 'But we do not attack or fight unless we ourselves are attacked.'

'It would serve you better to talk with Pacian,' Hanton said. 'They have some technology at their service. We didn't manage to save our semantics transmuter from the shuttlecraft when we landed, but the Avics taught us to speak their language with no difficulty whatever.'

'Very well. I shall be pleased to talk with Pacian. I found him friendly and helpful yesterday.' Clark nodded slowly as he considered. 'But I assure you that I will work only towards one end, and that is the safe retreat from this planet.'

'Trying to find the means of escaping might necessitate asking for trouble from the Brutans,' Hanton said. 'That wouldn't be wise, sir.'

'Perhaps not, but you may rest assured that I shall not risk our security or our lives. However the fact that we are stranded on this planet does not excuse us from the duty we have. If it is at all possible for us to quit this planet then we must do so, and not spare ourselves in effort or risk to accomplish it.'

'I agree with you, Commander,' Balfin said. 'I think the first thing we've got to find is a different method of transporting ourselves. That stroll through the jungle yesterday is out for future movements.'

'I'm inclined to agree with you,' Clark said. 'Hanton, find Pacian for me, will you, and ask him if I may talk with him as soon as possible.'

'Very well, sir.' Hanton got to his feet and departed.

I'd better get back to Mallory and Paine, Commander,' Magenta said. 'They'll both need careful nursing for some time.'

'Do what you can for both of them,' Clark said. 'We shall not be leaving this camp for a week at least. We'll need to let the activity we caused by our arrival to settle down before venturing out, and I'll spend the meantime getting to know what I can about our surroundings.'

'It would solve everything if we could steal a craft that would get us out of this,' Balfin said thinly.

'I don't think we shall find it so simple,' Clark retorted.

Pacian arrived, twittering a noisy greeting, and Clark shook hands with the alien. He studied the bat-like face, and almost pinched himself to discover whether he was dreaming. But this situation was packed with stark reality, and he sat down and considered what he had to say.

'Pacian, I want to thank you for what you've done for my people here. But for your help they would surely have died.'

'We are friends,' the Avic retorted reedily. 'We ask for

nothing in return. We know that if we had been in your position you would have helped us.'

'That is true,' Clark said. 'And if there is anything we can do to help you now, even though we are in a poor position, then don't hesitate to ask.'

'We have common enemies,' Pacian twittered, rustling his leathery wings. His beady eyes glinted for a moment. 'We have always fought on the losing side because our weapons have not been powerful enough to destroy the Ogrins. But the weapons you have are good enough for that task, and if I asked you anything at all it would be to turn your Lasers upon the Ogrins.'

'As much as I want to help you to prove our side of this friendship business, I'm afraid I am governed by strict laws issued by my planet for conduct on alien worlds,' Clark said. 'I cannot use my weapons on any alien unless it is to protect the lives of my men. We can fight only in defence, and then only when all other means have been exhausted.'

'I understand, and I agree with that. But the Ogrins will attack. They do often, and if you are here when they come, will you fight?'

'Of course! But the real enemy, I imagine, is the race you call Brutans. They are more civilized than the Ogrins. They are the masters of Muta, aren't they?'

'They are. We fear them more than the Ogrins, although the Ogrins hunt us for our flesh. But the Brutans seldom venture into the forest, and if we do not stray from the trees we are generally safe from Brutan attack. They have sensors around the limits of the forests and they know when we leave.'

'That means we are also trapped inside the tree line,' Clark said slowly. 'That's not so good.'

'If you tell me exactly what you have in mind then perhaps I can help you,' Pacian said.

'Sure. I'm coming to that now.' Clark took a deep breath,

restrained it for a moment, then exhaled sharply. 'My duty is to make all efforts possible to return to Earth,' he went on. 'I need a space ship to get away from Muta. Do you know if the Brutans have such ships?'

'I cannot say. We have never ventured beyond the limits of the trees. Those of our kind who have, never returned.'

'You've seen those skyrafts the Brutans use,' Clark said patiently, and Pacian nodded. 'Have you ever seen any craft larger than those?'

The Avic shook his head, and the dull feathers on the upper half of his body rustled softly. His massive chest swelled as he breathed deeply.

'We have never taken any interest in the Brutans,' he admitted. 'They kill for pleasure. They set traps just inside the forest to catch our people, and when they have caught some they kill them in cold blood.'

'The Brutans and the Ogrins fight?' Clark asked.

'All the time. The Ogrins will eat Brutan flesh if they cannot capture Avics.'

'And yet the Brutans have not wiped out the Ogrins, who are savage and barbaric!'

'They are slowly succeeding in that. But the Ogrins are hard to kill. Only your weapons kill them easily.'

'A fact for which I am grateful,' Clark commented. 'But I have to leave the forest, Pacian. I must check on the Brutans, try to discover at what level their science and knowledge of technology rests. If they have space craft then I want one of them. It's a fact that they have a weapon powerful enough to destroy our spaceships in orbit, and we had evidence that they possess a kind of radar that tracked our shuttleship down to the ground. If we're to get off Muta then I've got to find a craft suitable, and I won't get one skulking around in the jungle.'

'I wish we could help you, but it is impossible,' Pacian told him.

'It will be sufficient that you supply us with a base to work from,' Clark said.

'That has been arranged. You are welcome to stay here as long as you like.'

'But I'm afraid that our presence here will bring trouble upon your people. The Brutans may start an all-out search for us.'

'They often fly over the jungle, shooting indiscriminately into the trees, and they have killed some of our people like that, but they are content to remain outside the trees and leave us to our lives so long as we do not encroach upon their territory.'

'Have you any idea where the towns and cities of the Brutans are located?' Clark asked.

Again the Avic shook its head and ruffled its feathers. The nearest thing to a smile that it could manage appeared on its strange face.

'I am afraid we are very unhelpful in this matter,' Pacian said. 'But I must warn you that it will be impossible to leave the trees without arousing an alarm.'

'We can overcome that problem quite easily when the time comes,' Clark said. 'I shall be leaving here today, with one man, and I can't say when I'll get back. I would like a guide to show me to the edge of the forest.'

'I'll arrange for one of my people to accompany you, and you will need food and water to take with you. Do not eat any of the fruits of the trees in the jungle. Lieutenant Paine is dying because he disobeyed that advice.'

'I understand.' Clark started to his feet, holding out a hand to the Avic. But at that instant the hut tremored and tilted, and a strange low growling noise became evident.

Clark clutched at Pacian in alarm, frowning.

'What is it?' he demanded swiftly. 'Is it an earthquake?'

'No,' the Avic retorted in twittering tones. 'It's the Ogrins! They're attacking us!'

Clark snatched up his Laser and ran to the doorway of the hut. Outside he saw a scene of confusion as Avics scuttled and flurried hither and thither. Then he saw the massive and ominous figures of several Ogrins emerging from the denser part of the jungle. The sight of their fearsome appearance sent a pang of alarm through Clark, but he lifted the Laser, and saw out of the corner of his eye Kester Balfin emerging from the next hut, where Magenta was treating the two injured men. As the Avics deployed in terror, Clark prepared to fight.

Chapter Five

There were seven Ogrins, and they came at the huts with all the skill of natural hunters. Beams of discharged energy struck at them as some of the Avics turned to fight, but the Ogrins merely shrugged off the effects of the weapons and did not falter. Clark was frozen for a moment, but he realized the danger they were in and shook himself free of his paralysis. As he prepared to fight he saw a Laser beam flicker and strike at the foremost Ogrins, and he knew Balfin was already in action.

Clark hit two of the monsters and saw them fall dead instantly, and his confidence was restored after being shaken by the sight of the way the Ogrins shrugged off the Avic resistance. But they were no match for the Lasers, and Clark glanced around as he sized up the situation. If he were making this attack he would have sent some men around to outflank the huts. He saw movement among the trees and realized the Ogrins were thinking tactically. Three monstrous figures were appearing from the trees to the rear.

'All-round defence, Kester!' Clark yelled, and his voice went echoing eerily into the trees. He cut down another Ogrin making straight for him, and saw that Balfin had accounted for the others coming from the same direction. But the jungle seemed filled with the monsters, and Clark moved towards the hut occupied by his two sick men and Magenta. He caught a glimpse of Balfin turning to run towards the other flank, and he sensed that they had the initiative momentarily.

He saw an Ogrin with two Avics in its grasp, and Clark gritted his teeth as he sent a beam into the monster's large body. The Ogrin crashed to the ground, writhing in agony and the Avics fluttered free and went squawking into the trees.

Clark saw two Ogrins approaching the side of the hut where Magenta was nursing the injured, and one of them stuck a fist through the side of the flimsy structure. Magenta screamed thinly, and Clark, aware of trouble coming up on his left flank, paused and shot the attacking Ogrin before looking around for fresh trouble. The stricken Ogrin crashed down on the hut, demolishing it, and Magenta continued to scream from somewhere inside the heaped debris.

The second Ogrin threw a short club at Clark, who ducked behind a tree. The club struck the tree with such force that it tremored, and pieces of bark flew from the point of impact. Clark was impressed by the strength of the Ogrin, and leaned sideways around the tree and shot the giant.

Balfin was calling from the right, and Clark transferred his attention quickly, then swung the Laser. Balfin was being rushed by four Ogrins, and two of the monsters were carrying a type of energy blaster.

Clark wondered remotely how many Ogrins were in the raiding party, and he held his fire as he was about to emit energy, for a trio of panic stricken Avics was fluttering from a new attack and crossed Clark's line of fire. He darted to one side, intent upon relieving the pressure on Balfin, and he managed to catch one of the Ogrins before Balfin was overrun.

Then suddenly the attack faded, and silence came creeping back into the area. Clark moved forward cautiously, ready for more trouble, and Balfin appeared with the other Laser, peering around, tense and keyed up for action. There were more than a dozen dead Ogrins lying around, and several Avics had fallen in the short fight.

'Keep your eyes open, Kester,' Clark rapped. 'I want to check on Magenta. She had a close call.'

Balfin nodded, his eyes glinting, and he began to make a search of the area as Clark hurried back to the huts. Avics were beginning to reappear, trilling and twittering tremulously, and Clark tightened his lips as he reached the hut and saw the dead Ogrin sprawled across it.

He found it impossible to move the heavy body, and put the Laser back on his belt and used his hands to lift some of the debris. The hut was made of branches, and not difficult to tear apart. There was fear in Clark's mind until he saw Magenta, and he slowly and carefully freed the girl. She was conscious but dazed, her legs pinned down under the weight of the dead Ogrin. Clark wrinkled his noise at the fetid stench that arose from the dead Ogrin, and he shook Magenta's shoulder to attract her attention. She stared up at him with dull, shocked eyes.

'I'll get help,' he said. 'You're all right. Just stay quiet.'

She nodded and he arose and looked around. Hanton was coming towards him, followed by Searby, and Balfin was in the background.

'Over here!' Clark called. 'I need some help.'

They came at a run and looked down at the dead Ogrin. Clark tried to hold his breath, for the stench was terrific.

'Let's try and lift him off the hut,' he said. 'Magenta's legs are pinned underneath him.'

They took hold of the giant's body, and the four of them had difficulty in dragging it aside. Clark didn't get time to look closely at the alien, but he was impressed by its size, and was relieved that the Lasers had proved effective against them. They dragged aside the rest of the debris of the hut, uncovering Mallory and Paine. Both men were unconscious.

Magenta was shaken but unhurt, and she quickly recovered sufficiently to supervise the removal of her patients. They were carried into another hut, and Pacian approached Clark and Balfin as order was slowly restored.

'I have never known such a concerted attack upon us,' the Avic said. 'Something has stirred up the Ogrins. They rarely venture this far into the forest after us.'

'I think it was us they were after,' Clark said. 'Probably the weapons we used against them.'

'We would have been exterminated if you hadn't been here with those weapons,' Pacian retorted. 'Is it possible to make other such weapons?'

'If we have the time we'll go back to the shuttlecraft that Mallory crashed and remove the armament. You could use that.' Clark nodded slowly. 'If you set up those weapons around a permanent camp you would hold off anything the Ogrins threw against you.'

'We shall move camp now,' Pacian said. 'We have another even deeper in the jungle, and we must go to it until the unrest and activity around here dies down.'

'I'll be moving out immediately,' Clark said.

'What's on?' Balfin demanded instantly.

'I'll tell you when we're on the move! Your company is all I need, Kester.' Clark looked around. 'Have you checked that the Ogrin raiding party has pulled out completely?'

'I'll check now,' Balfin retorted. 'Give me twenty minutes.'

'Some of my men will accompany you,' Pacian said.

'I'll talk to the others, tell them what I plan to do.' Clark turned towards the hut where Magenta had taken the injured. 'We're leaving as soon as possible.'

He went into the hut, to find Magenta bending over Lieutenant Paine, and Hanton and Searby were watching.

'What is it?' Clark demanded.

'I thought the Lieutenant was coming to,' Magenta said. 'But he's still out.'

'How is Mallory?'

'He hasn't recovered consciousness yet. He's badly concussed.' The woman turned her dark gaze to Clark's face, and he studied her for a moment. 'Thanks for saving my life! She sounded breathless as she spoke.

'Glad I was able.' Clark took a deep breath. 'I'm moving out shortly with Major Balfin. I don't know how long we'll be gone, but don't worry if it turns out to be a week or so. Pacian is moving to another camp in a safer part of the forest and you'll all go with him. Remain with the Avics until we get back.'

'Where are you going, sir?' Hanton demanded.

'We're going to check out the Brutans. If they have any kind of a ship that's suitable for getting us off this planet then we'll have to lay plans for stealing one.'

'Then I figure we needn't concern ourselves about when you might get back,' Hanton said sharply. 'You won't be coming back. In the first place it's impossible to leave the forest without activating the sensors the Brutans have erected, and if you did manage to get clear of them you'd soon be spotted and picked up by the Brutans.'

'We shan't get anywhere skulking around in the forest,' Clark retorted. 'I would rather die in the attempt at escape than accept that I'm stranded here with this nightmare of aliens for the rest of my life. But apart from that it's our duty to try and return to Earth with the information we have. I'll leave one of the Lasers with you, Hanton, and you'll protect the rest of the party. Pacian will give us a guide out, and we'll arrange for another to meet us on the way back. Don't take any chances in here, and try to stay out of trouble.'

Hanton nodded. 'I'm all for trying to get away, sir, but I

feel that you'll be risking your life for no real purpose. We're trapped on this planet and there's no way out.'

'I'll check on that for myself, and if I am satisfied that we cannot get away then we'll sit down and try to work out what to do next. But I'm a hard man to satisfy, and I shan't quit trying to get off Muta until I've exhausted all logical efforts.'

'Good luck,' Hanton said.

'I'm thinking that perhaps Professor Searby should go with us,' Clark said. He looked at the older man. 'How would you feel about taking on a dangerous mission?'

'I was hoping you'd ask me,' Searby replied, smiling thinly. 'I may be of some help to you in determining the value or ability of any craft we come upon. I would like to go along. I've skulked around in this forest far too long, and if there had been someone here with the ability to fly a spaceship I would have attempted what you're planning now. It's the only chance we have.'

'Good.' Clark held out his hand. 'I'm glad you're thinking like me. Let's get ready. We'll pull out as soon as possible.'

Pacian soon organized their supplies of food and water, and when Balfin returned Clark was ready to leave. Balfin was enthusiastic about the trip, and agreed that it should be made. Pacian arranged for their guide, and Clark was satisfied that when they returned to the jungle they would be able to locate a guide to lead them to the new camp.

They set out with the Avic guide in the lead, and Clark turned once to glance back at the huts as they followed a faint path. He saw Magenta standing in the doorway of one of the huts, and when she waved a farewell he lifted a hand and acknowledged. Then the scene disappeared from view and they were enclosed in the living forest.

Clark soon found that the journey on the previous day had taken a great toll of his strength, and within minutes he was sweating and slowed by his exertions. He saw that Balfin was similarly affected, and was concerned by their apparent lack of stamina until Searby spoke from the rear.

'I think we should abandon this trip for a few days, Commander. It's obvious to me that you are not acclimatized to Muta. If you take a rest now you'll find that you'll be able to handle the trip with no discomfort later.'

'We'll push on,' Clark retorted doggedly. 'I've got the feeling that if we don't make the effort now it may be impossible to summon it later. What about you, Kester?'

'I'm doing all right,' Balfin retorted, and turned a sweating face towards Clark. He grinned and added: 'Let's keep going.'

Clark nodded and they went on, finding that after an hour their bodies accepted the strains of movement and they could continue without too much effort. It seemed that they were returning along the same route that had brought them to Pacian's camp the previous day, and Clark worried about it, afraid of ambush. But there didn't appear to be other living creatures in the jungle, and the air was stifling under the dark foliage.

It came home to Clark as they made slow progress that the situation in which he found himself was fraught with danger, and it became only too obvious to him that this mission was practically hopeless from the start. He could almost understand Hanton's lack of hope. They were far away from Earth. Space was too big for Man, took him into many situations that he was not mentally equipped to face, because none of his ancestors had ever been away from Earth. Therefore he had no instincts upon which he could call for help when needed, and no matter where he looked, there were too many reminders that he was on an alien world for him to be able to overlook the fact for long.

They halted at noon, although they could not tell the time by the sun because the sky was invisible to them through the foliage except when they reached small clearings, when their view was somewhat curtailed anyway. But the Avic was at home in this environment, and he moved with an assurance that Clark would have felt back on Earth.

They reached a stream and paused to rest and eat. Steam arose from marshy ground to their left, and Clark shook his head slowly as he gazed around. The water in the stream was dark and stagnant, and he wondered what kind of alien life forms frequented it. They didn't pause too long, and went on, filled with a sense of drudgery, sweating continually in the heat. They passed a clearing cautiously, and Balfin, carrying the only Laser they had brought along, halted in the shelter of a tree to escort them past the danger.

Clark looked into the clearing as he went by, and was almost safe when a strange sound caught his ears, faint at the outset but growing quickly louder. He paused and looked back at Balfin, who was peering at the sky over the clearing, and Clark tightened his lips when he spotted a craft swooping in towards the clearing. It wasn't one of the skyrafts they had seen previously but a more complex machine not unlike the shuttlecraft in which they had descended to the planet.

Balfin was behind a tree, the Laser ready in his hands, and Clark glanced the other way, motioning for Searby and the Avic to remain motionless. They watched the craft settling slowly to the ground. It fired rockets at the last moment to arrest its descent, then settled very gently upon extended legs.

Silence came and there was no movement around the craft. Clark imagined that the occupants were studying their surroundings before alighting, and he did not take his eyes off the alien machine. It was already in his mind that if they could capture the craft they might gain an invaluable advantage.

He saw movements behind the viewports in the side of the craft, and wondered at the origins of the occupants. Were they

Brutans? He had heard a great deal about the cold bloodedness of the race, but so far had not set his eyes on any examples of the species.

The Avic guide was coming towards Clark, who heard the faint sounds of the movement and turned his head quickly to caution silence. There was no expression on the Avic's face, but its movements were fast and nervous, giving Clark the impression that there was danger here. He switched on the transmuter as the birdman reached him, and the faint twitter that came to him was translated instantly.

'We must get away from here,' the Avic warned. 'That is a Brutan craft and they have sensors aboard that can detect our presence even when they cannot see us.'

'If that's the case then they've already detected us,' Clark mused. 'They've been sitting there for some minutes. I was wondering why they didn't alight.'

His forehead prickled coldly as he continued watching, waiting for some movement to herald the emergence of the craft's occupants. But suddenly a flaring light emanated from a small rod sticking out of the nose of the craft, and before Clark could move the light encompassed the nearer trees and dissolved them into a fine dust. The beam began to swing around as the craft seemed to spin upon its own axis, and trees were disappearing rapidly.

The Avic was grasping at Clark's arm, and he knew they had to get out of there. It was fortunate that the craft was turning away from their position or they would have been enveloped before they realized what was happening. Clark moistened his dry lips and turned to look at Balfin, who was crouching and aiming at the craft. Balfin was glancing towards Clark, awaiting orders, and Clark looked at the machine once more and realized that it would be deluging their position with the strange light before they could hope to get clear. He looked at Balfin once more and made a sweeping gesture with his hand towards the craft. Balfin nodded grimly and returned his attention to the target.

The craft was spinning slowly, and trees were disappearing easily under the bombardment of the strange ray being operated. Clark watched with a kind of fascinated horror as the falling trees vanished into dust, and the disturbance was creeping steadily towards Balfin's position.

Balfin was holding the Laser steady, and Clark wondered why the Major did not shoot. He began to tingle with anticipation, then fear, and the alien craft was turning all the time, slowly coming around to their position, bringing with it the certainty of total disintegration.

But the Major knew what his object was. He wanted the craft as whole as possible after evicting the Brutans, and he waited until the nose of the craft was coming to point directly at him. The falling trees marked the point at which the strange weapon was operating, and it came steadily closer to Balfin, taking in all the trees in an area of twenty feet from the edge of the clearing. Balfin expected the craft was using deflector screens for self protection, but there had to be a gap in those screens to enable the alien weapon to operate. He was waiting to put his shots in through that gap.

Clark found he was gritting his teeth. His hands were clenched and sweating. He was breathing shallowly, feeling breathless in the stifling atmosphere. Sweat ran down his face and trickled down the hollow of his chest. He could feel his nerves tightening intolerably.

Then Balfin sighted along the Laser weapon and fired, aiming for the muzzle of the alien gun. Clark watched intently, saw the Laser beam strike the front of the craft, and there was an immediate explosion. The next instant a bright flash enveloped the craft and a pall of smoke arose, blotting out all sight of the craft.

Balfin moved to Clark's side, his face showing amazement.

'What the hell happened?' he demanded.

The Avic was tugging at Clark's arm, calling urgently for them to move on, and Clark shook his head slowly. He would have given anything up to his right arm for that alien craft to have fallen intact into his possession. He motioned for Balfin to follow and moved away from the clearing, glancing back at the smoke-obscured craft as they struck into the jungle.

They hurried on for an endless period of time, until Clark was practically exhausted, and the Avic turned away from the invisible course he was following every time he sighted a clearing ahead. Once they heard the sound of an aircraft passing overhead, but failed to spot it through the dense foilage, and Clark was wondering what was going on. He fancied that the aliens were making a concerted effort to get at the intruders visiting their planet, and for a time he was concerned that Pacian might underestimate the forces building up against him and permit himself to be trapped.

They walked all day, and Clark was stumbling like an old man by the time the Avic called a halt. He sank down and lay on his back, sprawled over a mossbound root, and gasped for air. He glanced towards Balfin and saw that the Major was as badly pressed as himself. Searby, although a lot older, was not nearly so exhausted, and he grinned sympathetically as he came to Clark's side.

'You've done better than I thought you would, Commander,' Searby said. 'But in a few days you'll be able to make this trip without any trouble at all.'

'I guess the fact that we were cooped up on *Probe* 2 for months has something to do with it as well,' Clark gasped. 'But how far is it now to the edge of the jungle?'

'I've just asked the Avic, and he says thirty minutes walk from here will take us out of the trees. It will be night very shortly, and we'll have a better chance of getting clear of the mechanical cordon at the tree line if we wait till darkness.'

Clark sighed with relief. He would not be sorry to get into the open countryside again, despite the added dangers. But he felt oppressed by the trees around him, and longed for a lungful of sweet open air.

They ate and drank sparingly, and then Clark moved through the growing shadows to the Avic's side. First he thanked the alien for his help during the day, and the Avic rustled its wings with pleasure.

'Now what can you tell me about this mechanical cordon around the edge of the jungle?' Clark demanded.

'There are sensors set out, invisible to the eye, hidden where you cannot see them, but they record your passing and strange weapons operate in blanket fashion, deluging the areas where the sensors are activated with different types of energy beams to destroy all living cells.'

'Pacian said some of your people filtered through the cordon, but did not return. How did they get through?'

'There is a concealed tunnel through a hill on the edge of the trees. If you go through the tunnel you will emerge beyond the area of the cordon.'

'I wish I'd been told about it before we set out this morning,' Clark said. 'It would have saved me a considerable amount of brain-racking. Are there any dangers once we are through the cordon?'

'I do not know. None of our people have been that far and returned to tell us.'

That sounded ominous to Clark, but he said nothing. Balfin was sitting nearby, and had heard what was said. Now he spoke softly.

'I think we're going to have to move by night, Commander,' he said. 'Once through the cordon around the trees we can slip across country with no trouble at all. I had time to take a good look at the terrain as we passed over it on our way down. We'll have to make for one of the cities we spotted in the distance. It will be our only hope of gaining information.'

Clark nodded. Already his mind was flitting ahead, although he knew he could not make any hard and fast plans because he had no idea what to expect in the future. But he was certain before they set out on the most dangerous part of the mission that it was going to be extremely difficult, if not impossible, to gain any kind of success.

Chapter Six

Their Avic guide began to grow nervous as they reached the edge of the forest, and finally he halted and refused to go nearer the tree line. Clark could understand the alien's fear. He was not feeling confident himself, but he needed to know where the tunnel was located, and persuaded the Avic to show them the entrance. The alien agreed and they went on.

The hill reared up outside the jungle, with its lower slope inside the tree line, and Clark paused when they could see the starry night sky. Something akin to relief went through his heart when he saw the sky, and he was surprised for a moment by sight of two moons, one yellow and the other almost orange. Then he recalled the observations that had been made of Muta aboard *Probe* 2 before they swung into orbit, and the knowledge that had been forced out of his head by the shocking events since beginning the first orbit returned to his aid.

'This way,' the Avic said in reedy tones that were stilted with fear. 'The tunnel is about a mile long, and it will be completely dark. You'll have to feel your way through, but have no fears, the tunnel is straight and level.'

'And what can we expect to find on the other side?' Clark whispered. The moonlight was brighter than that of Earth's sattelite, but under the trees the shadows were dense, and it struck him as grotesque that he was standing here talking to a birdman who was rustling his feathers and showing all the signs of unrest one expected in a broody hen.

'I cannot say,' came the quick reply. 'None of our people who have got that far ever returned.'

'Then how come you know about the tunnel, and what it is like right through?' Balfin cut in.

'Some of our men have gone as far as the other end of the tunnel but no farther.'

'All right.' Clark nodded. 'We're on our own now. Thanks for bringing us this far. I hope you'll get back to Pacian's camp without trouble.'

The Avic nodded and turned away, leaving Clark peering at a narrow opening in a steep part of the hillside. When the alien had gone, Clark turned to Balfin and Searby.

'We'd better push on,' he said. 'Give me the Laser, Kester. I'll lead the way.'

'Let me go first, Commander,' the Major protested. 'I'm more accustomed to this sort of thing than you are. You'd better hold on to my belt so we don't get separated in the darkness. Searby, you stick close to the Commander.'

Clark secured a hold on Balfin's belt as the Major eased into the opening, and the Professor grasped Clark's belt. They entered the tunnel and shuffled forward, and almost immediately Clark knew it was going to be a nightmare passage. The air was stifling, dank and fetid, and their footsteps echoed eerily in the blank darkness. But Balfin struck forward boldly, the Laser clutched in his right hand, his left hand extended, his fingers moving along the side of the tunnel. He was trusting the Avic's description of the tunnel in order to make good time, but it took a lot of nerve to stride out as if he could see every inch of the way.

To Clark the tunnel seemed never ending. He dared not let his imagination have full control, for he was aware that they had not yet encountered any insect life on this strange planet.

The animal life was nightmarish, and he had every reason to suppose that the smaller creatures and beings would be equally grotesque.

But they reached the end of the tunnel without incident, and Balfin uttered a long sigh of relief when he finally thrust through a tangle of thick undergrowth and glimpsed the clear starry sky. Clark moved to Balfin's side, breathing deeply of the keen night air, and some of the depression that gripped him seemed to slip away as he stared around. Searby remained silent at their backs, content to let them make the decisions and the plans.

'Are we through the cordon, I wonder?' Clark mused aloud.

'I think it's my job to find out,' Balfin said. 'Stay put while I go forward a couple hundred yards. I'll check it out as quickly as I can. I doubt if there'll be guards on duty. I expect the Brutans have rigged up some kind of a force field, or a death trap that is activated by movement.'

'I expect you're right.' Clark nodded as he stared around. The bright light from the twin moons was disconcerting. Everywhere seemed bright as day, although the shadows were black and well defined. But details were visible, and Clark knew their moving figures would easily be spotted if there were guards patrolling the tree line. He fancied that even if guards were not on duty normally, the fact that aliens had landed on the planet might arouse the Brutans to some sort of extra activity.

Jumping to conclusion would not help his peace of mind, he realized, and he thinned his lips as he watched Balfin moving away. He saw the Major's figure all too clearly, and at each instant he was half expecting trouble to strike. But Balfin slowly vanished into the distance, and there followed a timeless period when there was nothing to do but stand in the shadows and wait out the sluggish time.

'Someone's coming!' Searby suddenly hissed, and Clark started and looked around. He saw three figures moving from right to left across their front, and knew at once that Balfin could not be one of them.

The moonlight was deceptive, but Clark judged the figures to be at least head and shoulders taller than average Earthmen. He clenched his teeth and narrowed his eyes as he tried to make out details. The strangers were thirty yards out, following the bottom of the slope of the hill, and they were dressed in dark clothing that concealed all but their outlines.

'Brutan?' Searby whispered, and Clark ducked, dragging the professor into cover, for the strange trio halted abruptly and were turning to survey the slope. 'Did they hear my whisper?' Searby went on in shocked tones.

Clark made no reply, and he took the small energy gun from his belt. The gun had been no use against the terrible Ogrins, but he was hoping that it might have some effect upon these newcomers, if the need for action arose. He peered down the slope, his eyes narrowed, his mind working on the chances at their disposal, and he tensed when he saw two of the newcomers starting up the slope towards their hiding place.

'They're probably carrying some type of sensor,' Clark said slowly. 'I don't think they could have picked up the sound of your voice, Searby. But stay down now. I won't shoot unless it's vital.'

The two strangers came closer, and Clark began to make out details. They seemed even taller than he had at first supposed, because they were down-slope and foreshortened, but as they drew nearer Clark realized they must be at least eight feet tall. They were humanoid in outline, moving forward swiftly on two legs, and they each had two arms. Clark saw they were carrying weapons, and recalling the type of weapon that had been operated from the craft they had encountered in the jungle, Clark knew he could not afford to take any chances. He crouched with the gun ready in his hand, and in the back of his mind was the fear that Balfin might return and stumble upon the third alien waiting below.

The two Brutans came on without hesitation, and Clark soon realized that they were making for the spot where he and Searby were crouched with uncanny accuracy. He tightened his grip upon the gun and waited for the first hostile movement. The two newcomers were closing the distance rapidly, and they were carrying fairly long rods in their hands, as yet not pointing in Clark's direction.

It was in Clark to fire, but he hung on, hoping against hope that they two would pass by. Then, when it seemed that they would stumble upon the entrance to the tunnel, a brilliant beam of light cut through the darkness and struck the pair. Clark blinked against the glare, realizing that it was Balfin in action, and he breathed a silent prayer of relief that Balfin had been selected to accompany him.

A second blinding flash darted from the middle distance, and Clark saw the third alien struck by the lethal burst of energy. He pushed himself to his feet, moving out of cover, and started towards the two aliens on the slope. He saw Balfin appearing below, moving towards the third Brutan.

There was not much left of the two aliens, Clark discovered, and his face was grim as he bent over to examine them. They were dressed in light cloth tunics, now tattered and burned, and their weapons had fused with their flesh. They were big men, very tall, and although it was difficult for Clark to ascertain their physical appearance with any accuracy owing to the damage caused by the Laser, he accepted that they were very similar to himself. He straightened as Balfin came hurrying up.

'You all right, Commander?' the Major demanded. 'I was

watching this trio for some time. There's a camp of them about a mile from here.'

'Did you get close to them?' Clark demanded.

'Sure! Crawled in as close as I could. They're the nearest thing to normal I've seen since we landed.'

'They look similar to us, but two feet taller,' Clark said. 'These three were thirty yards from us, Kester, and when they were exactly level with us they stopped and came straight for us, as if they knew we were here.'

'I spoke in a whisper,' Searby said slowly. 'It's possible they were carrying a sonic detector.'

'It's no use trying to check on what they were carrying,' Balfin retorted grimly. 'It's impossible to make anything of the mess I made of them.'

'Are we going on?' Searby demanded. 'We can't leave these lying here in the open like this. They'll be missed, and if they're found an alarm will be raised.'

'I'll get rid of them,' Balfin said. 'There's a pit not far from here. I almost fell into it on my way out, and when I dropped a stone into it I couldn't hear it strike the bottom.'

'I'll give you a hand,' Clark said. 'But I don't like this as a start to this mission. If the Brutans discover we're shooting on sight then they'll treat us as enemies and wipe us out.'

'I had to cut loose,' Balfin said sharply. 'I didn't know what their intentions were. It was a case of shooting first and asking questions afterwards. From what the Avics say, the Brutans are lustful killers, and we can't afford to take any chances.'

'You did the right thing,' Clark agreed without hesitation. 'But I still don't like it.'

They disposed of the bodies, then went on their way, moving in single file, slowly and cautiously. Balfin led, the Laser ready in his hands, and Clark looked around as they walked steadily. They were in the midst of farmland, and the fields were open and unhedged. They saw no buildings, no habitations of any kind, and Clark began to worry, because they had to find a hideout before the sun showed, and this land seemed devoid of sufficient cover.

Balfin dropped into a stream and they splashed across, waist-deep. As they emerged on the farther side there was a snorting sound and a quick movement of the shadows nearby. A few sparse trees fringed the stream, and Clark had been staring at them, afraid they might be concealing danger. Now he saw an animal of sorts charging at them, snorting and gnashing gutterally. Balfin paused and then moved forward a couple of paces to put himself ahead.

'It's a Byn,' Searby said. 'I've heard the Avics talk of them. They're half boar, half some alien form of life, and very dangerous.'

There was no time to say more. The animal, which was around four feet tall, came charging in recklessly, and Balfin set himself, then shot the animal, filling the shadows with brilliance that flared, winked, then died. The creature was stopped in its tracks, and Clark took a swift breath as his tension eased.

'Have they got any other shocks in this place we can expect to meet?' Balfin demanded, not turning his head. He was staring towards the trees. 'Are they wild animals, Searby?'

'They run wild, but they are bred by the Brutans for food. They have arms on top of their shoulders, but no hands. Each arm terminates in a curved horn that's sharp as a razor. There are great numbers of them out here on the plains.'

'Let's move on,' Clark said. 'We'd better be careful in further encounters, and try to evade trouble rather than shoot it down. We're leaving a trail that might easily be followed when the sun comes up.'

'I agree with you,' Balfin retorted. 'But this time I had no chance to take evasive action.'

Clark mentally agreed, and they went on. Time passed and the twin moons seemed to slide across the velvet sky. There were pungent scents in Clark's nostrils, and underfoot there was a short, grass-like vegetation bearing small flowers that gave off the perfume as their feet crushed tiny petals. Clark could only hope their feet would not leave a trail on the ground.

Presently the ground turned soft and became marshy, and Searby called a halt. They paused and closed, looking intently around, ready for any kind of trouble.

'We'd better skirt this marshy land,' Searby said. 'I heard the Avics talking about the marsh people who live further in. They're cannibals too.'

'It seems that dog eats dog on this planet,' Balfin said harshly. 'But what we want to find won't be lying around in any swamp. We'd better angle to the right now, staying close to the marsh until we sight one of the cities.'

Clark looked at the sky. The stars were fading, and the light from the moons was waning. He estimated that two hours would see the sun coming up.

'We're not going to make much progress between now and daylight,' he commented. 'I suggest we start looking for a hideout until nightfall again.'

'What's that up there?' Balfin demanded, and Clark looked in the direction the Major was pointing. 'It isn't a cloud, is it?'

Clark frowned as he tried to make out the dark object that was blotting out some of the stars. He saw that it was moving, and dropped to his knees.

'Get down,' he said. 'It's an aircraft.'

They dropped flat and lay motionless watching the large craft coming towards them. Balfin was covering the machine with the Laser.

'No shooting, Kester,' Clark warned thinly.

'Unless they start shooting at us,' Balfin retorted. 'It's hopeless, Commander. If we wait for them to show hostility we'd be dead before I could retaliate. The kind of weapons they carry, we don't stand a chance loosing off last.'

'I know, but we can't fight every single alien we come across. We'll wind up dead ourselves without ever having a chance of finding what we're looking for.'

They fell silent, watching the craft, which was moving very slowly. Clark fancied that the alarm had already been raised and the Brutans were searching for the aliens who were loose. Then he heard a pounding that might have been caused by a herd of stampeding animals, and when he raised himself to peer around he spotted a dozen Ogrins running rapidly through the night.

Balfin looked, and levelled the Laser.

'No shooting,' Clark warned. 'It looks as if that craft up there is herding those Ogrins.'

'Why aren't they trying to kill one another?' Balfin queried.

'Perhaps the craft hasn't sighted them yet!' Searby pointed out the distance between the Ogrins and the position of the aircraft.

'We could get lucky and have the Brutans calculate the Ogrins are doing our killing,' Balfin suggested.

They watched, and the Ogrins went thundering by only yards to their left. Clark suppressed a shiver as he stared at the giants. They would be at home in any nightmare, he told himself, and switched his attention to the sky. The aircraft was coming closer, descending imperceptibly, and suddenly the night was ripped asunder by darting beams of blinding light. Clark closed his eyes and lay still, and he became aware of a strange tingling sensation invading his system. He guessed it was the effects of the weapon being used by the aircraft, and when he raised his head he saw the beams striking down at the Ogrins. Some of the giants were already stretched out, and the others were separating, running swiftly into the night.

The aircraft sped overhead and Clark looked up, trying to check if it was a skyraft or one of the different type they had encountered in the jungle. He could not tell, and when the craft had disappeared in the general direction taken by the Ogrins he got slowly to his feet.

'Let's get out of here, and we'd better keep our eyes open for a ground search,' he said. 'It looks as if the Ogrins have been out on a raid of some kind.'

They moved on again in their original direction, and Balfin led as usual. But they had barely covered two hundred yards when the Major halted and lifted a hand to signal them to drop to cover. Clark crawled forward to Balfin's side, and the Major pointed to a moving figure ahead of them.

'An Ogrin,' Clark said through his teeth.

'A straggler,' Balfin said. 'He's coming this way.'

They waited tensely, and presently the Ogrin was close enough for them to see him clearly.

'He's got something slung across one shoulder,' Balfin whispered.

Clark narrowed his eyes and tried to pierce the gloom for details.

'It could be a Brutan,' Searby put in. 'It's moving slightly. Are you going to stop it?'

Clark considered quickly. Then he put a hand on Balfin's shoulder.

'Can you get him through the head, Kester?' he demanded. 'If that is a Brutan we could take him prisoner and try to get some information out of him. We're sadly in need of information.'

Balfin nodded and lifted the Laser, waiting for the giant to come closer. Clark glanced around, wondering about the aircraft and the other Ogrins, but the night was silent and still, and then Balfin fired, the Laser beam striking the Ogrin in the head. The tall figure crumpled to the ground and lay still, and the figure that had been slung across its shoulder went sprawling to one side.

Clark was on his feet and running forward almost before the Ogrin hit the ground, and Balfin joined him. They passed the motionless Ogrin and bent over the giant's prisoner.

'It's a Brutan all right,' Searby said, coming up quickly, his breathing laboured. He bent to examine the figure. 'And it's a female!'

Clark tightened his lips at the news. He bent over the alien and felt for a heartbeat, finding it pounding strongly, and he straightened and looked into Balfin's shadowed face.

'She's alive,' he commented.

'What are we going to do with her?' Balfin looked around. 'She could be the reason why the Brutans are attacking the Ogrins. I think we'd better get out of here, Commander. The question is, are we taking her along?'

'Carrying her is out of the question, and she's out of her senses at the moment.' Clark stared down at the motionless figure. The woman was a good seven feet tall, and heavily built. She was big boned and solid, with wide shoulders and hips and long limbs. Light coloured hair hung down to her shoulders.

'She's coming to,' Searby warned, and Clark saw the female begin to stir.

'Maybe we can tie her hands,' Balfin suggested. 'We shan't be able to control her once she sees us.'

Clark took a strap from his pack and attempted to bind the woman's thick wrists together, but gave it up after several attempts. The woman was coming to her senses, and she lifted her hands to her temples, groaning loudly as consciousness returned. Then she pushed herself up on one elbow and looked around, stiffening when she saw the dead Ogrin, then the three Earthmen.

Clark was ready with his semantics transmuter, and he spoke in what he hoped were reassuring tones.

'Don't be afraid. We will not harm you.'

She stared at them for a few moments, then spoke quickly in gutteral tones, her voice sending harsh echoes into the shadows around them. Clark waited, and she spoke again, quickly, imperiously. Balfin was covering her with the Laser, and she glanced at him, understanding the menace he constituted.

'Keep talking,' Clark said, although he knew she could not understand him. 'Be kind to us and give the transmuter enough to work on.'

She obliged, breaking into a tirade of seemingly angry questions, but she glanced from time to time at the dead Ogrin and seemed to know that they must have destroyed it and probably had saved her life.

Then the transmuter began working, and Clark sighed with relief when the unintelligible sounds were suddenly translated into English.

'You three are some of the aliens who have landed on our planet,' the woman was saying. 'Our people are searching for you. What are you doing now? Are you seeking to destroy us?'

'On the contrary,' Clark said into his microphone, and waited for his words to be translated. 'We are aliens and we have only one wish. That is to leave your planet peacefully as soon as possible. Our spaceship was shot down, like the one that came before us, and we are stranded here on Muta. Tell me, have your people, the Brutans, mastered space travel?'

She was silent for a moment, surprised because his voice was reaching her via the transmuter and in her language. Clark watched her large face, hoping she would not attempt violence. They would have to kill her to silence her.

'We have proved our friendship,' Clark went on smoothly.

'The Ogrin was abducting you and we killed him to save you.'

'Beware!' Searby called urgently. 'The aircraft is coming back.'

The Professor's voice reached the transmuter and was translated into the Brutan language, and Clark saw the woman glance up into the sky.

'Please do not attempt to communicate or signal our presence,' Clark said quietly. 'If you do we shall be compelled to kill you.'

The woman seemed to understand the threat, for she glanced at the watchful Balfin, then looked at the dead Ogrin. There was silence while they crouched and watched the alien craft moving silently through the darkness of predawn. . . .

Chapter Seven

The Brutan female got slowly to her feet after the craft had passed over, and Clark found her towering over him. She was perfectly proportioned to her size, and he felt a strange thrill in his heart as he let his gaze take in what details he could in the poor light. But he forced his mind to concentrate upon essentials.

'Where do you live?' he demanded. 'How did the Ogrins capture you?'

'They raided our farm. My parents were killed.' There was no emotion in the woman's hard tones.

'Where do the Ogrins live?'

'In villages on the edge of the forest. We are slowly exterminating them, but they are hard to kill. You must come with me to the town and I will hand you over to the security guards.'

'I'm afraid we cannot agree to that,' Clark said. 'We have heard that your people kill for the pleasure of it. We arrived in orbit around your planet in a ship carrying four hundred crew members, and all except four of us died when the ship was struck by a missle fired from the planet. It was the second of our ships to be destroyed in this manner. Your people were responsible, and we cannot permit ourselves to fall into their hands.'

'You will be picked up in a matter of hours from dawn,' the

woman said, and started walking rapidly in the direction Clark and his companions had been taking.

Clark found that he had to trot to keep at her side, and Balfin followed, his Laser ready for action. Searby was soon being left behind, and Clark reached out and seized hold of the woman's arm. She jerked herself free with no trouble and looked down at him.

'Not so fast,' Clark said. 'Let us talk.'

'I cannot help you in any way,' she intoned. 'If I were found in your company I would be killed along with you.'

'But we saved your life,' Clark retorted. 'Surely you have some gratitude or appreciation.'

'We are alien to your way of life, and it would be difficult for you to understand us. We are not concerned about dying. We kill to survive. We wage a constant war against Ogrins, Avics, Merscs and the wilder animals. Death is common among us, and we do not hold any great attachment to our relatives. My parents were killed a short time ago and this does not concern me.'

'What are Merscs?' Clark demanded. He hadn't heard them mentioned before, and he wondered what other type of life survived on this horrific planet. He felt they couldn't be any worse than the Ogrins.

'They live on the water, in the swamps, and they are little people, about half my size. But they are carniverous and they live on a diet of Brutan and Avic.'

Clark shook his head slowly as they walked on, and he held the woman's arm. She kept up her fast pace, and Clark was soon breathless, but she would not slow, and they went on and on through the darkness that attended the planet in the hour before dawn.

Eventually Clark spotted a cluster of buildings ahead, and when he saw they were making for them he commanded the woman to halt. She stopped and turned to face them, and

Balfin came up to Clark's side, holding the Laser ready.

'We are determined not to be captured,' Clark said. 'If you have no wish to die then you must do as I say.'

She considered for a moment, her shoulders hunched, looking down at them as if they were boys and she an angry adult. Clark could feel the beginnings of despair in the back of his mind. He knew he could not permit her to be killed if she refused to obey him, and a sense of impending doom tried to grip him.

'I will die anyway if I help you,' she said. 'The weapon you carry would make a quicker job of my death than the methods used by my people.'

'I can quite believe that,' Clark retorted. 'But there is no need for you to die. We do not want to kill you. We take no pleasure in bloodletting. Just agree to hide us until the next period of darkness and we shall leave you in peace.'

'And when you are caught you will tell my people that I hid you!' She shook her head. 'I will not help you.'

'Then you'll die,' Balfin said, lifting the Laser.

She bowed her head and stood waiting to be killed, and Clark clenched his hands. He shook his head as he looked at Balfin.

'We can't kill her,' he gritted between his teeth.

'That is what I gathered from your words,' she retorted with a low laugh, and turned and went on towards the buildings.

Balfin uttered a low curse and swung up the Laser. Clark pushed the weapon aside.

'It's our life or hers, Commander,' Balfin rasped.

'Let's go to the farm with her. If we have to we can make her a prisoner and hold her captive until we move on.'

'But if the Ogrins raided the place then there'll be a bunch of security guards buzzing around tomorrow,' Balfin retorted.

'That's a chance we'll have to take. We've got to start looking for a place to hide. We shan't be able to move during daylight.'

'That's all right by me, but I'm not turning squeamish about these aliens,' Balfin said harshly. 'They've already killed around eight hundred of our people. Don't be fooled by the fact that she's a woman, Commander. She's more cold blooded than any man I've ever met.'

'It's her way of life. She doesn't know any different!' Clark tried to make excuses as they hurried after the tall female. 'If we can make friends with her it will half the difficulties facing us. What we need is an ally who can get information for us. I can think of no one better than a Brutan female.'

'All right, we'll try it your way,' Balfin agreed reluctantly. 'But I'll kill her quickly enough if I have to. Our lives are forfeit on this planet. From what we've learned about these people so far we can have no real expectation of survival. If they want to fight then that's all right by me, and I'll play it according to their rules. No quarter and no mercy!'

'I'd go along with that if we had any chance of winning,' Clark said tensely. 'But we can't fight a whole nation, Kester. The best we can hope to do is find a suitable spacecraft and escape. If we can't manage that quickly then I see no chance for us. We'll either be killed or taken prisoner, or have to flee into the jungle and live out the rest of our days with the Avics.'

'I don't even fancy that,' Balfin said through his teeth, 'and I don't like the idea of being captured by these Brutans. I figure we're in a bad hole, Commander. I'm ready to listen to any reasonable plan for escape.'

'I'm trying to think of one,' Clark retorted.

They were almost running to catch up with the Brutan female, and Searby was straggling, evidently exhausted by their long trip. The woman glanced back at them, and lengthened her stride, and Clark saw they would soon be at the nearest of the farm buildings. If there were other occupants there then he guessed they would be discovered. He was aware that it was pointless trying to parley with the woman, and he took his personal gun from his belt, setting it for minimum emission. He fired at the big figure, and Balfin stared at him in surprise as the woman went down in a crumpling fall.

'What the hell!' Balfin exploded.

'I've merely stunned her,' Clark said through stiff lips. 'We can't take any chances, Kester. If she bursts in on others at this place then we're going to find more trouble than we can cope with. We don't have much time. Daylight is coming, and with it will come trouble. Let's bind her if we can, and gag her, then go check out the farm. If it is deserted we'd better try and find a hiding place there until tonight. Then we'll push on.'

'Now you're talking my language,' Balfin said. 'You hold the Laser while I bind her, Commander. We could dump her in that ditch over there if it's dry. We don't have a big time margin now.'

Clark mentally agreed, and they bound the unconscious woman and gagged her, then struggled to carry her into the ditch, which was dry and overgrown with weeds. They set her down gently and covered her over with undergrowth. Clark intended returning for her as soon as possible, and figured she would come to no harm where she was for thirty minutes or so.

'Now let's get on to the farm,' Balfin said, holding out his hand for the Laser. Clark handed it over and they went on, moving swiftly, leaving Searby behind once more. When they reached the outbuildings they eased into cover and examined the place.

'It looks deserted,' Clark said.

'I'll handle it,' Balfin retorted, getting to his feet. 'It's my job. Stay put with Searby, Commander. If I run into trouble there's no need for all of us to find it. I'll go through the place.'

Clark nodded, and lay looking around intently as Balfin moved forward. Daylight was beginning to creep across the plain, and to Clark it seemed that the nightmare was not ending with the coming of the sun. He watched Searby crawling in the last few yards, and realized that he shouldn't have brought the older man along. But they were committed and they had to go on taking their chances, regardless of the outcome.

'What's happening?' Searby demanded, flopping down at Clark's side.

'The Major is checking out the farm.' Clark did not take his attention from his vigil. He fancied that as soon as full daylight arrived there would be a large scale search of the area by the Brutans. They would be looking for Ogrins, without a doubt, but any extra activity was against Clark's plans.

Tense moments passed, and Clark was expecting trouble. Nothing had seemed to have gone right for them from the moment they detached from *Probe* 2, Clark thought remotely. But presently Balfin appeared, waving to them, and they got up and hurried forward.

'The place is deserted,' Balfin said. 'There's no one around here, only some farmyard animals in some of the other buildings. What happens now?'

'We'd better get our prisoner into the house and lie low,' Clark said slowly. 'Let's go get her.'

Balfin nodded. He seemed more cheerful now. They went back to the ditch and had a tough time dragging the woman out of it. She weighed as much as the two of them combined, Clark thought, and as the sun began to peer over a distant ridge he was able to get his first good look at her.

The Brutan woman was like an Amazon, he discovered. While she was not beautiful by Earth standards—her features were too broad and squat for that—she was enough like an Earth female to give Clark some faint stirrings of homesickness. She was still unconscious as they lifted her with difficulty, and Clark was hard put to get his hands around her limbs. They stumbled into the farm, and Searby was waiting at the door of the house to let them in.

Clark sighed with relief as they lowered the woman on to a couch. He moved to a window to peer out across the plain.

'I looked around from an upper window,' Balfin reported. 'I saw what looked like a town in the distance. I figure it's where we'll make for come nightfall. But it doesn't look large enough to contain what we need.'

'If we could pick up some kind of transport,' Clark said suggestively, 'we would cover more ground and make our attempt with less risk.'

'There are one or two smaller buildings around that I haven't checked out yet,' Balfin reported. 'I'd better go look them over now, although I doubt if they house Brutans. You'd better watch our female prisoner pretty closely, Commander.'

'I won't let her out of my sight when she regains her senses,' Clark said. 'Searby, you look around and find out what kind of food these Brutans eat and see if it's suitable for us.'

Balfin departed and Searby went through the lower rooms of the house. Clark remained with the prisoner, watching her intently. Daylight was upon them now, and the first rays of the sun were spreading across the ground outside.

Clark saw the woman was dressed in a short skirt of some heavy dark material, and an open-necked blouse. Her face was asiatic in appearance, dark and stolid. Sight of her made Clark think of Magenta Sabir, and he sighed sharply as he fought down his imagination and tried to keep the more important aspects of the situation in mind.

Searby came back shortly, pausing in the doorway to look at Clark.

'There's plenty of food here, Commander,' he reported. 'It is eatable. The Avics have some very much like it. It will sustain us with no ill effects.'

'Perhaps you can throw us some breakfast together then,' Clark said.

Balfin returned shortly, and there was a tight grin on his gaunted face. He glanced at the unconscious Brutan female and then turned his attention to Clark.

'You'll never guess what I've found in a shed outside,' he said.

Clark shook his head. He didn't feel like guessing games. Balfin stared at him for a moment, then widened his grin.

'One of those skyrafts we've been seeing in the air,' he said. 'Think you can fly it, Commander?'

Clark felt a surge of hope, but then tightened his lips. He shook his head.

'I don't think we could make good use of it even if we could fly it,' he said. 'We couldn't use it during the day, and it might be dangerous after dark.'

'Take a look at it anyway,' Balfin said. 'It might come in handy if we have to get out of here fast.'

'I'll wait until the girl comes to and talk to her about it. Let's get something to eat, then organize watches so some of us can start resting. It's going to be another tough night tonight.'

Balfin nodded. 'These Brutan males are around ten feet tall, aren't they?'

'That's what I gather, and looking at this female, I can quite believe it.' Clark studied Balfin's serious face for a moment. 'What's on your mind?'

'It would have helped if one of us could have masqueraded as a Brutan and gone into that town for a look around.'

Clark shook his head. 'Too risky,' he decided. 'We're going to have to do this the hard way.'

'That's what I was afraid of.' Balfin grinned tiredly. 'What are our chances of getting away from this planet, Commander?'

'Not good, I'm afraid.' Clark didn't want to talk about it. He was tired and dispirited, and yet he had to find hope from somewhere and use it to instil the same emotion in his subordinates. If he became hopeless then his men would quickly lose determination and ability.

'The woman is coming to.' Balfin moved across the room and stared down into the female's face.

Clark went across, and when the woman opened her eyes he spoke to her.

'I had to render you senseless for a time,' he said. 'But you are recovered now, and nothing else will happen to you if you do as you are ordered. We must stay here in your house until darkness falls again. It will be a long day, but you will have to endure it the same as we shall.'

She made no immediate reply, but stared intently into his face with large brown eyes. Clark stifled a sigh. She was going to be awkward, he knew, and that kind of complication they could very well do without.

'Be on your guard, Kester,' he said at length. 'I'll go check out that skyraft. Where is it?'

Balfin explained, and Clark left the house, carrying his personal sidearm. He stared around before walking out into the open, feeling uneasy as he gazed across the empty plain. Nothing moved out there in the bright sunlight, and the sky was empty. He wondered about it as he crossed to the shed Balfin had mentioned. Back on Earth if this situation had existed there would have been troops and aircraft out in force after a raid such as had been carried out by the Ogrins, but here on this alien planet no one seemed to care what happened.

He went into the shed and found the skyraft, his professional instincts instantly aroused. For a moment he stood looking at the craft. It was about forty feet long by ten wide, and the cupola to the rear was barely large enough for four persons. Clark walked around it, realizing that it was too large to pass through the doorway, and when he looked up at the roof he discovered that it would open.

There was a hatch in the rear of the cupola, and it opened to Clark's touch. He climbed into the craft and sat down in the pilot's seat, gazing at the strange control console, trying to understand it. The controls were few and apparently simple, and he felt an itch to try the craft but fought down the impulse. He was strangely indecisive, and it worried him. Normally he was quick-witted and fast to react, but since they had been on Muta he had been slowed down. He wondered if it were the atmosphere, and drew a sharp breath as he alighted from the craft and went back to the house.

Searby was almost through with making breakfast, and the smell of cooked food made Clark aware of his hunger. He went to where Balfin was watching their prisoner, and the Major looked up at him with interest.

'Any luck with the skyraft?' Balfin demanded.

'I think I could fly it if I had to,' Clark said, nodding. 'But I wouldn't test it for fear that we might be spotted.'

'It's obviously a runabout,' Balfin said. 'I expect every Brutan family has one.'

'That could be, and I've been figuring that all the craft we have seen were military ones.'

'From what we've seen of the Brutans so far I'd say they didn't need an organized police or military force,' Balfin commented.

Clark nodded slowly. He looked at the woman, who was still tied. She was watching him intently, great dark eyes staring into his face. He switched on the transmuter.

'If I untie you and give you food will you promise not to try and escape or raise an alarm?' he demanded.

She regarded him for a moment, then nodded slowly, and Clark moved towards her.

'Don't take any chances, Commander,' Balfin said thinly.

'We've got to feed her. We can't treat her harshly, Major.'

'I'm thinking of the fix we'd be in if she got away from us and raised the alarm.' Balfin was concerned. 'We're a long way from the forest.'

Their voices were picked up by the transmuter and the woman understood everything they said. She got to her feet when Clark had released her, and faced them, looking down at them from her great height.

'I will not betray you to my people,' she said.

'Why should we believe you?' Balfin countered.

She shrugged. 'I am interested in you. I know you are aliens, from a far distant planet. I would like to know more about you. It is obvious you are not as big as our men, but you have accomplished much.'

'I'll be glad to exchange information with you,' Clark said. 'Let's go eat, shall we?' He glanced at Balfin. 'Perhaps you will remain alert until I relieve you, Kester.'

'Sure.' Balfin nodded. 'But don't let that female get the better of you, Commander. If she does make a break for it and I get her in my sights I'll burn a hole through her.'

The woman smiled thinly and led the way into the kitchen, where Searby was serving out the food he had prepared. They sat down, and Clark watched the woman for a moment, afraid that she would suddenly try to trick him. She was too powerful for him to handle physically, and he felt that he could not shoot her down in cold blood if she did try to get the better of him. She seemed to sense his dilemma for she smiled and shook her head.

'Eat your food and do not worry. I will not attempt to trick you.'

Clark began to eat, and the food was not bad. But his mind

was not on the meal, and he tried to elicit information from the woman. At first she would not speak, and he was at a loss on how to proceed. Then he decided to try a friendlier approach.

'My name is Theron Clark,' he said. 'How are you called?'

She stared at him for a moment, then got up and went to a nearby cupboard. Clark watched her closely, his hand on his gun. But she came back with a tall jug, and poured creamy milk into large beakers, pushing one of them towards him.

'I am Ralip,' she said. 'I am alone here now. My parents were killed two weeks ago by Ogrins.'

'And you were attacked last night?' Clark shook his head. 'Why haven't the authorities sent troops to deal with the raid?'

'They chased off the Ogrins last night, and they know that by sunrise the Ogrins will have got back to their homes. You saved my life. We are not given to emotion. It is not bred in us. Life here is arduous, and we do not let our minds have any power at all to move us. But I thank you for taking the trouble to kill the Ogrin and free me.'

'It was my pleasure.' Clark smiled. 'Where we come from people are friendly. One man will help another if there is trouble, and all men will go out of their way to help a woman in distress.'

'I cannot see male Brutans doing that.' She chuckled in harsh tones.

'Will you give me the information I need?' Clark demanded.

'What do you want to know?'

'If your people have ships that are capable of leaving the Planet?'

'We have those ships. They fly between Muta and the other planets in the system.'

'The Brutans trade with their space neighbours?' Clark demanded.

'Of course! But you will find it impossible to steal a ship in which to escape. That is your plan, is it not?'

'It's the only chance we've got of escaping back to our own world.'

'And what would you do about Muta if you got back to your own world? Would other ships come to make war because of the two ships you have lost?'

'No!' Clark shook his head. 'Our people might try to make contact with yours, in the hope of creating friendship. But if they met with more hostility they would merely keep well away from Muta.'

'I wish I could believe that. I might be persuaded to help you escape if I thought you were speaking the truth.'

'I would not lie to you,' Clark retorted.

'Let me think it over. I owe you for saving my life. You have shown me kindness, and I would repay you. We are a proud race if nothing else, and a debt must always be paid.'

'Thank you!' Clark felt his hopes begin to rise. But at that precise moment Balfin called to him from the front of the house, and the Major's words sent a sharp pang through Clark's mind.

'Commander, we've got company coming. Three skyrafts are heading this way, and it looks as if they gonna settle down in the yard.'

Clark sprang to his feet, his teeth clenching, but the woman grasped his arm as he started for the door.

'You and your friends had better stay out of sight,' she said thinly. 'I'll go out and talk to them. They'll be police, checking up on the raid last night.'

'I have to trust you,' Clark said slowly.

'It is the only way. I have to go out to them. You can trust me. Stay under cover, for if you are seen it will be my life as well as yours that will be lost. Brutans are forbidden to aid aliens.'

'All right!' Clark nodded slowly. 'Get out there and do what you can. I'll trust you, Ralip.'

She smiled harshly at the sound of her name on his lips, and went through to the front of the house. Clark followed, stifling Balfin's protests when the Major learned the chance they were to take. They crouched by a window and watched intently, and it seemed to Clark that time stood still as they waited for the craft to come in and land. The girl was standing tall and erect in the yard, and Balfin was training the Laser on her back. But it didn't ease Clark's mind to know the woman would die if she betrayed them, for they would soon follow her into oblivion. He mentally crossed his fingers as he waited for developments. . . .

Chapter Eight

'She's not betraying us!' Balfin said hopefully after several minutes of conversation had taken place between the woman and four of the newcomers.

Clark nodded slowly. 'I think we can trust her,' he said, and smiled slowly. 'Correction! We are trusting her, and we'll have to go on trusting her. I don't see any other way out of this. We'll never make it alone!'

'I'm inclined to agree with you now.' Balfin sounded depressed, and Clark looked at him. They stared at one another. 'We are in the hell of a fix, Commander,' Balfin went on. 'I can't remember ever getting into a tighter spot.'

'Let's try and take it as it comes,' Clark said. 'It's the only way. We're still at liberty, and that's something. Look, Ralip is coming away from them.'

'They're leaving!' There was relief in Balfin's tones as they watched the Brutan men moving back to their craft.

'I'm hoping we'll never have to fight them,' Clark commented. 'There's not one of them under eight feet.'

They watched in silence as some of the skyrafts lifted steeply from the ground, and the woman paused by the door to turn and watch the others taking off. The craft swept away towards the distant forest, and then the woman turned and entered the house. Clark waited anxiously for her to report.

'They asked about the raid,' Ralip said, smiling thinly.

'They are only concerned about the Ogrins. Most of the raiding party were killed last night, and they're looking for wounded or stragglers.'

'They didn't mention the aliens who landed?' Clark asked.

The woman shook her head. 'They have not talked of you' She stared at Clark for a moment. 'I want to help you. Now that I've lied to the Authorities about the situation here my life is forfeit if they find you in my company.'

'We'll leave immediately, unless you have a hiding place where we can stay until nightfall!' Clark was eager to show that he had no intention of using her without consideration for her own position.

'There's a hiding place, but if you hide by day and walk by night you will never reach the place where the space ships are stationed.'

'You know where they are?' Balfin asked eagerly.

'I have been there several times to watch them take off and land. I could take you by air to the place and show you the big ships.'

'I couldn't walk around openly without betraying myself to your people,' Clark said.

'You would not leave the craft. Your two friends could hide here until we return.'

Clark glanced at Balfin, who was nodding slowly.

'Sounds like a good idea, Commander,' the Major said. 'If you could only get a look at one of their craft it would give you some idea of our chances. We've got to know what they're like and where they are. But that skyraft is big enough for more than a couple of people. Let's all go and stick together.'

'One of you will have to return to the forest to fetch the others of your group,' the woman said.

'But no one can move out of here without risking capture until nightfall,' Clark retorted. 'How long will it take us to look over the spaceport and return?'

'Half the day.'

'I'll stick around here with the Professor,' Balfin said. 'We'll be okay.'

'I'd rather we stuck together,' Clark retorted.

'There is an old saying about all the eggs being placed in one basket, Commander,' Frank Searby cut in.

Clark nodded. 'All right. I'll go joy-riding while you two lay up here under cover.' He looked at the woman, who was watching him intently. 'Where are the farm workers? You don't run this large place alone, do you?'

'There are no workers! We use machinery to do all the chores. I merely supervise. If I could afford a larger place I could run it unaided.'

'Good!' Clark was satisfied there would be little danger to Balfin and Searby. 'Where can they hide while we're away?'

Ralip led them through the house to one of the rooms at the rear, and they watched while she operated a hidden switch and revealed a large chamber behind a blank wall.

'This is where we hide when the Ogrins raid,' the woman said. 'You will be safe in here.'

'And if the Ogrins ever set fire to the house?' Balfin demanded.

'The house is fireproof,' she retorted.

Balfin and Searby entered the secret chamber, and before Ralip closed the door Balfin held out the Laser.

'You want to take this along, just in case, Commander?' he demanded.

Clark shook his head. 'I wouldn't get the chance to do much good with it if I got into trouble,' he said slowly. 'You keep it. If I don't get back for any reason then you'll have to go ahead with our plans without me.'

'I understand.' Balfin nodded. 'Good luck! Watch out for the route to the spaceport and make notes on the layout, if you get the chance.'

The door closed and Clark turned away. Ralip seemed eager to be on her way now, and they hurried out to the skyraft garage. Clark entered the machine and watched while the woman opened the roof and checked the motor. Then she came aboard and settled in the pilot's seat. She directed Clark to sit on the floor between the front and rear seats.

'If you are spotted inside the craft we will be destroyed. Stay down at all times. There are always a lot of aircraft over the town, and the police and security guards carry out spot checks. You will be able to see all you want from that lower viewport.'

Clark nodded, turning to peer out of the circular port set in the side of the cupola near the floor. Ralip started the motor and the next instant the skyraft lifted neatly out of the garage and soared into the sky. Clark felt his spirits lift as they whirled away, and he turned his head to peer down through the viewport. His brown eyes glittered as he watched the countryside disappearing swiftly beneath them.

This was the way to travel! The thought passed through his mind. He could see now that if they had continued to travel on foot they would have failed completely. He glanced at the big figure of the alien woman, and a sense of wonder stabbed through him. For the first time since *Probe* 2 was destroyed he felt a pang of hope, and felt that perhaps they were destined to escape this hostile planet.

They sped over a large town, and Clark looked through the port and stared at the wide streets and saw the tiny figures of people moving around. He was suddenly struck by the fact that there were no vehicles of any kind on the streets, and raised the point with Ralip. The woman smiled thinly as she glanced at him.

'We do not use street vehicles any longer. They went out years ago. They were slow and dangerous, and caused great pollution of the air. These craft are cheap and easy to operate, and they do not pollute.'

Clark nodded. He returned his attention to the ground, and they left the town behind and continued, heading, as far as he could judge, in a northerly direction. He saw that there was a countless number of skyrafts operating in the air over and around the town, and he stayed low between the seats, ignoring the cramps that began to assail his chest and neck. He was interested in everything he saw, and wished he could have had the opportunity to study the Brutans more closely, without the fear of being captured and killed.

They travelled for two hours, cutting a straight line across country, and Clark would have given a lot to have been able to sit in the other front seat and learn to fly the craft.

'Do you have weapons aboard this craft, Ralip?' he demanded.

'One powerful disintegrator for use against Ogrins. It is our duty to kill Ogrins wherever we see them.'

He took in that bit of grim news with a glitter in his eyes. Disintegrators were not pleasant weapons to play around with, and he glanced out of the port and studied some of the other craft flying around. Anyone getting triggerhappy with a disintegrator could do a lot of damage, he mused.

They bypassed two other towns, and then the coastline showed up. Immediately Ralip changed course and lost height, and Clark tensed when he spotted a vast complex of buildings and open spaces coming up.

'That is the place,' Ralip said. 'We are prohibited to fly over it. I must turn away now because the warning is flashing already. If I fly into the prohibited area I will be shot down without further warning.'

Clark nodded, staring hard at the ground. The woman took the skyraft on a circuit of the spaceport, staying outside the perimeter of the prohibited area.

'Lots of people fly around here watching for spacecraft,' she said. 'But not on a day like today. This is not a rest day. We cannot stay too long or we shall be intercepted by a security craft.'

'We want to stay out of trouble,' Clark agreed, 'but can you take us around just once more? I must impress the lay-out on my mind.'

She nodded, and her face was tense and tight-lipped as she glanced at him. Clark stared down through narrowed eyes as they made another circuit. He saw a number of strange craft on the ground near to the large hangars.

'Can you tell me which of those craft are the type that travel through space?' he demanded.

'The largest.' She turned the craft slightly, and pointed out one of the nearer craft on the ground. 'That is the type which travels to Sata. It will get you off this planet quite easily.'

Clark was silent until they had completed the second circuit. He studied the lay-out of the spaceport itself, and then the approaches. But Ralip turned away then and started the return trip to her farm.

'We cannot stay longer,' she said. 'We are under observation, and must not attract any attention.'

'Is there somewhere you can set us down in sight of the port?' he demanded. 'When we make our try perhaps you could drop us at the nearest point. But before we even think of making any attempt, I must get in close, preferably under cover of darkness, and find out what kind of obstacles will confront us.'

'We cannot land within sight of the port,' she replied. 'It is all a forbidden area.'

Clark said nothing as the skyraft began the return trip to the farm, and his thoughts were fast and calculating. Ralip was silent too, watching her surroundings carefully. Clark paid no heed to the woman, wrapped up as he was in his own plans, and it wasn't until he felt the craft lurch and rapidly lose

D*

height that he dragged himself from his thoughts and looked around.

They were not following the reverse course on the return trip, he was quick to notice, and stiffened when he spotted marshy ground beneath them instead of the solid, rolling plain. He clutched at the back of the seat for support as the skyraft tilted once more, and when he glanced at Ralip he saw she was fighting the controls, trying desperately to maintain control of the craft.

'What's wrong?' Clark demanded tensely, and there was a note of concern in his tones. She threw a quick glance across one broad shoulder.

'We're in trouble. The Marscs! Marshmen! They've got a tractor beam on us.'

'What are we doing over the marsh? This isn't the way we came when we left the farm.'

'I thought we'd pick up the rest of your people from the Avics. That would save you the trouble of marching back through the forest to get them.'

'That was thoughtful of you, but I wish you had mentioned it before setting out. I don't know where the rest of my people are right now. They were moving camp as we departed. We have to rendezvous with an Avic as soon as we get back into the jungle.'

'I'm sorry I didn't ask!' Ralip's voice was harsh with fear. The skyraft was tilting sideways, losing height, although unwillingly, as if some invisible force was trying to drag it bodily out of the sky.

'These Marshmen!' Clark said. 'What are they like?'

'Half my size, but very dangerous. They are our sworn enemies! We fight each other whenever possible. We have driven them into the marshes, but they come out on raids at times, and do a lot of damage and killing. They are fierce, and use a mixture of primitive weapons and modern ones.'

'It's certainly not a primitive weapon they're using against us now!' Clark observed, as the raft swung erratically and lost more height. He pushed himself up and climbed into the front seat. 'Which set of controls operate your disintegrator? I'd better make myself useful.'

Ralip pointed out the small box that controlled their only weapon, and Clark peered through the large forward viewport and studied the ground. There were immense stretches of open water, and a large number of trees, with solid ground here and there. They were just over the fringe of the marsh, but farther ahead Clark could see the country was closer, the vegetation denser and practically impassable.

He studied the ground, looking for signs of the weapon that was being used to bring them down, and he saw a patch of shimmering light that indicated the presence of released energy. He tightened his lips as he followed Ralip's instructions and brought the weapon to bear. When he thumbed a button on the side of the box a brilliant white beam darted earthwards, and the next instant the skyraft leaped and shuddered as the power of the tractor beam gripping it was released.

'We're free!' Ralip almost shouted in her relief.

'Let's get out of the area as fast as possible,' Clark retorted.

The woman swung the machine and they started away, but in the same instant Clark caught a bright burst of light somewhere below, and he glanced down, knowing instinctively that they had been fired upon. Before he could call to Ralip or do anything at all the skyraft leaped and turned upside down.

Clark fell heavily against Ralip, who was strapped into her seat and safe, and he was dazed as he struck his head against the solid wall of the craft. They were out of control, he thought in some confusion, and grabbed desperately at the seats to hold himself still as the skyraft described a number of hair-raising acrobatic movements through the sky.

Ralip was fighting for control, and Clark dragged himself

away from her, getting back into his seat. He clipped the seat belt into place, but found it too big, and there was no time to make any alteration. He instinctively went back to the disintegrator, but the craft was not steady enough for him to attempt to use it.

Again they were struck by a burst of released energy, and once more the craft went berserk. Clark saw they were losing height rapidly, and he thought their last moments had come.

'If we have to come down, try and get as far as possible from this spot,' he shouted. The cabin was filling with pale grey smoke, and it stung his eyes and constricted his throat.

Ralip glanced at him, and he was surprised that there was no fear in her expression.

'Get into the back seats and strap yourself down,' she said. 'You'll have a better chance of surviving the impact when we land.'

Clark obeyed her because it seemed the most sensible thing to do. When he was strapped into the back seat he looked down through the viewport, and saw they were getting away from the danger area. He could see a number of tiny figures on some firm ground, running hither and thither, manhandling a large machine that had a projecting tube. Clark figured it was the weapon that had been used against them, and he tightened his lips as he saw the tube being brought to bear once more.

'Take evasive action, Ralip!' Clark shouted. 'They're about to hit us again.'

The woman nodded without turning her head, and the next instant the skyraft was standing on end as she brought it around. A cold sweat stood out on Clark's forehead, because they were already damaged and he did not expect the craft to stand up to the strain. They went down fast, with so much acceleration that Clark felt himself pressed back into the seat. He stared through the forward viewport and saw the ground coming up at them. He closed his eyes, fearing the worst, thinking Ralip had finally lost control, but at the last moment the skyraft tilted and banked sharply, and they actually skimmed some trees as they went speeding across the surface of the marsh, with the trees between them and the weapon directed at them.

'That was too close for comfort!' Clark spoke harshly, and the woman turned her head to smile at him. 'Any time you want to join a crew of mine I'll be glad to have you. Where did you learn to handle a craft like this?'

'It comes with practise,' she replied, and now the smile was gone. 'It isn't the first time I've strayed into trouble. But I think we're safely out of it now. I'll take the shortest route home. Hold tight. We're going to have to stay almost at ground level. I don't know how seriously we've been damaged.'

Clark had considered his nerve as good as anyone's, but he could only feel admiration for this alien woman who had befriended him. He remained in the back seat and stared around from the various ports as they made for the farm, and the rest of the trip passed without incident. Finally Ralip turned to him, giving him a searching glance, and Clark, thankful that the cultivated plain was beneath them, lifted his gaze to her strong face.

'Something on your mind?' he inquired.

'I have a favour to ask you!'

'Anything! The way you've helped me, and got us out of trouble today, there's nothing I wouldn't give you, if it is within my power.'

'When you try to escape from this planet I want to go along with you!'

'To Earth with us?' Clark demanded, surprised.

'Anywhere away from this existence we lead,' she retorted. 'From what you have told me about your race of people I think I could be happy in their company.'

'We don't have much choice in risking our lives to escape,' he said slowly. 'We know we'll probably die if we remain on this planet. But you don't have to take any such chance.'

'I would rather die than remain. I'll do all I can to help you get away, but with the death of my parents I have nothing to hold me here. I don't look forward to spending the rest of my life tending this farm and fighting off the periodic attacks and raids that are made against us. Will you take me along?'

'Let us talk some more about it nearer the time,' he said. 'Right now there's too much to be discussed and planned. If you really want to go along and we find the means of escape then of course I'll take you.'

'Thank you!' She lapsed into silence, and Clark was thoughtful as they continued. Soon the farm appeared ahead, and Ralip leaned forward as she stared down at the spread of buildings. 'We have some trouble on our hands!' she retorted, her thin tones sending a pang through Clark. 'Look there beside my garage. It is the skyraft of Quartus, the local security chief. He's not with the craft so he must be in the house. I hope he has not discovered your friends.'

Clark peered down as they swooped towards the garage, and he saw the white craft on the ground nearby. There was no sign of activity around the farm, and the air of desertion made him wonder if a trap had been set for their return. But before he could broach the subject Ralip was putting the craft down neatly into the garage, and already there was a nine foot figure coming out of the house to meet them. . . .

Chapter Nine

'Pull forward the back of your seat,' Ralip instructed as she switched off the power. There's a storage space behind it. Get into it and remain silent until I come for you. I'll go out and check what's been happening.'

Clark obeyed quickly, and felt stifled as he got into the narrow space revealed by pulling forward the seat. He caught a glimpse of Ralip's face as she pushed the back of the seat into place, and then all sounds were muffled as she left the craft.

He switched on the booster of the semantics transmuter and lifted the microphone in an attempt to pick up voices. A moment later he heard Ralip's high pitched tones, and he knew the woman was nervous. Her voice came through the machine, and in English, and he listened intently.

'I am honoured by a visit from Quartus!' Ralip said.

'Ralip, I have been waiting here more than an hour! Why have you left the farm today? After the raid last night you knew I would be here to ask questions.'

'Your men were here at first light. I told them all I could.' Ralip's tones were lower now, as if she had made an effort to control her fear.

'A dead Ogrin has been found close to this farm, between here and the jungle.' The male Brutan's voice was hard and thick, unsteady and guttural. 'A number of Ogrins was killed last night by our forces, but this particular one died from the effect of an alien weapon, similar to the type used to destroy at least one of our patrol craft in the jungle. A number of aliens have landed on this planet and we are searching for them. Have you seen anything of strangers?'

'Nothing at all, Quartus! What do these aliens look like?'

'Similar to us in appearance, but not of our size. They appear to be of a size between us and the Marscs.'

'Are they dangerous?'

'All aliens are classed as dangerous. We have more than enough trouble with the Ogrins and the Marscs, without the addition of intruders arriving. Two large space craft were destroyed as the snooper patrol picked them up. But from each of them a handful of aliens escaped. They have been in action against us, and it is obvious from the reports I've seen that the aliens are living with the Avics.'

'I'll call you if I see anyone around who looks suspicious,' Ralip said. 'What do you want to know about the Ogrin raid that happened last night?'

'You were taken prisoner by an Ogrin, the one we found dead in mysterious circumstances. How do you account for the fact that he is dead and you are at liberty and unharmed?'

'I cannot account for it. I was being carried by the Ogrin when he was killed. I was stunned in the fall, and when I regained my senses I returned here, waiting for daylight.'

'Very well! But don't take any chances. I suspect the aliens will attempt to reach the spaceport at Rini and try to escape in a spaceship. It is their only hope of getting away with their lives.'

'Will they be killed if they are captured?' Ralip asked, and Clark tightened his lips as he awaited the reply.

'Without doubt! We cannot trust aliens, and will ensure that none get the chance to trick us. The general order is that all aliens should be killed on sight.'

'I'll watch out for them. Are they in this area?'

'We do not know. But they cannot eascape us. We will get them in the end.'

Silence came and Clark switched off the transmuter. He lay stiff and worried as he waited for Ralip to return to him, but long moments dragged by before he felt the craft tip a little as a great weight was placed upon the rear. The next moment the woman's voice reached his ears.

'You can come out now!'

Clark sighed with relief as he alighted, and Ralip gazed around cautiously before motioning for him to accompany her to the house. They reached the building and Clark waited in the kitchen while she searched the house for intruders. When she returned to Clark's side he saw that her face was wearing a frown, and her eyes seemed filled with concern.

'Did you hear what was said by Quartus?' she demanded.

'Every word.' Clark nodded. 'I told you it wouldn't be easy for us to escape, but what I learned makes me fear that it will be even more difficult than I anticipated.'

'I will help you, but if I am caught I will be killed with you.'

Clark nodded. 'The sooner we start making plans the better,' he said. 'If you will let my friends out of the secret chamber we can start plotting our next move.'

Ralip went off, to return a few moments later with Balfin and Searby following her. Balfin eagerly demanded to know what had happened, and Ralip began preparing food while Clark informed the other two of their experiences. When he had given them a complete account, Balfin sighed and shook his head.

'So it's going to be every bit as tough as we expected,' he said.

'Worse than I expected,' Clark retorted. 'It seems the local security chief is aware of the possibilities open to us, and he's expecting us to make a try for one of their space craft. I'm afraid we're going to have to shelve that plan for a spell. If we lay low until they begin to forget about us then the extra special precautions that are being taken now around the spaceport might be relaxed. I don't think we can try anything until the situation is returned to normal.'

'I'm inclined to go along with that,' Searby said. 'So what shall we do, return to the Avics for a couple of months?'

'It sounds like a good idea to me,' Clark said. 'I'm not keen on wasting time. We have to take into account the fact that another *Probe* project ship might be sent out to search for us in the way that we came looking for *Probe* 1. We can't wait around for a third disaster.'

'We'll have time before they arrive,' Searby said. 'We were down on the planet for months before you showed up, Commander.'

'But we have to take into account the time it will take us to reach a planet from which to call our base,' Clark said. 'I won't be happy until we are committed to escape, but I'm certain we shall only get one chance to escape, and if we make a mess of that then we'll never get clear.'

'So tonight we'll start back to the Avics and the jungle, is that right, Commander?' Balfin asked.

'That's it!' Clark retorted.

They were mainly silent during the meal that Ralip provided, and Clark could tell by the woman's face that she was downcast by his decision to return to the jungle. Later she moved to Clark's side as they waited for darkness to fall, and Clark could tell she was troubled as he looked into her eyes.

'Don't worry,' he said softly. 'I'm sure you can see the sense in waiting. When we do decide to make our try we will come this way, and you can travel the rest of the way with us. I'll take you along. We'll turn up after dark one night.'

'I shall be looking for you,' she replied. 'I wish I could go with you, but I fear there will be too many guards out in the darkness tonight, and if suspicion falls on me I won't be here to aid you when the time comes.'

'That's right.' Clark nodded. 'We'll need you when the time comes. Don't do anything to arouse suspicion against you. The time will soon pass and we'll be arriving before you realize it.'

Ralip nodded, and Clark felt a strange sense of wonder at the situation which had arisen. He sat with Ralip until it was time to leave, and tried to learn as much as possible about the planet and its inhabitants. By the time he called Balfin and Searby and they took their leave of the Brutan woman, he was certain that if they ever fell into Brutan hands they would die.

Balfin winced as he shook hands with Ralip, but called a cheery farewell, and Searby followed the Major, who was leading with the Laser ready in his efficient hands. Clark paused for a moment on the doorstep, unable to see Ralip's face in the shadows.

'Don't take any chances around here,' he warned. 'Watch out for the Ogrins. It will be a month at least before we return, so don't start looking too soon after our departure. But you can be sure that we shall show up'

She gripped his hand and Clark turned away. When he looked back after covering some distance he could still see her outline in the doorway. He sighed slowly, then inhaled sharply, and some of the tension left him as he hurried to catch up with Balfin. Then they were clear of the farm and retracing their steps of the previous night.

The moons gave too much light, as before, and they were very cautious as they headed in the direction that would take them back to the jungle. They moved slowly, checking their surroundings unceasingly, and lost track of time as they progressed across the plain. Clark began to think they had gone too far, and kept casting around for landmarks. They could not mistake the hill, however, and the forest beyond, and they moved slowly and carefully. Balfin maintained the lead, and Clark was thankful the Major had come along.

But Balfin suddenly went to earth, and Clark, at Searby's side, dropped flat almost in the same instant. Searby's breathing was heavy as he lay at Clark's shoulder.

'What is it, do you think?' Searby whispered hoarsely, and Clark, recalling that the three Brutan guards on the previous night had seemed to hear a whisper from thirty yards range, shook his head in silent reply and motioned for the professor to remain quiet.

The next moment there was danger prowling towards them. It took Clark a split second to note the four tall, gigantic figures that emerged from the shadows and came slowly forward towards them. Ogrins! Clark held his breath for a moment. They were out raiding again. But had Balfin been spotted before going to ground, or had the Major seen the bigger figures of the giants before being spotted himself?

Balfin was in control of himself, and did not move, but Clark knew the Major was ready with his Laser. It seemed that the giants would walk right into them, and Balfin would wait until the last possible minute before firing. The moments flitted by, and Clark was aware of his thudding heart and swiftly beating pulses.

Then the four Ogrins halted and converged, their voices like the disagreement of wild animals as they conversed in their alien tongue. Clark dared not move to boost the transmuter, although he would liked to have heard what was being said. But he figured the Ogrins as creatures little better than savage animals, and felt that they would have the same savage instincts and senses.

Presently the four began to move again, but in a slightly different direction, and it seemed that they would bypass Balfin on the right. Clark could feel Searby trembling at his side, and he slowly reached his right hand down to his waist to grasp the handle of his sidearm. The next moment there was a swishing in the short grass and the giants went shambling past.

Clark was prepared to let them go without a fight, for he wanted no trouble, but it suddenly came home to him that the Ogrins might be making for Ralip's farm. He clenched his teeth as he waited, and when the four Ogrins had passed by he called sharply to Balfin, the sound of his voice halting the giants in their tracks.

'Cut them down, Kester!' Clark shouted.

Balfin's reactions were so fast that the Laser beam was stabbing through the night like a brilliant white finger before Clark could complete his order. The four Ogrins were seared immediately, and Clark watched them going down with his eyes slitted, his hands clenched. The next moment he was upon his feet and moving swiftly forward.

'Let's get lost,' he said urgently, 'in case there's anyone else around and watching.'

They had barely started away from the area when bright lights flashed and several skyrafts appeared to blot out patches of stars overhead. The searchlights probed the ground, and Clark found himself huddled in a depression between Searby and Balfin as they sought cover.

'We've stirred up trouble,' Balfin muttered.

'I figured to give Ralip a break,' Clark said through his teeth. 'It looked to me like the Ogrins were making in that direction.'

'I was gonna cut them down whether you ordered it or not,' the Major muttered. 'But we've got trouble on our hands now.'

The probing lights suddenly converged, and Clark saw they had picked up two of the fallen Ogrins. Stabbing rays of raw energy lanced downwards, and the bodies of the Ogrins were disintegrated. The skyrafts began to circle the area, searching for movement, and Clark gritted his teeth as he lay upon his back and watched their dark shapes swooping and climbing. Time seemed to stand still, and the future was a blank expanse his thoughts could not penetrate.

When two of the craft suddenly landed and the tall figures of several Brutans alighted, Clark felt it was time they moved, and he led the way along the ditch, knowing it was taking them out of their way, but they had to break away without being seen and the extra distance would not matter if they managed to draw clear.

By slow degrees they managed to get clear of the area, and Balfin took the lead once more when they left the ditch. But the ground was getting soggy under their feet, and Clark felt a pang of concern as he felt his boots sinking into black muck to the ankles.

'Hold it, Kester,' he commanded, thinking of the Marshmen. 'If the Brutans put a cordon around the jungle to keep the Avics in then they've very likely done the same thing around the marshes to prevent the Marscs from attacking. I think we're walking into danger.'

'You could be right,' Balfin admitted readily. 'We're certainly a long way off the direction we had last night. We've got to angle left to get out of this bog.'

Clark glanced at the sky, ever on the alert for the first grim sight of a skyraft, but the sky was clear and starry, with no small black patches to signify Brutan activity. He stared for a moment at the twin moons, and wished it were the sky surrounding Earth upon which he was gazing. He suddenly felt a long way from home, and a sense of remoteness sneaked into his mind. He was already of the opinion that he would never see Earth again, but he fought off the knowledge and the attendant dark fears and returned his full concentration to their situation. Balfin was talking, asking a question, and Clark only caught the tail-end of it.

'Sorry, Kester,' he muttered. 'I didn't get that.'

'I asked if we should try to make the jungle in one swift march,' the Major repeated.

'We'll have to.' Clark did not pause to think about it. 'I don't see why we shouldn't reach that tunnel before daylight, and once in the safety of the jungle we'll be able to set our own pace without fear of discovery.'

A splashing sound was slowly becoming louder as they peered around, and Clark tensed, raising himself up to peer into the surrounding night.

'There's someone around,' Balfin said urgently, tightening his grip upon the Laser. 'Can you see anything, Commander?'

Before Clark could reply something hissed over their heads and dropped down neatly upon them. Clark felt wetness against his face, and threw up an arm, his fingers instantly tangling in a thin, sticky net. He heard Balfin curse, and the Major started to his feet, uttering a yell of startled anger. Searby remained on the ground, but Clark started up, tearing at the net, which seemed to mould itself about them, pinioning their arms and stifling them. It was no ordinary net, he remembered thinking remotely, and then he blacked out and knew nothing more . . .

Clark awoke to the flicker of firelight, the murmur of alien voices that were shrill and piercing. Above his head, when he looked up, a roof of reeds prevented him seeing the night sky. He tried to move, and discovered that he was bound hand and foot. He turned his head to one side and caught a glimpse of Balfin's figure, similarly tied, and Searby was on the other side of him. He did not speak, and could not tell if his companions were awake or still unconscious.

He slowly took stock of his surroundings, and when he moved the stinking pallet upon which he lay rustled and exuded a stronger reek of dirty water and rotting vegetation.

He lifted his head to trace the direction the voices were coming from, and spotted a group of a dozen men seated around the flickering fire.

They were small men, about half his size, and he knew with a clenching of his teeth that they had fallen into the hands of the Marscs, the Marshmen. He stifled the sigh that tried to escape him, and blamed himself for permitting the Ogrins and the Brutans to detour him.

The men were plainly arguing about something, and Clark fancied it was the fate of himself and his two unfortunate companions. He tested the bonds that held him, and found they were wet and tightening all the time about his wrists. Already they were cutting painfully into his flesh, and his fingers were throbbing sullenly, aching with the promise of pins and needles the moment his limbs were freed.

There were trees about them, no doubt sheltering the fire from above, and the splash of water and the mournful cries of alien nocturnal life created a strange backcloth to the nightmare scene. Clark told himself that he was not dreaming, and he glanced once more at Balfin, wondering if they had been searched and deprived of their weapons and equipment.

Presently one of the small men got up from his place at the fire and came under the rough shelter. He kicked Balfin in the ribs, waited for a response, and when there was none, came to Clark's side and did the same to him. Clark clenched his teeth against the retort which came to his lips and feigned unconsciousness, and there was no response from Searby when the Marshman kicked him. The little man went back to the fire and sat down once more.

Clark considered. He knew they could expect rough treatment from these small men. They lived primitive lives on the marshes, hunting Avics for food and fighting any strangers who crossed their domains. They were cannibals, Clark told himself, trying to recall all that he had learned about them.

He stared at them, watching the firelight flickering on their humanoid faces. If he stretched his imagination a little he could believe he was back on Earth, watching a group of campers relaxing for the evening, except that he could not understand their tongue and knew their outlook and attitudes were totally alien and unpredictable. He glanced at Balfin again, and saw the Major's eyes glint in the reflected firelight. He nodded slowly. So Balfin was playing possum, watching their small captors before taking a chance on revealing the fact that he was aware of his surroundings once more.

They were in a tight spot, and Clark realized that they might not get out of it. He tried to get free of his bonds, but they held him with no trouble, and tightened imperceptibly as the minutes passed.

The Marsc came from the fire once more and kicked Balfin again, and this time Balfin cursed strongly. There was a chorus of shouts from around the fire, and the next moment all the men were standing around their prisoners. Clark was kicked several times before he voiced his objections, and a further chorus of cries greeted the sound of his tones. Searby was seized and shaken hard, but there was no response, and Clark tightened his lips when he saw Searby released and noted the way the man fell back apparently lifeless.

Clark was grasped and dragged up into a sitting position, and he wrinkled his nose at the sour smell of these small men. He looked into small, sharp features and glinting dark eyes. The Marsc who had kicked him was evidently a leader of sorts, as he spoke to Clark in a brusque voice, asking a question, judging by his rising tones, but Clark could not understand. He shook his head slowly, glancing around, catching sight of their equipment and weapons lying in a heap nearby, and his eyes glinted as he took in the lines of the Laser that Balfin had been carrying. Then he saw the transmuter and a ray of hope filled him momentarily. If he could communicate with these little men he might be able to convince them that they were friends.

'Try and get my meaning,' he said authoritatively. 'Untie my hands and let me get my box of tricks.'

His words brought a silence to the little men, and he became the centre of attention. He motioned with his head towards the equipment, and the leader of the Marscs understood immediately. He went to the pile of equipment and picked up the Laser, turning to face Clark, and Clark turned cold when the terrible weapon was pointed at him. He shook his head furiously, calling loudly, and his apparent fear evoked gales of laughter from the little men.

The Marsc leader threw down the Laser and picked up several items of the equipment, holding each up for inspection, and Clark shook his head. It was evidently some game to the Marshmen, for they chuckled and slapped each other's backs whenever Clark shook his head. Then the transmuter was picked up, and silence came when Clark nodded eagerly. He motioned with his head, trying to get the Marsc to bring the equipment across to him, and eventually the little man did so, aware that the transmuter was not a weapon. He set the box down in front of Clark, then whipped out a fearsome dagger with a curved blade that glittered in the firelight.

Clark leaned away from the blade as it was thrust towards him, not with any intention of stabbing him but as a threat, and he stared at the bright metal as it passed very close to his face. The Marsc said something in his thin tones, and then moved around behind Clark. The other Marshmen watched intently, their small faces leering, set in hard expression of anticipation, and Clark feared that his last moments had come. The knife blade suddenly appeared over his right shoulder and eased down towards his throat, and he stiffened and closed his eyes.

Balfin shouted in anger and fear, certain Clark was about to be killed. But Clark kept his eyes closed and tried to prevent his imagination working. It was the worst moment of his entire life, and seemed to be his last.

Chapter Ten

The blade of the knife touched Clark's flesh, and he could not prevent a tremor passing through him. But then the Marshman moved away, leaving Clark swaying in a sitting position, and the others laughed joyfully at what had been a grim joke. Clark turned his head and opened his eyes, catching a glimpse of the Marsc leader moving around to Searby. Clark saw the knife blade moving in towards Searby's chest, and he called urgently, trying to attract attention.

The Marsc leader paid no heed, and with a quick twist of his wrist he slashed open Searby's clothes from the neck to the waist. Clark tensed, his eyes held by the slowly moving blade. One of the other Marscs called an unintelligible question, and the leader paused and reached out with his left hand, placing it upon Searby's chest. He shook his head, and Clark took it to mean that Searby was dead.

The next instant the Marsc leader had made a deft movement with the knife and sliced open Searby's chest. Horror spilled through Clark, and the gleeful shouts of the watching Marshmen hammered against his ears. Balfin roared out frantically, and Clark threw a swift glance in the Major's direction. Balfin was straining to get free of his bonds, but they held him tightly, and the horror that Clark felt was plainly visible on Balfin's heavy face.

Clark watched while the Marsc leader began to cut Searby's

body like a hunter preparing a steer for cooking. It came to Clark then that these men were cannibals, and the fact was borne out when a group of women appeared out of the shadows and grabbed the flesh, thrusting pieces on sharp sticks and turning to the fire.

'The fiends!' Balfin rasped, his tones tight with fury. 'Was Searby dead?'

'I think he was,' Clark said unsteadily. 'I hope he was.'

'So we know what we can expect!' Balfin redoubled his efforts to get free, and made so much noise that one of the Marshmen went to him and clouted him hard with a small club. Clark watched Balfin fall sideways and lie motionless, and once again he spoke to the Marsc leader, indicating the transmuter and trying to convey the message that he wanted his hands free.

The Marsc came to confront him once more, the blade of his knife red with Searby's blood. He spoke quickly and unintelligibly, and Clark shook his head, motioning to the transmuter. He received a kick in the face for his trouble, and fell sideways, his bound hands tingling and cramped.

The Marshmen returned to their fire, and Clark lay watching them through slitted eyes. He worked on his bonds again, wanting to get free. He was ready to die fighting, knowing what lay in store for them. They would be eaten in their turn, and the thought was so nightmarish that he could not encompass it.

Presently the Marshmen were feeding on Searby's body, and Clark was nauseated and ill. He tried not to watch, and was only too aware of Searby's mutilated remains lying beside him. The firelight flickering over the grim scene painted everything with a ruddy glow. It was a nightmare come true, and Clark felt that his sanity was buckling under the strain of the events which had taken place since their arrival on this alien planet.

There appeared to be around thirty to forty of the alien

pygmies grouped around the fire, and women and children were amongst them. They were probably a complete tribe, one of many that existed on the waterways of Muta. Clark knew he could not condemn them for their eating habits because it was their way of life, but the whole revolting business was foreign to his standards, and he closed his eyes and tried to keep himself mindless.

A foot kicked him in the ribs and he opened his eyes to find the Marsc leader confronting him once more. The little man peered down at him for a moment, the big knife still in his hand, and then he bent and slashed through the bonds around Clark's wrists. Clark stared up at him, unable to feel his hands. They were numb and swollen, and blood rushed through his veins as the constriction was removed. He was in agony almost at once, and had difficulty rubbing his hands in an attempt to chafe life back into them.

The entire tribe watched him now, some still chewing meat that was only half roasted over the fire. Clark stared around, his nostrils nauseated by the sweet smell of human flesh being cooked. He sensed that he was about to be killed. He was not afraid of the fact as it stood. Horror at what had happened to Searby seemed to have frozen his emotions. It was all like a bad dream that seemed never ending.

The Marsc leader held the point of his knife against Clark's throat, forcing Clark's head up so their gazes met. The blade nicked Clark's chin and he felt the sharp pain of it, then the trickle of blood down his neck. The Marshman said something in harsh tones, then moved back a pace, and Clark sat up slowly, still rubbing his hands.

He looked around and found he was the centre of attention once more. The leader of the Marscs snapped another string of unintelligible language at him, and motioned to the transmuter, apparently demanding to know its function. Clark reached out slowly for the box, and several Marshmen lifted weapons and waved them menacingly.

Clark switched on the transmuter and prepared to operate it. There was heavy silence around him, and all alien eyes were fixed on the red and green lights winking on the top of the transmuter. The Marsc leader held his knife ready to repel any treachery, and Clark moistened his lips when he was ready to speak.

'Say something,' he told the Marsc leader. 'Say anything. If we can communicate we may come to some understanding.'

The Marsc leader stared at him for a moment, then broke into a torrent of words. Clark nodded hopefully, waiting for the transmuter to operate. When the Marshman fell silent Clark spoke again, encouraging conversation, his mind still numb with the horror of what had taken place. But he felt he had a chance to get through to these little aliens, and he needed to convince them that killing him and Balfin would not be in their best interests.

The Marsc leader came closer once more, knife ready, and he asked a spate of questions. Clark waited, and the next moment the unintelligible words were transmuted into English. He nodded slowly, and saw the surprise which came to the Marsc leader's face as his own words were transmuted into the alien language.

'We are aliens,' Clark said quickly. 'We have come to this planet in friendship. We are not Brutans, who attack you on sight, or Ogrins, who kill you for food. We are travellers, and we ask you for hospitality.'

He knew his words sounded incongruous after the fate that had overtaken Searby, but if he could gain a breathing space for himself and Balfin then they might find a way of escape.

'What machine is that you are using?' came the swift reply. 'How can it turn your words into my tongue and let you understand what I say?'

'If I explained how it worked you wouldn't understand,' Clark said. 'We are not enemies of your people. Quite possibly we could help you. The weapons we carry are powerful enough to kill Ogrins. Even the Avics have no weapons powerful enough to do that.

'We take you for Brutans. They are good to eat and so are you.'

'Where we come from we do not eat the flesh of men. We do not kill every stranger who comes our way unless he threatens us.'

'You came into our territory. Under our laws that means you die.'

'We were escaping from Brutans and Ogrins,' Clark said.

'You fight Brutans and Ogrins?'

'Yes. We have killed many Ogrins. We are friendly with the Avics, and have helped them fight the Ogrins.'

'We eat Avics. If we do not kill you will you show us where the Avics are camped?'

'I do not know where they live, apart from being in the jungle. If you fight Brutans and Ogrins and we do the same then that makes us friends.'

Clark realized that his assumption was too simple to be taken seriously, but he could think of nothing else to say. If he could get these cannibals to accept him and Balfin as friends, or at least not regard them as enemies and potential meals, then they might have a chance of surviving this situation.

'If you fight Brutans and Ogrins then you would fight us. We have fought with you and that makes us enemies. We have eaten one of your companions, and plan to eat another of you tomorrow.'

Clark sighed heavily. There could not be any kind of an argument against that logic. These aliens had life worked out to simple rules that all added up to the same thing—survival.

He realized that he had to obey those same simple rules if he wanted to live.

'The two of us are very small,' he said tightly. 'If you are short of meat then we will kill some Ogrins for you.'

'Ogrin meat is bitter. Your meat is good, better than the Avics or the Brutans. We heard there are more of you in the jungle, and we shall find the Avic camp before very long and take all of you.'

That sounded ominous to Clark, and he fell silent. He tried to figure out what to say that would interest these little cannibals and take their minds off their next meal. His hands were free now, and if he could remain so for a little longer then he might get the chance to grab the Laser. With that in his hands he would even up thc odds considerably.

He glanced in Balfin's direction and saw the Major had regained his senses. Clark had to fight hard against the impulse to look towards the weapons on the ground. He stared into the Marsc leader's face.

'Do you have weapons powerful enough to kill Ogrins?' he demanded.

'We catch them with our nets and drown them,' came the grim reply. 'The weapons the Brutans and Avics use taint the flesh. You are of no use to us except as food.'

Clark fell silent, and the Marsc leader came forward with his knife at the ready. He kicked the transmuter away from Clark and motioned for Clark to lie down. All eyes were upon Clark, and he slowly obeyed, aware that the rest of the tribe was alert and ready for any attempt to escape. Clark felt his spirits sink, and he dropped flat upon his back. The Marsc leader bent over him, and in that instant Balfin's voice roared out, echoing across the small camp.

'Fight 'em!' the Major yelled, and there was a scuffling and thudding as the women and children started away out of danger. Clark reached up for the Marshman, grasping the wrist of the hand that held the knife, and he twisted sideways as the cannibal tried to plunge the weapon into his chest. In the background there was a confusion of voices and noises as Balfin, evidently free of his bonds, made a dive for their weapons.

Clark found the Marsc leader surprisingly strong, and had difficulty in retaining a grip on the pygmy's wrist. The alien was astonishingly quick, with instant reflex action, and Clark was hard put to keep the point of the knife out of his flesh. He was desperate, and rolled quickly, dragging the smaller man off balance and to the ground. Aware that a number of knives and clubs were nearby, Clark sought to get his adversary between him and the rest of the tribe, and he was barely in time. As he twisted around to face the gathered pygmies a club struck the ground at his side, and a knife whirled towards him, the point digging into the ground a scant few inches from his left hip.

The pygmy was as strong as Clark despite the disparity of their size, and Clark realized that he had to get on his feet in order to make his weight tell. He got to one knee, using the weight of his upper body, and out of the corner of his eye he saw some of the other pygmies coming to the aid of their leader.

But Balfin was already at the pile of equipment, his clutching hands reaching out for the Laser. Some of the Marshmen were starting towards him, and a knife whizzed by him, but he grabbed the Laser and went into a forward roll with it, going down and over, his hands sure upon the weapon, his nerves taut, his mind filled with desperate determination because he knew that if they failed to make a break now both he and Clark would wind up dead.

Balfin came up on one knee, the Laser levelled in his grip, and he was facing the fire and the group of Marscs. Some of the vicious little men were already coming at him, and he gritted his teeth as a club narrowly missed his head. He hoped the Laser had not been damaged, and he thumbed the button and a darting beam of white brilliance snapped out and assailed the tiny men.

Pandemonium struck the Marscs instantly, and a dozen of them went down so quickly they never knew what killed them. Balfin clenched his teeth and swung the Laser, careful not to catch Clark, who was wrestling with the leader of the Marscs, and he sent short streams of death into the densely packed racks of the Marshmen.

In a matter of seconds the situation had changed completely. Those aliens who had not been destroyed were intent upon saving themselves, and the campfire was totally deserted except for the remains of the pygmies who had died. Even women and children had been caught by the Laser beam, and Balfin was trembling inwardly as he swung around to check his rear. Then he started towards Clark, who was on his feet now and trying to hold the Marsc leader.

Balfin struck savagely at the alien's head, and Clark released the pygmy as he fell unconscious. For a moment both men froze, staring at one another. Then Balfin drew a quick breath.

'We'd better get out of here, Commander,' he said.

'Let's not leave any equipment behind,' Clark said. 'We're going to need everything we can carry. And turn the Laser on Searby's remains, Kester. We can't leave him for the Marscs to finish off.'

Balfin nodded grimly and went to the spot where Searby's remains lay. He turned the Laser upon them and then came back to where Clark was busy sorting through the equipment that had been taken from them. There were no signs of the Marscs now, although the shadows around them were echoing with strange calls and sounds.

'We don't know the way out of here,' Balfin said, and Clark looked up at the stars.

'Give me a couple of minutes and I'll try to locate some of

the stars I noted last night,' Clark said. 'Watch our backs, Kester. They'll try and overpower us if we give them the chance. Remember those nets they use. If they can trap Ogrins and drown them then we'll have to be very careful.'

Balfin crouched, the Laser ready in his hands, and he stared around grimly, peering into the shadows.

'I figure we'd better hole up somewhere, Commander, until the sun shows,' he suggested.

'If we do that we'll be asking for trouble from the Brutans.' Clark checked his handgun, and then stuck it into his belt. He massaged his wrists for a moment as he straightened and looked around. Then he picked up the transmuter and put it on, strapping it to his chest. 'I'm ready ready to go now. We'd better stick close together and try to cover all directions.'

'We're probably in the middle of the marshes now,' Balfin said. 'If so we're gonna need a boat or something.'

'Let's take a look around anyhow. I don't want to stay at this spot for a moment longer than necessary.'

Balfin nodded slowly, and he fired a precautionary shot from the Laser, swinging the muzzle and burning down the crude habitations of the Marscs. There were anguished yells from the surrounding darkness, and Balfin's blood ran cold for a moment as he considered what faced them.

'I'm ready to go,' he said in a grating tone, and Clark took out his sidearm and readied it for action.

They started from the camp area, and almost immediately clubs and knives came silently through the night. They dropped to their knees and Balfin fired again, sending stabs of brilliant death in all directions. A silence followed and they got up to go on, but had barely covered any distance at all when there were furtive sounds in the shadows all about them.

'We're not going to get out of this!' Balfin spoke through his teeth, and his lips were hard and pulled back in a snarl of defiance. 'I'm up to my knees in water, Commander, and the ground underneath is barely taking my weight. We'll need a boat of some kind or we'll be in bad trouble.'

'There must be some craft around here,' Clark said. 'Let's move to the right.' He lifted his gun and fired when he fancied he saw movement just ahead, and the brightness of the flaring weapon almost blinded him for several moments. He kept blinking as they moved off to the right, and the water was getting deeper with each step.

Soon they were up to their waists, and the darkness closed in impenetrably. They were silent, and when they paused to listen they heard nothing but the slap of water here and there and the gentle sighing of a dark breeze.

'That slapping sound,' Balfin said softly, his mouth close to Clark's ear. 'Sounds like water on the bottom of a boat, Commander.'

'That's what I was thinking!' Clark peered around, his eyes still affected by the flashes of their weapons, and he fancied he made out a straight line in the darkness, an unnatural outline that could belong to a raft or boat.

They paused and Balfin diminished his height a little, trying for a silhouette.

'It's a boat okay,' the Major said slowly. 'Better let me go ahead to check if there's anyone aboard.'

Clark nodded, half turning to guard their rear, and he heard a series of splashing sounds not far away. They were still under observation, he reminded himself grimly, and was ready for any attack with the strange nets that had made them captive before. He glanced back towards Balfin and was surprised to find the Major several yards away, moving swiftly and silently through the water towards the alien craft.

Balfin held the Laser ready, and his keen eyes were closed to the merest slits. He didn't care now he had the Laser in his hands. He would take on all-comers without fear. He saw a small figure rear up on the flat boat ahead, and he cut the instinctive action which almost had him using the Laser. If he fired he would get the boat too! He moved in, and discovered that the boat was a little more than a long dugout—a tree trunk that had been hollowed and adapted for marsh use. He saw water churning where the Marsc who had vacated the boat was swimming, and he fought down the impulse to use the Laser. He peered around, satisfying himself that they were safe from attack for the moment. Clark was coming towards him, and together they hurriedly climbed into the frail craft.

Clark took the Laser and sat in the bows, peering around alertly, while Balfin picked up a heavy sweep-type oar and stood up in the stern. They began to move out as the Major put his weight on the oar, digging one end into the mud under the surface and poling them away from the Marsc camp area.

Balfin ducked several times as he heard heavy objects whizzing past his head in the dark, and there were faint splashes around them as they moved away to signify they were under some kind of attack. But the Marshmen were cautious, too afraid of the Laser to come to close grips once more.

Clark watched all quarters, twisting this way and that to ensure they did not come under sudden attack. He fancied he saw another boat out to the right, following them at a safe distance, but the shadows were deceptive, and he did not fire to give away their position.

Minutes later they were well clear of the area, and it seemed that all dangers were past. Clark heaved a long sigh as Balfin substituted a light paddle for the long oar, and then they were making good progress across an open stretch of water. There was a second paddle in the boat and Clark picked it up, holding the Laser across his lap. He dipped the thin wooden blade into the smooth water and exerted his strength, adding his weight to their primitive mode of propulsion, and the light craft fairly lifted and surged along.

'We're well out of that, Commander,' Balfin called at length. 'But have you any idea where we are?'

Clark had been keeping an eye on their surroundings and at the same time trying to look at the night sky. He knew the night was well advanced, and it seemed to him that their troubles were not over by a long way. He turned his attention to the sky once more, and after a few moments had to admit that he did not know where they were or what direction they should take. As far as he was concerned they were totally lost.

'We'd better try and make dry ground somewhere, then go on from there,' he admitted finally. 'We don't know where those Marshmen took us, Kester, after they captured us.'

'You're right,' the Major agreed without hesitation. 'I think we'll be all right once we strike dry land.'

Clark looked around, afraid that they might be heading into more trouble. These Marshmen knew the area intimately, and they would not be keen for two prisoners to escape. He paused in his paddling and checked the Laser. They would not be taken alive the next time. He would prefer to fight to the death than rely upon the mercy of the alien pygmies.

They began to tire. Their wrists had been cruelly bound for some considerable time, and Clark didn't have any feeling in the little finger on his left hand. He ached in every muscle and his back felt as if it were broken, but they paddled on, their horror over their experiences forcing them on when muscle and sinew cried enough.

When he glanced backwards, Clark saw Balfin straining at his work in the stern. He continued for several more moments before calling a cessation.

'I'm just about done,' Clark said. 'Let's take five minutes, Kester. We need to listen for sounds of pursuit.'

They stopped and the boat slowly lost way. In the ensuing silence they heard nothing that was not natural, and Clark was ready to believe that the Marshmen had decided against fighting men armed with weapons such as the Laser. They had probably cut their losses. But he did not blind himself to the possibilities, and until they were clear of the marshes they could not afford to believe their enemies had quit.

'How long do you think we've got before the sun comes up?' Balfin asked as they went on once more.

Clark stared at the sky again, his eyes narrowed. He shook his head as he failed to come to a decision.

'It's hard to say. But I figure that the Marshmen couldn't have taken us far from firm ground in the time they've had at their disposal. We didn't leave Ralip's farm until sundown, and we travelled for a long time before falling in with the Marscs. I think we're not so badly off as we imagine, Kester.'

'I hope you're right, Commander,' came the firm reply.

Clark felt tiredness trying to swoop into his mind, and he fought it with all the mental strength he could muster. He kept looking around, ready to drop the paddle and grab the Laser, but there was no sign of impending trouble anywhere within the range of his vision. Time passed and a strand of worry attached itself to his thoughts. It enlarged and became twisted as further time elapsed, but he said nothing to Balfin. It wouldn't help to indicate the obvious. If they were not under cover before sunrise then the trouble they'd experienced at the hands of the Marscs would be as nothing to what they could expect from the Brutans or the Ogrins.

A black shadow stretched away on either hand and before them, Clark noticed, peering ahead, and it was low and heavy. A spurting hope touched his mind, but he killed it instantly. They paddled on, and the black outline drew imperceptibly nearer. Balfin had spotted it and now ceased paddling.

'What is it, Commander?' he demanded hoarsely.

'I'm hoping it is dry land,' Clark replied. 'Let's push on a bit.'

They did, and a few moments later the prow of the ungainly craft ran aground. The impact came so unexpectedly that Clark was thrown forward heavily, and he lost the Laser as he pitched out of the craft. He landed on his face in a foot of water, but there was firm ground under his body and he started up instantly with relief flaring in his mind. Balfin was coming towards him, grabbing up the Laser, and they hastily took their equipment and scrambled out of the marsh.

'Don't stop yet,' Clark said after they had left the water behind. 'I shan't feel safe now until we reach the jungle.'

'If we're anywhere near the point where they took us into the marsh then we're moving in the right direction now,' Balfin said.

Clark studied the stars and after some moments he agreed.

'I think we are on the right track again,' he commented. 'We'd better move apart a bit, Kester, just in case. I'm not keen on any more nasty surprises. 'We'll cover each other. You take the Laser. You're better with it than I am.'

Balfin chuckled harshly and moved slightly to the right and they went on.

Now the immediate dangers were past Clark found his mind becoming inundated with horror. When he recalled the events that had taken place in the camp of the Marshmen his mind tried to rebel against the agony of remembering, and he clenched his teeth as he walked stolidly through the darkness. He pushed one foot before the other without conscious thought, and they went on through the indistinct shadows, crossing alien country with only their primeval instincts to aid them.

'Commander!' Balfin's hard whisper came out of the darkness to Clark's right, startling him out of his thoughts, and he swung around quickly to check his surroundings, feeling a little guilty because he had permitted his alertness to fail. He heaved a long sigh when he found no trouble, and then looked towards the spot where Balfin was down on the ground. He dropped quickly and began to move in cautiously, coming up on the Major's left.

'What is it?' he demanded in a harsh whisper.

'Straight ahead,' Balfin said tightly. 'I saw a light flicker. It didn't last long. Might have been a campfire unmasked for a moment. The Brutan patrol we met on the way out of the jungle had a covered fire just back from the tunnel. I figure we must be getting close to the jungle.'

Clark nodded, filled with relief. He peered in the direction Balfin pointed out, but could see nothing. Then his gaze slid to the right, and he frowned as he tried to make out details.

'That blacker area over there, Kester,' he said softly. 'It could be the jungle, huh?'

Balfin would not commit himself immediately. He studied the area.

'Could be,' he admitted at length. 'We've got to find that hill though. Shall I go on ahead of you, Commander? No sense both of us walking slap into trouble.'

'I fancy we'd better stick together, to cover each other,' Clark said. 'Let's take it easy, but keep going, and make a detour around the spot where you figured you saw the light. One thing to remember. I think these Brutans can hear a whisper from thirty yards so let's keep it quiet from now on.'

Balfin went ahead slightly, and Clark gripped his energy gun as he followed. They were tense once more, aware that now was approaching the most dangerous part of their attempt to return to the jungle and its sanctuary. They had to get through the Brutan cordon!

Suddenly Clark felt the ground rising under his feet and he peered around, hoping against hope that this was the hill where the tunnel was situated. But he could not accept that they were so fortunate after what they had experienced. He was prepared for more disappointment and danger, and he tightened his grip on his weapon as they went on more slowly.

When a harsh challenge was shouted out of the darkness near them Clark went instantly to ground, watching Balfin's broad back as the Major flung himself down. Echoes fled quickly, and tension rose up inside Clark like a flowing tide. The challenge was repeated, coming unintelligible from the darkness, until the transmuter Clark was wearing picked it up and translated it.

Clark thumbed the button that turned the instrument off, but not before the harsh voice relayed its warning in English.

'Halt! You are under observation. Stay still and report what you are doing in a prohibited area!'

Clark clenched his teeth, for it was a Brutan shouting, and he and Balfin were the only strangers here. It looked as if their present run of bad luck was persisting, and they were going to find trouble on the last stretch to safety!

Chapter Eleven

Balfin was unmoving and silent, despite the repeated challenge, and Clark knew the Major would swing into action the moment danger struck, But they didn't want to fight! If they could withdraw and break contact they would be able to slip away into the darkness and lose themselves without trouble. Clark stared into the direction from which the voice had come, and his lips tightened when he saw a movement in the shadows. The next moment a tall figure appeared, advancing cautiously, a rod-like weapon held ready for action.

Clark hoped Balfin would not fire, but he dared not call a warning. The Brutan came on, and Clark, knowing Balfin's exact position, feared the Major would be discovered. But yards short of Balfin's spot, the Brutan halted and stood peering around. The next moment another Brutan voice called from the darkness ahead, its owner invisible to Clark.

'You're seeing things that are not there!'

'I saw something, I tell you,' the first guard retorted. 'I not only saw something, but I heard a sound. These sonic detectors don't make any mistakes.'

Clark thinned his lips as he listened. He had been mystified by the apparent ease with which the Brutan guards at the tunnel had picked up Searby's whisper. Now he knew how it was done. He shook his head slowly as he considered. A sonic detector was just another set of odds stacked up against them.

But the guard was apparently satisfied that he had been mistaken for he turned away and disappeared once more in the direction from which he came. Clark began to breathe easier, and after a few moments he moved forward slowly and carefully to Balfin's side. The Major turned to speak, but Clark pressed a hand against his mouth, cautioning silence. They communicated with signals, and Balfin moved to the right and they crawled away.

It seemed to Clark that they were on the right hill, and his relief began to swell in his mind as they began to cast about for the tunnel entrance. Balfin, who had been out of the tunnel and returned to it from a distance, suddenly touched Clark's arm. He put his mouth to Clark's ear and spoke softly.

'Follow me. I got my bearings.'

Clark nodded and peered around as they went forward, and he fancied he saw movement in the background. There were guards all over the place, and they were alert and ready for trouble. Then Balfin paused, and Clark saw the Major easing through a screen of bushes into the tunnel beyond.

They stood up thankfully in the tunnel, and Clark held on to Balfin's belt as they went forward. The total darkness was welcome. At least they could not be spotted in here. But the trip seemed never ending, and Clark found his nerves overwound by the time they emerged on the slope that led down into the jungle.

Balfin did not hesitate, but plunged down the slope until they were well within the tree line. Then he halted, breathless, and leaned against a tree trunk, his face a pale oval in the shadows. His shoulders were heaving as he looked at Clark.

'We've had our share of troubles this trip, Commander. I guess there were times when I figured we would not see this jungle again.'

'And we lost Searby!' Clark felt a pang stab through him as he thought of the episode of their nightmarish contact with the

Marscs. 'But we're not out of the woods yet, Kester. We've got to come back this way, then try to steal a Brutan spaceship. The Brutans will be expecting us to attempt something like that, according to that security chief I overheard talking to Ralip. I reckon it will be an impossible task, but our only alternative is to remain on this hellish planet for the rest of our lives.'

'And that period may not be so very long, according to what has happened to us so far,' Bafin commented harshly. 'I've never known a place where so many creatures are waiting to eat you.'

'Dog eats dog,' Clark said. He looked around, peering into the shadows. 'We're not entirely safe in here, remember. But there should be an Avic around watching for our return. I don't figure they'll be expecting us for a few days more, so we might have to wait around.'

'I can track our way back to that camp we stayed at,' Balfin said, 'But not until daylight. Shall we rest up now?'

'You sleep while I stand guard.' Clark tried to see the sky but could not. 'I don't think there's more than a couple of hours to sunrise.'

They settled down, and Clark sat with his back to a tree, the Laser ready in his hands. Balfin stretched out and was asleep within moments, and Clark listened to his companion's steady breathing. He didn't think that he could have made it this far if Balfin hadn't been along.

He dared not let himself sleep, although he was exhausted. He kept staring around, and his ears were keened for the slightest unnatural sound. His thoughts moved sluggishly, and he tried every trick he knew to remain at peak alertness.

It seemed to him that reality had ceased to exist from the moment *Probe* 2 had been destroyed. He could barely recall any part of his life before that terrible moment. It needed a great effort on his part to picture the faces of his parents back on Earth, and for some time he could not bring to mind an image of his brother Vern, who had evidently died in the destruction of *Probe* 1. If he ever got back to Earth he would have to break that grim news to his parents, he knew, but at the moment that eventuality seemed too remote to be considered.

He tried to get his thoughts back to duty. It was his responsibility to get the survivors off this planet and back to Earth. He was mindful of the fact that *Probe* 3 would be sent to check on events around Muta, and it would certainly share the same fate as its predecessors unless something was done to prevent it reaching Muta orbit. But when he thought over what they had to do to get off the planet his mind sank into despair. Even if the Brutans were not expecting an alien attempt to seize a spaceship the task would have been well nigh impossible, but with their full expectation of such an attempt, Clark was certain they could not succeed.

But the alternative, as he had told Balfin, was to remain for the rest of their days on this planet, and he knew he would rather die attempting to escape than face the possibility of remaining in the jungle for the rest of his life, fighting off Ogrins, Brutans and Marscs. He knew they wouldn't always be so fortunate as they'd turned out to be on this trip, and one by one they would find themselves cut off and taken, to be killed or eaten.

Two hours passed and Clark found his range of vision slowly increasing. Thin rays of sunlight began to lance down through the foliage, and he reluctantly shook the Major and brought him back to reality. Balfin stared around for a moment, then looked at Clark with disappointment in his pale gaze.

'I was dreaming,' he said slowly. 'We were up there in *Probe* 2, pulling out of Muta orbit. Then I had to open my eyes to this nightmare. I always thought nightmares happened while you were asleep, but it seems to work the other way around in this place.'

Clark nodded. He got up and stretched, and after they had eaten part of their survival kit rations they prepared to move out. Balfin went off with the Laser to look around and search for signs of their track on the outward trip, and returned to Clark within fifteen minutes, claiming to have found it.

'I haven't seen anything of the Avics, but I suppose they wouldn't show up too close to the edge of the jungle.' Balfin wiped sweat from his forehead and grinned tightly. 'If you feel like a stroll through the trees then we can move out, Commander.'

Clark nodded and they collected together their gear and set out.

It soon became apparent to Clark that he was in for a rough time. He was practically asleep on his feet, and stumbled and sprawled often over the treacherous roots and undergrowth. But Balfin set a hard pace, and Clark would not call out for a reduction in their progress. The sooner they linked up once more with Pacian and the Avics the sooner they could do something about their predicament.

Time passed, seemingly dead slow to Clark, but they made progress and eventually reached the spot where the Brutan craft had landed in the clearing in its search for them. The craft was still there, a heap of useless metals, reduced to practically nothing by the power of the Laser, and Clark paused for a moment just inside the tree line and stared at the destruction. It had all been so unnecessary.

Violence was not a prerogative of Earthmen, he thought as they stumbled on. Most forms of life lived with violence as a main characteristic. It was the way of Nature, and Nature seemed omniscient and all powerful, governed by the same basic rules right through the Universe. But these alien forms of violence were too much for Clark, and he longed to be off the planet and back amongst his own kind.

Balfin paused after some hours and turned a sweating face towards Clark. The Major's shirt was open to the waist and sweat gleamed upon his tough body. He waited for Clark to join him, then sat down.

'I've been ready for a halt ever since we started,' Clark admitted. 'I figure we'll take a few days rest when we get back to camp. We'll have to lie low for some time to let the Brutans think we're never coming out of the jungle. Once they relax their vigilance we'll find it easier to make our attempt.'

'One throw, win or lose,' Balfin said, chewing a protein tablet. He swigged it down with water and slammed the stopper back into the canteen with the heel of his hand. 'I came on this expedition because I was looking for action and excitement. I certainly got more than I bargained for. Why did you volunteer for this trip, Commander?'

'My brother Vern was aboard *Probe* 1.' Clark thinned his lips for a moment. 'I figured to find out first hand what happened to him.'

'I'm sorry he didn't make it!' Balfin looked away for a moment. 'I don't figure any of us are going to make it either, huh?'

'If we don't it won't be for the want of trying,' Clark said heavily, and a grin touched Balfin's dusty lips.

'That's what I like about you, Commander,' he retorted. 'We come with the same frame of mind. I never admit defeat either.'

'I figure we would have been finished long before now if you hadn't been along, Kester.'

'That's the way I feel about you,' Balfin retorted. 'You've done fine so far, considering what we're up against. I'm happy to leave the rest of it to your judgement.'

Clark shook his head as he considered. He felt that he

couldn't walk another step, but he pushed himself slowly to his feet.

'We should be hitting Pacian's old camp before long, huh?' he demanded.

'A couple of hours, I reckon.' Balfin grunted as he heaved himself upright. 'Things have been quiet since we came back into the jungle, huh?'

'Perhaps too quiet!' Clark looked around.

Balfin checked the Laser, and his blue eyes glittered as he started forward, looking for the trail they had left previously. Clark followed him once more, and they went on and on through the undergrowth.

When they reached the clearing where Pacian had his camp, they found it deserted and desolate. The dead Ogrins, killed in the attack, still lay motionless where they had fallen, but the Avics killed in the raid had been removed. They edged into the clearing, fearing an ambush, but Balfin quickly searched the area and came back to Clark with the news that everyone had gone.

'I've found tracks, Commander. They must have been left by the Avics when they moved to the new camp. Are we gonna stay here the night and go on in the morning?'

'It's been a hard day and I'm whacked,' Clark admitted. 'In any case, we'd get only a few miles before darkness came, and then we'd have to sleep rough in the jungle. I don't think I fancy that. There's no telling what other strange animal forms live on this planet. I figure we won't be losing much time by staying here tonight.'

'I agree with you.' Balfin nodded. 'There are some supplies in one of the huts. Shall I fix some food?'

'Give me the Laser and I'll remain on guard until it's ready.' Clark looked around, shaking his head as a pang of doubt struck him again. They were so far from home and their chances of returning seemed to be diminishing hourly.

Balfin handed over the weapon and went off to one of the huts. Clark settled down in the brush and forced himself to full alertness. He stared around into the impenetrable jungle until Balfin called him thirty minutes later.

After they had eaten they felt easier, and shadows were beginning to creep down into the forest.

'We'll have to take turn about on guard,' Clark said, his eyes narrowed as he studied the deserted camp. 'The Ogrins know of this place and they might come back.'

'I'll take first watch if you want to sleep, Commander,' Balfin said instantly. 'You look all in. I guess I am more accustomed to this way of life than you. I'll take six hours, then call you, and you take over until it's light enough for us to go on.'

Clark agreed, and went into a smaller hut to sleep. He lay down on a pallet and closed his eyes, and the next moment, it seemed, Balfin was shaking him awake and whispering in his ear. Stark reality caught Clark and he left the hut with the Laser in his hands, settling himself down in a vantage point and fighting his tiredness. Another six hours sleep would have made him more suitable to another day of slogging through the jungle.

Time passed slowly, and he became cramped as he waited unmoving and cold. Dawn came eventually, and he waited for thirty minutes after he could see across the clearing to ensure there was no possibility of another Ogrin attact. But the forest was silent and still, and again Clark was struck by the eeriness that was created by the absence of smaller forest life. There were no smaller creatures or birds, no natural sounds anywhere, and it worried Clark, made him think that unseen things were slinking through the undergrowth, scaring away the usual lower order of life.

He went to awaken Balfin, and they breakfasted quickly. Clark was stiff and sombre, but impatient to get on. He felt they were in the grip of a situation over which he had not the smallest control. Whatever their fate was to be, they were hurrying towards it without the ability to stop and consider their intentions or actions.

Balfin picked up the faint trail the Avics had left on their move to Pacian's new camp, and soon they were pushing forward through the undergrowth once more. The ground seemed softer in this deeper recess of the forest, and Clark found his feet sinking in sometimes up to the ankle. He soon became tired once more, and made hard work of following the seemingly untiring Balfin.

Suddenly Balfin went to ground, and Clark dropped flat in his tracks, his instincts at work despite the fact that his mind was filled with diverting thought. At first Clark feared the worst, but the forest echoed with trilling and twittering, and he began to rise, aware that they had found some Avics. Balfin was getting to his feet, and amongst the trees appeared the strange figures of several birdmen.

Clark had to use his transmuter to understand what was being said, and soon discovered that these were from Pacian's camp, preparing to make for the edge of the forest to await Clark's return. They were delighted that the trip was now unnecessary, and assured Clark that another hour's journey would take them into the new camp.

Clark lost some of his tension now they had company, and he plodded on within the party as they covered the last lap. He was dripping sweat by the time the scouting Avics called out that the camp was in sight, and Clark was filled with relief.

Magenta and Hanton came running across the clearing from the cluster of huts as soon as word reached the camp of Clark's return, and Clark looked into Magenta's smooth face, telling himself that he hadn't expected to see her again. She almost threw herself into his arms, such was her excitement, and Hanton stood back, watching, looking around for Searby.

Pacian came up, twittering excitedly, and Clark held up a hand.

'How are Mallory and Paine?' he asked.

'Lieutenant Paine didn't survive the trip here,' Magenta said softly. 'We buried him, Commander.'

'And Mallory!' There was an edge to Clark's tones. He had bad news to impart.

'Lieutenant Mallory is conscious and making progress. How did you get on? Were you successful?' The urgency of the situation was obviously almost too much for the woman. Her dark gaze slid to Balfin's hard, tired face, and she looked at Clark once more. 'What happened to Professor Searby? He didn't come back with you!'

'Let's get into one of the huts and have some food. I'll give you a report while we're resting. I'm not an old man, but I've never felt so tired before in all my life.'

'It's the climate and conditions,' Hanton said grimly. 'It takes a long time to really adjust to it. But what about the Professor, Commander? Is he all right?'

'He's dead!' Clark tightened his lips and shook his head. 'It's a nightmare to even recall it.'

They were silent, and Pacian led the way to one of the huts. Clark sank down on a pallet and tried to relax, but his nerves were taut and his mind was still clutched by the unreasoning horror that had assailed him the moment he'd opened his eyes to find himself a prisoner of the Marscs.

Balfin began to tell the others of their experiences after leaving the forest, and Clark listened intently, his teeth clenched. It all sounded too bad to be true, but he relived every instant of it, feeling the horror drawing tighter in the darker recesses of his mind.

There was silence after Balfin ended his narrative, and then Pacian ruffled his shoulder feathers and twittered gently. Clark turned up the transmuter.

'The Marscs have always been our enemies. They come into the forest hunting us at times, and they think nothing of marching several days to catch us. We fear them more than we fear the Ogrins.'

'Did you have any luck looking for a way off the planet, Commander?' Hanton demanded.

Clark explained his trip with Ralip, and Hanton's eyes gleamed.

'That sounds promising, sir! But will we be able to grab one of their ships?'

'I fear they will have a tight security ring around the space-port.' Clark's eyes glittered as he recalled the view that had met his eyes when Ralip's skyraft had circled the spaceport. 'We're going to have to sweat it out for a week at least before we think of moving on.' He glanced at Pacian. 'Can you put up with us for that length of time?'

'You are free to stay as long as you wish,' the Avic retorted. 'We are pleased to have your company. Let me know if there is any way we can help you.'

Clark thanked the alien. 'Are you safe from attack here?' he asked.

'As safe here as anywhere in the forest. There is nowhere perfectly safe for us. But I don't estimate any attacks being made against us at this spot. We have never been attacked by Marscs or Ogrins in this area.'

'Then we'll sit it out for a week before contemplating any movement,' Clark decided. 'He glanced at the intent faces watching him, saw worry in Magenta's beautiful features and resignation on Hanton's tough face. He glanced at Balfin and knew that Balfin was prepared to back him up in anything he decided to do. 'We'd better get all the rest we can,' he continued. 'When we do move out it will be hard and dangerous. We'll have to move fast and be prepared for anything. In a week Mallory should be well enough to move, but in any case we shall have to wait for his complete recovery. But that won't mean we shall be sitting around doing nothing constructive. There are plans to make and details to work out.'

His words fired them with some determination, but Clark himself was far from feeling confident. With the horror of their brush with the Marscs still fresh in his mind he could only think that perhaps the only safe course for them was to remain here in the forest with the Avics. It would be a mean kind of existence, but at least they would be alive. On the other hand the prize that glittered seemingly out of reach, the means to return to Earth, seemed important enough for them to take the risks required.

Clark tried to relax when the others left the hut, and he settled himself to sleep. For two nights he had practically been without sleep, and his thought processes were slow and erratic. He closed his eyes and tried to ease his aching body, and with the knowledge that whatever lay ahead of them was still in the future, he blotted out his weariness and despair and gave up the unequal fight to maintain strict control of his senses. He slept.

Chapter Twelve

The following days passed slowly, and as Clark observed, they spent most of the time talking over plans and ideas. A week after their return to the forest, Clark found himself in a better frame of mind. Some of the horror that had assailed him in their brush with the Marscs had faded into the background, and once again he was feeling optimistic. He did not diminish the fact that the odds were against them, and he fancied they would not be able to successfully complete the last part of their mission, the stealing of a ship capable of carrying them away from the planet. Even if the Brutans were not on their guard against such an attack, he figured their security measures would be more than sufficient to prevent the casual stealing of a spaceship. In any case, Clark feared that no such ship would be just sitting on a launchpad waiting for them to board it.

But he kept his mind occupied as much as possible and tried not to brood upon the climax. Whatever transpired, they would be totally committed, and if they ran out of luck, or lost the initiative, they would pay with their lives. It was a gamble, and they had to take the chances or sentence themselves to this living nightmare of remaining on Muta with the Avics for company and the Ogrins, Brutans and Marscs for enemies.

Lieutenant Mallory made good recovery during the passing week, and at the end of that time he was walking around normally. He had been sullen and morose for the first few days, no doubt fully aware that his panic-stricken flight which had wrecked the shuttlecraft and injured him had really smashed their chances of escape. But as the days went by he slowly found the nerve to face his colleagues once more.

Clark said nothing of Mallory's lapse, but he was aware that Mallory was likely to break again under pressure, and made a mental note not to trust him completely in any future operation. He watched Mallory's face while they talked over their intentions, and noted the set expression which showed on the man's pale features, the hunted look which showed briefly in his dark eyes.

Balfin was the mainspring in the plot to steal the spaceship. He sat for hours with Clark, discussing all the possibilities, pointing out the apparent pitfalls and estimating their chances. But they finally agreed that a great deal depended upon the aid they could expect from Ralip when they returned to the farm, and Clark was only too aware that if the situation there had changed a great deal since they'd left then they would have to revise all their plans.

The Avics did what they could to help, but that aid consisted mostly of information that really wouldn't help. None of the Avics had ever seen the spaceport or a spaceship. None of them had left the forest. But they all knew something about the Brutans, and Clark listened to all he could about their major enemies.

Finally Clark decided they were ready to make their attempt. He felt that the longer they delayed the less hopeful they became. Mallory was well enough to make the tough trip through the forest, and they would not force the pace. The Avics agreed to accompany them to the edge of the forest, and Clark was thankful for their help.

They set out at dawn and to Clark's relief he discovered that the past week had helped him a great deal in becoming acclimatized. The going was still rough, but he took it in his stride, and by the end of that first day he was well pleased with their progress. When they made camp, with Avic guards out to screen them, they ate in the growing shadows, then talked before sleeping.

'We'll be out of the forest by tomorrow evening,' Clark said at a short briefing. 'Get all the sleep you can tonight, because tomorrow will be a hard day and we've got to go on without halting once we're out of the trees. It's a long walk to the farm, and we can expect no other help until we get there.'

They turned in, and slept soundlessly until dawn, thoroughly exhausted by their physical efforts.

Next morning they went on, and Clark began to feel the effects of being hemmed in by the tall trees. He longed for open countryside, despite the fact they would be more vulnerable to detection. The hours passed slowly, and during the afternoon Pacian came back from the leaders to talk with him.

'We are near to the spot where your craft crashed,' the Avic said. 'Do you want to visit the place? Is there anything aboard that might be of help to you?'

'We'll give it a miss,' Clark said without hesitation. 'The Brutans are aware of its location and most probably they have set a trap around it. There are one or two items aboard I could do with, but I'd rather go without them than take any kind of a chance now.'

The Avic nodded and went back to the leaders, and Clark wiped sweat from his brow and told himself that they were nearing the end of the toughest part of the hike. He was impatient now to get out of the trees, to be able to stand up and look into the distance. He was accustomed to peering through a hatch at illimitable space, and the close confines of the trees made him chafe inwardly.

Presently Pacian returned, twittering softly, and Clark

fancied there was some kind of trouble. But the Avic had news.

'One of our scouts went close to the clearing where the shuttlecraft lay, and he reports that it is gone.'

Clark thought about that, a frown on his rugged face.

'The Brutans?' he demanded.

'Most likely. They had probably taken it to their city to examine it.'

'It's of no use to us. It was broken beyond repair!' Clark did not want to become too single-minded, but he knew their only chance of escape lay in capturing a spaceship.

They went on, and as shadows began to fall amongst the trees the Avics became excited. Finally a halt was called and Pacian came up quickly.

'We are a mile from the tunnel and dare not go closer until the sun has gone down,' the Avic announced. 'We can do no more for you. But we shall wait until you enter the tunnel before returning to our camp. I hope you will be able to get away from Muta, Commander. If you do you must warn your people not to venture here again.'

'Don't worry!' Clark smiled thinly. 'We'll give Muta a wide berth next time.'

They spent the time waiting for darkness by eating and preparing for the last phase of the trip. Clark was beginning to feel nervous, because so much of the next part of their plan depended upon Ralip, and until they saw the Brutan woman again they would have no idea of the general situation.

When it was dark enough for them to leave, Balfin went on ahead with Hanton, each carrying a Laser, and Clark took his leave of the Avics. He shook hands with Pacian and then the Avics turned and faded into the jungle. Clark looked around, staring into the deserted areas, feeling that the Avics were still watching them and would continue to do so until they were safely into the tunnel, and Clark could not help wondering what would have become of them if the Avics had proved to be enemies instead of friends! He dared not dwell upon the thought and turned his attention to his own party.

Magenta and Mallory was standing close together, and Clark peered at Mallory, wondering how he had taken the tough march. Mallory's teeth glinted as he forced a smile.

'I'm all right, Commander,' he said tightly. 'Don't worry about me. I can keep going.'

'The worst part of it is over,' Clark said. 'When we get out of the tunnel it will be all open countryside. Let's move on, and stay close to me now.'

They moved along the faint trail that Balfin and Hanton had left, and when the ground began to rise Clark knew they were close to the hill and the tunnel. He finally halted and made Mallory and the girl stay down while he went ahead to contact Balfin, and now there were tiny fears in the back of his mind, trying to take hold of his imagination and attention. He felt the Brutans might have discovered the tunnel and had set a trap there for them. But there was no other way out, and if they had to fight for their passage then they would do so. There could be no turning back now.

A whispered challenge came to his ears and he replied instantly, moving in to find himself covered by the Laser in Hanton's hands.

'The Major has gone through the tunnel to check the other side,' Hanton said. 'We're doing all right so far, huh, Commander?'

'If the rest of it goes as easy as the first phase then we'll have nothing to worry about,' Clark retorted. 'But after this there must be no talking. The Brutans appear to have some kind of sonic detector.'

He could hardly make out Hanton's features, and they could not see more than a yard through the gloom. They crouched together and waited for Balfin's return, and the minutes seemed like hours.

Presently there was a faint rustling sound from the direction Balfin had taken, and the next moment Balfin appeared. He was breathless from his exertions and sat for a moment taking deep breaths.

'The way is clear as far as I can tell,' he said at length. 'I went through the tunnel and checked outside it. There's no sign of guards. I expect a week of waiting around with nothing happening has put them off.'

'I hope you're right.' Clark started to his feet. 'I'll fetch Mallory and Magenta and we'll go through the tunnel. We can't afford to waste any time. It will be a close thing as it is to get to Ralip's farm by dawn.'

Balfin nodded, knowing only too well what lay before them, and Clark went back to where he had left Mallory and the woman. They were waiting for him, silent and still, and Clark led them back once more. When they reached the spot where Balfin and Hanton were crouching the Major got up instantly and started away. They followed him closely, moving slowly and silently.

Passing through the tunnel proved to be no less nerve racking than the previous times, Clark found, and they held on to one another in the total darkness. When they emerged finally they dropped into cover while Balfin went forward to check out their route.

Clark warned the others not to speak or make any noise under any circumstances, and they waited, finding a keen wind in their faces. The moons were not showing in the sky and Clark was thankful that the night was much darker than their previous trip. But the moons would be showing later, and by that time he wanted to be well on his way to Ralip's farm.

Balfin returned, moving stealthily, and he dropped down beside Clark.

'That camp is still where I saw it before, but the men there are not on duty. I didn't see any guards prowling around. I figure they've got over the scare when we first landed, and this camp is merely a routine station to guard against Ogrins and the like.' There was no emotion in Balfin's soft voice, and the news heartened Clark.

'Okay, Kester,' he said. 'Lead off and we'll start making good time. So far so good!'

They went on, remaining in close contact in the darkness, and as time went by Clark felt his spirits begin to soar. If they managed to avoid trouble then there would be few complications in this phase. It would make the last part seem more possible to accomplish.

But Hanton, on Clark's right, was suddenly going down, and Clark spotted movement in the sky at the same time he caught Hanton's movement. The others were going down, and Clark looked up as he hit the ground, making out the ominous shape of a skyraft coming silently towards them. It could only be spotted by the blanking out of stars in the background, and it was perfectly silent.

They lay still, and Clark found his nerves tightening. He hoped neither Hanton nor Balfin would fire at the craft, unless it attacked them, and he turned his head slowly as he followed its progress. It went right over them, but did not deviate from its course or lose any speed. It disappeared in the direction they came from, and Clark took a deep breath as he waited until a safe period had elapsed.

Balfin got up to go on and they hurried to keep him in sight. Clark looked around, seeing Mallory and Magenta together, and the woman seemed to be helping Mallory. Clark waited for them to draw level, and he leaned towards Mallory.

'How are you making out?' Clark demanded.

'Beginning to feel the pace a little now, sir,' Mallory admitted. 'How much farther to the farm?'

'Several hours yet. I'll tell Balfin to lose pace a little. It will be better to arrive later than schedule than have trouble because we're moving too fast for you. Just take it easy.'

He went on then, increasing his pace to catch Balfin, and the Major turned his head as he glimpsed Clark's shadow gaining on him. Clark opened his mouth to ask the Major to slow his pace, but before the words came a shaft of brilliant white light stabbed down at an angle from the dark sky, striking the ground a hundred feet to their left. Balfin fell to the ground, sweeping out an arm that knocked Clark flying, and as he rolled, Clark caught a glimpse of the other three dropping to ground.

The skyraft had swung around and come back, and they had not heard it. Now it blotted out the stars as it zig-zagged slowly around the area, sending blasts of pure energy at the shadowed ground.

Fortunately the first blast was also the nearest to them, and Clark lay motionless, his mind tight with fear, watching the imperceptible movement of the craft. The others did not move, and Clark was relieved that Hanton had not attempted to retaliate with his Laser.

Presently the skyraft moved away again, and they watched it for some moments, deluging areas of the ground with death, and the farther away it went the easier Clark began to breathe.

'That was too close for comfort,' Balfin said shortly. 'Do you figure they've got detectors aboard that picked up signs of us?'

'I don't think so!' Clark shook his head. 'If they had, that first shot would have been a whole lot closer. Let's get moving again, Kester. We can't afford to drop behind schedule.'

Balfin nodded and got slowly to his feet. 'We'll have to keep a better watch after this,' he vowed.

Clark went back to Mallory and Magenta as they went on, and put an arm around Mallory, getting his right shoulder in

Mallory's left armpit. Mallory put an arm around Clark's shoulder, and it was obvious to Clark that Mallory had taken about enough. With Magenta on the other side of Mallory, helping with her light strength, they continued.

They went on without further incident, although they saw activity in the distance, and several skyrafts seemed to be involved in the shooting. There was no noise, and the bright, stabbing beams of energy were striking the ground several miles away. Some answering flashes were directed skywards, and Clark figured there was another Ogrin raid in progress. But they did not halt, and Balfin went on tirelessly, leading the way without hesitation.

The moons appeared above the horizon, one following the other after an interval of twenty minutes, and Clark did not like the pale light that infused the velvet night. The stars seemed all the brighter now, and when Clark gazed around he could see the faces of his companions quite clearly.

Time passed and Clark felt the burden of Mallory sapping his strength. Mallory was becoming weaker, sagging in the arms of Clark and Magenta, and finally Clark had to call a halt. He lowered Mallory to the ground and left Magenta sitting beside him while he went on to Balfin.

'Mallory can't go any farther under his own power,' Clark said. 'I've practically carried him the last two miles. I figure we're gonna have to carry him or leave him for a spell.'

'How can we leave him?' Balfin demanded. 'We couldn't get back for him before daylight.'

'If we got Ralip to use her skyraft we could pick him up around dawn,' Clark said.

'That's if the situation is as we left it over a week ago,' Balfin said slowly. 'What happens if we get to the farm and find it impossible to use the skyraft? When daylight comes Mallory will be spotted.'

'How far to the farm now, do you reckon?' Clark demanded.

'Must be a couple of hours at least. I think I know exactly where we are, but it's difficult to tell in this light.'

'We've got nothing we can use to rig up a stretcher,' Clark said. 'We can't sling him across a shoulder because it would be too uncomfortable for his injured ribs.'

'Two of us could carry him between us,' Balfin said. 'I think Hanton could help me. We're both big men. If you'll take the lead, Commander, we'll handle Mallory.'

'Okay, let's try it.' Clark took the Laser. He waited while Balfin and Hanton organized themselves, then started off in the lead. Magenta came to join him and Balfin and Hanton, carrying Mallory between them, followed a few paces in the rear.

Clark adjusted his pace to those behind him, and he stared around, his eyes ceaselessly searching his surroundings. He felt vulnerable in the moonlight, but his increased field of vision enabled him to check his direction more easily, and he was certain the farm was not so far ahead.

Balfin called for a halt an hour later, and they sat on the ground in a group, breathless and tense. Mallory stretched himself out and lay breathing heavily, and Clark was worried about the future. If Mallory became too weak or ill to move then they would have to lie up in cover somewhere during the long hours of daylight, and he suspected there would be considerable activity in the area when the sun came up. But he said nothing to the others, and waited patiently until Balfin was ready to go on.

As he and Hanton picked up Mallory the Lieutenant tried to get away from them, and he fell to the ground as they lost their hold upon him.

'Leave me!' Mallory said in ringing tones. 'I ain't too keen on going through with this. Leave me here and I'll take my chances with the Brutans in the morning.'

'You're going along with us,' Clark said. 'Just stay quiet. We're not far from the farm now. We'll be able to rest up there all day tomorrow. You're tired now, Mallory. We're all tired. But you'll feel better when you've had some food and rested up.'

They went on once more, and soon Clark saw dawn creeping into the sky. He felt a sense of urgency seeping into his mind, and he hoped they would not have trouble finding the farm. He went on relentlessly, pushing one foot before the other, finding the effort becoming increasingly more difficult to find. When he glanced back and saw Balfin and Hanton staggering under the weight of the now semi-conscious Mallory he clenched his teeth and prayed for a chance to succeed. They had been up against it from the moment they had detached from *Probe* 2. There had been the promise of success right from the start, but now the situation was tightening up against them, and in the darker hours that came upon them, Clark found his determination and hope foundering.

Magenta recalled his attention to his surroundings, and he thinned his lips as he looked around, blinking when he realized that he had let his thoughts wander—a dangerous practice under the circumstances.

'There are buildings ahead,' the woman reported softly, and Clark took a swift breath of relief. He narrowed his eyes and saw the outbuildings of Ralip's farm, and a sigh gusted from him as he felt his determination strengthen once more.

'Get down and stay down,' he said in low tones, and turned as Balfin and Hanton lowered Mallory to the ground. 'Come with me, Kester. We'll go check out the house. It's almost dawn and we need to get under cover.'

Magenta moved to Mallory's side to examine him while Balfin came towards Clark, and Clark turned instantly, tightening his grip upon the Laser as he started towards the farm. They went on in silence, bent almost double, moving slowly, watchful and alert, and Balfin was ready to use the Laser should the need arise.

They skirted the small garage that housed the skyraft, and then got their first glimpse of the house itself. Clark halted in surprise as he peered through the shadows. The outline of the house was not tall and smooth, as it should have been. The roof and the upper storey was crumpled and in ruins.

Balfin went to ground instantly, and Clark followed quickly. For a moment they stared at the house, then looked at one another, and in the early morning they could see nothing more than the pale oval of their faces.

'What the hell happened here?' Balfin demanded hoarsely. 'There's been trouble for sure. The house is practically knocked flat.'

Clark shook his head slowly, his mind enveloped by shreds of shock. There was an image of Ralip's heavy face on the screen of his mind, and he was already fearing the worst, although he tried to prevent the working of his imagination. He pushed himself slowly to his feet and started towards the ruins, and when Balfin arose, Clark turned on him.

'You'd better stay down and cover me, Kester, just in case,' he said.

Balfin nodded and dropped flat again, and Clark went forward alone, the Laser ready in his hands. He heard his footsteps echoing as he crossed the open space before the house, and he stumbled several times as bits of rubble turned underfoot. As he drew nearer to the ruin he saw more clearly the extent of the damage, and his mind kept trying to tell him that they were finished, for without Ralip's help they could not possibly make it to the spaceport.

He dared not call Ralip's name or give any indication of his presence. He found the front of the house blocked to his feet and walked around the shattered building, wondering how it had come to be destroyed. But more important—what had happened to Ralip herself?

There was deep shadow around the rear of the building and Clark moved slowly, his nerves taut. He found the kitchen door closed and obdurate against his attempts to open it, and the slight sounds that he made echoed away into the surrounding grey shadows. He started to go on, to make a complete circuit of the house, and turned a corner to find three tall figures confronting him with rod-like weapons levelled in their hands.

Clark halted instantly, too shocked to think of using the Laser, and the three figures closed upon him immediately. One of them spoke sharply, in Brutan, and Clark waited for the transmuter to give him the question in English. It came through in a few seconds.

'Who are you and what are you doing here?'

Clark knew it was too late to try and resist. He was covered by three weapons, and even if he managed to use the Laser they would surely cut him down before he managed to get all three of them. They were out of sight of Balfin, who would not know what was happening, and Clark figured that if he surrendered without trouble the Brutans might take him away immediately, enabling Balfin to spot them, and sight of himself under restriction by Brutans would enable Balfin to understand the situation. The others might be able to get clear.

Clark's thoughts were fast and furious in that split second as he contemplated, and then he raised his hands above his shoulders.

'I am one of the aliens from the spaceship that was destroyed in orbit over a week ago,' he said resignedly, and waited for his words to be translated. 'I surrender myself to you.'

His words convinced him more than the weapons covering him that he had come to the end of his escape attempt, and all he could do now was prevent these aliens learning of the presence of Balfin and the others. Someone had to escape, and Clark meant to do his best to see that the others avoided capture. But he mentally consigned himself to his fate, and as he stood watching the three Brutans his hopes for his own future sank way below zero!

Chapter Thirteen

'Where are your companions?' the apparent leader of the Brutan trio demanded. 'You are wearing a transmuter and can understand my language. Answer now, and drop that weapon you are holding. It cannot avail you in this situation.'

Clark got the words after a slight pause, and he let the Laser fall from his right hand. It thudded on the hard ground and Clark felt that the small sound was the knell to his own doom.

'I am alone,' he said, having no intention of admitting to the presence of the others.

'What are you doing here?'

'Looking for food!'

'You were looking for the woman who lives here. She has befriended you.'

'A Brutan?' Clark demanded scornfully. 'You should know better than that.'

'We have arrested the woman. She was identified as flying her skyraft around the spaceport, and it is supposed that you were with her.'

'I have not made contact with any alien on this planet,' Clark said.

Their voices were echoing slightly against the wall beside them, and Clark let his shoulders slump a little as he lowered his hands to his side. Daylight was beginning to filter through the shadows, and he could see a crimson glow in the sky to the east. He took a deep breath and recalled how sweet daybreak was back on Earth, and his breath quivered in his throat as emotion struck him.

'You will accompany us! Walk towards the front of the house and do not try to escape. You will be interrogated at headquarters. You are an alien, and it is suspected that you have killed Brutans in your activities since landing.'

They stepped aside for him, and Clark felt dwarfed by them as he moved forward. He saw one of them bend to pick up the Laser, and then he reached the front corner of the house and stepped around it. As he reached the corner he saw Balfin coming across the yard towards him.

In the split second that he was out of sight of the Brutans, Clark hurled himself sideways. Balfin saw him, had halted at his appearance at the corner, but when Clark hurled himself flat Balfin was alerted. He dropped to one knee when he caught sight of the tall figures of the Brutans appearing. For a moment he hesitated, and heard the shouts of the big aliens. Then he fired the Laser and cut them down, blinding Clark with the flash.

Clark closed his eyes and gritted his teeth. He heard the strange crackling sound of Balfin's attack, and for several seconds he could not see properly. He sat up, blinking, when Balfin reached him.

'Where the hell did they come from?' Balfin demanded. 'I got the shock of my life when you appeared around that corner, then threw yourself down. I guessed something was wrong, but I didn't figure it was as wrong as that.'

'You saved my life, and probably the whole situation.' Clark got unsteadily to his feet. He looked around anxiously. Daylight was coming in now, and the fiery tip of the sun was just showing above a distant ridge. 'We're in trouble, Kester.' He quickly narrated what he had learned from the three Brutans.

'Hell, we're in bad trouble! What are we gonna do, Commander?'

'Ralip's skyraft!' Clark was grasping at straws and he knew it. 'It barely made it back from that flight I made to the spaceport, but it might have been repaired. I don't know when Ralip was arrested.'

'You figure to go right ahead with this plan we made?' Balfin stared into Clark's face.

'You get a better idea?' Clark kept his gaze steady. 'Can we get back to the jungle and the Avics? And if we do, are we going to spend the rest of our days with them?'

'I don't want to go back.' Balfin sighed heavily and shook his head. 'I want to get back to Earth. I'll go through hell with you, Commander, but I don't think there'll be much chance of coming out the other side.'

'We could take the skyraft to the perimeter of the spaceport and look over the place. If there's a chance of getting away we'll take it, but I have no intention of throwing our lives away in a suicide bid.' Clark turned and looked at the dead Brutans. 'We'll have to conceal their bodies.'

'I'll take care of that while you look over that skyraft.' Balfin spoke grimly. 'We've got to get moving. The sun is coming up fast. Did you get any idea on how to fly one of these things when Ralip took you up?'

'I think I can get us where we want to go,' Clark said. He started away across the yard. 'I'll call the others in. We've got to get out of here fast in case those three have friends.'

Balfin went across to the dead Brutans and picked up the Laser Clark had discarded. He tested it in a short emission, and Clark was surprised it still worked. He took it and hurried away across the yard, and when he reached the garage he paused and looked for Hanton and the others. He saw Hanton's head and shoulders sticking up out of a depression, and waved a hand, beckoning them to come in. He waited until he saw Hanton and Magenta helping Mallory forward then went into the garage.

Clark paused in the doorway of the garage and stared at the empty space where the skyraft had stood. A bitter sight escaped him as he turned slowly and went out. Another setback, and the worst so far. He stared around the yard, his dark eyes filled with a bleak expression.

Hanton came up, supporting Mallory, who seemed semi-conscious.

'What was the shooting, Commander?' the big gunner demanded.

'Just a little trouble the Major took care of. Can you make it across to the house?'

Hanton nodded and went on, taking most of Mallory's weight. Magenta paused and looked into Clark's taut face. She had a gaunt expression on her smooth features, but her eyes were bright.

'Another setback, Commander?' she asked

'We've got a little trouble on our hands,' he admitted. 'Let's go over to the house and get under cover. Then we can talk about it.'

They started across the open ground, and Clark saw that Balfin had already dragged the bodies of the dead Brutans out of sight. Hanton was helping Mallory through the doorway of the house, and Balfin stood at the left front corner of the shattered building, watching their surroundings.

Clark and Magenta were twenty yards from the house when Balfin yelled.

'Skyraft coming. Get under cover!'

Clark grasped the woman's arm and hurried her into the house. He closed the door and went to a window, peering out anxiously at the sky. There was a skyraft visible, still a long way off but obviously making for the farm.

'Stay in cover and don't go near to the windows,' Clark said. He went to a side window and peered out, catching a glimpse of Balfin pressed back out of sight of the yard around the corner, his back to Clark. 'Kester!' Clark called, and the Major turned quickly.

'We need that craft, Commander,' Balfin said. His face was tense and there was a fine sheen of sweat on his forehead.

'I agree with you! I'll cover it from the front of the house. If it lands we've got to take it without damaging it. Let's see who gets out of it and how many there are before we do anything.'

'They could be coming to check on the men we killed,' Balfin said. 'They didn't have any kind of a craft here, so perhaps they were dropped off and now they're to be picked up.'

'Okay. I'll go back to the front door. Stay out of sight.'

Balfin nodded and grinned and Clark turned away, moving back to a front window. Mallory was lying on the floor with Hanton and Magenta bending over him.

The skyraft was coming in to land. It swung around the farm first, and Clark was afraid that Balfin might be spotted. But the craft, painted black and white in large squares, eased down to drop into the dust twenty yards from the front of the house.

Clark stayed back from the window, peering out cautiously, and he narrowed his eyes when two figures alighted from the craft. One he recognized instantly as Ralip, and he felt a surging of hope as he stared at her large, heavy face. Her companion was dressed in a dark leathery uniform, a big man, almost nine feet tall, and carrying a rod-like weapon in his hands. He spoke to Ralip, who seemed downcast and subdued, and they came slowly towards the house, Ralip leading, the man following closely, his face showing impatience and bad humour.

The man suddenly yelled loudly, and echoes fled around the yard. Clark could not pick up what was said on the transmuter. He turned up the volume and waited. Ralip was coming straight to the door of the house, and Clark tightened his lips as he peered at the waiting skyraft. There didn't seem to be anyone else aboard the craft, and his hopes began to rise. This man with Ralip was the local security chief, Quartus. Clark had seen him after Ralip brought him back from the flight to the spaceport.

Moving away from the window, Clark checked the Laser, and he motioned for Hanton and Magenta to remain still. The next moment the door was opened and Ralip entered. She came into the room and paused, not seeing Clark at first. But she saw Hanton and Magenta hunched over Mallory, and Clark saw her expression change as she looked around. Then she spotted him, and Clark went forward swiftly, stepping into the open doorway, the Laser levelled in his hands. He confronted the Brutan, who stared at him stolidly, not showing surprise. The rod-like weapon in the Brutan's hands was pointing to the left, and Clark knew he had the advantage.

'Drop your weapon,' Clark ordered, and the transmuter translated his words. 'You are under the cover of another weapon to your left.'

The Brutan turned his head instantly, and saw Balfin, moving forward from the corner. He opened his large hands and his energy gun dropped to the ground.

'Come in,' Clark invited, moving backwards, and he felt dwarfed by this huge man.

Quartus entered the house and Balfin showed up at his back, closing the door. For a moment there was silence. Then Clark looked at Ralip, who was staring at him as if unable to believe her eyes.

'What happened here, Ralip?' Clark demanded.

'They came after you had gone back to the forest. They said I knew something about your movements. My house was destroyed and they took me into the city to make me tell what I know.'

'But you lied to us, Ralip,' the Brutan said. 'You know the penalty for aiding enemies of the State.'

'We don't have to go into that,' Clark said. 'There isn't much time. We are taking that skyraft out there and flying to the spaceport, where we'll take the first available spaceship out.'

'That will be impossible,' Quartus said instantly. 'The security has been doubled. You would never get away with it.'

Clark grinned as he adjusted the transmuter. He nodded.

'We'll get away with it or die in the attempt. Under your protection we should have a better chance than trying it alone.'

'I will not help you.' There was a determined note in the Brutan's tones.

'We don't need your help beyond the use of your craft,' Clark said. 'Kester, find something to tie our alien friend with, and make sure he cannot get loose inside of several hours.'

'Leave it to me,' Balfin said. 'But I figure it would be safer if we took him along. Some of his friends might drop in just after we leave, and they could get in touch with the spaceport and warn them what to expect. We'd walk into real trouble.'

'You're right. But tie him anyway. We are no match for him physically.'

'You won't get away with this,' the Brutan said sharply.

'Then we'll all die trying,' Balfin retorted. He motioned for Hanton to help him, and Clark kept the Brutan covered until he had been securely tied.

'Ralip, do you still want to go along with us?' Clark demanded.

'I do! You can see what they have done to my home, and after this they would kill me for helping you.'

'There's a chance we may not succeed.' A grim note touched Clark's tones.

'I have no chance at all staying here,' she said.

Clark nodded. 'Can you fly that machine you arrived in?'

'Yes. We should have no trouble getting to the spaceport because Quartus is the most powerful man in this district. His craft is painted so everyone knows it is his. We should be able to land on the spaceport without being challenged.'

'Are there regular flights by spaceships?' Clark demanded.

'Of course. One ship leaves every day on a regular run.'

'What time?' Clark was watching Quartus intently, and although the Brutan was tied he intended taking no chances.

'At noon!' Ralip was frowning, trying to calculate what Clark was planning.

'It has been cancelled,' Quartus rapped.

'That's another chance we'll take.' Clark was thinking swiftly. 'I don't think we'll have much chance of dropping in at the spaceport and finding a craft sitting there waiting for us to steal it. But if we show up a couple of minutes before a scheduled flight blasts off then we'll have a chance of catching it.'

Balfin nodded. He was testing the knots in the rope he'd used to bind the Brutan.

'With this guy along we shan't get much trouble from their security,' he said. 'I'll stick close to Mr Quartus and keep him sweet.'

'All right. Now we'll have to spend some time here if we are not to arrive at the spaceport too soon, so let us be careful. You tell us when we should leave, Ralip, to get to the scheduled flight a few minutes before it takes off.'

The woman nodded, and now there was a spark of hope in her expression. Clark was feeling the same way. He grinned.

'We could do with some food,' he said.

'I'll see what they left for us,' Ralip promised.

Clark was tensed up now, and time seemed to stand still. He made Hanton stand guard with a Laser, and after they had eaten he took a turn himself, standing by the front door, watching the sky and the approaches to the farm. But there was nothing moving out there in the brilliant sunlight. Balfin remained close to their prisoner, guarding him with the other Laser, and Magenta watched the rear of the house.

If they were discovered before their departure, Clark intended taking off in the skyraft and making an attempt to bluff their way clear. Time went by, and his spirits rose accordingly.

Finally Ralip indicated that they ought to be moving, and Clark went with her to the skyraft. It was a larger machine than the one Ralip had used, and it was more heavily armed. Clark felt his spirits rise still more as he looked around the interior.

'You're sure you can fly this with no trouble?' he demanded.

'I can fly it,' Ralip said. 'You'd better have Quartus in the front beside me, so you and your companions can sit in the rear and cover him. Don't give him a chance to overpower you. He could ruin everything.'

'We're only too aware of that,' Clark said. 'Don't worry about Quartus. You just concentrate on getting us down beside that spaceship within a few minutes of her departure.'

He went back into the house and helped carry Mallory out. Then Balfin escorted their prisoner, and Quartus was seated in the front seat beside Ralip, with Balfin sitting behind the Brutan, the muzzle of the Laser pressed against the big alien's spine.

Clark got into the craft and closed the door. Ralip looked around then turned to the controls, and the next moment they were lifting into the air and swinging away from the farm. Balfin caught Clark's eye and grinned, and Clark smiled, feeling the weight of responsibility lifting a little from his shoulders. There was nothing else he could do now. They were committed. This was the last phase of their bid to escape, and if they succeeded all their troubles would be over. He dared not let his thoughts dwell upon the alternative.

A metallic voice suddenly filled the cabin with a stream of unintelligible sound, and Ralip leaned forward and turned off the communicator.

'Turn it on,' Clark said instantly. 'If Quartus is supposed to report in or answer that call then we'll arouse suspicion by maintaining silence.'

'We can't take the chance on him giving the true situation,' Balfin said in great concern.

'Gag him!' Clark spoke with quick decision. 'We don't need him to say anything.' He waited until Balfin had carried out his order, and the big Brutan was livid, but cowed by the muzzle of the Laser that Hanton was pressing against his left ear. 'That's better. Wait a minute, Ralip, before turning on the communicator.'

They went on in silence while Clark set to work on the transmuter. He knew the many uses of the instrument, and he hastened to instruct the small computer control. When he was ready he switched on and spoke in English into the microphone, and his words came out of the transmuter in Brutan, in the voice of their captive.

Ralip glanced over her shoulder in surprise, and Clark grinned as he looked at their captive. Quartus was staring at the transmuter as if he couldn't believe his ears.

'This is a great little machine,' Clark said. 'I've programmed it to use your voice wavelengths, Quartus, and your tongue. I can give any order I require in my own language and it will come out of this box as if you had spoken. Now you can turn on the communicator, Ralip. Let's hear what's being said.'

Ralip glanced at him again, and there was doubt showing in her expression, but she turned a switch and a harsh voice gave forth with another string of unintelligible words. Clark waited for the message to be translated, and it came through quickly.

'Security Callsign Seven. Come in District Leader Quartus.

Please report your position. Vector Three has indicated Ogrin activity.'

Clark hesitated, nervous now, aware that if he used a wrong procedure he would alert the people at the other end of the communicator.

'Security Callsign Seven,' he said into the transmuter, the microphone close to his mouth. Ralip was holding the change-over to transmit until he had finished speaking, and Clark was using a Hold button on the transmuter itself to prevent the message being transmitted until it was complete. 'This is District Leader Quartus. I am busy with an investigation into the whereabouts of the aliens who landed on the planet a week ago. Keep me informed of progress in Vector Three, but designate my assistant to the operation. I will call in when I have anything to report.'

Clark cut out then, and thumbed the Hold button. The message was repeated in Brutan in the voice of their prisoner, and Clark was tense and nervous as he awaited reaction from the Brutan operator. Silence filled the cabin for a few tense seconds, then the harsh voice spoke again, running on in a gibberish of meaningless words. When the voice fell silent Clark motioned for Ralip to switch off the communicator, and he let the message record from the transmuter.

'Security Callsign Seven. District Leader Quartus, your message received and understood. Subleader Angmer will direct operations in Vector Three. Will stand by for your progress reports on whereabouts of aliens. Security Callsign Seven out!'

'You've done it,' Balfin said in excited tones. 'They fell for it, Commander. I think we're beginning to see a glimmer of hope.'

Quartus shook his head angrily, and Clark took a deep breath as he stared down at the ground. The skyraft was travelling at a tremendous speed.

'We're not going to arrive too early, are we, Ralip?' Clark demanded.

'I will make allowances for the speed,' the woman retorted. 'I will set you down inside the spaceport within three minutes of the take off of the regular space flight.'

Clark was content with that. He glanced at Magenta, and then looked at Mallory, who was conscious once more and beginning to sit up and take notice. Mallory looked at Clark and shook his head slowly.

'You should have left me behind, Commander,' he said weakly. 'I'm not gonna be much use to you.'

'If this goes the way I plan it then there'll be nothing for anyone to do except get off this craft and transfer to the spaceship,' Clark said with a confidence he did not really feel. His pulses were beginning to race and his heart was already thudding powerfully. 'Ralip, aren't you getting too close to the marshes where we had that trouble last week?'

The woman nodded and veered to the right, and Clark studied the ground, thinking of the incident with the Marscs. He did not want to come into contact with those cannibalistic pygmies ever again.

The communicator became animated again and the harsh voice called Quartus once more. As the message came out of the transmuter in English Clark tightened his lips.

'Security Callsign Seven. District Leader Quartus please give your exact position immediately.'

Ralip turned and gave Clark a worried look. Clark shook his head.

'Leave the communicator off for a bit,' he said. 'They'll think Quartus has left the craft and is making investigations.'

The woman nodded, but she was clearly uneasy, and the message came through several times in the next few minutes.

'How long to the deadline we have to make?' Clark asked Ralip eventually.

'Fifteen minutes,' came the firm reply, and Clark clenched his teeth as nervousness began to stab through him.

'I don't know how we are going to handle this.' Clark went on. 'We've got to get to that space ship before they seal the hatches. Then once we're aboard we've got to overpower the crew and blast off immediately.'

'What about the defences they've got?' Balfin demanded. 'You're not forgetting the power of the missiles that destroyed *Probe* 2, are you, Commander?'

'I'm not forgetting them, and I'm trying hard not to think about them,' Clark retorted. 'I'm going to take a chance that when we blast off the Brutans on the ground won't know what is really happening, and before they get around to shooting down one of their own craft we might be out of Muta orbit and in the clear.'

'That's a long chance, Commander,' Mallory said thinly.

'We've been living on borrowed time ever since we detached from *Probe* 2,' Balfin snapped angrily. 'Give the Commander a break, Mallory. He's not calling the shots, and he's done everything right so far. We'll ride with him all the way now.'

Clark tightened his lips as the moments passed, and now time seemed to be fleeting by instead of dragging. They were rapidly approaching the coast, and their critical time was almost upon them. The communicator came on the air once more, and this time there was a brusque note in the operator's tones.

'Security Callsign Seven. District Leader Quartus, report your position immediately regardless of security.'

'They're getting anxious for some reason,' Balfin said. 'What do you make of it, Commander?'

'I don't know! Probably I haven't used the right jargon for Quartus. But we've got to stall them for time. Once we hit that spaceport then nothing else will matter.'

The operator came on again, demanding urgently for the

position of District Leader Quartus. Clark didn't want to push his luck by talking to the operator again, but he didn't want to have an alarm raised for any reason. He thought for a moment, then spoke into the transmuter.

'Security Callsign Seven. This is District Leader Quartus. Stay off my wavelength. I repeat. Stay off my wavelength. I will call you when I want you.'

Clark motioned for Ralip to switch on the communicator, and then let his message repeat in Quartus's voice. They sat waiting tensely for the operator to come on the air again. There was a click and a slight buzzing sound. Then the Brutan spoke again. The transmuter translated for them.

'Security Callsign Seven. District Leader Quartus, are you in trouble? I repeat—are you in trouble?'

Clark shook his head as he glanced at Balfin, who was staring at him with one eyebrow raised in silent query. Clark glanced at Ralip.

'How long now to the spaceport?' he demanded.

'Five minutes. The spaceship is due to leave in ten minutes.'

Clark moistened his lips. He leaned over the seat and turned off the communicator, then spoke into the transmuter.

'Security Callsign Seven, this is District Leader Quartus. I am not in trouble. I am at the farm of Ralip Rabba and I have apprehended some of the aliens. I will report shortly. Please stay off my wavelength until I call.'

He sent the message and they waited tensely. Clark stared down from a viewport, catching a glimpse of the coastline, and he took a deep breath for a moment. They were banking on this attempt, and if it failed they were finished. He tightened his lips as another message came through the communicator.

'Security Callsign Seven. District Leader Quartus. Do you need assistance?'

'Security Callsign Seven! This is District Leader Quartus. I do not require assistance. I am on the point of leaving the Rabba farm.'

Clark was becoming nervous as he waged a verbal war with the unknown Brutan operator. He saw Ralip looking at him and there was concern on the woman's face. Then the operator came through again, and his words sent a pang of premonition stabbing into Clark's heart.

'Security Callsign Seven! We have plotted your position from the moment you left headquarters with Ralip Rabba! You left that farm one hour fifty-five minutes ago. Please report the situation now! If you are in trouble then indicate its character and we will assist you.'

'Security Callsign Seven! This is District Leader Quartus! I am not in the habit of repeating orders. I warn you to stay off my wavelength. I am in control of this situation and will report as soon as possible. I am in the process of capturing all the aliens landed from the second alien ship destroyed last week. Plot my course by all means, but stay off the air.'

Clark switched off then, and his face was set in harsh lines as he stared through a viewport. Balfin was sweating, his pale blue eyes glittering in the sunlight. He caught Clark's eye and nodded.

'The spaceport is just ahead,' Ralip announced. Her voice was tight and nervous.

'Circle the perimeter,' Clark said, forcing himself to remain calm. 'You've been out here before, haven't you, Ralip, to watch the spacecraft take off?'

'Many times!' The woman nodded, not looking around now.

'Point out where the space craft usually stands!' Clark was craning forward, trying to get his first glimpse of the spaceport. He saw the complex, and noted several large craft on the acres of smooth concrete. A tight knot of anticipation and worry began to swell inside him, and he found he was breathing shallowly, tensely. Mallory was beginning to mutter angrily, and Clark looked towards Balfin.

'What's on your mind, Commander?' the Major demanded instantly.

'We'll try and get down as close as possible to the ship, and you've got to get out of here and aboard the craft as quickly as possible. You've got the other Laser, Hanton, and you'll have to cover the rest of us while we transfer to the spaceship.'

'Will do, Commander,' the Gunner said, tightening his grip on the Laser in his hands.

They began to circle the vast complex, and Clark found himself almost breathless with excitement. There were some skyrafts in the air, but none of them in the space over the spaceport. Clark saw quite a number of emplacements around the perimeter, and they were manned. A string of coloured flares suddenly blossomed in the sky, and Ralip instinctively veered away.

'Keep going around,' Clark ordered. 'We're committed now. We can't cut and run. Can you pick out which ship is the one we want, Ralip?' He glanced anxiously at the woman.

'They've always gone up from that area over there!' Ralip pointed to the right.

Clark leaned over and peered through a viewport and saw two large craft almost side by side in the area indicated.

'Two of them!' Balfin rapped. 'What gives?'

'Is this some of your work, Quartus?' Clark demanded, looking at the silent Brutan, who had turned his head and was staring at him with glittering eyes.

The man nodded slowly. He was gagged and unable to speak, but the animal-like sounds he emitted seemed to convey his great pleasure.

'We're getting out of this alive,' Balfin said angrily. He jabbed the muzzle of his Laser against the Brutan's skull. 'If we don't make it, Quartus, then neither will you. Make up your mind to that. I'll have an eye on you the whole time, and if it looks like we are gonna fail then I'll burn a hole right through you.'

'What are those two craft, Ralip?' Clark demanded. 'Which one looks like the regular flight craft?'

'The one on the right, I think,' came the uneasy reply. 'I can't really tell. Sometimes they use one type and sometimes the other.'

'We're on our way down now,' Clark said tightly. 'I guess you better drop in between them, Ralip. We'll try one, and if that isn't right we'll take the other.'

'I doubt if we'll get the opportunity to change horses in midstream, Commander,' Balfin rapped. 'We've got company coming up to join us.'

Clark saw the group of skyrafts lifting from the spaceport itself, and he clenched his teeth. There were still shoals of flares erupting overhead, and now the communicator began chattering again, but Clark had switched off the transmuter and he did not know what was being said. He stared down at the two craft they were making for. One looked deserted and derelict, with closed hatches and apparently no state of readiness for flight. The other had an airlock open, with a ramp leading up to it, and as he studied it, Clark saw a couple of Brutans moving around in the airlock.

'If Quartus put two craft together to fool us into making an attempt then I figure the one with the open airlock is the decoy,' Clark said. He knew this was a life or death decision 'To get through that airlock we'll have to land between the two craft, and that could be a death trap. Ralip, take the one on the right. We'll be covered by its hull from that open invitation.' He glanced at Quartus as he spoke, but there was no expression on the Brutan's heavy features. He did not know if he was guessing right or not. 'Straight down,' he snapped. 'Let's get in there, Ralip. Stand by, Kester. We'll go into that ship together and take the flight deck.'

Balfin nodded. Ralip sent the skyraft dipping low over the complex, and Clark looked around and saw a stream of sky-rafts coming in fast pursuit. He knew it would be touch and go. They wouldn't get any kind of a chance to duck out if their first guess proved wrong. He lifted a hand to the handle of the door at his side, his teeth clenched, his eyes narrowed.

'Hanton, cover us with the Laser, and keep Quartus under guard the whole time. Ralip, soon as we get out you help Magenta with Mallory. Get him on the ship as quickly as you can.'

They did not speak, but heads were nodding furiously. Clark saw the ground swinging as the skyraft veered a little, and then they were dropping straight down to the smooth ground beside the spacecraft on the right.

Before they stopped moving Clark had the door open and was leaping out of the skyraft. He pulled his sidearm as he ran the few yards to the airlock of the giant ship. Punching an activator, he was slightly surprised when it worked and the airlock door opened. He was about to step into the craft when Balfin thrust past him and opened the inner door. The next instant Balfin was rushing inside, and Clark paused in the doorway to look around.

He saw Ralip and Magenta struggling to get Mallory out of the skyraft. Hanton was already outside, crouching beside the raft, his Laser ready, one eye on the motionless figure of Quartus, still in his seat. A glance at the sky showed Clark a dozen skyrafts swooping down, and he tensed as he expected bursts of fire to strike at them. Then he turned and entered the ship, running along a corridor to the flight cabin up front.

Balfin was in the cabin, confronting one frightened Brutan mechanic.

'Take him with you,' Clark rapped. 'Get back to the airlock and hurry our people aboard, Kester. Let me know as soon as everyone is safely on. I'll get to grips with this.'

Balfin nodded and motioned for the Brutan to precede him. When they had departed Clark looked around the alien ship, his professional curiosity aroused. But there was no time for him to try and learn. He knew he needed Ralip's command of the Brutan language to enable him to decipher most of the unintelligible labels on the controls confronting him.

He was standing in a spherical room containing a mass of apparatus and machinery. Several seats were mounted before consoles overflowing with panels and switches and screens, and he tightened his lips, trying to use his knowledge of spacecraft to aid him in this impossible task. He crossed to what appeared to be the main control console and experimentally flicked a few switches. Red lights flickered on, winked, and went out to be replaced by green dots. Dials began to register, and he moistened his lips as he wondered how he would ever get this monster off the ground. He began operating all the switches on the console.

Moments later Ralip appeared, her face tense, her eyes showing a great deal of concern. Clark had forgotten his own fears in his interest, and he switched on the transmuter and hurriedly asked a host of questions.

'The others are aboard,' the woman said. 'How can I help you?'

'Tell me what these labels say,' Clark said quickly. 'You can fly a skyraft so you've got a mechanical mind. Help me get the main drive started.'

The woman stared at the mass of panels and switches, and began reading out the labels. Clark followed her intently. He clenched his teeth when he felt the ship jar slightly, and a frown touched his forehead although he did not break his concentration. They were under attack! The knowledge passed across the face of his mind and disappeared. He felt sweat trickling fast down his face, but he ignored it. He placed a hand over a pattern of tiny white lights and a panel of indicators in front of him flickered into life.

Slowly he went through the sequence of animating the circuits of the ship. Ralip interpreted for him, and Clark knew that but for the semantics transmuter he would have been hopelessly bogged down.

He left the cabin and ran back to the airlock, feeling the ship jarring several times as he did so. He came upon Mallory lying on the floor, and Hanton was at the airlock door, his Laser in his hand.

'Where's Balfin?' Clark demanded. 'I'm as ready as I can be to try a take-off. You'll have to be strapped down before we can move.'

'The Major is outside trying to get Magenta in, Commander,' Hanton said.

'What happened to her?' Clark asked, snatching the Laser from Hanton. 'Watch the airlock. Take my gun.'

He went through the airlock and peered outside. The skyraft was where they had left it, and Balfin was crouching down beside it, using his Laser against the skyrafts peeling out of formation and swooping down at the spacecraft. Magenta was sprawled on the ground beside the Major.

Clark tightened his lips and ran across the concrete to the skyraft, and Balfin turned a grinning face towards him as he paused in taking on the enemy.

'We've got to get out of here,' Clark said. 'Grab Magenta and let's go.'

'Leave her, Commander,' Balfin said. 'She's dead. It was Mallory's fault. He pulled away from her as she was helping him out of the skyraft. I sent Ralip to help you soon as I could. She could have handled Mallory, but I figured you would need her in the control cabin.

'You figured right.' Clark tried to keep his eyes off the dead woman. 'Come on, Kester. There's nothing left here for us to do. We've got one chance, let's take it.'

'You go on ahead and I'll follow you. These skyrafts are hitting the spaceship. If they damage it we'll never get off the ground.'

Clark paused to take on a skyraft that came wobbling down to attack, and he saw it disintegrate under the power of the Laser. He ran back to the airlock and turned to fight again, while Balfin hurried to join him. They entered the airlock and Clark sealed the door. Then they entered the craft and Clark dropped the Laser and started running for the control cabin. He entered, to find Ralip still switching on various banks of controls.

'I have discovered the control computer,' the woman said, smiling widely. 'It is in operation. There is a preset programme of flight which should take us into orbit.'

The craft swayed, and Clark tightened his lips. He turned as there was movement at his back, and he saw Balfin and Hanton carrying Mallory. Towards the back of the cabin there was a row of couches, and Clark motioned for them to strap themselves down. He went to the command console and strapped himself into the upholstered seat facing it. Ralip came to his side. She was not scared any longer.

'You must press this button to set us in motion,' she said.

Clark nodded, and his right thumb hovered over the button.

'Get yourself fastened to a couch and I'll make the effort,' he commanded. 'Let's get out of here if we are going to make it.'

She hurried away, and Clark felt the craft jar again. He could feel tension building up again. This was the great moment. Either they would blast off the ground or they would remain dormant, doomed to capture and certain death. He moistened his lips, afraid that an anti-climax was about to hit them. Then he saw Ralip was on her couch and he thumbed the button. He blacked out almost instantly as the ship blasted off the ground and reached for orbit. . . .

Clark came to his senses to find himself hanging over the straps holding him in his seat. There were bleepers sounding insistently, and he blinked at the rows of flashing red and green lights before his eyes. He saw a large blank screen to his right and punched a button beneath it, bringing an image of Muta to life on the screen. His ears were buzzing and his head ached, and when he touched his face he found blood drying at the corners of his mouth.

Turning, he saw the others unstrapping themselves from the couches, and Ralip hurried to his side. Clark looked around.

'We'll need a defensive screen around us, Ralip,' he said, shaking his head. 'They'll fire missiles at us.'

She turned to consider the controls, then flipped a few switches and depressed some buttons. Two more screens became animated, and Clark stiffened when he saw a dozen bright dots showing on the smaller screen.

'Missiles,' he gasped.

Balfin hurried to his side, staring at the screen.

'They're missiles all right,' the Major declared. 'This is where we get it like *Probe* 2 did! Have we any deflector screens on this ship?'

'I don't know, and I wouldn't know how to operate them if we had.' Clark spoke through his clenched teeth. 'Hold tight. If we can get out of orbit we'll be able to outrun them. We can chart a course later, but right now we're pulling away from Muta.'

He stabbed a long forefinger at the main drive button, and Balfin went spinning away across the cabin as acceleration blasted through the ship. Clark felt himself being pressed back into his seat by invisible hands, and he stared at the screens in front of him. He knew by the sudden movement of the planet towards the lefthand side of the screen that the ship had suddenly altered course under the driving force of the acceleration, and he glanced at the smaller screens. The missiles seemed to be losing speed, dropping back, and he clenched his hands as he waited and watched. He didn't care where they headed so long as they cleared Muta.

Moments later Balfin came crawling back to his side, and the Major arrived in time to see the white dots of the missiles flaring harmlessly as they exploded out of range. The sphere of the planet was edging right off the larger screen and Clark knew they were out of orbit and putting space between themselves and the nightmare that had existed from the moment they detached from *Probe* 2.

Balfin was grinning widely, relieved because they had accomplished the impossible. But Clark was in no mind for celebration. As far as he was concerned the hardest part was still to come. He had to navigate their course back towards Earth, and there were signals to be sent. He supposed *Probe* 3 would already be on its way to Muta, and the necessary warnings had to be issued. He glanced at the big screen, and now Muta had shrunk to half its former size and was rapidly decreasing all the time.

Clark took a deep breath and tried to kill the remnants of the horror that still clung to the inner recesses of his mind. He had his duty to steady him, and he got out of his seat with determination filling him. There might be pursuit! He had to take that into consideration. Then there was the matter of writing up a report! He shook his head slowly as he tried to find words to put substance into the half-formed thoughts in his mind. The report would have to wait. Each moment of time took them farther from Muta, and time was what he needed to quell the horror of what they had left behind.

For the first time since *Probe* 2 had been destroyed he found himself aware that he had time. They had dragged themselves clear and now the future was stretching before them once more, illimitable, like Space itself!